SINS OF TWO FATHERS

ALSO BY DENIS HAMILL

Stomping Ground

Machine

House on Fire

3 Quarters

Throwing 7's

Fork in the Road

Long Time Gone

SINS OF TWO FATHERS

A Novel by

DENIS HAMILL

ATRIA BOOKS

New York • London • Toronto • Sydney • Singapore

ATRIA BOOKS

1230 Avenue of the Americas
New York, NY 10020

ISBN: 0-7434-6298-X

First Atria Books hardcover edition October 2003

10   9   8   7   6   5   4   3   2   1

ATRIA BOOKS is a trademark of Simon & Schuster, Inc.

Manufactured in the United States of America

For information regarding special discounts for bulk purchases,
please contact Simon & Schuster Special Sales at 1-800-456-6798
or business@simonandschuster.com.

For my brother Tom, who always makes it all add up

SINS OF TWO FATHERS

SOMEWHERE IN THE MIDDLE . . .

Thursday, July 27

Hank Tobin hit bottom.

Lower, Tobin thought, watching the white-bearded parkie spear a fast-food wrapper with the pointed pole and stuff it into the big, green Department of Parks garbage bag. *I've sunk past the bottom into the subbasement of hell.*

He shifted on the wooden park bench, gripping the pint of Stolichnaya concealed in the brown paper bag. *Like a park-bench bum,* he thought. He hadn't had a drink, not one drop of alcohol, in four years. Hadn't really been tempted. The booze had helped wreck his marriage, had clouded his thinking on the night he wrote the most reckless newspaper column of his life, had strained his relationship with his kids. But right now he was hungry for a drink. For escape. He needed something to make the pain of his son, Henry Jr., facing life in prison go away.

Tobin gripped the sealed bottle cap. Contemplated twisting it, like a suicidal man with his sweaty finger poised on the cold trigger of a pistol. He knew if he turned the cap, broke the seal of his sobriety, that this time there would be no going back.

He watched a group of children in the Marine Park playground squeal through the sprinklers. He used to take Henry here as a kid, when Laurie was still in diapers. Julie would open a big picnic basket she'd have prepared at home—cold chicken cutlets, tubs of salad, pretzels, fruit, cold lemonade, and peanut butter and jelly sandwiches for the kids. They'd all eat and toss crumbs to the birds. Then Hank and Julie would play for hours with the kids on the swings, the seesaws, the sandbox, and the sprin-

1

klers. It seemed like yesterday. And then as Tobin drew a deep, humid New York breath, it felt like two lifetimes ago. Part of another man's sweet and happy and normal life.

He cinched the vodka cap in his hand, sweating, gazing around the park.

Almost a quarter-century earlier he'd walked hand in hand in this park with Julie when he was still courting her. Now, four years after the divorce, he was trying to summon the nerve and the precise words he would need if he ever worked up the courage to knock on Julie's door asking for her help. If he couldn't find those words or that courage, he'd crack open the bottle of vodka.

Julie lived three blocks away, but he knew he had to get the words perfect because Julie didn't suffer fools. Especially Tobin, who was the biggest fool in her life.

Tobin knew that when his world tilted off its axis, when the wheels spun off his life, all the hot babes, front-page stories, boldface gossip items, best-selling books, movie deals, and A-list parties added up to nothing but a grubby mirage. It was a piss-poor substitute for a good marriage and a close family.

When you need help, Tobin thought. *There is only one place to go to circle the wagons and fight back. To save your kid. To ask for help. Home. But that's if Julie will even open the door for me.*

The parkie put the spear and the bag into his idling Parks Department truck and grabbed a broom and a handled-shovel and approached Tobin, the peak of his army-green uniformed hat pulled low over his sunglasses, visoring the blinding morning sun. The parkie's face was gaunt and yellowish. Tufts of white hair spilled from under the hat. He looked like a down-on-his-luck Santa with a part-time summer job.

"Excuse me, fella," said the parkie, sweeping up cigarette butts and candy wrappers from behind and under Tobin's bench. He collected discarded newspapers, bunching them under his arm, wearing work gloves for his dirty chores.

Tobin shifted on the bench to let the man do his job and said, "Sorry."

"Sorry" was the operative word for Tobin's life now. No detox ward, rehab, or AA meeting could rescue Tobin this time. No twelve-step program could turn this one around. No loud, breast-beating, quick-fix Hank Tobin column would save his son from jail.

The great Hank Tobin is powerless, neutralized, impotent, Tobin thought. *Exposed as the fake I could never look in the eye in the mirror. When others offered praise, congratulations, and awards, I secretly knew that the career was held together with smoke and mirrors and bluster, like some manufactured boy band. Maybe before I became an asshole, swallowed by my own self-importance, there was a time when I was a pretty good reporter and not such a bad guy. I must've been a decent man once. Or else a great woman like Julie Capone would never have given me a second look, never mind married me.*

Then she gave me two great kids. We had a special marriage. A wonderful, nutty, loving family. A helluva life. Then came The Column. And I threw away all those things that really mattered. For cheap headlines, talk shows, gossip items, fancy restaurants, deals, glamour, celebrity. For The Column, which I wore like a suit of armor to protect myself from the truth of my own inadequacies.

And as I wrote myself into a figment of my own imagination, only two people knew I was a fraud—Julie and me. So Julie filed the divorce papers, but I wrote the script.

Now my son's life is on the line and all my celebrity, fame, and connections are useless, Tobin thought. *I wrecked the lives of strangers with my arrogant, self-aggrandizing, and reckless newspaper column. And instead of bringing the long overdue bill to me, the piper is making my kid pay. My son is paying for my sins.*

Oh . . . my . . . god. What did I do? What do I do? Where do I turn? Who can I trust?

He tightened the grip on the vodka bottle cap as the parkie groaned, checked his watch, and sat on a bench facing Tobin, across a six-foot-wide cobblestone pathway.

"Time for my five-minuter," the parkie said, sitting with the bright sun behind him, making him a dark silhouette to Tobin. "Scorcher."

"Yeah," Tobin said, hiding the vodka bottle next to his leg.

"At least the kids are cool," the parkie said, nodding toward the children in the sprinkler, a rainbow arcing through the frail mist.

"Kids are always cool, period."

"Used to bring mine here once upon a better time."

Tobin nodded. "Me, too."

"Ah, well, funny how things turn out later."

"I'll say."

"When they're this age, you think nothing'll ever go wrong for them."

Tobin nodded, his blood screaming for booze, and said, "Oh, man . . ."

"You and them both figure that you'll always just be there to protect them."

"Yeah," Tobin said, squinting at the parkie.

"You stand behind them on the swings, make sure they don't fall," the parkie said, nodding toward a couple of fathers pushing their kids on the toddler swings. "You stand under them on the monkey bars to make sure they don't get hurt. You check the sandbox for glass and needles before you let them dig. When they come shivering out of the sprinklers, you wrap their little defenseless bodies in big warm beach towels, and hug them in your arms. You hold their tiny hands when you walk them home to make sure they're safe. You promise yourself that if anyone ever tries to hurt your kids that you would die, surrender your very life, to save them. You would hurt anyone who ever hurt your kid. You try to be the daddy that your daddy never was to you and . . ."

Tobin shielded his eyes with his left hand, gripping the vodka with his right, peering at the white-haired silhouette, and said, "Hey, I know you, buddy?"

"I know from the way you look at the kids that you're a father," said the parkie.

Tobin nodded and pulled a photo of a man named Kelly from his shirt pocket. Except for the hair and beard, the parkie sort of resembled the bald man in the photo.

"Like me," the parkie said, standing up. "Just another father who misses his kids."

Tobin squinted at the old parkie, whose dark wraparound shades reminded him of the wary eyes of a horsefly. A welcome rolling breeze blew in from the direction of Jamaica Bay across the flat meadow of Brooklyn's Marine Park, sweeping between the two fathers. The parkie checked his watch, dropping some of the old newspapers. He stamped his foot on a loose front page of the New York *Daily News*. Tobin glanced down at the headline that was about his twenty-two-year-old son, Henry Jr., facing twenty-five-to-life in jail for something that Tobin knew his son didn't do. Which Tobin believed was a frame-up. He was convinced the man in the photo had set up his son to get even with Tobin for a hurtful column he'd written a long time ago. *Could this be him in the flesh?*

"What makes you think that?" Tobin asked the old parkie, gripping the bottle, palming the photo.

The parkie bent, grimacing in pain, and picked up the newspaper page. The man's hat fell off his head, and Tobin thought he saw the man's hair move as a single piece, like a loose wig. The parkie caught his hat, jammed it on his skull, and straightened the wig as he stood with a half-smile. He stared at Tobin, who saw his own distorted reflection in both lenses of the bubble sunglasses, like an out-of-body experience. The parkie balled and twisted the front page of the newspaper in a slow deliberate gesture, as if strangling someone.

The parkie walked to his idling truck and climbed behind the wheel, his white wig now askew on his head. He gunned the engine and shifted the gear into drive.

"Because you and me are a lot alike," the parkie said. "So much alike that you will now feel the pain I have felt for the past ten years, Hank Tobin. You are going to know what it is like to have your son suffer for the sins of his father, which is the worst pain any man will ever know."

Tobin lurched toward the parkie's truck. But the parkie hit the gas and sped off into the blazing sun.

Tobin held the vodka bottle in his hand, staring at it and then at the disappearing truck. If he had any doubt before, Hank Tobin now knew more than ever that he would need to summon the courage to ask Julie to work with him to help save their only son. He didn't know if he could find that courage as he stood staring at the bottle of booze. . . .

ONE

Monday, July 24

Three days earlier, when he arrived home from overseas, Tobin needed his fix.

Hank Tobin had no idea that after being away covering "The War" that he was about to get involved in the biggest battle of his life here at home in his country. His city. In his own family.

Right now he just knew he needed his byline fix.

Dressed in an arctic-blue, lightweight Brooks Brothers suit and pale-yellow Ralph Lauren tie, Tobin stepped off the El Al plane into the International Arrivals Building at JFK, itching for a copy of the New York *Examiner.* After collecting his single Gucci bag, he carried it and his Dell laptop computer through Immigration to the long Customs line. Except for two plane passengers who were reading his latest best-selling book, *Bulletins from the Abyss,* he hadn't seen his name in print in six weeks while away covering the usual madness in the Middle East. While the world continued to focus on the body count in Iraq and the future of Iran and Syria, in Tobin's first week in the Middle East he decided to go to Israel, to what he considered to be the point of origin of the Middle Eastern inferno. It was still in flames. In the first week he'd filed six different columns on six different suicide bombings—one on a twenty-two-year-old bomber, one on the family of a victim, one on a coffinmaker, one on a special Israeli anti-suicide-bombing task force, one on a Hamas woman who had trained to be a bomber but had a change of heart, one on a bombmaker, and another on the Jerusalem police bomb squad.

Since his mother was born in Ireland, Tobin had long ago applied for and obtained an Irish passport. He now held dual citizenship and Irish and American passports. When Tobin traveled overseas, he always kept his American passport in his hotel safe and carried his Irish passport in case he was stopped or snatched by American-hating terrorists. Or confronted by a crazed skyjacker looking for an American hostage. Raised in Brooklyn by a single mother from Dublin, Tobin could do a fair Irish accent, certainly good enough to fool the ear of a Middle Easterner. Plus the Irish passport made ordinary citizens in that always-percolating region of the world open up more when he interviewed them with his fake Dublin brogue, flashing his Irish passport imprinted with the golden harp.

Tobin even carried a letter on an *Irish Evening Standard* letterhead, stating that Henry Tobin Sr. was on assignment for them in the Middle East—or the Balkans or South or Central America or Asia—depending on the circumstance. And Tobin did file occasional pieces for that Irish newspaper, using the byline Henry Tobin Sr., to differentiate it from his popular New York *Examiner* Hank Tobin byline. He carried copies of his Irish newspaper stories as proof that he was an Irishman.

So far the ruse had worked. On this last trip, Arabs treated him better than other American journalists. Maybe it was the full salt-and-pepper beard and the thick mane of graying hair that the fundamentalists liked. As soon as Tobin was awarded a column fifteen years ago, he started wearing designer suits and ties and growing the beard, thinking it gave him an authorial gravitas, the "look" of a true *author,* a cross between Ernest Hemingway and Tom Wolfe. Whatever it was, the Irish passport, the conservative suits clashing with the rebellious and now trademark beard, or just his disarming personality, more people talked to Tobin than other journalists, and he was treated with less hostility.

Tobin had filed the suicide-bombing stories from Israel, then he'd spent a week in Afghanistan, a week in Saudi Arabia, five days in Indonesia, three days in Somalia, and another week in Iraq, filing columns about the local reaction to America's slow-motion, never-ending war on worldwide terrorism.

I'm getting too old for this shit, thought Tobin, delighted to be back in "safe" New York City as he inched through customs. *The Middle East. What a fucking place! Five more years of reporting and I'll be fifty, and I can sit back and just write the column and the novels at home and never go back to shitholes like that again. Give me the moon over Manhattan.*

There was a time, before the Twin Towers went down, when he could do all the foreign reporting he wanted at home in New York City by riding the subway. If he wanted to do a piece on Arabs, he took a subway to Atlantic Avenue or Coney Island Avenue in Brooklyn and just walked into any store with a Halal sign in the window and listened to animated rants about the Israeli tyranny. If he wanted a Jewish counterpoint, he only had to travel a few neighborhoods to Midwood or Boro Park to talk to impassioned Jews, some of them as militant as the Hamas and Al Qaeda factions of the Brooklyn Arabic population. If he wanted to interview Chinese immigrants about a downed spy plane in mainland China, he could get all the quotes he needed over a bowl of wonton in the Chinatowns of Flushing, Queens, Sunset Park, Brooklyn, or lower Manhattan. He found all the Russians he needed sunning themselves on the Brighton Beach boardwalk, got the Greek point of view as they tended their fig trees outside two-family homes anywhere in Astoria. Caribbeans shared their thoughts over jerk chicken in Crown Heights, and Dominicans were outspoken in the salsa clubs of Washington Heights. He could interview Albanians in Moshulo Park, Indians in the many restaurants of Curry Row on E. Sixth Street in Manhattan, and publish all the Poles fit to print in Greenpoint.

And most of them knew Hank Tobin from his column in the *Examiner,* a true populist voice of the common people.

But ever since he became the highest-paid marquee columnist in New York—and brand-name book author, an Oscar-nominated screenwriter, and a radio and TV personality, with an autobiographical TV series about his exploits in development in Hollywood—his editors and his readers expected Hank Tobin to travel to the world's hot spots to file his unique and colorful you-are-there dispatches, sparkling with lyrical prose and ballsy, detailed, and fastidious reporting that had won him a second Pulitzer Prize two years earlier.

But right now he was happy as hell to be home.

Home, where people recognized him on the street, where New Yorkers asked Hank Tobin to sign columns when he sat courtside at the Knicks, or in box seats at the Mets, or ringside at the fights. Home, where he always got a good table at impossible-to-get-into restaurants with waiters who knew him on a first-name basis.

But before a veal chop in Elaine's, pizza in John's, pasta at Rao's, steak at Peter Luger's, or even a hot shower in his Central Park West penthouse condo, or a night in the company of a beautiful woman, Tobin itched for a copy of the New York *Examiner.* To see his byline. To get his fix. Since he was a kid reporter, when he saw his first byline over a story about a Brooklyn rent strike in *Flatbush Life,* some magical elixir, superior to the blood of life, scorched in his veins and pounded his heart.

Even when he won his first Pulitzer Prize, and strode to the podium at Columbia University, Tobin accepted the plaque and held up the check and pointed to his name on the "Pay to the Order Of" line and quipped, "It's always great to see your name in print." The J-students roared. But Tobin was serious. When he saw his name on his column—*Hank Tobin*—in twenty-point type, and his thick-haired, full-bearded, squinty-eyed take-shit-from-nobody photo logo, it always assured him that his life was meaningful and worthwhile and respected. *Tobin mattered,* he thought. Even when he was feeling low and empty and alone over not having his ex-wife Julie or Henry and Laurie in it anymore, his name and photo on The Column gave his life purpose, definition, value. Even as he put on a fake modesty by claiming that the power he wielded was in fact the might of the big-city newspaper, not The Column, deep in his heart he believed that Hank Tobin's column packed special wallop. He thought of it as a second personality. His twin. He'd once read an interview with a famous über-model, maybe it was Cindy Crawford, who'd said she dealt with her enormous celebrity by thinking of her public persona as "The Face." Every morning she awakened as a normal human being, with mortal needs, moods, disappointments, fears, phobias, flaws, zits, wrinkles, and self-doubts. And then it took several hours to put on "The Face"—washed, conditioned, blow-dried, and sprayed her famous hair. Then applied layers of foundation, liquid makeup, lipstick, mascara, eye shadow, rouge, highlighters. Until, one step at a time, like the words, sentences, and paragraphs of his column, she became flawless—"The Face." Which was her mask. Tobin understood what she meant. There was Hank Tobin, the man, and there was Hank Tobin, The Column. Which was another kind of mask. His wife, Julie, had warned him for years before their divorce that Tobin had worked so hard at developing the mask, with no time for *the man* who was also a husband and a father, an integral part of a family and a home and a private life, that *the man* had become the mask. Hank Tobin was The Column.

Bullshit, Tobin had said. He could differentiate. But he knew that it was The Column that had made him a New York *player.* And that people befriended the logo and the byline more than Hank Tobin, *the man.* Still, Hank Tobin, *the man,* had created The Column, and he was convinced it had its own organic power that was autonomous of the clout of the *Examiner*. Tobin was sure he could move to another paper and have the same impact. But Julie argued that then his power, influence, and clout would come from the might of that new paper, which in turn got its power from its readers. Just like the power of her gold shield, when she was still on the force, was derived from the NYPD. Which got its power from the citizens. But Tobin believed the man controlled The Column, and so he was in control of his life. And The Column.

The Column also helped wreck his marriage. So did the Other Woman—Mona Falco.

Still, right now, Tobin needed his *by Hank Tobin* fix. Sure, of course he'd read his own columns online overseas, checking that the editors and copy editors had not mangled his carefully chosen words. But reading a column online did not evoke the same tactile sense of power in Tobin as holding the newspaper in his hands. He used to thrill in riding the morning rush-hour subway, incognito in a hoodie and shades, watching New Yorkers from every ethnic and socioeconomic walk of life read his column on the way to work. He loved seeing the paper tremble in the hands of the readers when he made them angry or caused them to laugh. Sometimes they would rattle the paper, roll it up, and slap it against their open palm, or nudge a friend and read a section of it aloud. He'd seen one guy get so incensed he actually spit on his column. Sometimes he'd see people tear it out, to show it to others or save it for posterity. He'd received copies of his column in the mail, spotted with bird droppings. One reader—he assumed it was a man—had even used it as toilet paper and mailed it to him at the *Examiner*.

Tobin loved ink on paper. He hated the ephemeral detachment of cyberspace. When the Hank Tobin column appeared in print, in a real newspaper—with people gripping it in their hands, the ink rubbing off on their fingertips, some of them moving their foreign lips as they read it, learning English and the idioms of New York in the process—he felt like he had physically touched his readers in a personal fashion. Three times a week he entered their lives, became a part of their daily routines, altered their thinking. *Your words, your ideas, your opinions manipulated their emotions,* he thought. *You were as powerful on a weekday morning as the engine of the train that propelled them through the black veins of the City of New York. You had a voice as loud as the million collective readers who read The Column.*

Hank Tobin knew his foreign correspondence transported those people who rumbled to their daily mundane jobs to the exotic, thrilling danger zones of the universe, where he showed them with exploding verbs and concrete nouns what he saw firsthand with his own eyes. He delivered the rest of the world—the sights, sounds, smells, tastes, and feel of a place, framed by history in the making—to the people of the capital of the world. Even when he wrote columns at home about his native New York, Hank Tobin helped them cope with their big, broad-shouldered city by pointing fingers at the thieves and scoundrels who robbed their tax dollars and exploited the trust they invested in them. Sometimes he just made his readers laugh on a humorless Tuesday. Or made them seethe on a happy Thursday. Or detonated an investigative bomb about police brutality or dirty judges on a lazy Sunday morning.

Hank Tobin was New York, a big loud mouth in the big bad city.

And now he was getting impatient waiting on the goddamned Customs line to get into his native city. In the days before the Trade Center attack, he was VIP'd right through the gates of his city. He knew the airport cops, Customs agents, and Immigration people from columns he'd written over the years. But ever since, everyone was a possible perp. Air travel had become a test of human endurance. Coming into JFK, he found the airport was always crawling now with Federal agents—FBI, ATF, DEA, INS, Customs, CIA, Office of Home Security, even Interpol guys. Besides these plainclothes teams, armed National Guardsmen patrolled the busy lounges, exits, entrances, snackbars, saloons, and security checkpoints. And Port Authority airport cops also scanned the new arrivals streaming into a wounded New York that remained the prime target of international terrorists because of its symbolic landmarks, such as the Empire State Building, Statue of Liberty, and United Nations. *And because there are more Jews in New York than there are in Tel Aviv,* Tobin thought.

"Anything to declare, Tobin?" asked the Customs agent named Fanning, whom Tobin had interviewed years before on a drug-bust story. He'd even shared a few beers with Fanning, before Tobin hung up his tankard four years ago, after the divorce.

"Only my genius," said Tobin, plopping the carry bag and laptop-computer case on the examining table.

"You still using that same Oscar Wilde line, Tobin?" said Fanning, unzipping the bags and giving them a cursory search. "Come up with something original, will ya? You're the big writer. Besides, my job is lookin' for contraband, and Wilde was a major bone smuggler, wasn't he?"

"Your political correctness astounds me, Fanning."

"Sorry, but I even gotta check *you* with the eye-in-the-sky now," Fanning said, checkmarking Tobin's bags with a yellow pencil. "How's the wife and kids?"

At the mention of his family, Tobin felt a void in his gut, a panicky sinking sensation like an elevator with snapped cables falling in a black shaft.

"Great."

"That kid of yours is giving you some run for the money, huh? Some run of page ones on that new paper."

"No shit? I've been away. . . ." He felt a surge of pride in his twenty-two-year-old son, Henry Jr., an ambitious, impatient, fledgling journalist who in Tobin's absence had taken a full-time job on a brand-new New York daily newspaper called *The Globe,* which Tobin had never seen and which did not yet have an online edition.

"You're doing the work of the Lord, Fanning," Tobin said, patting Fanning on the shoulder.

"Then put something in the collection plate, humpo," he whispered. "Careful outside, they're searching for some urine-colored watch-list mope. Since the war, they're always watching."

Tobin nodded and moved on, looking for the familiar face of his driver, Ali from Bell Taxi. The car-service account was one of his many newspaper perks. When he returned from a trip, Ali was always waiting. This time Tobin didn't see him.

Once past the security line of the terminal, Tobin noticed a six-pack of Feds wearing tinted shades and earpieces, as subtle as blood spatters on a wedding gown, standing behind an unmarked counter, scanning a bank of computer monitors. Tobin figured they were studying closed-circuit video images from the "eye-in-the-sky" cameras that Fanning had referred to, a ceaseless stream of multiethnic faces of the new arrivals. They were obviously searching for someone in particular. The "urine-colored" watch-lister, probably an Arab, that Fanning had mentioned.

Tobin noticed the Feds perk up, growing alert and animated, like a family of cats setting into predator mode. He glanced from the excited Feds to a swarthy-faced Arab man. Back to the Feds. His double take brought another Fed to Tobin's side, touching his elbow.

"What are you watching?" asked the Fed, his face so badly scarred by acne that at first glance Tobin made him for a burn victim.

"The melodrama," Tobin said.

"Pretend you don't notice," said the Fed. "Look at me. Me only. Good. Smile. Who are you?"

Tobin laughed, "Hank *Tobin* from the New York *Ex—*"

"Smile. Like we're old friends. There's an individual we're watching."

"If I noticed that, he probably did. He's on the watch list?"

"Shake my hand, then walk to the men's room. . . ."

"Hey, pal, you never showed me any ID."

"Are you being uncooperative?" asked the Fed. "If you make me ID myself, I'll detain you. If you don't do as I say, I'll think you're aiding and abetting the individual we're watching."

Tobin thought that being detained, hassled, strip-searched, and interrogated could make a pretty good first-person column. But he was tired and it was too much of a pain in the ass. Leave that to a young reporter. Besides, most readers would agree with the Feds erring on the side of caution in these jingoistic and jittery days.

"Actually, I could use a leak," Tobin said, laughing, shaking the agent's hand, and sauntering toward the men's room. He passed the swarthy-faced Arab who cleared Customs, carrying a briefcase, dabbing his sweaty face with a hankie. Just as the Fed who'd stopped Tobin and the rest of the Feds circled the man, guns drawn.

Panic shivered through the terminal.

Tourists screamed and babbled in a dozen different languages.

A flight attendant banged into the ladies' room. A Hassid shielded himself with his suitcase. A skycap shoved away his bag rack, dove behind a pillar, shouting, "Third time this week! Fuck me and the planes these Mohammeds ride in on."

Tobin spun. Plopped his bags on the ground. Looped his press card around his neck on a chain. Twisted the nib of his Mont Blanc ballpoint and started scribbling notes in a narrow Reporter's Notebook that he always carried in his back pocket.

"No shoot!" the swarthy Arab shouted.

Other passengers scattered. The Arab was forced to his knees, hands yanked behind his neck. The Feds shouted: "Stay down!" "Don't move!" "Lay flat!" "Face Mecca!"

Uniformed airport cops and National Guardsmen fanned out. Pointing weapons. Studying frightened faces. Searching for terrorist colleagues.

The terminal hushed like a requiem mass, as if everyone was holding the same breath. In the stillness the sound of Tobin's ballpoint scratching the paper was as loud as the ticking of a bomb.

He glanced up at the Feds handcuffing the Arab and turned a page of the notebook. One young guardsman aimed his rifle directly at Tobin and said, "Stop fucking writing shit down."

"What?"

"Hard of fucking hearing?"

Tobin tapped his press pass. "I'm a reporter and I'm not embedded with you, pal, and this is still the U.S. of—"

"U-S-of-shut-the-fuck-up and stop writing shit down," the guardsman said. "Or you'll see what the fuck happens. Law says shut the fuck up and stop writing shit down."

"What law says that?"

"Am I having a fucking problem with you?"

Tobin studied the young kid. Maybe he shaved twice a week, eyes as blue as a fairy-tale sky, nail-bitten index finger pulsating on the steel trigger of the M-16, and decided the best place to fight for the First Amendment or the Fourth Estate was in his column or in a courtroom. Not in an airport in these paranoid times.

He put away his notebook and pen and watched the Feds search the Arab. They opened his pants, explored inside his underwear, and ran a scanner over his body and shoes. "I do nothing," the Arab shouted. A stocky, red-haired Fed cupped his hand over the man's mouth. "Dummy up," the Fed said.

Two other Feds lifted the Arab under the arms and dragged him on his tiptoes across the polished-tile floor of the airport and through an unmarked gray door into a fluorescent-lit room and slammed the door. Two National Guardsmen took positions outside the gray door. The whole process took under a minute.

"Write any shit you please now," said the guardsman. "It's a free country."

For the next ten minutes Tobin searched for Ali, his driver. He used the time to check his voice messages at the *Examiner,* punching in his password code on the keypad of his cell phone. The airport was back to normal business as he listened to the messages of several readers saying he'd done an outstanding job in his foreign trip. A few crank callers told him he was a kike lover. A few said he was a Jew hater. He skipped over a dozen calls from flacks pitching stories for columns, including a call from the Police

Commissioner's flack and one from a spokesman for the State Department. Then came one from a man with a voice that was electronically scrambled.

"Hey, Hank, this is LL," the voice said. *"Thank God you're back. I was starting to worry I'd have to do all this without you. You remember me, don't you, Hank? I'll never forget you. Hey, I tried to give you that scoop your kid had on page one of his new paper today. But you were still away. So I gave the tip to your kid. Did a nice job. I have more stuff for you when you're ready, Hank. Big stories. Very big stories. Your column changed my life. Now I'm gonna change yours. I'll be in touch. We only have six days, counting today, and then I'm outta here."*

The man hung up. *Creepy,* Tobin thought. Unlike most crank callers, who just vented, cursed him out, or called Tobin an asshole, this guy used a voice filter. And sounded confident. Like a man at a control panel. A voice coming out of a grave. A man on a mission. Tobin needed to urinate.

From his left, Ali, the dark-skinned Pakistani car-service driver, hurried over and grabbed Tobin's bag and his laptop. "Sorry to be late, Mister Tobin," Ali said, shaking his head and exhaling in frustration. "But there was so much security. They stop me and searching my trunk two times. I'm parked in the lot across the street. Can't park outside."

"I'll meet you in the car, Ali," Tobin said, heading for the men's room, passing a newsstand where an Indian man wearing a turban and Nehru shirt stood behind the counter. The gray-bearded Indian newsie looked nervous, fidgety, as Tobin stood on line to pay for the *Examiner, Daily News, Post, Times,* and *Newsday.* After handing the Indian newsie a ten-dollar bill, in an afterthought, Tobin grabbed a copy of a new New York daily called the *Globe,* which was a thin broadsheet, as opposed to a tabloid like the *Examiner.* While he was away, his son, Henry, had dropped out of NYU in his senior year, stopped writing freelance for the *Village Voice,* and took a full-time job on the new daily that everyone predicted wouldn't last six months. In a barrage of e-mails and transatlantic phone calls, Tobin had tried to talk Henry Jr. into staying in NYU and freelancing for the weeklies. But the precocious kid had developed a fierce competition with his father, especially since Tobin and his son's mother finally divorced four years earlier, after two years of on-and-off bickering and trial separation, and wanted to go head-to-head with the old man on a rival daily. It worried Tobin. He didn't want to humiliate his own kid. But he wasn't going to write beneath his own intelligence and professionalism to let the kid shine, either. He wished Henry had graduated college, taken his first daily newspaper gig in

Los Angeles or up in Boston or down in Miami. Then come to New York to kick a little ass after Tobin turned fifty, and was ready to navel-gaze his way through one column a week as a learned elder sage.

"Anybody buying this new paper?" Tobin asked.

"You are, sir."

"I mean, do a lot of people buy it?"

"I see nothing, sir," the Indian newsie said. "I hear nothing. I say nothing, sir."

"You came to America for that, huh?"

"I love America. Have a nice day, sir."

Tobin crossed the terminal and stepped into the men's room, followed by a janitor wearing an orange vest who pushed an industrial mop and bucket and who immediately began to swab out those of the dozen toilet stalls that were not occupied. Two stalls were occupied and three other men stood at urinals. As he relieved himself at an empty urinal, Tobin thumbed through the *Examiner* and found his column in his fixed spot on page two, the squinty eyes peering back at him like the double barrels of a shotgun. He panned his name H-A-N-K T-O-B-I-N. *It belongs on a column slug,* he thought. *Three good strong syllables. Followed by 800 words to live by.* He reread his lead.

> Tehran, Iran—"Sources in this city and in the Pentagon tell me we'll be sending body bags home from here on our next stop on the Axis of Evil Express, to take citizens' minds off the economy back home, unless . . ."

Good, he thought. *They didn't mess with the lead. That'll make Foggy Bottom nuts. No wonder the State Department flack called me. Now he'll give me something fresh from their point of view.*

The janitor moved to a new stall, flushed the toilet, and mopped as Tobin scanned the rest of the column and saw nothing amiss, just a wrap-up of his six-week trip with an ominous drumroll of more war to come.

He glanced at the *News* and *Post,* which had the same lead story about a Queens Judge named Nikolas Koutros taking bribes to fix two cases. Maybe he'd follow that one up. He'd interviewed Koutros a few times, met him at several Democratic Party political functions over the years. He started out in the Brooklyn Democratic machine and was transferred to Queens to replace a judge who had been convicted in a different bribery case. So he was a judge who took over for a judge convicted of taking bribes, who was now accused of taking a bribe. *You couldn't bribe somebody to make up a story like that,* Tobin thought.

Tobin had some good contacts on Queens Boulevard, which was paved with six wide lanes of old bribes and other assorted political machine felonies. *Newsday* had a graphic on the sagging economy on page one. He glanced at the various stories on the front page of the *Times*. *Great paper,* he thought. *But like reading your fucking lease.*

He zipped up, washed his hands, dried them, and then snapped open the *Globe* and saw a story tagged EXCLUSIVE about a possible Al Qaeda sleeper cell on Coney Island Avenue in Brooklyn bannered across the top of page one. He read the well-written, vivid lead, filled with action verbs and specific nouns, about a source telling the reporter about the comings and goings in the basement of a certain apartment house near Avenue J.

The reporter, working on a tip, was on the scene just as a joint NYPD-FBI Anti-Terrorist Task Force led the superintendent out of the building in handcuffs after discovering the bomb-making materials and pro–Al Qaeda and anti-Israeli and anti-American literature in the super's tool-and-equipment room in the basement.

Reads like me, Tobin thought. He was so impressed with the lead that his eye popped up to the byline to see who'd written it. His heart thumped when he saw the byline: *by Henry Tobin Jr.*

Not bad, kiddo, Tobin thought. *Weak source but great lead, great details . . .*

The men's room door banged open and the swarthy Arab whom the Feds had rousted only 10–15 minutes earlier rushed in, tie askew, face sweaty, hair tousled, covering his mouth with his hand. He lurched toward a just-mopped toilet stall and made it in time to heave into the bowl. The janitor paused, his back to Tobin, flapped his arms and shook his head, and ran the mop over the next stall, the strong smell of disinfectant stunning the room.

"You okay, pal," Tobin asked, expecting a gun-wielding Fed to burst through the men's room door. None did. The others in the men's room zipped up and exited in a rush, without stopping to wash their hands.

"I fine. Thank you. . . ."

"Fine? Hey, didn't they just handcuff you and drag you into a room?"

"Wrong man," he said. "They say . . . I am the wrong man. They apologize."

The janitor half-turned, as if hanging on every word. Tobin glanced at him, squinted from the strong disinfectant, and looked back at the Arab.

Tobin walked to the stall door, pulling out his ballpoint and his notepad, holding his press card in his hand.

"That's it? They just cuffed you, dragged you into a room, tossed you, grilled you, and shoved you out? And apologized?"

"Check my papers," the Arab said. "They make some calls. Then I hear they catch right man in London."

The Arab emerged from the stall, wiping his mouth with toilet paper, sweaty and trembling. Tobin introduced himself, showed his press card, and gripped his ballpoint. "Wanna talk about what they did to you?"

"No!"

"Why not?"

"Three times I have been stopped already," he said. "I make trouble, they never give me visa again. My family is here. Forget it. Wrong man, they apologize. It's okay."

"It's not okay to do this to people," Tobin said. "Maybe if I write a column—"

"No! No! Please. It's just the times we live in now. No more trouble, please."

The man washed his face, dried it, and hurried out of the men's room as the janitor moved to yet another stall, flushed the toilet, and slapped the mop into the pissy tiles.

Tobin followed the Arab out of the men's room and watched him hurry, head bowed, through the terminal carrying his briefcase, out of the exit, and to a taxi rank where he climbed into a waiting cab.

Tobin watched him go as his cell phone rang. The caller ID was blocked. He answered anyway. "Yeah."

"I was starting to get worried you wouldn't get back in time to be a part of this," the voice said. *"So, what did you think of your son's story?"* It was the same mechanical voice as the one on the voice mail at work. Knowing that the screwball caller had his private cell-phone number sent an army of ants parading up Tobin's spinal column.

"Who's this?"

Tobin looked around the terminal. He saw scores of people speaking on cell phones, pay phones, hard-line, land phones behind ticket and security counters.

"This is LL, Hank," the man said.

"LL? As in Lex Luthor?" Tobin said. "This some kind of bad joke?"

"Close. But your kid scooped you. You read his story. Big story, no?"

Tobin searched around, eyes darting to the men's room. He hurried to it, banged open the door. One man urinated at the urinals. The other people were gone. The janitor's orange vest hung on the mop handle that stood upright in the big bucket.

"Yeah, big," Tobin said into the phone. The guy at the urinal turned, frowned.

"I have scoops for you, too. Gotta get them in before the dot of noon, July 29."

"I don't take tips or scoops from blind sources," Tobin said, exiting the men's room and striding for the exit. "Especially from people who don't ID themselves when they call my private number. And who know my movements. . . ."

He scanned the terminal again, trying to spot the mystery caller.

"That would be foolish," LL said.

"Yeah? Why?"

"Because I know things you need to know."

"Like what," Tobin said, crossing the street with the light to the airport parking lot where he could see the black Bell Taxi Towncar waiting, motor running. He pirouetted to see if he was being followed. He wasn't.

"About your future. Just think of me as yesterday's papers and tomorrow's headlines. And then after July 29, my suffering will end and yours will begin."

"This is a mind fuck, pal, and I'm hanging up," Tobin said. "I'll worry about my own future, and you are now part of my past."

Tobin disconnected, climbed into the car-service vehicle, and sped toward Manhattan. Ali took the Van Wyck to the Grand Central Parkway to the Long Island Expressway toward the Mid-Town Tunnel. The Towncar climbed the LIE rise revealing the island-long skyline of Manhattan spread out before them like a shrine to Western civilization. Tobin gaped at the empty patch of blue sky that was once blocked by the World Trade Center and was reminded that he was going home to a place that was forever changed.

A cop at the toll plaza waved for Ali to pull over. The cop peered in. "License, registration, and pop the trunk. Roll down the back winda, keep your hands in view."

Tobin's window powered down, and the cop peered in.

"Hi," Tobin said.

The cop pointed at him and nodded. "You're whozis, from the paper. . . ."

"Hank Tobin."

"Yeah," the cop said, as a second cop searched the trunk. "You wrote about my son once. Walter Brody?"

Tobin had no memory of anyone by that name. "Oh, yeah, sure . . ."

"Little over twelve years ago, now," the cop said, as the second cop slammed the trunk lid. "Nice column. You spelled his name wrong. But what the hell. I gave up the sauce like you since, too."

"Sorry . . ."

"Not as sorry as I am," the cop said. "I miss him every day since I buried him. Never caught the fuck who did it, either. Anyway, be good. Keep writin' the great stuff."

Ali sped into the tunnel, and Tobin searched his brain for the murdered son of the cop. He couldn't remember. He was probably still drinking when he wrote it.

Once out of the tunnel Ali drove uptown on Third Avenue. Tobin's cell phone rang again. Another blocked call. He answered. "Tobin," he said.

"*LL,*" said the filtered voice. "*Hey, I'm trying to give you a tip on a good story.*"

"Give me your name first."

"*LL . . .*"

"Here's a tip from me to you," Tobin said. "Give your tips to someone else."

"*I'll give it to your son. It's more than you ever gave him.*"

This time LL hung up on Tobin. *Who is this guy?* he wondered as he glanced out the rear window at the iron centipede of traffic, then sat back and finished reading his son's story in the *Globe*. Wishing he'd written it.

TWO

Tobin stepped off the elevator in his penthouse condo, deprogrammed his alarm by punching in the date of his marriage to Julie—4/4/80—and dropped his keys into a silver bowl on a small mahogany table by the front door.

Magenta summer light shone through the cathedral windows and reflected on the white Italian marble foyer floors from the sky that he felt a part of perched this high over the gigantic city. He put his bags down and walked across the deep-pile champagne-colored rug of the living room to the southern exposure of the wraparound terrace.

The cityscape was a granite-and-glass mountain range, all glistening peaks and shadowy valleys of ceaseless life, a throbbing, pulsating, never-resting free-for-all of people and ideas and stories just screaming to be told. By Hank Tobin. He knew only a few thousand of those people. Millions knew him. More than the Mayor, or the City Council, or any other cheap politician, this was *his* city.

Tobin shuffled through his mail. Most of his bills went directly to his accountant, but he always had his checks mailed directly to his home. He liked seeing, feeling, and reading his name on the checks. The way his readers held his column and his books in their hands. He also wanted to know what was coming in before his accountant sent money out. He xeroxed all the checks so he could audit his accountants—especially after the Enron/Arthur Anderson scandal—to be sure they didn't cook his books. The bills he left to them, even though he knew he should be looking at them, too.

He glanced at two six-figure checks from his publisher, royalties for his last two books, and another from his talent agency minus the fifteen percent fee, as a seven-figure advance on his next book. He didn't even open the screenplay residual checks from the Writers Guild. Another high six-figure check from his literary agency for the TV series he'd developed based on his own life, the pilot of which was ready to be filmed. If the series caught fire, he would collect "Created By" fees like an annuity every week without writing another word, for as long as the show ran, and into syndication beyond the original network broadcasts.

He shit-canned the invitation to the Cannes Film Festival for another film he'd written that had no chance of winning any award but which had been accepted into the festival. The last time he went to Cannes on a film he'd written was a disaster.

Before that trip almost five years before, Tobin and Julie's marriage was turbulent. He'd spent months away in Hollywood doing endless rewrites on the script in preproduction. Then he took a sabbatical from the *Examiner* column to be on the set every day for sixteen weeks in Dublin and Los Angeles.

One hazy, Guinness-logged night as he sat in the after-hours lounge of the Shelbourne Hotel, Mona Falco arrived out of the Dublin rain, wearing an Irish wool hat and matching Aryn sweater, skin-tight jeans, and knee-high boots. Her gorgeous mocha face was an exotic rarity in a land of translucent white faces. Even as they drank deep into the night, Tobin had no intention of bedding Mona Falco. By three A.M., in a moment of boozy weakness, his ego swollen by the idea that Mona had traveled three thousand miles in pursuit of him, he found himself naked in bed in Mona Falco's room.

They kissed and fondled, and as they reached a sweaty frenzy, he'd gone abruptly flaccid and cold. An embarrassed Tobin blamed his manly failure on the booze. But he knew the reason he could not perform was because the guilt of betraying Julie had made him as limp as his character, as weak as his loyalty to his wife. He mumbled an embarrassed apology, collected his clothes, and fled to his own room, leaving Mona Falco lying in a frustrated and injured sprawl on the Irish linen sheets.

Mona checked out the next morning.

Upon his return to New York, Julie suspected that he was having an affair with a policewoman named Mona Lisa Falco, whom she'd heard Tobin had dated during a trial marital separation. Julie, also then a cop, had heard on the NYPD tom-toms that Mona Falco had taken a vacation to Ireland at the same time Tobin was over there working on his movie. Julie had made one single telephone call to the Shelbourne Hotel and asked for

Mona Falco's room. They told her there was a "Do Not Disturb" on her line. There was no answer at Tobin's room.

"I add one and one together, and I come up with two cheating fucks," Julie said, before Tobin even unpacked, smashing the Waterford crystal tea set he'd bought her.

Tobin remembered the look on his son Henry's face, a puzzle of cracked loyalties. His daughter, Laurie, gave him the benefit of the doubt but had suspicions that her dad had cheated on her mom, at an age when she had just started dating.

Henry adored his father but hated him for hurting his beloved mother, who'd held this family together while Tobin was off chasing his career in South American, Africa, Asia, Belfast, and the Middle East for The Column. Sure, the column supported the family, and that was his job. Julie knew that was his life when she married him, just like he knew her cop schedule also kept her away from home on holidays and weekends.

But then Tobin chased a second screenwriting career in Hollywood, involving ritzy parties, awards shows, foreign locations, wallowing in the glamour, big money, and on-the-make women. Being an absentee father was one flaw. Cheating on his mother wounded Henry because he saw how much it hurt hardworking Julie, who'd dedicated every spare minute to her kids.

Tobin denied the infidelity with Mona Falco, rationalizing that it didn't really count because guilt had saved him from himself. He wanted to believe that sex without penetration or orgasm wasn't sex, like temptation is not sin. It was another shallow self-deception. He'd gotten naked in bed with another naked woman while married. But Tobin knew that if he admitted it, his marriage was over. So he added it to his mounting cargo of denial, part of which was misinterpreting celebrity for talent.

Tobin and Julie argued daily for months but somehow stuck it out. They saw a counselor. The kids also unloaded their baggage to the same shrink. The family was held together with truces, cease-fires, and peace talks. When Tobin's film was selected for the Cannes Film Festival, he'd felt this desperate need to go, afraid he'd miss something, aching after so many years of having his nose pressed to the Hollywood glass window to be a part of that sizzling cinema party. He wanted to go mingle with the rich, make deals with indie prods, meet big stars, pitch script ideas to hot young directors. He'd convinced Julie it was vital to his career that he go, even though it meant missing Henry's high school graduation.

"Go get it out of your system," Julie said. "At least you won't be with Mona Fucking Falco."

Two days later Julie's mother called her to say she should open up to the gossip page of a certain rival New York tabloid where there was a gossip item and photo of Hank Tobin being kissed by a topless actress in a thong bikini. The "actress" had had a walk-on in his movie, a dancer in a strip-bar scene. Tobin had been scheduled to do a photo-op with the legitimate female star of the film, as part of the official studio promotional campaign. That photo shoot was supposed to happen at 10 A.M. But that morning a man who said he was from the publicity department called his room and asked if he could be on the beach at 9:30 A.M. instead. Tobin said sure.

When he showed up, the starlet who'd played the stripper rushed to him, topless, her ass bouncing in the string bikini, and threw her arms around Tobin, kissing him on the lips. Dozens of photographers snapped photos.

In the soft focus background of the photo that ran in a rival New York tabloid stood a smirking Mona Lisa Falco.

On the phone, Tobin told Julie that the "ambush" photo was obviously set up by the rival tabloid's photographer to embarrass Tobin during a newspaper war. It didn't matter when Tobin said he couldn't even converse with the young gorgeous wanna-be star because she was a Bulgarian who could speak no English. Then Julie told him she didn't care half as much about the bimbo starlet. But she told him to look at the chick in the background. Tobin put down the phone, searched for the photo that had been faxed to him, and said, "Oh, my God."

" 'Oh, my *Mona,*' is more like it," Julie said.

Tobin swore he didn't even know Mona Falco was in Cannes. "She must've come here on her own," Tobin said.

"Sure, the NYPD Policewomen's Association runs a charter flight to the Cannes Film Festival every year, Hank," Julie said.

It didn't matter to Julie when Tobin swore to her on the lives of their kids that he had never slept with that topless starlet or Mona Falco or anyone else in Cannes. The item and the photo had humiliated Julie and the teenage kids. Henry wouldn't even get on the phone with Tobin. All of Henry's pals were asking him if his old man could fix them up with some sloppy seconds. Laurie's girlfriends said little. To her face. But she heard the whispers and the snickers behind her back at Blessed Sacrament High.

Tobin tracked down Mona Falco, demanding to know why she was there, following him, mugging for the camera in the background.

"You sent me the round-trip ticket and a voucher for a prepaid hotel room," she said, showing him the envelope and typed note.

She claimed she'd tried tracking him down but didn't know which Cannes hotel he was staying in. "Then I got a call this morning saying you'd be at a photo-op on the beach at 9:30 A.M.," Mona said. "So I showed up to meet you, but security wouldn't let me near you."

"I never sent this ticket or voucher, Mona," Tobin said. "You're just trying to wreck my marriage, my family!"

Confused and insulted by the accusations, Mona flew home.

Tobin was baffled. Was Mona a stalker? Or was he being set up by the rival paper with Mona? As well as the starlet? Did someone at a competing tabloid learn that Mona had been one of his NYPD sources? *It's so goddamned weird,* he'd thought.

Tobin didn't win any awards that year at Cannes. But when he got home, he was presented with a set of divorce papers. It was the first time he didn't like the way his name looked in print. The locks on his one-family home on E. Thirty-eighth Street in Marine Park, Brooklyn, had been changed, and his bags were packed.

"Please let me explain," he said to Julie.

"No. Go be Hank Tobin."

The door slammed. Tobin stood on the stoop, locked out of his house, out of his family. Neighbors watched from stoops, or as they watered lawns and put out the garbage. All of them had seen the picture of the half-dressed babe kissing him at this place called Cannes.

The memories still depressed him now, four years later. It wasn't just an emotional plunge. It caused a physical reaction—his scalp itched, his fingers trembled, and his skin flushed with clammy sweat. Indigestion rose in him like bile.

He needed air. He stepped out onto the terrace, shuffled past the new Cannes invitation, which didn't interest him in the least now that he was single, and looked south toward the vanished Trade Center. The hole in the city gave him a better view of the sprawling green and gray expanse of his native Brooklyn. He wondered what Julie was doing over there right now, who she was with, tried to imagine her daily routine. Coffee and oatmeal with raisins for breakfast. Then the papers. She probably didn't read his column anymore. Then the gym where she'd work her cute little butt off on the treadmill and the butt buster and grunt her way through four-sets-of-fifty on the ab-cruncher. Then some light free weights and an aerobics class and a step class. Home, a shower, shopping for dinner. And then maybe a date, afterward, with some asshole cop, not worthy of her. Every time Tobin thought of Julie getting undressed in front of another man, then letting him touch her, her touching him, doing the intimate special things she had always done with him, it strangled him with jealousy. And regret. No one was better in bed than Julie. No one was better out of it, either.

Even though most of the women he'd dated since his divorce were five or ten or fifteen years younger than Julie, all educated, attractive, and gym-toned, none of them had that special oomph, that lusty turbo charge of pure three-dimensional womanhood that Julie brought to bed. Or that sense of confidence Julie had when she walked a city street, unafraid of almost anyone or anything. Anything except closed spaces. She was a desperate claustrophobic, and Henry Jr. had inherited the phobia.

From the beginning Julie was the soul of his column, often giving it the fresh ideas, angles, and perspective only a woman might think about when writing about a major news event. She was more than a sounding board. She was a synthesizer. She was also a funny, sarcastic, ironic son of bitch. In those early years, the best lines in Hank Tobin's column were often Julie's. Tobin didn't realize just how good Julie was, of course, until he slept with and walked and talked and spent time in the company of others. He couldn't remember the last time a date gave him a line that he'd used as a lead or a kicker to a column. Julie had given him hundreds.

He stared at Brooklyn some more, that vast inexplicable swatch of the world that was as much a metaphysical state of mind as it was a physical place. If Manhattan was the brain of New York then Brooklyn was its pounding heart. He raised his arms and let the winds blowing off the Hudson cool his damp body, gulped the fresh air, rolled his head on his neck, and exhaled with a loud sigh. Julie was living over there, smack in the middle of it, in the same little house where they'd raised their kids when he was a struggling general-assignment reporter.

After the divorce, Julie had rebuffed Hank's offers of buying the family a bigger and grander home. "You aren't buying your way back in, Hank," she said. "Put your money in trust for the kids if you want, but I won't take it."

Tobin stepped back inside and saw that his home answering machine was full and pressed the play button. "Hank . . . or should I say *Hank*

Tobin . . . just a reminder that tomorrow night is our son Henry's twenty-second birthday," Julie said. "Thought you might want to say hello to him, if you have a free minute in your calendar. Hope you're safe wherever you are because your kids still love their father."

Julie's voice was so icy Tobin half-expected frosty breath to puff from the answering machine. The next message played: "Hi, Hank, it's me, Dani. Call me as soon as you get home. Miss you."

Dani Larsen was blond and beautiful and as sweet as one of her sunny TV weather forecasts. She'd told him so many times that she wasn't looking for a lasting relationship that he feared she was. But she was just so . . . *nice.* He saw her a couple of times a month when he was home in New York.

Then came the smoky voice of Mona Falco. "Hi, Hank, Mona. Just a call to say hi, to tell you how good your columns were from over there, how happy I am you're safe. And to say I'm still so single it should be a felony. Listen, let's just catch up and say, hey. For old time sakes. We really should talk anyway. About your son. I'm hearing things you should *know.* It's important. Call me. Hank. No strings . . . bye, bye."

Tobin figured it was a ploy. Mona invented things to get him on the phone. To pressure him into seeing her. But he wanted to avoid her, didn't want to be seen in public with her, where some paparazzo might snap them together, for Julie and his kids to see.

The next message brought a smile to Tobin's face: "Dad, Laurie, a reminder, tomorrow's Henry's birthday. Don't forget like you forgot mine, old man. Bye . . . I miss you and really, really love ya. I aced all my courses. So you owe me something expensive. Something with four wheels, maybe, and I don't mean skates, Daddio. I'll be out on Long Island chilling. Be back day after tomorrow. Can we have breakfast? Leave me a message on my beeper-phone mail."

He called Laurie back, got her machine, and left a message asking her to meet him at the Carnegie deli for breakfast in two days at nine A.M. If he didn't hear from her, he'd assume it was a date. Laurie had suffered from the divorce. He knew she still wrestled with resentments that her father had probably cheated on her mom, even though Tobin still denied it. And with Tobin missing from the house, she rebelled, played hooky, failed some high school classes, refused to take any prep courses for her SATs, and wound up going to Kingsborough Community College, located right on Manhattan Beach, just ten minutes from the house. Laurie was taking a summer semester, hoping to earn enough credits and a high enough grade-point average to get a transfer to a four-year school like Brooklyn or Hunter or one of the upstate SUNY schools like New Paltz.

Kingsborough had its good points, including a beautiful sprawling campus with its own private beach overlooking Jamaica Bay, Breezy Point, and the Rockaway peninsula, and was considered the best community college in the much improved City University of New York system. But Tobin had hoped she would have gone to New York University, like her brother, or Columbia or Harvard.

Tobin assumed a lot of the responsibility for Laurie's academic drift. He tried to rationalize her situation by reminding himself he had gone to Staten Island Community College and did okay.

The next message was from his editor, Tracy Burns, in her usual clipped sentences: "Tobin? Burns. Nice job over there. Now throw a change-up. Do a birth instead of a burial. Call me, I could use a sympathetic ear."

Tobin knew that meant that forty-nine-year-old Burns had busted up with her thirty-seven-year-old boyfriend again. Tracy Burns's high cheekbones, long legs, and sassy confidence made her more attractive than most women half her age.

She and Tobin had long been attracted to each other, but they knew even one roll in the hay could ruin a beautiful friendship. Burns had been dating a handsome younger novelist who wanted to move in with her and maybe marry her. She passed. Burns thought marriage and monogamy were both ridiculous and unworkable ideas. "I love kids, but as some ink-stained sage once said, 'The greatest enemy of people in our trade is the perambulator,' " she said.

Burns was so newspapery-cynical that she often edited Tobin's girlfriends. "That weatherchick you're boinking just about qualifies you for statutory rape."

"She's gonna be thirty-one," Tobin said.

"We talking her IQ or her tits?"

"If I said that in the newsroom, I'd be fired," he said.

"Subtract her age from mine and that's how old I was when I lost my cherry."

"That's why you're an editor, and she does the weather."

"I owe you a raise for that."

"But she probably makes more money than you because she does TV."

"Make that a demotion."

Tracy Burns was great misanthropic fun, a terrific editor, a good friend, but there was also something very sad about her. This was a woman who would never know the joys of kids on Christmas morning. She would never marry, and she would not keep a steady boyfriend. She lived for today's edition of the paper because she was never satisfied with yesterday's paper.

I'll call her later, he thought.

Tobin picked up the portable phone to call Henry to make birthday plans when the next message marbled him in midact. He stared at the answering machine as he heard the same filtered voice he'd listened to on his cell phone and *Examiner* voice mail.

"Hi, Hank," said the mechanical voice. *"LL here. Just a reminder, tomorrow is your son Henry's birthday. Don't miss it like you missed his high school graduation when you went to Cannes four years ago."*

Tobin looked around his thirty-by-thirty-foot living room; at the two Stickly couches and arm chairs with the deep-brown suede cushions; the blue, red, and gold Persian area rug; the ceiling-to-floor bookcases; the framed original art on the walls, a prized Pollock, signed Warhol, some excellent reproductions of Matisse, Pissaro, Monet, Manet, and a few lesser-known modern artists from the galleries on Fifty-seventh Street and Soho.

He was almost afraid to move, as if the man attached to the mechanical voice were hiding here in his bachelor pad, watching him. *Who is this fucking guy?* The phone rang in his hand, startling him. His heart raced. He whispered, "Hello."

"You get my message about our son?"

"Yes, Julie, I was just gonna call him."

"Good. Bye."

"How are you? You okay these days?"

"I don't do small talk with big shots. Just double-checking, see ya."

"Knock it off."

"You want to ask me about the kids, fine. Don't ask me about my life."

"Okay, how's Henry?"

"I guess he's doing great on that newspaper. The pay sucks, but he's only twenty-two. He pissed me off dropping out of NYU. That goddamned school cost you over a hundred grand in tuition. . . ."

"Forget the money."

"No, I won't. I don't want him to forget it and become some spoiled rich kid who thinks Daddy's money is always gonna be there."

"That's a legitimate concern."

"You bet your ass. I busted my buns for twenty-two years on the job to get myself a half-pay pension. And I never asked you for one penny in alimony, just child support."

"I know, Julie. I offered more. . . ."

"Keep it and spend it on your bimbos. I want these kids to take my values into life with them, not *yours* and—"

"I know the song, Julie," Tobin said. "You've been singing it for so long they play it on the oldies station."

"Hey, get fucked, Tobin."

"That can be arranged," he said, trying to brighten the conversation.

"Not with me it can't," she said. "Besides, I'm too old for you now. I just ordered Girl Scout cookies from one of your dates. Who baby-sat for them while you were away, anyway? Don't tell me . . . Mona Falco? She must be pushing forty now. She the den mother for Troop Tobin?"

"Cheap shot. How's Laurie?"

"The best. She works, she aces school, she goes out with a yuppie guy named Mario with a business degree from Colgate, who's about as exciting as a Weight Watchers dinner. But I don't think you'll ever see him out of work or getting bailed out at night court, either. And I don't think he's got cheating in him. Yet. But all men are dogs who eventually look to bury their bone in any hole they can dig."

"Who you seeing?"

"My kids, my personal trainer, and my shrink."

He heard the beep of a call interrupt. "Can you hang on?"

"Call-interrupting is rude, and I have a thirty-second threshold for it."

Tobin laughed and switched over to the incoming call, "Hello?"

"LL here, Hank. Your ex-wife, the one you're still nuts about, she's seeing a real asshole detective named Zach Moog. Maybe you should tell her he's not really separated from his wife like he tells Julie. And, for Christ sakes, don't forget tomorrow is your son Henry's birthday."

Tobin's skin pebbled. Rage boiled in his skull. "Who the fuck is this?"

"Like I said, yesterday's papers and tomorrow's headlines, Hanky Panky. I have a great scoop for you. . . ."

"Eat shit, pal."

LL laughed heartily over the phone as Tobin switched back to Julie.

"Sorry, Julie, have you been getting any calls from a . . . Julie? Julie? Julie you still there?"

Dead air. "Shit!"

He hung up. The phone rang again. He answered and realized all he'd done was put LL on hold. *"We really need to talk, Hank. I have information for you,"* LL said.

Hank hung up again and walked through the dining room, passing the massive teak dining table, circa 1855, bought at an upstate auction of an old inn that was being torn down for a modern motel. The wooden chairs that surrounded it weighed forty pounds each, made of matching oak with red velour cushions and polished brass tacks. The Waterford crystal chandelier that hung above the table came from the same auction.

The calls from this LL, whoever he was, were bothering Tobin. *Could it be Henry himself,* he wondered? Busting his balls, trying to spook him, looking to throw him off his game, as he competed with Tobin as a new player for an opposing paper? Who else would have his work, cell, and home phone numbers? And know when he was arriving home, on which flight, at what time? Plenty of people, maybe. Almost everyone at the paper could have figured all that out. But was it Henry?

Or maybe it was someone from the paper, he thought. *Some ambitious upstart. Or an aging, disgruntled hack still doing general assignment after thirty thankless years. Or some jealous chick I never called back. Maybe it's not even a guy. Maybe it's a woman, with that voice filter. Tracy Burns. Or Julie. Maybe she called me from her cell phone as she spoke to me on her house phone, and used the voice filter. Good way to throw suspicion off her. Nah, Julie wouldn't waste her time. Wait, could it be Mona Falco? Would Mona jeopardize her job like that? Head of the NYPD Hate Crime Unit making crank telephone calls? Too nutty . . .*

He entered his master bedroom, which was furnished with a king-size four-poster bed with a polished oak headboard carved with Celtic designs that also served as a bookcase with matching oak end tables. An entertainment center faced the bed. He had three spare bedrooms, one for each of his kids and one that he used for his office, looking out over the emerald treasure of Central Park.

Women loved Tobin's apartment. And every one who'd ever visited offered new design suggestions. But he liked it the way it was. His kids rarely visited, opting instead to meet him at a restaurant. *I date my kids,* he thought.

He plopped on the bed and dialed Henry. His son's machine answered. "Henry, this is the old man," Tobin said onto the tape. "How about we go to Peter Luger's for steak tomorrow night and catch the Mets game. Something tells me it's also your birthday. Hey, that piece in the new paper today was ter-rif-ic. Just be careful of blind sources. Sometimes they can lead you down blind alleys. But hat's off. I'm very proud of you, big guy. Call me and let me know if you can fit me in between all the babes and bylines. Love ya. . . . Dad."

He hung up, stared back out at Brooklyn, and thought of Julie.

THREE

Tobin spotted his waiter through the Elaine's crowd and waved for his check. The waiter nodded as he delivered plates of food to another table along the brick wall of the famous Upper East Side restaurant that attracted the biggest names of Broadway, politics, the law, Hollywood, publishing, music, TV, and media. Reporters often stopped into Elaine's with detectives or other law-enforcement sources they used on stories. You couldn't really afford to eat in Elaine's on a print reporter's salary, but you could buy a cop a drink at the bar and stargaze and rub elbows with the high-paid columnists, editors, and TV news people.

Tobin had spotted a guy who looked familiar staring at him from the bar, mid-thirties, and fierce, dark-Irish good looks. He knew he'd seen the guy before, maybe a face from his Brooklyn past or from some other old column he simply couldn't remember from his drinking days. Tobin nodded to the handsome guy, who was a good six-three, muscles bulging under the sharp imitation Armani, red-striped blue silk tie knotted on a $50 white shirt. The guy had "civil service" encoded on his wordless glare, his unblinking eyes wicked with whiskey. He sipped from a rocks glass. *Asshole,* Tobin thought. *One of those "You-probably-don't-remember-me" guys from my past. A grievance collector who wants to put me in my place.*

Tobin broke the stare and finished his veal chop without looking back at the glaring guy at the bar. Dani Larsen left half of her main-course arugula salad on the plate and sipped her sparkling mineral water. She checked her gold watch a fourth time. Tobin's agent, Esther Newberg, sat at the next table with his book editor, Maxwell Issenoff, glancing at Dani and then at Tobin with mild amusement.

"Sure you don't want a decaf-cappuccino?" Tobin asked, opening the top button of his light gray Cerrutti suit jacket, dipping his linen napkin in his imported Italian Pellegrino water, and dabbing a spot of calf blood from his blue silk tie.

"I have to be on the air at four-thirty," she said. "It's nine-fifteen now. Maybe I'll have a mint tea at your place."

"I don't now and never will have any mint tea."

"I have some with me," she said. "And my toothbrush."

She always brought a change of clothes, her own tea, toothbrush, condoms, packets of Equal, and a breakfast Nutra Grain bar, too, Tobin thought.

The waiter brought the check to the table, and Tobin snapped his credit card on it without looking at the price. "Thanks for dinner," Dani said.

"Bugs Bunny's dates eat more than you."

"I'm a weatherchick, a mannequin that tells you whether or not to take your umbrella to work in the morning," she said. "I'm not allowed to *eat* eat! If they let me go general assignment, maybe I could eat something I truly love, like a goddamned hot dog at a Coney Island triple homicide. All these stories you told me tonight that you didn't have room for in your columns are more interesting than anything I've ever done on the air."

"War ain't dull, Dani."

"How can I get Bernie to assign me to real news stories like that?"

"Start by asking."

"I do but he says I give great weather," she said. "I could file a sexual harassment grievance for saying that."

"Don't. He's just old school. And the boss."

"But I hate weather. I want to cover murders, fires, elections, *wars.* I want them to send me over to the Middle East. I wanna be Ashleigh Banfield, Christiana Amanpour."

"Write Bernie a memo."

"Help me with it. Bernie's your friend. You know what should be in it."

He knew she was hinting that he should give her boss, his old pal Bernie Zachbar a call encouraging him to give Dani a shot at general assignment.

"Write the first draft, and I'll look at it," he said.

She brightened, grabbing his hand as the front door opened and Tracy Burns, his editor, entered with a woman he didn't know. Elaine, the loveable but take-no-bullshit owner, approached her, and they exchanged cheek kisses. "I'd like a table near a single, gainfully employed, heterosexual man, please, Elaine," Burns said.

"The table you don't need a reservation for," Elaine said. "For the single straight guy with a j-o-b, you need a gun to kill me for him first."

Burns laughed, looking youthful and full of energy, her big eyes darting around the restaurant. She flicked her eyebrows at Dani and winked at Hank.

"Hey, Tobin, I hope you're not using an *Examiner* credit card to pay for your prom," she said.

"Hey, Trace, you know Dani Larsen?"

"Sure. I watch her every morning to see if it's a good or bad hair day."

Oh, Jesus, Tobin thought. *She's already had two wines. Trouble.*

"Actually I'm looking to do general assignment," Dani said.

"General Hospital isn't hiring? Just kidding, kid, you have a great face for general assignment. If Tobin thinks you have all the right stuff, you'll excel."

"You were the best teacher I had at Columbia, Ms. Burns," Dani said.

"Really?" Burns said, and Tobin knew she didn't remember Dani. "Thanks, kid. I remember you now. . . ."

"You gave me an A," Dani said. "I was a brunette then. You said blondes had more fun in TV news."

"Right," Burns said. "And that's not the only place. Obviously."

"What's tomorrow's wood?" Tobin asked, referring to the headline story, glancing back to the bar. The guy who'd been glaring at Tobin was gone.

"Actually, I'm embarrassed to say, we chased your son's story," Burns said. "The Arab they busted could be connected to the blind sheik. Wish you had your kid's source."

Tobin nodded. Elaine came over and told Burns that her table was ready. Burns smiled, looked at the table next to a gay couple, and shrugged. "Maybe they've got the inside scoop on Martha Stewart," she said. "Good luck with your general assignment, kid. If you need a reference letter, call me. Your date has my number."

Burns drifted toward her table. "She's a character," Dani said.

"Nut job," Tobin said and excused himself and walked to the men's room, saying hello to a few actors and producers and directors he knew at the tables along Elaine's wall of fame. One bald, baggy-faced producer with a stunning blond woman, at least twenty years his junior, said he'd read the proposal for Tobin's new book that afternoon and was going to bid on the movie rights with Tobin's West Coast book-to-movie agent, Ron Bernstein, in the morning.

"Man, wouldn't that be great, us working together," Tobin said. "The deal is I always get first crack at the script."

"Of course," the producer said.

Tobin gave the producer a thumbs-up and thought how obvious it was that the beautiful blond arm-candy was with him for his money and Hollywood power. He stepped into the bathroom and walked to the single urinal and relieved himself, wondering if others thought the same thing about him and Dani. Behind him, the door of the toilet stall opened with bang.

"You really think you're hot shit, don't ya, Tobin?" said a slurry voice, booming over his shoulder. Tobin half-turned and looked at the hard-eyed guy from the bar, zipping up his pants.

"Actually," Tobin said, "I'm taking a warm piss, if that's what you mean."

"You don't remember me, do you?"

The big guy stepped in front of him, chest out, an intimidating bully-cop move.

Tobin zipped up and said, "No, and with that attitude, I don't want to, either."

"You and someone I loved like a father usta be best friends."

"Yeah? I have lots of friends."

"You forget the old ones. The way you dumped your Brooklyn wife when you got Manhattan famous."

Tobin took a step toward the big guy, put his finger in his face, and said, "You're out of fucking line, pal."

Tobin made a move for the door. The big man threw the deadbolt into the latch.

"I know all about you, Hank 'Forget-Where-You-Come-From' Tobin. Forget everybody including your once-upon-a-time best-buddy Jimbo."

He didn't need to mention Jimbo's last name. There would always be only one Jimbo in Tobin's life. He'd been one of Tobin's boyhood pals. He died on September 11, running into the North Tower with the jaws-of-life to pry people loose from a trapped elevator. The people in the elevator got out. Jimbo and four guys from his midtown firehouse didn't.

"Jimbo always was and always will be one of my best friends," said Tobin. "You must be his nephew. . . ."

"Godson," he said.

"Sorry . . . right, it's been a while, but Jimbo always talked about you like you were his kid brother. Victor, no?"

"*Vincent.* Vinny Hunt. And Jimbo was more than a big brother to me. More like the father I never had. I loved him."

"I did, too. Sorry, Vinny, the kid Jimbo always talked about. You're a cop, right?"

Tobin washed his hands, dried them, and held out his right hand.

"Captain," Vinny Hunt said, letting Tobin's outstretched hand dangle in midair like the arm of a tollbooth. "And not a kid. I'm thirty-seven years old."

"Hey, sorry. And I'm very sorry about your loss."

"Then how come you never made Jimbo's funeral?"

"I did," Hank said, putting his hand in his pocket, fiddling with change.

"I didn't see you."

"St. Saviors, 9:30 A.M. mass, November 28, a week after they found his remains, and made the DNA match," Hank said, pulling out his wallet, and removing a laminated funeral palm card given out at the church. "I stood in the back. I wore shades. I said my prayers and made my private peace with Jimbo."

Vinny Hunt looked at the funeral palm card and swallowed hard. Someone knocked on the bathroom door. "In a minute," Tobin shouted.

"You didn't write about it. How come?"

Tobin shrugged, played with the change in his pocket, and nodded. "Maybe because Jimbo's death wasn't a *job* to me. I'm a reporter, Vinny, not a poet, not a holy man. Maybe I didn't think I could do Jimbo justice. Or maybe because I just didn't have the balls he had."

"You gotta have balls to go to all the war zones. . . ."

"A lot of reporters have more balls than me," Tobin said, trying to defuse this potentially explosive, half-drunk cop. "We all dealt with Jimbo's loss our own way. I sent a private letter of condolence to Penny, and we had a long private talk."

Vinny took a deep breath and sighed. "Oh, Christ, now I feel like a shitheel," he said. "Me and Penny, we don't talk much. Matter fact, not at all."

"You should. She's a good egg."

"She never liked me. . . . I shouldn't be telling you all this family shit."

"Okay," Tobin said. "So how about them Mets?"

"If you were there at the funeral, then I owe you an apology, Tobin."

"Jimbo called me Hank."

"Whatever. Maybe I should've asked Penny if she heard from you before I came all the way up here to make an asshole outta myself. . . ."

The knocking on the door grew louder. "Go shit in your pants," Vinny shouted. Tobin could see that Vinny still wanted to punch somebody. Anybody.

Tobin smiled and said, "Ya know, maybe Penny thinks you don't like her. I mean you were like family to Jimbo, right? This stuff happens a lot with in-laws. A wife can get jealous of the time her husband spends with his relatives. Or old friends. Especially if they're single. Human nature."

"That was the problem. I'm single, and when Jimbo went out and got his load on with me, she blamed me. She figured if I was out runnin' around with single women there'd be single women runnin' around Jimbo and . . ."

The knocking on the door turned into banging.

"She can't be jealous anymore. Jimbo would probably have wanted you and her to patch things up, especially for the sake of his kids. Right now those kids—two boys, right?—could really use an uncle. Or a father figure like Jimbo was to you in their lives."

Vinny Hunt looked Tobin in the eyes, and nodded. "Matter fact, I'm his oldest kid's godfather. So I hear ya," Vinny said and took out his own wallet and handed Tobin an NYPD business card that said he was Capt. Vincent Hunt, NYPD Intelligence Division, located in the Brooklyn Army Terminal in Bay Ridge, Brooklyn.

"Let's have lunch sometime," he said, as a barrage of thumps rattled the bathroom door. "You ever need anything on the QT, about anything or anyone, my unit, my guys, they can find out anything. The chief of the unit is my PD rabbi, and he lets me run it with a free hand. I got undercover Arabs, undercover Israelis, undercover mobsters. You ever need anything verified on the shit that's going on, call. You need help, call. Unlike the Feds, you can rely on what we tell you."

"Sounds great," Hank said. "Not a big fan of the Feds, huh?"

"I hold them responsible for Jimbo. But that's a long story I'll tell you sometime."

The banging increased. "I think we better open the door," Tobin said.

They both laughed. "By the way, that Dani Larsen is some hot piece of—I mean, one great-looking broad."

"Yeah."

"She has some fan club, tell you that. Even Jimbo's teenage sons drool over Dani Larsen. You serious about her?"

"I'm not looking for a soulmate, Vinny. She's a date."

"The first time I ever seen her on the TV news I thought, wow, there's a girl a guy just wants to marry. You don't see many of those."

"No, you don't," Tobin said. "In fact that only happened to me once."

"Yeah, me too. Didn't go as planned. But still trying."

Vinny unlatched the door, pulled it open to reveal a celebrated actor and the middle-aged producer he'd spoken with a few minutes earlier. "Jesus Christ, guys," the actor said. "You getting chummy in there, or what?"

"Fellas, at long last meet Deep Throat," Tobin said.

"That's where I'll put my fist you ever knock like that again," Vinny Hunt said.

Burns stopped Tobin as he walked from the men's room back to his table. He grabbed the back of a chair and leaned over Burns, noticing Dani Larsen watching Vinny Hunt as he walked toward the door. She flashed her sunniest weatherchick smile. Vinny stuck a finger in the corner of his eye, like a bashful kid, nodded to her, and said hello.

"You're not serious about that training bra cadet, are you?" Burns asked.

"I'm not serious about anybody," Tobin said, glancing toward Dani conversing with Vinny Hunt. Both of them looked toward Tobin, who pretended not to notice them. But he watched them in the reflection of a pair of beer-logo mirrors.

"Speaking of kids, your son isn't a bad reporter," Burns said.

"He should've stayed in school."

"You didn't."

"True," Tobin said, watching Dani Larsen scribble on the back of a business card and hand it to Vinny Hunt. "But that was a different time."

"I think your date likes the big dick in the fake Armani."

"You have a delicate way with words."

"Well, he's about six-three and he is a detective, isn't he?"

"Yeah."

"Like I said, big dick."

"She's entitled to make contacts," Tobin said. "Listen, I might do something on Nick Koutros, the bribe judge, for Thursday. Not sure yet. Enjoy your dinner."

"Enjoy your *dessert*."

"I'll try," he said, watching Vinny Hunt leave and Dani watching him go.

"You should pick on somebody your own age," Tracy Burns said.

"You, too."

She nodded and smiled, and Tobin walked to his table. Without sitting he signed the credit-card slip, left a thirty percent tip, and stuffed the receipt into his jacket pocket.

"Ready?" he said.

"Sure," Dani said, standing, pulling her overnight bag over her shoulder, and taking Tobin by the hand. It made him feel foolish and self-conscious.

As they approached the door, a gang of loud young reporters entered in a laughing flourish. "We gonna kick ass and take some names," he heard one familiar voice shout and then from the center of the pack he saw his son, Henry, a few beers past deadline, effusive as a lead actor on opening night.

"Hey, big guy," Tobin said.

The other young reporters hushed in the presence of the legendary Hank Tobin.

"Hey," Henry said, awkward and surprised, looking from his father to Dani Larsen. He noticed that her hand was in his. Tobin let go of her hand and reached it out toward Henry. They shook.

"Introduce us to your old man, Henry," said one of his *Globe* pals.

"Just because you kicked his butt today doesn't mean we don't want to meet him," said another.

Henry looked from Tobin to Dani again and said, "Guys, this is my old man."

Tobin took special care to shake each one's hand, ask their names, what they were working on, wishing them luck on the new paper. The young reporters, men and women, seemed thrilled to be speaking with the unassuming Hank Tobin.

Then an awkward little silence ticked in the doorway, actors waiting for a cue.

"I'm Dani Larsen," Dani said, filling the dead air and extending her hand to Henry. "That was an awesome story you had on page one today."

Henry shook her hand, mumbled a "thanks," and looked Dani straight in the eyes.

"You get my message about the Mets game, Henry?" Tobin asked, studying his tall lean son, strong and loose with a swimmer's body. Henry was an attractive blend of his father's dark-Irish genes and his mother's chiseled Italian features, his face ignited by big baby-blue eyes that burst out of some hybrid Viking/Celtic ancestry. Since grammar school those blue eyes and thick brows made even good girls go nutty over him.

"Yeah."

"Sound okay?"

"Actually, I'm a Yankees fan, Pop. I'd rather go to see the Cyclones. Even though they're a Mets farm team, I root for them because they're from Brooklyn. Grab a Nathan's dog instead of a Luger's steak, if it's all the same to you."

"All the way out in Coney to see a farm team?"

"They're a Brooklyn team. And we used to go to Coney all the time."

Tobin nodded, realizing he'd sounded like an elitist snob. "Great. Always wanted to catch a game down at KeySpan Park. We'll talk in the morning, no?"

"Yeah."

"You okay?"

"Great," Henry said, staring at Dani Larsen.

"Nice to meet you," Henry said.

"We'll talk tomorrow," Tobin said.

"Great."

"That was a helluva piece today," Tobin said, in front of Henry's friends.

Henry nodded and said, "Thanks."

Henry nodded and walked to the bar with his newspaper buddies, the way Hank Tobin had done after thousands of deadlines over the years.

"Ready?" Dani asked.

Tobin stared at the group of young reporters, saw someone hand his son a beer, and watched him guzzle in his splendid, sudsy youth.

FOUR

Tobin imagined Julie answering her Brooklyn door. Dressed in a robe, her hair wet from the shower, startled and thrilled to see Tobin on her doorstep. He imagined Julie telling him that the kids were not at home, wouldn't be back for hours. He imagined her inviting him in for a cup of coffee. And following her into the kitchen, where she rose on tiptoes to reach for the coffee on the high shelf in the left-hand oak closet. Next to the fridge that was covered with magnet-secured family photos of Henry and Laurie and dozens of photos of Hank and Julie down on the sands of Coney Island. Pushing strollers through the Brooklyn Botanical Garden. Playing softball in an annual Brooklyn saloon league. And family shots of the whole Tobin family on Christmas, Easter, Fourth of July, and Thanksgiving. And on the kids' birthdays. He envisioned himself walking up to Julie from behind as she reached for the coffee. And wrapping his arms around her waist. He could hear her emit a soft, wounded moan, a sound that said, "Come in, all is forgiven, come back to me, the kids, and the family." And Hank loosened the belt of the robe, pulling it down over her narrow shoulders. Leaving her standing naked and warm and freshly showered, her back arching as she clutched the top of the freezer door. He imagined cupping her full breasts, the breasts that nursed his children, and kissing her long, soft neck. He imagined dropping his pants and entering her from behind as he gazed at the montage of family photos. Filling Julie with every inch of his love for her, he felt himself thrusting harder and faster, erupting in torrents, thrusting deeper and more urgent as words he couldn't even hear bellowed from his mouth.

"Wow," Dani Larsen said as Tobin collapsed on her, spent and panting. "You on something?"

"I don't need Viagra," Tobin said, rolling off her. "Yet."

"That was really something."

"Yes, it was."

"Too bad you called me *Julie*."

He stopped his panting, held his breath, and looked at her betrayed young face. She hoisted herself out of the bed, searching for her itsy-bitsy thong panties, revealing all her near-perfect nakedness as she circled the big four-poster bed. She was gym toned, wasp waisted, small breasted, and natural, her skin as taut as the hide of a bongo.

"Sorry," Tobin said.

"Me, too. It's the third time you've done that."

"Strike three?"

"I do weather, not sports, Hank."

"I feel like an asshole."

"If it's any consolation, that makes two of us," she said, pulling on the panties and then wiggling herself into a pair of jeans.

"You're leaving?"

"I have to be on the air at four-thirty," she said, covering her breasts with a loose blouse. "It's almost midnight. If I grab a cab, I can still wedge in three hours' sleep."

"Stay."

She looked at him, eyes wounded, and flashed the weatherchick smile. "Even when I was growing up poor in Scranton, dreaming of someday being a big-city reporter, I never slept three in a bed."

"Let's not get too self-righteous," Tobin said. "I saw you give that cop your card."

"You mean the tall, shy, big-shouldered babe of a guy?"

"Him."

"He asked for an autograph for one of his nephews who lost his fireman father on September 11," she said. "What was I supposed to do? Say no? I don't even know his name. But you know what the hunk said to me before he left?"

"That you were a hot piece of ass?"

"I wish," she said, hoisting her overnight bag onto her shoulder and walking to the penthouse door. "He said I was lucky to be with such a terrific guy like you. Asshole that I am, I said, 'I know.' "

Tobin climbed out of bed, in rugged good shape for a man his age, his beer belly long gone from abstinence and his muscle tone firm if not rippling from push-ups, sit-ups, crunches, and dumbbells.

"I'm sorry, please stay," Tobin said, pulling on a pair of Jockey underwear, feeling too naked to be naked.

"You're a nice guy. But my advice? Only date chicks named Julie. Bye, Hank."

He watched her walk with erect self-dignity across the gleaming Italian marble floor that reflected the crazy, dazzling cityscape of Manhattan. Dani unlocked the door and left. And never looked back. Gorgeous.

Tobin stared at the closed door for a long time, alone in the big, opulent, and silent penthouse. He locked the door, grabbed the cordless phone, and walked to the terrace. Manhattan shone before him like the biggest illuminated target on earth. He gaped south through the black hole in the skyline, and focused on the darkened prairie of Brooklyn where Julie slept in a house filled with pictures of the fractured family.

He dialed a number on the telephone. It rang six times before an unhappy man's voice said, "This better be fucking good."

"Bernie, this is Hank Tobin."

"At this hour?" asked Bernie Zachbar, the legendary TV news director who was Dani Larsen's boss. "I got a four-thirty broadcast staffed by a collection of knuckleheads suffering from anchoritis, and you call me at midnight for what? Is the Chrysler Building still standing?"

"I need a favor."

"I owe you a few. But, Christ, can't it wait till the roosters have their coffee?"

"I'll never sleep unless I ask you right now."

"What, Hank?"

"You got a weatherchick named Dani Larsen. . . ."

"Everybody wants to meet Dani Larsen. . . . Wait a minute. You're already doing her, aren't you?"

"No," Tobin said. "That's why I can ask for the favor now. The kid is dying to do general assignment. She has more balls and pride than you know. She's ready, Bernie."

"She's the most popular weatherchick in morning New York, Hank. . . ."

"She's thirty-one," Tobin said. "She already gets ten, maybe fifteen years chopped off at the end for being a dame. Don't take any more away now."

"You serious about her?"

"No, it's just her turn," Tobin said. "Can you do it?"

"Done," he said.

"Don't tell her I called you. Let her think she got it strictly on merit."

"Okay. And, speaking of upstarts, that kid of yours, Harry . . ."

"Henry."

"Yeah, good reporter. But tell him to be careful of blind sources."

"I already did."

"Don't call me this late anymore, Hank."

"Thanks, Bernie," Tobin said and clicked off the phone and continued to stare south at Brooklyn.

The phone rang in his hand. He looked at the caller ID window that indicated that the number was Private. He answered and said, "Yes, Bernie."

"LL here," the filtered voice said. Tobin shivered in the hot summer night air.

"Look, what do you want, pal?"

"Wow, I thought that big guy was gonna clock you up in Elaine's."

He's a stalker, Tobin thought. *Dangerous. Mark David Chapman, Hinckley.*

"There are consequences for crank calls, guy."

"I'm just trying to help, Hank."

"Great, then let's meet, come out in the open."

"Oh, by the way, your son has another terrific piece on the front page of the morning Globe. *I offered it to you, but, hey, you weren't interested."*

Tobin said, "Do me a favor, will ya? You're probably well intentioned. You obviously have some good inside information about things. But I'm too old for anonymous phone calls. I don't need any new sources. If you don't want to meet me, don't want to give me a name, please, I say this as politely as possible, lose my number. Call Jimmy Breslin at *Newsday.* Call Steve Dunleavy at the *Post.* Call Mike Daly at the *News.* But leave me and my son alone, okay?"

"I wish I could, Hank," LL said. *"But like I said, I owe you."*

LL hung up. And Tobin stared off at Brooklyn, ants marching straight up his spine.

FIVE

Tuesday, July 25

Every time Tobin walked into a newsroom in the new century he got depressed. He was raised in the newsrooms of the 1970s when a constant *rat-a-tat-tat* of a hundred Royal typewriters and the AP, UPI, and Reuters Teletype machines provided a staccato soundtrack to a city room that matched the jackhammer tempo of the city street. In those disco days reporters used to call to each other across the smoky hodgepodge of desks, shouting for phone numbers, the names of sources, quoting their best lines, trying out leads on each other, busting a million balls. Reporters would bellow "COPY!" to copyboys who'd run to deliver one triple-spaced page of copy at a time to grisly, unshaven, middle-aged male editors waiting with lethal heavy black pencils at the city desk. People scrambled at deadline. Presses were stopped. It was a helluva job.

"Hey, Hank, wassup?" said a young city-desk editor named Tammy Kwon as Tobin entered the wide expanse of the *Examiner* city room, sporting a perfectly tailored blue-pinstriped Versace suit with pale-blue shirt and blue silk tie with red stripes. Kwon sat slouched in front of a computer terminal, as if waiting for a late train.

"Hey, Tammy, what's the good word?"

"You used 'em all," said Kwon, as she edited and moved copy to the copydesk with the bored click of a mouse.

In places like the old *Daily News* on Forty-second Street, legendary metro editors like Sal Gerage used to edit with one foot propped on a desk, Pall Mall dangling from his lips, a half-quart can of Rheingold Beer in his left hand, a pencil on one ear, and a phone attached to the other, shouting things like, "Fuck you, we stand by our story" to flacks from City Hall to police headquarters to the halls of the City Council. Reporters told bawdy jokes, made disparaging ethnic and gender remarks about each other, and were generally politically incorrect. And funny. Tabloid newsrooms were filled with noise, imagination, energy, balls, and laughter. A city room was a mirror held up to the frenzied city it covered. This was all based on the theory that fun newspapers came out of fun newsrooms. Few people ever got rich working for newspapers, but if the job was fun, then eager, hard-working, and talented people would make it a life.

By the new century, technology and political correctness had neutered newsrooms. Computers had replaced the manual typewriters. Telex machines were obsolete as wire services poured over the soundless Internet. No one shouted across the newsroom anymore as reporters now e-mailed each other silent, sneaky, and often mean little messages. No one shouted for copyboys because the job category had been eliminated. Copy was moved electronically. New kids were called "interns" and did mostly clerical chores for school credit. Alcohol was so verboten that anyone who came back from a three-martini lunch even a little bit tipsy would be called on the carpet. Do it twice and you were fired. The Sal Gerages were replaced by Brooks Brothers yuppies who sipped decaf lattes, deploying troops at formal morning-news meetings.

When Tobin entered the *Examiner* newsroom in the new skyscraper near Times Square, it was like walking into Metropolitan Life. Reporters with journalism degrees from prestigious universities sat at computer terminals clicking away at keyboards. A reserved, self-conscious din that never rose above the volume of a knuckle-cracking contest replaced the great, thunderous, exciting roar of the newsrooms of yesteryear.

Not that Tobin felt some cheap, syrupy nostalgia for the "good old days." He loved progress. He enjoyed an evolving city and world. He relied on faxes, modems, the Internet, voice mail, e-mail, and cell phones. He was spoiled by twenty-four-hour cable news, five hundred satellite channels, DVDs, global locating systems. And his Palm Pilot stored all the names and numbers and information he needed to feed the insatiable appetite of The Column. They were all amazing and vital new tools that in many crucial ways had improved the business of reporting and editing. But too often the human factor, the artisan's physical attachment to the craft, the pencil-and-paper, cut-and-paste, ink-under-the-nails elements of newspapering that brought reporters physically closer to their stories, and therefore their readers, had been lost. Technology could never replace the good pair of shoes a reporter needed to trudge through the dirty city snow and climb four flights of squeaky tenement steps to do a look-see piece of reporting on a triple homicide on Christmas Eve.

Tobin always looked for the footprints in a story. Searched for the details that showed that the reporter had put in the legwork and looked people in the eyes. The telling gesture—roll of the eyes, chattering teeth, sweat on the brow, smirk, scowl, or grimace—that accompanied a quote often spoke louder than the words. He liked to point out that the psychologist Ray Birdwhistell did studies indicating that only thirty-five percent of human social exchange is verbal, the rest nonverbal body language. The human face alone is capable of over a thousand different expressions, many of them mixed and emotionally cross-pollinated. Just as radio cannot deliver what TV can, no amount of technology will ever replace Johnny-on-the-spot, up-front, look-see reporting.

Technology made reporters lazy. The human factor was diminished. And with the decline of the human factor and the rise of political correctness, a lot of the "juice" or adrenaline of the newspaper job was lost. So was a lot of the fun. When you lose the fun, you lose the best talent. Talented people with loud voices and quick wits and limitless imagination simply would not submit themselves to being brought up on sexual harassment charges because of a comment like, "Gimme a fuckin' break." Or, "You look nice in that dress." Not for $50,000 and $60,000 a year. You could make that as a cop, with a twenty-year half-pay retirement.

A lot of the best talent had gone to write for TV news, or Hollywood, or hip magazines. Some wrote books. Some of the city's best reporters became flacks. Most columnists didn't even come into the office anymore, preferring instead to work from home where they could stay under the radar, avoid office politics, and be judged solely on their work.

But Tobin still liked to come into the city room, to talk to reporters and editors, to use the clip morgue, and get what was left of the "juice" of the dying newspaper business. Tobin liked people who made newspapers. He also liked to be around people of his guild who viewed him as a star, even if many of them were filled with private envy, open resentment, and unspoken contempt. He always made a point of saying a personal hello to the ones he knew did not like him, hoping his attentions might win them over.

"That was a great lead in yesterday's story on Koutros, the bribe judge," he said to an overweight female reporter named Phyllis Warsdale, who usually said little more than a perfunctory hello to Tobin. She was what the older, jaded, cynical newspaper people called a "serious journalist," someone who saw journalism as a calling, an earnest vocation, and adhered to all the rules and formal tenets. Warsdale would never cross the line, never stretch a quote to make it fit the story, or play sleight of hand with the facts to make the story more lively and readable. She was an old-school tabloid editor's nightmare but good to have around to give the paper a spine of credibility.

"Thanks," she said, startled but flattered as she refilled her coffee cup at the coffee machine. She always wore a spotless dark pants suit, white blouse, her hair short and never a strand out of place. Her reporting was as fastidious as her grooming. Tobin had never seen her eat a single morsel, not one pretzel, in the seven years he'd known her. She was heavy, but she worked hard at fighting her weight, which came not from gluttony but a bad genetic hand dealt at birth that she toiled to overcompensate for with sterling professionalism. She had a pretty face, a sly little smile, and if she ever lost thirty pounds, TV would snatch her up.

"I learned most of what I needed to know by the end of the first graph," Tobin said. "The rest was just a helluva good piece of writing and reporting."

"Thanks," said a disarmed Warsdale, sipping black coffee from her Styrofoam cup. "But I'm having a hell of a hard time following it. I tried getting copies of the original files on the two cases—the one Koutros is accused of taking bribes on. I'd like to talk to the arresting officers who screwed up the arrests. But the city says both files are classified. What bullshit. It's like the Giuliani years. Worse, because they're using the all-purpose 'national security' or 'antiterrorist' climate as a shield. What the hell does a corrupt Queens judge have to do with terrorism and national security? It's nonsense. I had to file an official Freedom of Information Law request. The FOIL could take almost a week. Plus, Queens Boulevard is paranoid. No one is talking."

Tobin saw his opportunity. "Hey, I know a few people who've been around since Donald Manes. . . ."

"Who's Donald Manes?"

"A Queens borough president who killed himself when he got caught in a parking-ticket corruption scandal in the eighties during the Koch administration—before your time. But Nick Koutros, the bribe judge, comes out of his old political club. Originally from Brooklyn but got transferred to Queens after that old scandal to fill in a vacancy left by a dirty judge. My guess is there's more to come, and I know a few guys who got burned and did time back then who probably know who else is on the take."

"Really?"

"I can get them to talk to you anyway. Maybe they can steer you the right way. Remember that if a judge gets caught, it usually means there's been a pattern. That means he's taken money from a lot of lawyers. Those lawyers usually come from big firms that support the campaigns of judges or other pols who appoint them. They also cultivate other judges. So if they have a paper trail on him, Koutros is gonna look to cut a deal. He'll name names rather than spend fifteen years in the can. Some of the old mummies I know might know who those names are gonna be."

Warsdale grew excited and said, "Why aren't you writing this?"

"It's your story, not mine. I was gonna do it as a companion column, but if you're the one being stonewalled by the NYPD, City Hall, and Queens Boulevard then you're the one who should do it. Maybe I can do a sidebar column off your main. When you crack yours open a little more, you can show they're crooks; I can say it. Hold on."

Tobin searched his Palm Pilot and wrote down the names of three people on a sheet torn from his Reporter's Notebook. "Al Collins is a bail bondsman, knows every crook in Queens, on both sides of the bench. Ira Stein has been chasing ambulances since they were horsedrawn. And Lou Baratta clerked for a corrupt judge named Wilson, who forgot him in his will. Baratta fell on a grenade for Judge Wilson about fifteen years ago, did time for him, and knows exactly how to follow the money. He also knows where more skeletons are buried than the potters' field gravedigger. These days he's the manager of an airport motel where the machine pols bring their goomattas."

"What's a 'goomatta'?"

"Nothing, what's a 'goomatta' with you?"

Warsdale didn't get the joke, just scrunched her nose.

" 'Goomatta' is a mistress," Tobin said. "Baratta runs a cheaters motel, Phyllis—the kind of place people go to exchange dirty money. Like bribes and kickbacks. I know for a fact that Baratta also worked out a deal with the Queens courts to use his motel as a place to sequester juries. So he gets his commission and splits it with the county clerk. They also use it as a place to stash guys in the witness program."

"I can say you vouch for me?"

"Of course," Tobin said. "We work for the same paper, don't we?"

Warsdale was speechless at first. She sipped her coffee and said, "I don't know how to thank you . . . Hank."

"Go kick some ass. Sorry . . . we still allowed to say that around here?"

"Right now, you can even call me 'toots,' " she said, hurrying toward her desk, coffee spilling from the cup.

He moved on through the city room, nodding to reporters and editors from sports, features, boroughs, and national sections. He passed the small windowless offices of subeditors and the darkened, empty Op-Ed page, gossip, and political columnists. They were all home working in their pajamas and would send their 800 words in by modem. He passed a larger office that had a window looking out onto Times Square, heading for his messy desk that he requested be located amid a cluster of other reporters' desks, giving him a more modest, one-of-the-troops profile in the city room.

A janitor wearing a pea-green uniform emptied Tobin's overflowing trash can, and swept popcorn kernels and pretzel crumbs from around his desk, collected empty Coke cans and a crumpled pretzel bag from his desk top, and moved on to the next desk. *Someone's been sitting at my desk,* he thought. His desk was always a mess, like a minilandfill of old notebooks, press releases, readers' mail, yellowing newspapers, and reference books and magazines. But he never left behind foodstuffs, a hangover from his childhood tenement days when the cockroaches would invade anything edible or drinkable left out overnight. He could forgive someone using his desk in his absence. But that someone had used it to picnic and left the litter behind pissed him off.

"Hank!"

Burns's voice was raspy with wine. She must have stayed late in Elaine's.

"Someone had a birthday party at my goddamned desk," he said, stepping into her office, carrying his mail.

Burns looked as sexy as an editor dared in a tailored gray skirt suit with navy blue pumps accentuating her rock-hard calf muscles under black stockings. She sat on the edge of her desk and snapped open the morning *Globe.*

"Forget that, you should have your son arrested for elder abuse," she said. "He beat the shit out of his old man again this morning."

"I gotta subscribe to that paper," Tobin said, walking behind her and reading his son's lead over her shoulder. Her perfume was subtle and expensive.

Henry Tobin Jr.'s story was about a plumber with a Middle Eastern name who had been arrested after Joint Terrorism Task Force agents searched his locker the night before in the Empire State Building and discovered blueprints for the building's ventilation system along with a jar of liquid arsenic. The man, Abdul Mohammad Aziz, of Coney Island Avenue in Brooklyn, a father of four from Yemen, swore he knew nothing of the blueprints or the poison. But Henry Tobin Jr. reported that an unnamed source claimed there were also anti-American and anti-Israeli newspapers and pamphlets found in the locker, with literature linking Aziz to the blind sheik Omar Abdel Rahman and Osama bin Laden. When Henry asked JTTF spokespeople to comment on this report, they would neither confirm nor deny. Henry also drew a connection between the maintenance man he'd written about in Brooklyn and this plumber, with his blind source claiming they both belonged to the same Brooklyn mosque and suggesting that Arab terrorists had infiltrated the maintenance staffs of some of the city's skyscrapers.

"Good story," Burns said. "Gives the reader a real Imodium moment."

"It scares me shitless, too, because I wish Henry had a named source."

"I wish we had his *blind* source."

Tobin knew the source was this crackpot LL, who had been calling him, pissed off about some old slight or column. He didn't tell Burns anything about it. Yet.

"You gonna do the bribe judge?"

"Nah, let Warsdale run with it until she can plant her flag a little deeper."

"Big of you. So, you and that weathergirl a May/December item?"

"Nah."

"Half your age plus seven?" she said, hopping off the desk, walking behind it, counting on her fingers. "Cut off would be twenty-nine. You're right."

"Your steady is half your age plus eight," Tobin said.

"But he's a novelist," she said. "That makes him world-wiser even at thirty."

"Maybe we should double-date, and your novelist and my weather-chick could get it on," Tobin said.

"I'd cut off his three-piece set," she said. "But I know he's out banging other young broads. That's why I threw him out. He calls it research. I call it whoring."

"You ever think that you're also research?"

"I'm sure there's an older woman in his new novel. And then he'll move on for good. But he's a slow writer."

"How long did you suspend him for this time?"

"He's been out for a month. He'll be out for at least another month."

He smiled and changed the subject.

"I might do a piece on coming home from the war to the war at home."

"Ugh! Please, enough with the friggin' war. If it's gonna be a navel gaze, make the readers laugh. You're still good for a couple of laughs, aren't you, Hank?"

"Depends on who you ask," he said.

Tobin leaned back on his swivel chair at his desk, called his son, Henry, at the *Globe,* and got his voice mail. He told Henry he'd meet him in front of Nathan's for a hot dog at 7 P.M. before the Cyclones game.

He scrawled through his e-mails, printing those he thought he could use in his comical mailbag column, copying snippets of letters and giving comical one-line zinger replies. He also sliced open a few envelopes with his letter opener. The column would take maybe two hours, more a typing job than a piece of writing.

The phone on his desk rang. Hoping it was Henry, he snatched it up and said, "Tobin, *Examiner.*"

"Did you get your mail yet?"

The ants scrimmaged on his flesh again at the sound of LL's voice. "Goodbye."

"There's a letter there from me," LL said.

Tobin cradled the phone, dropped the stack of mail on his desk, watched it fan out like a hand of cards. He scanned the envelopes and spotted the return address on one consisting of two letters: LL. The address under it spooked him to the marrow. It was the Marine Park address of the house where Julie and his kids lived. Frenzy burst in him. He struggled for control.

He remembered that some anthrax victims had died just from handling the contaminated envelopes. He took a deep breath. Sweat oozed on his chest and back and drooled from his armpits. Tobin rolled his swivel chair away from his desk, staring at the pile of letters. Other reporters noticed. They cupped telephones. Most stood and backed away from their computer terminals.

Warsdale approached, carrying a notebook, a big smile splitting her face. "Hank, I got in touch with Collins and I can't thank you en—*what's wrong?*"

"I might have a poison pen pal. Get *out!* Pass the word."

Warsdale backed away, spun, murmured to several other reporters as Tracy Burns hurried from her office, walking toward Tobin. "I have an idea for some of the art to go with your mailbag col—" She stopped in midstride and halfway through the sentence when she saw an ashen Tobin gaping at the mail on his desk and at Warsdale and the other reporters around him backing away and bolting for the exits, covering their mouths with hankies and their shirts.

"Hank?"

"Call security, Trace," Tobin said, his tongue a leathery lump in his sticky mouth.

"*What?*"

"Got a spooky phone call about a letter. . . ."

Burns wrapped her arm across her nose and mouth and shouted with muffled urgency, "Hank, get outta that chair, and get the hell out of here!"

Tobin stood and turned, and as he did, he saw the entire city room— reporters, editors, photographers, interns, janitors, cartoonists, secretaries—stampeding through the exits.

SIX

Tobin joined the exodus on the stairwells and down into the glass and steel and marble lobby and out into the sun-splashed streets of Times Square. People blew their noses, coughed up phlegm, and spit on the sidewalk in desperate attempts to expel toxins from their respiratory systems. Most avoided Tobin as if he were a leper.

The seven-million-dollar-a-week NYPD Operation Atlas high-alert antiterrorism plan, put into effect at the start of the Iraqi war, responded with lightning speed to the anthrax alert at the *Examiner*. As soon as the NYPD Bomb Squad and NYPD Hazardous Materials Unit arrived with two special emergency vehicles, Tobin was placed into a fully equipped, quarantined ambulance where his hands and mouth and nose were tested and swabbed by FEMA workers in bio suits. His clothes were removed for testing, and he was given a robe. He took a few items from his jacket pockets and slid them into his robe pocket. A nervous Pakistani city doctor wearing a silver bio suit took blood and urine and checked his lungs, heart, and pulse, and gaped with a lighted scope into Tobin's eyes, ears, and down his throat. The doctor offered Tobin the antibiotic Cipro. Tobin turned it down.

A little more than an hour later Detective Mona Falco of the NYPD Hate Crime Unit entered the "bus"—as the ambulance workers referred to the ambulance. She clipped her gold shield on the belt of her pleated black pants and said, "HMU took the letter on a lights-and-sirens race downtown to a special Department of Health bio lab where a robot opened it in a tank."

"And?"

"All they found inside were eleven sheets of paper," she said, flipping her memo book. "The first page was a typed note that read: 'Hank: The following ten pages are the last decade of my life. Thanks. LL.' The other ten pages were blank. No powder. No threats. The pages were checked for toxic chemicals, but so far nothing. The postmark is from a post office in Marine Park, Brooklyn, your old neighborhood, Hank."

"He used my . . . Julie's home address."

"I know."

"Creepy."

"I could have a radio car watch her house."

"Oh, she'd love that. Especially if she knew *you* sent it. Please, no."

"I have nothing against Julie. You okay?"

"No."

"I mean physically?"

"Fine."

"The air in the newsroom came up as clean as a tabloid newspaper ever gets."

"You're a laugh riot, Mona."

"We're gonna start letting people back into the building in a few minutes. Did this guy, this LL, or whoever he is, say anything on the phone about Jews or Arabs? Blacks and whites? Gays or lesbians? Abortion or animal rights? Anything that could be construed as a threatened hate crime? Is he after you because of one of your columns, Hank? Something you wrote about race or bias or right-to-life issues that he doesn't agree with?"

Tobin looked out the back window of the ambulance at the crowd of *Examiner* reporters and staff crowded behind police barricades onto a street corner across from the newspaper building. The entire skyscraper had been evacuated and emergency vehicles from NYPD, FBI, FDNY, and FEMA closed off the intersection, their lights flashing. Armed National Guardsmen circled the entire city block on which the *Examiner* building was located. News crews from every TV station in town were on the scene.

Word had spread that the building was evacuated because of a possible anthrax-contaminated letter to star columnist Hank Tobin. The all-news radio and national cable stations were already beating the story to death.

"No," Tobin said to Mona Falco. "He never mentioned any kind of racial, political, religious, ethnic, or sexual bias. If this is a crime, I wouldn't categorize it as a hate crime, Mona. He's just some kind of crank."

"I left you a message about your son."

"I was gonna call, I swear."

"Sure you were. I wanted to give you a heads-up that the Feds want to know all about how your son is getting these exclusives."

"He's a good reporter, just like m—"

The ambulance door opened again. This time two men in plain suits and ties entered. "Hank Tobin?" asked the steel-eyed black agent with a flat mid-American twang. He chewed gum like it was a second source of oxygen.

"Yo."

The man flashed a wallet with an ID card and small shield. "Special Agent in Charge Luke Cox, FBI, Joint Terrorist Task Force. This is my partner, Cyril Danvers."

"Hey," Tobin said, looking from Cox to the red-haired Danvers.

Cox nodded to Mona Falco, smiled in a sheepish way, as ordinary men often do in the presence of beautiful women. "Good afternoon, Detective Falco."

"Hi, Luke."

"Would you like anything, Mona?" Cox asked. "Danvers here'll get you coffee, soda, whatever you need."

"No, I'm fine, thanks, Luke," Mona said.

Tobin could see that Cox was smitten with her and that Mona knew it, using all the right body language to make him squirm.

"How about me?" Tobin said. "What, I'm not pretty enough to rate a coffee run? How about a double ice latte, my man, Danvers?"

Danvers just stared, said nothing. Cox chewed his gum and said, "Okay, no beating around the bush, Tobin. Is this some kind of tabloid publicity stunt to boost circulation and book sales?"

Tobin looked at Cox and the silent Danvers, who reminded him of a middle-aged Archie from the comics. Then at Mona Falco, who shrugged.

"You might not be beating around the bush," Tobin said. "But you are pounding your pud, Cox."

Cox grinned and folded a fresh piece of chewing gum into his mouth and chewed in a juicy squish. "Why'd you refuse Cipro?"

"Because it's a debilitating antibiotic that was overused during the first anthrax scare," he said. "I'll wait for the test results. Some of us learn from mistakes."

"Wasn't because you knew what was in that envelope?"

"I don't have Clark Kent's X-ray vision."

"Maybe you mailed it to yourself."

Tobin turned to Falco and asked her if she knew the postmark date on the envelope. Falco flicked through her memo book and said, "Three days ago, July 22."

"I was in Iran," Tobin said.

Danvers raised his ginger eyebrows and looked at Cox, who chewed his gum and smiled, and said, "So, maybe your wife mailed it for ya."

"When my *ex*-wife has something to say, she says it to my face," Tobin said.

"Or in court papers," said Cox.

"You sniffing in my underwear drawer, Cox?"

"Or maybe your kid sent it," Cox said. "The one with all the hot tips for his page-one stories. He seems to know every move we're about to make before we do. If someone hit the lottery the way Henry Tobin Jr. scores page-one exclusives, you'd be the first one to write a column saying the game was rigged, Tobin."

"So what are you saying here? That my kid sent me a letter filled with *blank* pages and made crank calls to me so he could get a story?"

"Or maybe you saw how good he was doing, and you figured this was a way of getting yourself back on page one," Cox said, chewing and swallowing. "Where you could sell a couple of books and newspapers."

Tobin laughed. "Right, and I put my wife's home address on page one."

"Maybe," Cox said. "And you said that's *ex*-wife, no?"

"Does your partner know any English?" Tobin asked, nodding toward Danvers.

"Affirmative," said Danvers, sitting up straight.

Tobin said, "Good, because maybe you can explain this to Cox...."

"Special Agent in Charge Cox," Cox said, chewing faster.

Tobin said, "I did not, my *ex*-wife did not, and my kid did not send this letter. It came from a crank reader. Maybe I overreacted, but if this is a false alarm, that's all it is. I don't need cheap publicity to sell books. I'm already a best-seller, and the *Examiner* doesn't need stunts to sell papers. We do it with talent. If we need hot copy, all we have to do is write another story about how you geniuses at the FBI can't prevent terrorism."

"Press hoaxes don't help, Tobin."

"You like to blame the press, but you guys screw up case after case: Wen Ho Lee the *alleged* Chinese spy, Richard Jewel the *non*–Atlanta Olympics bomber, losing the evidence in the McVeigh trial, letting Robert Hansen, the FBI Soviet master spy, operate under your noses for fifteen years, blowing the Zacarias Moussaoui evidence. You came up with more than ten blank pages before September 11 and three thousand full coffins by September 12."

"We don't have any blank pages on you," Cox said. "Or your publisher."

"And now I'd like to thank you for just giving me tomorrow's column."

Tobin removed a small tape recorder from his robe pocket. Cox stopped chewing his gum when he looked at the little red light indicating that it was recording.

"I'd like that tape, please," Cox said.

"I bet you would. But it belongs to the *Examiner*. And in this state you can tape-record any personal conversation you have with another person."

"You better not print the contents of that tape."

"Is that a threat, Agent Cox? We gave you people sweeping new powers, but we haven't revoked the First Amendment. Yet."

Cox stared at Tobin and the tape recorder. He stopped chewing. "This interview is finished," he said and nodded for Danvers to open the back door of the ambulance.

Tobin said, "Maybe you ought to start smoking to help kick that chewing-gum habit, Cox."

Cox gave Tobin one last glare before he stepped out into the sunshine.

"That was stupid," Mona Falco said. "He's one of the top JTTF agents. Washington listens to him. These guys have a lot of clout these days."

"I don't like guys who chew gum when they rag my family. It's a quirk."

"It's not smart to rag Cox."

"He's nuts about you, Mona."

"Get lost," she said, smiling. "He just has old-fashioned manners."

The Pakistani doctor who originally treated Tobin leaned into the back of the ambulance. He was no longer wearing a bio suit. He handed Tobin his clothes and said that based on the negative toxin tests, Tobin was free to go.

"I have a column to write," Tobin said.

The doctor shrugged, left the ambulance, and closed the door as Tobin pulled on his clothes. Mona Falco sat on a gurney, her short dark hair revealing all of the sharp angular bones of her beautiful mocha-colored Italian-African-American face. Her sensual full lips were the inspiration of hundreds of male-partner, locker room jokes, squad car fantasies, and juvenile police-station men's room graffiti. She looked at least five years younger than her thirty-nine years and at five-foot-five she was a trim and athletic woman but too short for modeling, and she had no desire for the world of make-believe drama.

Mona loved being a cop, especially a detective, and she had a tenacious, reassuring, disarming talent for getting suspects to talk. Women trusted her; men wanted to. Mona Falco was as even-handed a cop as Tobin had ever met and so the Hate Crime Unit fitted her like a velvet glove. Which she wore to weed the city of hate mongers, bigots, and fanatics.

But Tobin wondered how she could bring herself to do the job every day, protecting the civil rights of Arabs after losing her only sibling, a twin brother, in a classified Special Ops mission immediately following the terrorist attack on a U.S. Marine barracks in Beirut in 1983.

"I worried about you when you were away," Mona said. "I worried about you today as soon as I heard the call. You're a rotten bastard. But I worry about you."

"Why?"

"Wish I knew. The only time you ever call me is for column fodder."

"You're dangerous, Mona, you know that. If I spent an hour alone with you again, I might not be able to control myself."

"Is that so bad?"

"I can't let my kids believe their mother's theory that I was involved with you while I was with her," Tobin said. "I can't let them think I dishonored their mother that way. That I'm a deceitful, cheating bastard who wrecked the marriage, the family."

"That means I'm the plague in your life? Forever?"

"I'm no good, Mona. Find a guy worthy of you. Marry him."

"Admit it, the reason you won't date me is—"

"Don't you dare play the race card."

"What frigging race card? You're playing the race card by suggesting a race card. It never crossed my mind."

"Sorry," he said, smiling.

"I think, no, make that I *know,* that the reason you won't date me is because you're afraid it would mean you'd never get your wife back."

"I don't think anything will ever get Julie and me back together," he said, buttoning his shirt. "I just can't live through a second divorce, this one from my kids. They are my only family now."

Mona already knew Tobin had no brothers and sisters. He didn't have to mention again that he'd never met his father or that his Irish immigrant mother had been buried for over twenty-five years. He'd told her all that, little by little, over the years.

"Since the divorce, more than ever, I need my kids to respect and love me, Mona. My favorite day of the year—the day all my Christmases and birthdays come at once—is Father's Day. Maybe because I never celebrated Father's Day in my life until I had my own kids. More than ever, I need someone there on Father's Day. Or the rest of the year isn't worth living."

"So I shouldn't wait for your call? Ever?"

Tobin the columnist didn't want to lose a great source. Tobin's male ego didn't want to lose the affections of a beautiful woman, either. A mean, selfish, insecure little part of him wanted Mona to continue loving him even though he didn't love her back.

"I'll call."

"Other men call. I rarely answer. But they call, Hank. Cops, politicians, reporters, bankers. White, Asian, black like me. They think I'm pretty. They think I'm sexy. They think I'm smart and fun. They want to go out with me, Hank."

"How many are married?"

"Well . . . some are, but . . ."

"At least I'm a single asshole."

"If you're divorced and I'm single, why don't you call me?"

He looked at her, thought how silly he was in rejecting the advances of this stunning woman. But she was right. An open affair with Mona Lisa Falco could kill what tiny glimmer of hope he had left that someday he could get Julie back. Julie wouldn't resent other women in Tobin's divorced life. But she was convinced that Mona Falco was the Other Woman in the marriage. If Tobin was ever to have a second chance with Julie, he couldn't carry on an open affair with Mona Lisa Falco. And Mona was the kind of woman who would want it out in the open.

"I'll call," Tobin said.

She stared at him, pouted, and kissed him on his lips. *Oh, man,* he thought.

"Between me and you," Mona whispered, touching his face. "Just like the Feds, people in NYPD are wondering about your kid's sources. Tell him to be careful. I know if he gets hurt, you get hurt."

Mona had been a reliable source for over ten years, when he met her covering some forgotten bias crime in Brooklyn. She'd just started in the Hate Crime Unit then, had just made detective. And she was eager to climb the ranks. There was an instant, unspoken mutual attraction. But neither acted upon it because Tobin was married, and she was engaged.

One night, in a bar called the Mariner's Inn, after covering a perp walk in a Crown Heights race-attack case, Mona and Tobin stopped for a beer as she gave him confidential information on the case for his column.

After four beers, Mona sobbed and said she was a failure. Her first engagement, to a black man named Burke, ended when he admitted that he didn't want to have children with a woman who wasn't one hundred percent black. "I was nineteen and he made me feel like I was passing for black," she said. "He made me uncomfortable in black circles because my mom was white and my father was a black man who abandoned my mom when me and my brother were babies. We never used my father's name. We were raised using my mother's maiden name, Falco, instead of my father's name, John Wolf."

Mona said her fiancé dumped her and later married a black model. She met her second fiancé at a wedding on the Italian side of her family. He was the son of her mother's friend. He was a great dancer, wore Versace suits, drove a Cadillac, and took her to four-star restaurants. He was a perfect gentleman. She moved into his luxurious Soho apartment. He had lots of disposable income. He proposed, said he wanted children.

As a precaution Mona said she used her detective skills to investigate him. And learned he was a liar. He led a double life. She had agreed to marry him thinking he had a top-level auditor's job in Goldman Sachs. But she soon learned that her husband-to-be was actually a low-level clerk who supplemented his income as a bookmaker, taking gambling action on ball games for the mob.

She'd been living for three years with a man who had a secret life.

She left him.

When Mona confided all this to Tobin, he said it was better to learn all this about the guy now instead of after a wedding and babies. That night, after several drinks, Mona came on strong to Tobin.

Tobin's marriage was already shaky. He and Julie fought constantly about how much time he spent on work instead of with his family. Julie had suggested a trial separation. Tobin resisted it. He also resisted the temptation of Mona Lisa Falco.

But two months later, much of which Tobin spent on assignment out of town or out in late-night saloons with sources, Julie said she needed a separation from "you and your goddamned column."

Three months after separating from Julie, Tobin ran into Mona Falco on a story involving the serial killings of homosexual runaways. Mona was the detective in charge of the hate crimes. Tobin was in the third month of his separation from Julie. They had dinner, as friends.

Tobin drank too much wine, topped with two cognacs, and this time he said, "Well, we're both single now. I'm game, if you're still game."

It was Mona's turn to say no: "I don't want to be a rebound-misery fuck."

Tobin accepted the rejection. He let Mona Falco drive him home to his new one-bedroom Greenwich Village sublet where she kissed him good night at the door.

A week later Tobin and Julie reunited. Then he went to Ireland on the movie. Before he left, Julie told him she didn't want to know what he did while they were separated, but that he was now again part of a *marriage*. "Cheat on me," she said. "You cheat on our *family*."

Two weeks later Mona Lisa Falco showed up at the Shelbourne Hotel in Dublin.

Even though that interlude had been a sloppy, drunken, unconsummated fiasco, Mona had fallen hard again for Tobin. She couldn't help confiding her feelings to a few policewomen friends back home.

And soon rumors of a Hank Tobin/Mona Lisa Falco affair spread through the tight fraternity of women detectives in Brooklyn. Julie overheard a couple of female detectives speaking about the affair in a locker room.

When Julie confronted Hank about Mona Falco in Ireland, he stammered, sputtered, and ran out of lies. Julie refused to believe that it was a mere drunken one-night stand. Using her medal-winning investigative skills, Julie launched her own private investigation into Mona Lisa Falco and Hank Tobin.

Julie dug through Tobin's old Xerox copies of *Examiner* expense forms and found receipts for meals eaten in restaurants she'd never eaten in, paid for in cash. She snooped in his old notebooks, searched through his old columns, and matched them with Falco's arrest records, and learned that Mona had been one of Tobin's secret sources inside NYPD for over five years. Julie had always assumed Tobin's sources were men. But now she knew one of his main sources was the beautiful Mona Lisa Falco. The one he met in saloons late at night. Hank and Mona were a tag team.

She dug into Mona Falco's background, learning she had a Sicilian-born mother and a black father named John Wolf, who'd cakewalked on the wife when she was still pregnant with the twins. The kids were born in Trapani, Sicily. After the twins were born, Mona's mother traveled from Trapani to New York in search of John Wolf. She never found him. She overstayed her visitor's visa and won permanent residence in a general INS amnesty. Julie tried to discover what happened to the father. But none of the John Wolfs she traced had any connection to Mona Falco or her mother.

Julie solicited classified military information about Mona's twin brother, who she said was killed in a Special Ops retaliation mission after the terrorist attack on a U.S. Marine barracks in Beirut in 1983. Julie ran into roadblocks in her search, but she was a tenacious detective. Digging into Mona Falco's dirty laundry became Julie's hobby, involving vital-records searches in New York and in Sicily and genealogy traces. She even began tracing her own family tree to try to verify an odd detail her grandfather had told her about her own bloodline. But mostly she focused on Mona Falco. Julie's cop instinct kept telling her that something wasn't kosher about Mona Falco.

Then, after the Ireland incident, came the photo from Cannes.

Julie filed for divorce. Tobin was crushed. He pleaded with her to reconsider, told her he wanted his family back. But Julie was unmoved and proceeded with the divorce. After an official one-year separation, the divorce was granted.

Julie gave up her obsession with Mona Falco. She stashed away her file on Mona's background and moved on with her life as a single mother.

Ever since, Tobin had kept his distance from Mona Falco, hoping that someday he'd win Julie back. But Mona still called him. For Mona Falco, who'd rejected so many men, Tobin was the one who got away.

But here she was in the ambulance, outside of his newspaper building, this time investigating a case in which he was involved.

"You'll really call me, Hank?" Mona said, moving toward the ambulance exit.

"Soon," Tobin said, pulling on his second loafer. "Right now I gotta go write."

Tobin opened the ambulance door and stepped out into a mob of reporters, cops, soldiers, and citizens. He spotted Julie pushing through the crowd with his son, Henry. He knew that his daughter, Laurie, was at the beach out in the Hamptons and hadn't yet heard about the incident. Julie gave him a tight little smile and mouthed the words, "You okay?"

He nodded. Julie lifted her sunglasses and winked at him. *She winked at me*, he thought. *She came, she worried, she still cares.*

Then from the side he saw a dozen microphones jabbing at him.

"Hank, please." He turned and saw Dani Larsen, her eyes pleading for an on-camera interview. "Over here . . ."

He looked at her, her first New York general assignment gig, and it was covering the guy who had called her by his ex-wife's name as he made love to her the night before.

"I'll give a brief general statement and then give you an exclusive."

Tobin glanced at his son, Henry, who just glared at Dani Larsen, and then checked his watch and turned away into the crowd, looking back at his father as he left.

Julie moved toward him, her little smirk broadening to a smile, lifting her sunglasses again and dabbing her blue eyes with a hankie. She brushed past a man in his fifties with jet-black hair and matching beard and old-fashioned mirrored aviator shades. Tobin found it odd that the man wore golf gloves.

He focused on Julie, beautiful and coming his way, smiling. Because she had taken so much care to shelter it from the sun over the years, her glowing face was still wrinkle free. Her dark shiny hair hung through the back strap of an NYPD baseball cap, and she wore snug, old, sexy blue jeans, a clingy striped polo shirt, and small white designer sneakers. Smiling like that at him, pushing her way through the morbid crowd, in a time of family crisis, Julie looked perfect. Flawless. She looked like the one and only woman meant to be his wife.

He reached his hand through the crowd for Julie. And she groped for his. She clutched his hand and pulled him toward her. Ready to kiss and embrace him. Then the smile faded. She looked closer at his face. She crushed his fingers in her fist as she wiped lipstick from his upper lip, blatant red on the tear-dotted white hankie. Julie looked over his shoulder and her face recoiled, like she'd just been shot. She shook loose of his hand as if it were rat. She took a step backward. She yanked off her sunglasses for a better look, shielding her eyes with her ringless left hand. Tobin followed her eye line to Mona Falco stepping out of the ambulance, her bright red lipstick glistening in the late-morning sun. His heart sank. Dread filled him.

"Julie, wait. . . ."

He turned back toward Julie, but a hundred sweaty faces swirled in front of him, the sun blinding him. When he located Julie in the glare, she was backing up, looking from Tobin to Mona and back again, her eyes like the tiny shattered windows of a dollhouse. Julie turned and pushed her way through the undulating crowd, joined an embittered-looking Henry, brushing past the man with the jet-black hair and beard, and without looking back they hurried off together.

News crews and reporters encircled him.

"Shit," Tobin said.

SEVEN

After Tobin gave Dani Larsen the one-on-one interview at his desk, the film crew packed up the cameras and the lights. Dani and Tobin drifted away from the others.

"Thanks," she said.

"My pleasure," he said. "And hat's off on the general-assignment transfer."

"Did you call Bernie Zachbar about me?"

"You got the gig on your own hard work."

"Why don't I believe you?"

"Hey, you got here fast, you got the exclusive, you asked good questions, some tough ones, good follow-ups, you look terrific, your diction is flawless. Besides local, it'll probably get fifteen to twenty seconds on network. You won the job because you can do the job, Dani."

She looked at him as her crew finished packing behind her.

"I'm sorry about last night. I guess I got a little insulted. You've been so good to me. Introduced me to people, gave me great advice, inspired me, made me laugh. I don't sleep around, really I don't. But you were special and I guess I hoped you thought the same about me, and so when you called me by your wife's name, it just hurt and I—"

"Stop, I'm the one who should apologize," he said.

"I know I always pick your brains, but can I give you some advice?"

"Sure."

"Either go back to your wife or get on with your life."

"You're a poet."

"I'm a *woman.* You're a good guy. I sort of hoped we could have gone somewhere. Maybe we could still—"

"Any chance of that just ended, Dani. Some wise editor once said, 'It's fine to cover the circus as long as you don't sleep with the elephants.' You just covered the Hank Tobin circus, which you don't wanna join anyway. Believe me."

She blinked, looked a little sad. Her producer called her and told her they needed to get back to the station to edit for the four o'clock news cycle.

"You mean that makes you off-limits?"

"At least I won't get your name wrong again," he said.

She nodded, a little bewildered. "I have no regrets about the times we had."

"Oh, man, me neither," he said.

"Gotta go. See ya. And thanks for calling Bernie."

She smiled, but Tobin saw a twitch of regret tug the corner of her mouth. She turned and hurried off. *Another good one bites the dust,* he thought.

He turned to walk back to his desk and noticed many of the people in the city room glancing or staring at him. A few laughed and murmured. Some diverted their eyes. Others ignored him, as if he were a sideshow embarrassment. Hank Tobin had a way of glomming the spotlight with loud columns, gossip items, best-sellers, talk-show appearances. And now even an anthrax scare. He was used to mixed reviews, never let them bother him, believing that any publicity was good publicity so long as they spelled the Tobin name right. Those who didn't like him, his high profile, star salary, book deals, movie contracts, or his work could drop by his apartment and polish his Pulitzers for him any time they felt like it.

He plopped in his chair, placed his tape recorder and notebook on the desk, and typed his slug onto the screen, and started to bang out The Column.

TOB26JULY
BY HANK TOBIN
ATTENTION ALL DOGS: BEWARE OF FEDS.

Two days ago, after six weeks of witnessing the frightening anti-Americanism in the Middle East, I returned home to witness firsthand The Feds of the new America in action as I stepped off an airplane at JFK. In the time I spent in the bloody dunes and exploding streets of the world's tinderbox, I never once was treated the way I saw agents from

six different branches of our Federal Government treat a single innocent passenger of Middle Eastern extraction as he stepped through the
doorway of America. If the man were a dog, the Feds who accosted,
handcuffed, and dragged him for interrogation would be charged with
cruelty. But because he was an Arab, and they were Feds, the Consti-
tution did not apply.

But more about that incident later.

First, let me tell you what happened to me yesterday, after Federal
authorities were alerted to a suspicious letter I received here at the
Examiner. The newspaper building was evacuated. Citizens and emergency vehicles clogged Times Square, the crossroads of the world. I was
quarantined in a special ambulance to be tested for possible anthrax
poisoning.

Then I received a visit from a pair of agents from our allegedly new-
and-improved FBI. And it was my turn in the doghouse.

Instead of offering words of support and promoting a sense of
safety, the head Fed, Luke Cox, Special Agent in Charge of the New
York Joint Terrorism Task Force, treated me as if he were a dogcatcher
on the scent of a rabid hound. Instead of being debriefed as a victim of
a threat or a hoax, I was put under the interrogation lamp, in a classic
case of blaming the victim.

His partner was polite and shall remain nameless here. But Agent
Cox—who should be wearing a rent-a-cop square badge and checking
bags at the Staten Island ferry—didn't know that I had a tape recorder
rolling as they grilled me. As you will read here, Cox made a complete
horse's ass of himself.

But that's not the point. If the Feds treat a white American—in this
case a newspaper columnist who has more recourse than the average
citizen and the power of a New York daily newspaper behind him—in
this fashion, I shudder to think how they treat John Q. Citizen. Especially if he's of Middle Eastern decent.

Here then is a portion of the FBI's Q&A with me. . . .

Tobin then transcribed the most contentious excerpts of the encounter
with Cox, word for word. He left out references to his son Henry's stories
in the *Globe.* Then he referred to his notebook to recount the scene at the
airport the day before—which would read as two days ago in the next day's
edition of the *Examiner.*

He put in the confrontation with the acne-scarred Fed, named him, the National Guardsman, named him, too, and talked about how the Arab visitor had been seized by six Feds, handcuffed, and dragged through an anonymous gray door. *"That gray door represented in microcosm the new threshold of the United States of America. Visitors and citizens are being rounded up by Federal dogcatchers and dragged like stray mongrels through that gray door into the dog pound of the post-9/11 America."*

He talked about how he ran into the Arab in the men's room about fifteen minutes later and how the man vomited from panic and was too terrified to give his name or criticize the agents for fear of being denied a future visa to visit his family.

Tobin hammered his 800 words like horseshoe nails toward a "kicker," which in a reporting/polemic column like this often echo the lead, to give it an ironic symmetry.

This is how the new America creates life-long enemies. By treating visitors and citizens like dogs. And training those dogs to Beware of Feds.

"Good read," Burns said. "I'll fix a few of your mixed metaphors, and you slip from first to third person a few times. Since you're part of the story, let's keep this one first person throughout. But if I were you, I'd call my accountant and prepare for an IRS audit. And bang goes your FBI sources. Any Fed caught talking to you after this will be transferred to Anchorage. But guess what? This Cox guy is right on the money. That hoax letter and this column *will* sell more newspapers and copies of your book."

"That's called gravy," Tobin said. "But screw these guys. I'm tired of everybody trembling in fear of being labeled a traitor if we criticize the government because we're at war. We're at war to preserve things like the First Amendment."

Burns burst into laughter and hummed a few bars of the "Star-Spangled Banner." "All of a sudden Citizen Tobin is a 'serious journalist,' " she said, laughing. "You've bent more rules in this racket than old man Hearst."

"Well, Aristotle said the main purpose of all writing is entertainment," he said.

"See, even that's a paraphrase to fit your argument."

Burns picked up her phone, called the desk, and told Tammy Kwon to "refer the Tobin column on a page-one skyline. Something like 'Tobin

Leashes Feds.' Matter fact, show me a mock-up if we take the column out-side for the first five or six graphs under the wood and then jump to three," Burns said, and hung up.

Which meant there might be a Hank Tobin column logo and a refer-ence to his inside column above the New York *Examiner* logo across the top of the front page. Or the column might actually run across the bottom of page one and be continued on page three. One way or the other it would kick up a shit storm in FBI headquarters and make the *Examiner* letters page and web site and Tobin's voice mail and e-mail box sizzle with read-ers ranting about similar situations, some calling him a commie traitor, oth-ers calling him a Jew-hating, Arab-ass-licking cocksucker.

Tobin would be interviewed by talk-radio hosts, TV cable people. Bernie Zachbar would dispatch Dani Larsen to ask Tobin for a copy of the tape to play on the air. Then he'd make her get an official reaction from the FBI as to the fate of Agent Cox. Tobin, who owed Zachbar for giving Dani Larsen her shot, would give her the tape as an exclusive. And then Zach-bar's favor would be repaid.

"Our marvelous guild will be watching you," Burns said.

"Did I tell you that you look beautiful today, Trace?"

"You've been looking at women in burkas for too long."

"No, really, you look terrific, Trace."

She nodded, even seemed to blush. "Yeah?"

"Yeah."

"Thanks, Hank," she said, in a quieter girlish way, folding her arms across her chest.

She kept smiling as he walked straight to his desk and picked up the phone and dialed a number that had been in his head for twenty years.

"Hello?"

"Julie, it's me, Hank. Listen, please let me explain about Mona Fal—"

"Good-bye."

"Julie, please, she was there on official duty, you have to believe me. . . ."

Julie hung up. Tobin slammed down the phone, turned, and Burns stood behind him holding his tape recorder, which he left in her office.

"You better keep this somewhere safe."

"Thanks."

Burns shook her head and walked back to her office. Tobin watched her go. *Great gams for an old dame,* he thought. The phone on his desk rang.

"Tobin, *Examiner* . . ."

*　　*　　*

"I see you got my letter," LL said.

"Listen to me, this is getting old fast."

"So are we, Hank."

"What the hell do I have to do with your last ten years?"

"Everything, Hank."

"You could spend the next ten in a cage for stunts like that one this morning."

"For what? All I did was send you a letter. Sorry I caused all that trouble. I didn't threaten you. I didn't say one cross word about you. Or your wife and kids. I saw your wife, Julie, was there today. And Henry. That was nice that they were concerned. Laurie couldn't make it. She's out in West Hampton, at the Bath and Tennis Beach Motel, with her boyfriend, Mario, who drives a red Camaro. . . ."

"You get a charge out of stalking my family?"

"Can I give you some advice?"

"I don't take advice from people I don't know."

"But take it from someone who failed miserably as a father, you really should spend more time with your kids. They're older now. You missed the boat on some of their best years. But if you spent half the time you do with different women with your kids—dinners, a show, a ball game, a walk in the park, a weekend in the Hamptons, or up in the mountains—they'd probably love it."

The home truths that LL mentioned in his calm, monotonous tone hit supersensitive buttons on Tobin's guilt panel.

"Hey, guy, fella, LL, or whatever you call yourself, I don't need fatherhood lessons from you. I need you to butt out of my family life."

"A man can be judged by how good a father he's been. By that standard, I failed. It's too late for me. You still have some time."

"Okay, I hear you. Thanks for the advice. Now, please, stay away from my family and please stop calling me."

Tobin hung up. And picked up the phone and called his son.

EIGHT

Tobin watched a high, deep fly ball sail toward the three-quarters moon that dangled over the inky Atlantic Ocean. The breeze blew the American flag inward toward the stands of KeySpan Cyclones Stadium, where the Brooklyn Cyclones were playing the Yankee Single-A farm team. The smell of gunpowder from the pregame fireworks display still hung in the stadium bowl. It smelled like modern Jerusalem.

"That ain't going nowhere," Henry said.

"Isn't," Tobin said. "And that ball's outta here, kid."

He followed the flight of the ball past the nightlights of the Cyclone roller coaster and the Wonder Wheel that illuminated Deno's and Astroland amusement parks. Hurdy-gurdy music rode the salty wind that delivered the mixed aromas of hot dogs, knishes, French fries, and the sea. The ocean-whipped air currents kept the ball in play.

The Cyclones left fielder shagged the fly ball at the wall.

"Okay, so my round," Tobin said.

He hailed a beer guy, leaned across Henry, who'd insisted on sitting on the aisle (where Tobin had always sat when the kid was a kid), and bought his son his second tall, foamy Budweiser and toasted him with his container of Diet Coke. They shared a bag of peanuts, cracking them, and dropping the shells on the ground.

"Enjoying the game?"

"It's the top of the first, Pop," Henry said, as a sweeper in his fifties, wearing a Cyclones maintenance uniform and Cyclones hat, swept up the shells in the aisle and in the row behind them. "I would have enjoyed it more if I had time to go home and shower and change. But I worked till deadline."

72

"Well, you enjoying it so far?"

Henry looked at his father, removed his suit jacket, and said, "Great."

"What'd you write for tomorrow?"

"Pay fifty cents and find out. Like you always told me when I asked you."

Tobin nodded, watched his son take a deep slug of the beer and drop shells onto the cement aisle floor. Within seconds a sweeper swept them into a handled dustbin. Henry was sweaty, with a five-o'clock shadow. Tobin realized he had never been there to witness Henry nick his way through his first adolescent shave. He wondered when he'd started shaving. *Must've been after the divorce,* he thought.

"Henry, I gotta tell you I called up that synagogue-firebombing story. Hell of a piece of reporting. Talk about right place, right time."

"Thanks, Pop."

"Jesus, how'd you get there so fast?"

"Tip."

"Some tip. From who?"

"You asking me to reveal a source, Pop?"

"No, but be prepared that other people will. You get exclusives like the ones you've been getting, law enforcement will start looking hard at you and your work."

"First Amendment hasn't been suspended yet, has it?"

"Not yet."

Henry shrugged, gulped half a cup of beer, and shouted. "Brook-lyn!"

Tobin tried to remember being twenty-two. He couldn't pinpoint it. His twenties were like a giant ice floe, all frozen together and floating in a sea of beer, pot, college, chicks, madness, most of the details submerged.

Tobin said, "You ever feel like maybe going for a weekend to the Hamptons?"

"Sure," Henry said. "I might go with my friends next weekend."

"Oh . . . sounds good."

Another batter came to the plate, dug in, scratched his crotch, spit like a Roman fountain, and took a called strike. The Cyclone fans, including Henry, applauded.

"What about the mountains? Maybe you and me, maybe we could go fishing? Or camping? Or something?"

Henry turned to him, frowning, half-smiling, and said, "Pop, I'm twenty-two. We never went fishing or camping in our lives. When I was a scout and asked you to volunteer for the troop, you told me you loved 'the great indoors.' Now you wanna go fishing and camping?"

Henry laughed, drank some beer, wiped his upper lip, jammed the beer between his thighs, megaphoned his hands, and shouted: "Brook-lyn!"

"I just thought maybe we could make up for lost time."

"Pop, is this one of those time-to-reassess-our-priorities spiels? Because if it is, deal me out. Time comes, it goes. You can't get it ba—"

The batter smashed a line drive toward short, and the shortstop made a diving catch, bringing Henry and most of the other fans to their feet, chanting: "Brook-lyn! Brook-lyn! Brook-lyn!"

Henry joined the fans in jabbing his finger into the Brooklyn sky. Tobin felt an odd, empty disconnect.

"Great fucking catch," Henry said, sitting down and taking a gulp of beer.

"Great . . . so is that a no?" Tobin asked.

Henry turned to him in his seat. "To what?"

"Camping, fishing? We could even stay in a lodge or something."

"Pop, not for nothing, I'm a general-assignment reporter. I don't get four days off a week like a columnist. I get two. And when I get spare time, I spend it with my friends or a chick. The way, you know, *you* do. I'm not trying to insult you or anything but that ship sailed. A long time ago. Jesus Christ, you don't know who or what I am anymore. You don't know who I date. Where I buy my clothes. What my hobbies are. You paid for it, but I bet you don't even know what kind of car I drive."

"I'm talking about us, father and son. Who cares what you drive?"

"The car isn't important, but it's just part of the pattern. Sorry, Dad, I really don't mean to be glib, or sound resentful. But you don't just cram for a fatherhood final over a long weekend in the mountains, eke out a passing grade, and say everything's okay. You wanna get closer, let's do it organically. In increments. Like this. A lunch here, a dinner there, a night at the fights. Like this. This is cool. It's a start, Pop. Enjoy the game. Pass the peanuts."

Tobin sat through two more innings, watched his son devour four beers, which worried him because he feared Henry had inherited his booze gene. Henry talked about the batting averages and fielding percentages of the Cyclone team. He talked about what a great shot in the arm this ball-park and the team was for Brooklyn. Whenever Tobin tried to turn the conversation personal again, Henry evaded it, with inside-baseball gab.

Before the bottom of the fourth, Tobin watched his son order a sixth beer and another bag of peanuts. Tobin offered some cash, but Henry insisted on paying.

Henry's cell phone rang. He took it off his belt clip, checked the caller ID, shrugged, and answered. "Tobin," Henry said, echoing the way Tobin answered his phone. Then Henry listened, his eyes widening and half-turned from his father. "Oh . . . hi . . ."

Tobin tried not to look like he was eavesdropping as he eavesdropped. He noticed Henry check his watch, and lean forward. A hungry, anxious, bit-biting urgency seized him. Alarms rang in his head. Henry's eyes blinked, and he took a fast gulp of beer as he checked his watch against the time on the scoreboard, ignoring the Cyclones batter who launched a home-run drive to right field, bringing the fans to their collective feet.

"Give me an hour," Henry said. "That way I can change, like you say. Yeah, I know what you're talking about. Okay, I'll wear it. Sure."

He clicked off the phone and stood. A little wobbly.

"Your guys just put up three runs," Tobin said.

"Dad, look, sorry but I gotta go."

"Go," Tobin said, looked at him, concerned. "Go where?"

"Wouldn't you like to know?"

"A chick?"

"Nah."

"You're not going on a story with six tall ones in you, are ya?"

"I'm good. No pro'lem."

Jesus Christ, Tobin thought. *He's going on a job half-tanked.*

"Henry, it's your birthday. I was gonna take you to Lundy's rawbar, maybe Pip's for a comedy show. We were supposed to be together. . . ."

"You, above all people, are not gonna tell me that, are you, Pop? How many birthdays, holidays, Little League games did you miss to chase stories?"

"But you've been drinking."

"You drank your way through your first eighteen years in this business, Pop."

"I'm not proud of that."

"You did okay," Henry said, checking his watch. "Look, I have to go."

Tobin grabbed Henry's arm and said, "I'm not letting you drive."

Henry broke free of his father's grip, stared him in the eyes. "Yo, Pop, I'm twenty-two years old today. You lost your moral authority when you cakewalked four years ago. You lost your legal authority over me last year. I have a job to do, and nobody stands in my way of doing that. Especially you."

Henry moved up the aisle, the leather heels of his Italian loafers clicking on the cement aisle, his suit jacket dangling from a finger over his shoulder, and tripped over a step in the incline. He brushed past the sweeper who stood at the top of the aisle.

Tobin watched him go, apprehension gripping him as his son hurried from the ballpark as the fans chanted "Brook-lyn! Brook-lyn! Brook-lyn."

NINE

A half hour later Tobin bought a hot dog at Nathan's, slathered it with their spicy mustard, and walked up onto the boardwalk. In the distance he could still hear the chants of the Cyclones game echoing from the stadium. Coney was booming, lines forming for the rides of the amusement parks, the fast-food stands mobbed. He strolled the wooden planks by the Brooklyn sea, eating his frank, observing the young couples carrying Kewpie dolls, wary of the malevolent gangstas out on a night hustle and the young bums pan-handling for change by the kiddie park. He was soothed by the plethora of uniformed cops patrolling in cautious pairs.

As he walked to the railing bordering the beach where he'd left a zillion childhood footprints, where he'd kissed dozens of Brooklyn girls in bikinis on sizzling afternoons, he remembered one particular day when he brought Julie to bay Twenty-two. He'd bought her a meatball hero and a Coke from Mary's Sandwich Shop, and Julie Capone sat in her skimpy bikini, her olive complexion and blue eyes reflecting the colliding rivers of Irish and Italian blood. He remembered that her hair was dyed blonde then, cut in short, punky layers. A ballsy twenty-one-year-old rookie cop, Julie had stolen Tobin's imagination six months earlier on the freezing February day he first encountered her as she awkwardly clerked a domestic disturbance that ended in murder in East Flatbush.

He'd been scanning the police radio in the *Examiner*'s Brooklyn cop-shack and raced to the scene of a domestic disturbance. Julie, on foot patrol, had responded first. She was a nervous wreck, worry crumpling her pretty face. Tobin, a police buff, had reported dozens of these scenes before and knew the ropes. He helped P.O. Julie Capone secure the scene before

77

the detectives and forensic teams arrived—telling her to touch nothing, to detain witnesses. He scribbled the make and license number of a Mercedes Benz that fled the scene.

In return, Julie gave Tobin the inside details of the murder, which he turned into a tough, tragic, lyrical feature piece that was a classic anatomy of a "little" murder in the big city. A string of similar offbeat, colorful pieces would lead Tobin to his own column.

The day they met, Julie was commended by brass for doing everything right before the DTs arrived. She preserved the scene, kept the crowd away, and handed over live witnesses and several statements with names and phone numbers. Julie also gave the detectives the plate number of the fleeing Mercedes. All of which led to a fast arrest of a major drug dealer. The "domestic disturbance" turned out to be a drug-turf-war murder and led to the arrest and conviction of a top dealer. An innocent woman was just collateral damage in the feud. The celebrated bust placed Julie Capone on a career path to the homicide squad.

The next day Tobin called Julie at the precinct to check on a few details for his story. Julie said she couldn't talk. Tobin asked if he could buy her dinner. She was hesitant. He promised it was strictly business. They ate in Brennan and Carr on Nostrand Avenue and Avenue U, which made the best roast beef sandwich on the planet. He'd always remember that she arrived dressed in tight jeans, high oxblood boots, wearing a forest green Irish-wool turtleneck sweater with matching scarf and skull cap, blasting in from the snowy February street with apple cheeks and a big dazzling smile, shivering and wringing her small bare hands. She wore no rings. It was love at second sight.

They drank beer and ate beef and talked murder and later they drank more beer and talked about plans and dreams and laughed at each other's morbid homicide jokes and how murder had brought them together. Tobin walked her to her Toyota Corolla in the restaurant parking lot, giving her a bold open-mouthed kiss good-bye. When he was finished kissing her, she yanked the back of his hair and kissed him back. She tasted like beer and sounded like Brooklyn and laughed like a teenager. "Oh, my God," she said, jumped in her car, and sped away as if afraid of what she was feeling.

The next week they went to a movie and afterward dinner at Fiortino's. Over the following weeks Tobin scanned the police radio and accidentally-on-purpose met Julie at other minor police calls. On days off they met for pizza at Spumoni Gardens or Joe's of Avenue U for calamari and clams. Or

Nathan's for a hot dog when the first buds of spring popped over Brooklyn and the Coney Island carnies opened the arcades for the season. They made love on the fifth date, after eating home-cooked lasagna served with red Chianti in her Spartan garden apartment in Bensonhurst.

On the seventh date she knew he was a little nuts when he asked her to wear her police hat, opened tunic, badge, and gunbelt to bed. But she did it and liked it, getting a naughty kick out of Tobin's antiauthoritarian streak. She drew the line at bringing handcuffs into bed.

Then on a hot July day five months after their first date, Tobin drank cold beer under the hot Coney Island sun. *The way Henry did at the ballgame tonight,* Tobin thought. *I banged down at least a six-pack before dragging Julie kicking and screaming into the surf.*

He dunked her under the water that day, pulling her farther out until they were shoulder-deep in the sea. Then he stole her bikini top. She laughed and laughed, demanding it back, half-enjoying the risqué freedom of swimming topless. He refused to give it back, half-drunk with beer and July heat, waving it above his head like a victory flag for all on the beach and in the surf to see. A rowdy, randy crowd of Brooklyn guys formed, cheering: "We want tits! We want tits! We want tits!" Julie grew angry, her fierce Irish-Italian temper rising with the mounting waves. A crowd gathered as Tobin swung her bikini top, hoping to get a peek at her perfect breasts.

"Give me the goddamned top back, Hank, or I'll tear you balls off," she'd said.

"Not until you give me an answer."

"Answer to what, asshole?"

He reached into the little pocket of his bathing suit and pulled out a diamond engagement ring and said, "Whether or not you'll marry me."

He held out the diamond ring that exploded with summer sun. Julie's eyes bulged, she leapt in the air, breasts heaving for all to see, and grabbed at the diamond ring.

"You bet your ass I'll marry you!"

The guys on the shore chanted: "Tits! Tits! Tits!"

Julie looped her arms around Tobin's neck and kissed him in the Coney Island sea as the tide sucked outward revealing them at waist depth. Strangers applauded as he put the ring on her finger and pushed her under the water, with her yellow bikini top.

That night, in Tobin's little basement apartment of the Marine Park house they would eventually buy from the landlord, they made love four times. They tried a fifth, but Tobin conked out a little before dawn, still inside the woman he would marry three months later. Nine months after the wedding Henry arrived.

It all started here in Coney, Tobin thought, leaning now on the board-walk railing looking out into the darkened sea.

He took out his cell phone and speed-dialed a number.

Julie said, "Hello."

"It's me."

"Who's me?"

"Hank."

"I'm supposed to know that? Henry need to talk to me or something?"

"No. Henry split early—"

"Jesus Christ, you fucked up his birthday again?"

"No, he split early on a story. I wanted to explain about this after-noon. . . ."

"None of my business . . ."

"Please don't hang up, Julie. Hear me out. I'm standing here in Coney, and I was thinking about you and me and that day when I proposed to—"

"Good-bye."

Julie hung up.

He hurried back to his silver Lexus parked in the KeySpan Stadium lot and drove down busy Surf Avenue, snaked around Emmons Avenue past night neon that reflected on the boat-bobbing tranquility of Sheepshead Bay. His dashboard clock told him it was almost ten o'clock. He aimed like a homing pigeon to the house on E. Thirty-eighth Street. The old yellow house looked compact but perfect—the lawn trimmed tight, the rose-bushes clipped at fierce right angles, a fresh coat of yellow paint offset by forest green shutters, making the two-story house appear cared-for, sturdy, and immaculate. Like Julie. Rather than a piece of real estate, it looked like a part of a family. It was a home more than a house.

He scanned the block and saw familiar neighbors gabbing on red brick stoops, drinking canned beers, smoking cigarettes, listening to the Mets game on boom boxes as their kids goofed off on skateboards and played rap music on portable CD players. Hanging out on the stoop until after the Mets games ended saved thousands of dollars in air-conditioning over the course of a summer.

Christ, he thought. *It's a wax museum. These same people were on the same stoops when I left four years ago.*

Part of him shuddered at the running-in-place lives they led. But another part of him, the part that brought him here tonight, envied them and the solid, happy simplicity of their working-class lives. They had their kids with them. They were with spouses they loved and trusted and relied upon in life, partners who cushioned the slow, agonizing hobble into old age. Tobin thought they were blessed because they believed in something that was very, very important—*family*. For all the collateral bullshit that went with the debate—abortion, premarital sex, infidelity—Hank Tobin resented that the right-wing neoconservatives had made "family values" their issue. Family wasn't an ideology. It was a life source. As essential to existence as water and food and oxygen. *Without family, some kind of family, you don't really have a life,* Tobin thought.

When Tobin's family splintered, so did his life. He tried to replace it with The Column, but it didn't work. He missed Julie, the sounds of his kids in the morning, the silly domestic spats, and the dinner-table gab and the laughter.

He climbed out of the Lexus and heard all conversations on the neighboring stoops hush as he chunked closed the heavy car door. Tobin nodded to some of the old neighbors. They nodded back. *They'd have enough gossip for a week,* he thought.

He rang the bell to the house he bought when he was still making $25,000 a year.

He heard movement from inside, saw lights going on in the vestibule, heard the double locks being turned, and then the door opened. Julie wore a seersucker bathrobe and a towel turban on her head.

"Oh, Jesus Christ," she said.

"Don't give all these nosy bastards a show."

"Scram."

"Let me come in, please. I *need* to talk to you."

"Not interested," she said, guarding the entrance, smiling at the neighbors who watched from across the street and next door.

"It's about Henry."

She opened the door. "If this is a scam, I'll get my fucking service revolver and really put on a show."

Tobin stepped into the vestibule. Julie stood between him and the inside door.

"What about Henry?" she asked.

"He drinks too much." He could smell the girlie soap and the Herbal

Essence shampoo and the Oil of Olay wafting off her damp, heat-radiating body.

She blinked. Twice. "Yeah?"

"I'm afraid he's gonna get in trouble."

"He gets a DWI maybe he learns a lesson. Meanwhile nothing me or you say will stop him from having a few beers. He's just following in his father's footsteps."

"Cheap shot."

"So's you coming here using that as a bullshit excuse to invade my life. I'll mention his drinking to Henry. I'm sure you already did. Thanks. Good-bye."

"He got a phone call, left the ballpark early, and went on a story half-tanked."

"Like I said, father's footsteps. . . ."

"It's a different time, Jule. The news business is different now. He can get humiliated. Blacklisted. If he makes mistakes covering the kind of stuff he's writing about, he could take a fall. I had two Feds tell me today they think he might be manufacturing these stories he writes. I don't think it's true, but he's chasing blind leads. He could get set up. I'm afraid of the public spectacle."

"You afraid for him? Or for what it'll mean to the great Hank Tobin's reputation?"

"Cheaper shot." But he had to admit, that worried him, too.

"Are you ready to watch your son be publicly ridiculed?"

She bit her lower lip, took a deep breath, looked Tobin in the eye, and said, "He's a grown man, Hank. He's the same age I was when I made my first big collars. The same age you were when you chased headline stories. That I fed you. He has to sink or swim on his own. Don't try to be the over-protective father now. You're kinda late."

Tobin nodded, her words slicing through bullshit. He nodded, grabbed the doorknob to leave, turned, and said, "Mona Falco was just working the case."

He gazed into her face, beautiful even without makeup.

"That's none of my business. And I'm none of yours. Good night."

His eyes drifted down to her breasts where the nipples protruded through the damp cotton robe. He imagined her underneath the robe, knew all the special places where she loved to be touched and caressed and kissed. He grew aroused. She followed his eyes to her breasts, folded her arms across them.

"Can we have dinner some night, Jule?"

"Nah."

She opened the inside door, put on a big showy smile for the neighbors, and made sure she spoke loud enough for the neighbors to hear when she said, "Thanks, Hank, so nice of you to drop by."

He nodded, pushed a smile on his face, and stepped outside. And looked straight at the face of a guy he knew from Julie's police past, a detective named Zach Moog who climbed out of a Jeep Cherokee carrying a small bunch of prepackaged Korean-deli-bought flowers.

Tobin knew that Moog had been partnered with Julie in the Special Victims Unit. Moog often called her at home, leaving messages on her beeper. Tobin had heard rumors over the years from cop friends that Julie had a vengeance-fuck-fling with Moog after she first learned of Tobin's affair with Mona Falco. Tobin didn't believe it at the time. He always thought Julie was too proud to let any Tom, Dick, or Harry into her bed. *Especially any Dick,* he thought.

Tobin didn't know that Julie had kept in touch with Moog. But here he was, saying hello with flowers these days. It made him wonder about the old rumors.

There is no cure, treatment, or bromide for the human jealousy virus, he thought as he watched Moog approach. *You developed HJV in diapers. It gets worse with age, remains chronic over a lifetime. There's only one known cure—embalming fluid.*

Those in HJV denial suffered worst from it in times of midlife crisis.

As Tobin rummaged his memory, he unearthed old late-night phone calls, before the introduction of Caller ID. He recalled that when he'd answer he could hear the mindless whiskey din of a saloon in the background, a smoker's phlegmy breathing, followed by mumbling, rattling hang-ups. He didn't think a lot about those calls at the time. Now they had Zach Moog imprinted on them.

Tobin also remembered one particular night, maybe six or seven years ago, when Julie was in the shower a little after ten P.M., saying she had to run out on a case that just had a major development. Julie's incessant beeper ring caused him to root in her pocketbook, where he never snooped, digging past her service revolver, handcuffs, mace, and gold shield until he found her beeper. He just wanted to shut the damn beeper off. When he grabbed it, searching for the shut-off button, he couldn't help reading the illuminated message in the little display window. When decoded from numbers to letters on a telephone pad, the message to Julie spelled out I LUV U.

Tobin only knew about this mostly teenage beeper-code-sending-rage because Mona Falco had once sent him a similar message, long before they ever slept together. Mortified, Mona apologized for it the next day, saying she'd been tipsy.

Now Tobin remembered a dozen other times when Julie had to run out on late-night cases, after her beeper sounded off. He remembered other phone calls, lots of them, that Julie would get at night, which she would answer and then take the phone into the bathroom to speak privately, claiming it was about a confidential case the details of which she had to keep secret from her newspaper-columnist husband. Her line was that if stuff ever leaked she would be the prime suspect of the leak. She said that if she was ever brought in for a NYPD General Order 15 interdepartment investigation interrogation into a press leak and given a polygraph, she wouldn't have to worry about lying.

Tobin always approved. He often had to shield the names and conversations with his confidential sources. Especially NYPD sources. The one he shielded with the greatest care, of course, being Mona Falco.

So now, six years after those phone calls, after the beeper message, Moog seemed startled when he saw Tobin walking from Julie's house. Moog nodded in a smirky way and said, " 'Sup, Tobin?"

Moog rolled his shoulders, shot his cuffs, and gave Tobin one of those smug, flared-nostrilled looks that seemed to say, *That's right, I'm fucking your bride, asshole, and so what are you gonna do about it?*

Tobin stared into Moog's eyes. They didn't look altogether real, like little blue decals pasted on Ping-Pong balls. Moog held the stare as Tobin glanced at Julie, a game of chess played on the stoop. Julie just stared at him as Moog passed Tobin, smirking, and handed her the flowers. Moog kissed Julie on the lips and entered the house that Tobin had bought with scrounged-up dough in the early years, writing freelance articles for boxing, travel, and skin magazines. All so Moog could enter while Tobin was left on the stoop.

This is how murder happens in New York in July, Tobin thought.

Tobin knew Julie dated and had boyfriends, but this was the first time he had seen her kiss another man. He felt ill. He imagined Moog exploring her naked body beneath the seersucker robe, kissing her in all the places he knew so well and missed so much. In his house, his bedroom, his bed, where he had made his children with Julie.

Julie looked back at Tobin, and closed the door.

Tobin took Flatbush Avenue, the busy commercial street that was the spine of Brooklyn. He used to pick up Julie in their dating days, and drive down Flatbush Avenue when they went to "The City" to see a Broadway show or to eat in Chinatown or to swig beers on MacDougal Street. Julie used to pop out of her basement apartment in Bensonhurst, dressed in short skirts, high heels, her face gleaming, smelling of the familiar shampoo and Opium perfume, and plop in the front seat of his beat-up old Ford Mustang. Tobin would hold her hand as he drove, the way he drove now, all the way down Flatbush Avenue, passing Brooklyn College, where he'd gotten his degree in English Lit., never taking a single journalism course. He'd pass the little storefront of *Flatbush Life*—which some reader once called "a contradiction in terms"—a community newspaper where he took his first job before moving on to the *Village Voice* and then the *Examiner,* telling her that one day he would have his own column.

He was lost in reverie as he jockeyed past the dollar cabs and the groaning buses, picking up night workers on their way to nursing homes and municipal hospitals and all-night diners. He put on the oldies station and jolted through the once all-Jewish neighborhood that was now mostly Caribbean and African-American, passing Erasmus High, where he'd gone to summer school twenty years after Barbra Streisand and Neil Diamond sang together in the glee club. When it was still one of the best high schools in New York, a prep school for then prestigious Brooklyn College. Today Erasmus had one of the worst academic records in the public high school system.

He cruised past the eerie, darkened stretch of Flatbush Avenue sandwiched between the inky vastness of Prospect Park and black-night void of the Brooklyn Botanic Garden, approaching the granite literary cathedral that was the main branch of the Brooklyn Public Library, heading for the Manhattan Bridge, when his cell phone rang.

Let it be Henry, he thought. *Telling me he's okay, that he wants to have dinner after all.* He plugged the earpiece of the hands-free cell-phone contraption into his left ear, pushed the white button to answer, and said, "Tobin."

"Don't hang up, Hank, your kid could be in a jam," LL said.

Adrenaline gushed through Tobin, like a mainlined stimulant. "You got a beef with me, fine, take your best shot. But don't you dare fuck with my kid."

"You have no time to waste, Hank."

"What, where? Come on!"

"You know the mosque on Forrest Avenue?"

"Yeah, some of the clowns from the 1993 Trade Center bombing were associated with it. The blind sheik's Brooklyn HQ. Why?"

"I hope you're not too late. I got a tip. I tried to give it to you first. You ignored it. So I gave it to your kid. Again. But I just found out this might be more than I thought. I hope you're not too late."

"Too late for fucking wha—"

Tobin heard a hurtling whisper of steel against steel. As he drove down Flatbush the sounds of an explosion followed by panicked human screams poured into Tobin's ear.

"What the fuck is going on?"

"Oh, my God, I'm getting all this on film. . . ."

The phone went dead. Tobin screamed into the dangling black ball in front of his face. "Getting what on fucking film? What? Talk to me, god-damn it! Where's my son? Where's Henry?"

But the line was dead.

TEN

Tobin saw a pair of wooden police horses blocking the entrance to the Park Drive of Prospect Park. He yanked a mad left toward it across three lanes of oncoming traffic. He swerved around a B-41 bus. Sent a Brownstone Car Service station wagon screeching up onto the sidewalk of the parkside where it came to rest, popping its hood on the metal fence. Tobin drilled up onto a small grassy knoll next to the entrance. He rocked past the police barricades. And sped onto the Park Drive. He looped around the darkened park where hundreds of people strolled on the closed-to-summer-traffic roadway in the ghostly glow of decorative sodium-vapor lampposts. People dispersed as Tobin raced past. He rounded Grand Army Plaza, scuffing rubber as he squealed past the Third Street playground. He whipped by the Picnic House and the Long Meadow, blaring his horn and flicking his high-beam headlights. Citizens dove for cover, cursing him, giving him the finger. One bare-chested teenager smashed a beer bottle off his back window.

Tobin hit seventy-five mph as he swept around the ballfields, dotted with make-out, summer-love couples. He rode the brakes as he exited into Park Circle with his hand pressed flat against the blaring horn. Cars, buses, and trucks spun to stops at crazy angles. Tobin jigsawed through the knotted traffic circle. He accelerated up Coney Island Avenue, blowing through a half-dozen red lights. In the near distance he could see the first orange hue of flame. He smelled acrid fumes on the humid air and then the billows of smoke blew down the grim stretch of gas stations, body shops, and auto-parts stores. Sirens pierced the Brooklyn night.

Helicopters now buzzed in the sky, beaming searchlights on the tenement rooftops. Fire engines, police cars, Bomb Squad trucks, ambulances, and various unmarked cars with cherry lights spinning converged from north, south, east, and west directions into the intersection of Forest and Coney Island Avenues in the middle of the Arab community that began settling there in the mid-1980s.

The commercial street was clogged with Arab businesses, a casbah of electronic stores, fruits and vegetable shops, dry goods stores, Halal butchers, and a dozen Arab restaurants, kebob houses, and bakeries with signs stenciled in Arabic script. Middle Eastern music, drums and sitar music, accompanied by the warbling of some anguished desert banshee echoed from a record store.

Four radio cars formed a traffic barricade a block from Forest Avenue, uniformed cops diverting morbid, rubbernecking motorists, only letting emergency vehicles through. Tobin made a sharp right, parked in a bus stop, jammed his press parking placard in the dash, looped his Working Press card around his neck, and rushed down Coney Island Avenue with his Reporter's Notebook and small Radio Shack tape recorder in one hand and gripping a ballpoint with the other.

Tobin searched for Henry.

Pushing through the sweaty mob of weeping, angry Arabs in the smoky night, glaring at the flaming Al-Koei Mosque on Forest Avenue, Tobin couldn't see his son. Firefighters rushed in and out of the ornate building with the turreted Taj Mahal design, stretching hose, and chopping through a side door. Other firemen yanked pieces of the front doors and sections of window frames onto the sidewalk.

Tobin knew that in the initial chaos he had his best chance at access to the scene. Before barricades were thrown up and top NYPD and FDNY brass, Feds, and officious ballbusters from the Mayor's office arrived and cleared all the press out of the way.

He positioned himself behind an FDNY deputy chief in a white fire hat who talked to an NYPD lieutenant. Tobin turned his back to them, scribbling notes, as if reacting to what he was seeing in front of him instead of eavesdropping.

"Anyone left inside?" asked the police lieutenant.

The deputy chief said, "My guys pulled out a cleaning lady. She's fifty-fifty, ate a lot of smoke, minor burns on arms and legs, on her way to KCH. They'll probably copter her over to Cornell to beat the infection. The

Imam says there's no one else inside. Our guys didn't find anyone else. As soon as first response finished the search, the place went up in a poof. Definitely a delayed accelerant. The marshals will know fast."

Tobin's heart soared. It meant Henry was not inside.

"Witnesses mentioned a yellow van, SUV, something like that, racing from the scene," said the police lieutenant.

"Cocksuckers," said the deputy chief.

Now Tobin's reporter's sixth sense shifted into overdrive. He called Tracy Burns on her cell phone and told her he was going to file a second piece for the sports final. He told her what he already knew, about the fleeing yellow vehicle, the injured cleaning lady, and that it was a suspected arson. She grew excited. She'd hold the presses. Reporters and photographers were enroute. Tobin told her to send someone to the New York Presbyterian Medical Center burn unit, the best on planet Earth, to wait for the victim. "I want everything you can give me on the vehicle you saw fleeing the scene," Burns said. "Details. Give me Hank Tobin stains-on-the-tie, dirt-under-the-nails details. And don't, for chrissakes, let your own kid beat you."

Tobin hung up and moved into the crime scene like a predator. He scanned the tableau, a scramble of firemen, cops, and EMS workers, flashing lights, crackling radios. Outraged locals fell to their knees to pray or shook fists at the sky and shouted in Arabic. Some wept. The mosque flames lit the scene in a hellish glow, sparks spitting into the night air like little shooting stars. Dueling arcs of water shot from high-powered hoses crisscrossing in the orange haze, exploding off the building in showers of dirty diamonds. Heavy-booted firemen and emergency-unit cops splashed through sooty streams that ran into blackened puddles.

Tobin fanned smoke from in front of his face when he noticed two animated bomb-squad investigators standing with a fire marshal near the corner diagonal to the inferno. Wearing fire-retardant gloves, they poked through clumps of smoking debris, sniffing hunks of smoldering and charred wood. Tobin drifted toward them, checked his watch, wrote the exact time and date on the cover of his notebook, with the words "Mosque Bomb," and began to scribble a few descriptive notes. The climate. Sounds—sirens, police radios, hose water, axes on wood, shouting, crying, gasps, crackling fire. Stars in the sky. Crescent moon. Acrid smell. Lack of wind. Size of crowd—two hundred, and growing. Faces. Emergency vehicles—he stopped counting at twenty-six.

He scribbled some fire images, metaphors, similes, and active verbs. All the while he inched closer to the bomb-squad guys and the fire marshal, half turned away as if not paying attention. He pressed the RECORD button on the small tape recorder and sandwiched it between the front and back covers of the opened notebook, the built-in microphone wedged against the metal spirals, taping a secret record as he took notes.

He introduced himself to a weeping Arab woman, dressed in a modi-fied open-faced burka called a "hijab," getting her reaction to the fire. She said her name was Johara Sadat, and that she was a close friend of the injured cleaning woman, Nahira Shakoor, mother of six, and that she was a nonpolitical person who loved Allah and prayed every day. And that she was certain that this was arson because Allah would never let a fire start in their mosque by accident. "This is the handiwork of the infidels," she said.

"Could this be a response to the war in Iraq?" he asked. "Or the bomb-ing of the Midwood synagogue?"

"If it is, the infidels are striking out at the wrong people," she said. "We are peace-loving people here."

As his tape recorder preserved Johara's quotes, he eavesdropped and took notes on the banter between the animated bomb-squad guys and the fire marshal.

"No Molotov," said one bomb-squad cop, handling a piece of smoking wood with a special protective glove.

"Willie Peter will make you a believer," suggested the fire marshal, pointing to sizzling white dots on a piece of the charred wood. "Snow flakes?"

"Ya think? Need a fuckin' T round. Probably no shortage of them in this neighborhood. Matter fact, you'd expect them to be firing them out instead of in."

"Could be hump-jockey intramurals, too."

"Maybe an RPG-7. They love 'em almost as much as yogurt."

While the Arabic woman ranted, part of it knee-jerk rhetoric, some of it heart-felt grief, all of it impassioned and angry, Tobin scratched notes and searched the growing crowd for Henry. He didn't see his son working this story. He probably already got what he needed and was rushing to the paper or home to file for the Sports Final edition.

Tobin taped the Arab woman as he focused on the conversation between the officials. From old columns on the bomb squad and fire mar-shals, he understood most of their slangy shorthand. "Willie Peter will make you a believer," was an infamous chant of Vietnam-era soldiers. They were saying that in order to do this much damage and cause such an instant blaze it would have taken a round from a Russian-made RPG-7, a rocket-propelled grenade, fitted with a thermite round that would release inflammable white phosphorus particles, nicknamed "Willie Peter." The RPG-7 was a favorite weapon of Arab terrorists, and since September 11, 2001, the FBI and ATF guys were forever searching mosques and Muslim centers on "anonymous tips" looking for caches of these kinds of rocket launchers that they feared could be fired from small boats in Jamaica Bay at jumbo passenger jets as they took off from JFK and LaGuardia.

Now the bomb-squadies and the fire marshals were suggesting an RPG-7 was used on the mosque. *Odd,* Tobin thought. They theorized that it could have been warring Muslim factions or "hump-jockeys," also known as "camel-jockeys," taking out rival houses of worship in some kind of jihad civil war. Maybe Iraqis getting even with Kuwaitis or Qataris for letting America use their airfields in the war? That seemed far-fetched.

But Tobin also thought some rage-filled Vietnam vet who managed to smuggle home an RPG-7 could have launched the attack and now used it on a mosque. *Maybe a disgruntled old vet who lost a relative in the Trade Center,* Tobin thought. Or maybe someone who lost a kid in Afghanistan or Iraq. Or maybe a local JDL guy who wanted to get even with Muslims, any Muslims, for losing a relative in a Jerusalem suicide/homicide bombing. Or in retaliation for the unsolved synagogue bombing.

But how did this wacko LL know about it in advance? Tobin wondered.

Scribbling notes, he felt a warm presence by his side and smelled a familiar perfume. Mona Falco said, "You know something I should know, Hank?"

"I know that meeting you twice in one day is more than a coincidence."

She waved a night edition of the next day's *Examiner.* His column was bannered across the top of page one, with the tough attack on Cox, the top FBI guy from the Joint Task Force. Falco nodded toward Cox and Danvers, who stood speaking to the police lieutenant and the FDNY deputy chief. Cox hadn't seen Tobin yet, but he held a rolled up copy of the *Examiner* in his left hand, smacking it against the palm of his right hand.

Falco led Tobin to the rear of a fire truck, out of Cox's line of vision.

"I know you're gonna regret this," Falco said, referring to the front-page story.

"What's life without a little regret?"

"Um . . . a better life?"

"I love the way you say 'um.' "

She smiled and asked, "Your ex wasn't happy to see me . . . us, today was she?"

"Um . . . life is filled with regrets."

"How was your, um, birthday with your son?"

Tobin said, "Sorry, I don't discuss my private life with my kids with anyone."

As emergency lights licked across her beautiful face and the flames of the mosque reflected in her eyes, she leaned closer to him. Her breath on his ear was warm and thrilling, and the smell of her perfume stirred places in him he didn't want to rile. "The Joint Task Force knows your kid already filed a story on this bombing, exactly twenty-eight minutes after the first 911 call came in. In time to make the morning *Globe.*"

Tobin felt relieved by further proof that Henry was okay. It also made him eager to file his own column.

"You filing for the Sports Final?" she asked.

He nodded.

She said, "Between you, me, and better days, we were watching people from this mosque for the bombing of the Midwood synagogue. You were away then. . . ."

"I know about it."

"This mosque was connected to the 1993 WTC bombing. We think they're also connected to Al Qaeda sleepers. This whole neighborhood is a fundamentalist Muslim stronghold. Since Iraq, the call for jihad and suicide bombers on American soil has brought more nuts out of the woodwork. Maybe they lobbed a grenade at themselves, to deflect scrutiny, or to get sympathy. We're also investigating whether this bombing is a tit for tat for the synagogue. You can print that as gospel, just don't use my name."

"What about this yellow car that was seen fleeing?"

"So far we've been told it was a Jeep, an SUV, a panel truck, a Yeshiva bus, and an ice cream truck. Take your pick. All we know is that it's mustard-colored."

"I owe you."

"Call me."

He nodded and walked off in the direction of his car. Television news crews arrived, set up, and filed live remotes from the scene. Gangs of print reporters stood behind police barricades as the Mayor arrived with his top aides and the Police Commissioner. And now Tobin saw Cox and Danvers walking directly toward him.

"Good evening, Mister Tobin," Cox said, smiling, tapping the rolled-up *Examiner* with the front-page story quoting him verbatim against his palm.

"You think so?" Tobin said. "I think it's a bad night for New York and the country and Western civilization. But that's just me."

"Do we have the tape rolling again?"

"Nah. Even you wouldn't fall for that twice."

But it was running, sandwiched between the covers of the Reporter's Notebook.

"Please step behind the police barricades, Mister Tobin," Cox said, chewing a wad of gum, banging the rolled *Examiner* against his right palm. "This is a crime scene. We have so much evidence to collect. Thank you very much, sir."

Tobin sat at his New York *Examiner* desk banging out a present-tense, you-are-there second column, action-packed with details, picture images, sights and sounds and smells, shoring it with strong verbatim quotes from the Arab woman and the unnamed law-enforcement official—Mona Falco. He wrote a hip, educational riff on RPG-7 with a Willie Peter loaded shell. He added a wicked "nut graph," a Hank Tobin polemic on what it all meant to the city and the nation and the world, giving the column his loud voice and a ballsy point of view. Then he reinforced his argument with ominous quotes from the Arab woman, winding his way to a tough, grim, portentous kicker.

Burns popped out of her office. "Twenty minutes, Tobin. Can't hold it longer."

Tobin nodded. His phone rang. He grabbed it and said, "Tobin, sorry, deadline. . . ."

LL said, *"Don't hang up. Check your e-mail."*

"I don't have time for your bullshit."

"Check the mail from yourself to yourself."

Tobin clicked onto his *Examiner* e-mailbox and opened a message labeled "Mosque Bombing Pictures." The sender's address was his own private e-mail address. LL had somehow learned his password and tapped into Tobin's private e-mail address to send him an e-mail at his newspaper address. He clicked on the "You Have Pictures" box.

A series of digital photos opened before his eyes on the screen. The first photo showed a mustard-colored Explorer with tinted windows superimposed against the Al-Koei Mosque. The second photo showed a long, dark device protruding from the driver's window. The third and fourth photos showed a missile being fired from the Explorer in a streaking muzzle flash. The fifth photo showed the projectile exploding through the windows of the mosque. A sixth photo showed the mosque in flames.

Tobin stared in utter disbelief.

"You want more details?" LL asked.

"Shoot."

"Appropriate choice of word. The shooter wore blue jeans, white sneakers, and a blue Nike bomber-style jacket," LL said. *"Dark hair, gold watch, white guy. He paced up and down in front of the mosque, talking on a cell phone for ten minutes before the attack. He got into the yellow Explorer and drove by and fired from inside and sped off."*

"You could see all that in the dark?"

"You don't want it, fine, I'll give it to your kid for an update."

"No! I want it."

LL hung up. Burns strode to Tobin's desk. "Ten minutes, Hank, and I—"

Her jaw dropped when she saw the sequence of photos on his computer screen. "Jesus fucking Christ . . . that what I think it is?"

He nodded and whispered, "The source is blind."

"He takes pretty good photos for a blind guy."

"You wanna go with them?"

"Pope's pecker pious?"

Burns did a scrolling speed-read of Tobin's column, nodding, excited, snapping her fingers, banging the desk top. "Oh, baby," she said, moaning. The breaking news, exclusive details, and startling Zapruder-like pictures, all stacked against a looming deadline percolated in both of them like high-octane stimulant drugs. Stoned on news.

"It gets better."

"Give it to me, baby. All of it."

"Physical description of the shooter. But like I said, the source is a cipher."

"Gimme more."

"Six foot, dark hair, blue jeans, gold watch, blue Nike bomber-style jacket, white sneakers. White guy."

"I love it."

"How can I attribute it?"

"To an anonymous source," Burns said. "Maybe as a mystery hacker. Add a disclaimer down low saying we have no idea if the photos or the description are authentic but in the public's right to know everything we know as we learn it, we are providing what we know at press time."

"Iffy . . . you wanna go with it?"

"It's your column, Tobin."

"It's your paper."

She raked both hands through her thick hair, exhaled, put her hands on her hips. "We have five minutes till drop dead."

"Look. It's vague enough where we can't get sued. It can't hurt anyone specific. It's history's first draft, Trace. We have an obligation to give the reader what we have. Every inch of me says this is news. I'm okay with it if you are. You okay with it?"

"This is the computer age. Sometimes a source comes at you via cyber-space. If we don't go with it, someone else will, and I'll cut my wrists."

"Between you and me, it's my son's source. If we don't use it, Henry will."

"Okay," Burns said, checking her watch. "I'm okay with it if you are. Your call."

He typed the description of the alleged bomber and did another graph about the photos at the top, did a fast spell check, and held his finger above the SEND button for ten seconds as Burns watched.

"We have one minute, Hank," she said.

He looked at her. She looked at him.

He hit the SEND button.

Which sent Hank Tobin's life straight to hell.

ELEVEN

Wednesday, July 26

Tobin had the scrambled eggs with lox and rye toast, no butter, and coffee. Laurie had a fruit cocktail and coffee. They spent much of the time over breakfast talking about his time in the Middle East. And the previous day's anthrax scare and mosque bombing.

His cell phone rang twice, the caller ID window flashing Mona Falco's familiar phone number. He didn't answer. He wasn't going to spoil his breakfast with his daughter. Especially by talking to the woman his kid's mother blamed for the bust up of the family. He let the voice mail take the messages. It was probably about The Column. He didn't give a damn what she had to say about it. He'd deal with business later.

He knew that all over the city New Yorkers were reading a pair of his columns, two ass kickers, if he had to say so himself, that would probably cause a shit storm by the end of the day. The Feds would be furious at him, but they'd have to follow his leads to trace the mosque attacker.

But Laurie hadn't read the columns yet; she'd slept all the way in from the Hamptons. Tobin picked her brains about her mother and Zach Moog.

"I made a deal with Mom," she said. "I don't comment on her love life, or lack of one, and she doesn't bust my buns about the guys I date. I love her to death, but she tries to measure all my boyfriends against you."

"Really?"

"That's more than I should have said. One thing for sure, I don't want a stepfather named 'Moog.' But don't ask me more, Dad, please. I love you and Mom both and hate you both almost as much for not being able to work things out. Pretty stupid, too, you ask me. Both of you are *old*. You're never gonna find anyone as good as each other again."

"Jule . . . your mom wants no part of me."

"A lower profile might help. You know, try dating out of sight of Page Six."

"There's rats everywhere. Anyway, how are you? Who's Mario? What crime family is he from? I wanna run his yellow sheet."

"After you're finished racial profiling, we need to talk about something."

She gulped water. Tobin said, "Don't tell me you're—"

"Get the check. We'll talk while you drive me home."

Tobin drove over the Brooklyn Bridge and said, "Where's this Mario guy?"

"He's kinda afraid to meet you."

"Why? How old is this son of a bitch?"

"Chill. People are intimidated by you, old man, that's all."

"Why? Why's he intimidated by me?"

"The bullcrap tough-guy pose you do in the column, I guess. I tell him you're really a marshmallow. What about you? You seeing anyone new besides the weatherchick and Mona Falco?"

"Mona Falco is just a source. Let's talk about you." He ramped off the bridge and looped around to the entrance of the Brooklyn Queens Expressway heading for the Gowanus to the Belt Parkway to Marine Park. "You said you had something very important to talk to me about in the car. Talk to me."

Laurie fell into a long silence, gazing out at the sun-gilded harbor. He said, "Please tell me this is not literally a pregnant silence."

Astonished, Laurie said, "How can you say something like that to me?"

"How old is this Mario?"

"Twenty-one."

"You really think he's gonna stick around and raise a family?"

"You mean you think he'd split like you did?"

Tobin glanced over at her, the little dagger piercing his heart. "C'mon, I never wanted to leave, baby. You know that."

She nodded as he rumbled along the Gowanus Expressway, the traffic thin and breezy on the outer rim of Brooklyn. "I believe you, Dad. I really do."

"I'd do anything to make that up to you."

"Okay, how about a car?"

Tobin looked at her, the Lexus jolting toward the Belt, saw her slouching on the bucket seat, peering up at him with an innocent yet conniving face that looked like Julie when she was much younger.

"You little con artist. That what this is about? This the big father-daughter talk that might cause a scene?"

"I'm nineteen, Dad. I need wheels."

He shook his head, took a deep breath, relieved as hell that his kid wasn't knocked-up, planning an abortion, or ready to drop out of school to marry some Brooklyn knucklehead so she could have a kid when she was still one herself.

"You really ace everything in school?"

"Well, one B, in Spanish. Aced everything else."

"The B troubles me."

"You bought Henry a car, and he had two C's."

"I did?"

"You can't remember? You drinking again, Dad?"

"No! I've just been so busy. My accountant handles that kinda stuff. Buying a car is a pain in the ass. Paperwork, insurance, registration. I just told Herb to pay for it."

"I never ask you for anything."

"I wish you would."

"Okay, I'm asking."

"No, I mean, I wish you would ask me for real things, more than cars or cash or clothes. Father and daughter stuff. I dunno, maybe we could go away to the Hamptons."

"Yeah, right, I'd really look cute spending a weekend in the Hamptons with my father. You writing comedy these days, too, old man?"

"I missed you while I was over there. I covered stories about kids your age, girls planning weddings, who chose instead to blow up themselves and other kids their age on buses or in shopping centers or discos. I worried about you."

"Ditto, Daddy. I worried about you, too."

"I wanna be a better father to you and Henry."

"Oh, God . . ."

Tobin looped past Coney Island and exited at Knapp Street and drove down toward the house on E. Thirty-eighth Street.

"I'll call Herb and tell him to buy you the car."

She reached across and kissed him. "I loved you before you said that."

"What else is going on? You serious about this Mario?"

"Don't you even wanna know what kinda car I want?"

"I don't really know one from the other," he said. "I know a Rolls-Royce is out of the question. So's the one Magnum PI used to drive, what's it called? It's red."

"Ferrari."

"Yeah, no Ferrari."

"I don't want one of those big gas-guzzling monsters like Henry got."

Tobin braked for a light near the corner storefront that had once been Jahn's ice cream parlor when he dated Julie. Now it was a Russian restaurant.

"Mario must be Italian, which means he must know about cars," Tobin said.

"More ethnic profiling."

"What's Mario suggest you buy?" Tobin asked as he made a right along Avenue U. To his left Caribbeans played cricket against men wearing turbans on the meadows of Marine Park where Tobin had played football and baseball as a kid.

"Mario says that if you're gonna spend as much as you did on Henry's car, I might as well get a Benz or a Beemer."

"As in Mercedes or BMW?"

"You not as played as you look, old man."

"So what are we talking here? Bottom line?"

"I read a story Mom was reading about you in *New York* magazine that said you're the highest-paid columnist in New York. Then there's the books, the movies, the TV show. God, how embarrassing is that gonna be? Anyway, I asked Mom how rich you were, and she smacked me off the back of my head. She doesn't want you to buy me high-end because the insurance will be also be high-end. But I want to pay my own insurance. I don't drink, so you don't have to worry."

"Jesus Christ, kid, what's the price tag?"

"Henry's cost thirty-eight large."

"Thousand?"

"For thirty-eight hundred you can't get Rollerblades anymore."

"I spent thirty-eight grand on Henry's car? What the hell does he drive?"

"My Beemer would be much more economical on gas, Pop, and has a better resale value than his Explorer."

As he approached E. Thirty-eighth Street, Tobin said, "Henry drives an Explorer?"

"Yeah," Laurie said, laughing. "He bet me that you didn't even know what he drove. He wins. Again."

"What color is his Explorer?" Tobin asked as he made the left onto E. Thirty-eighth Street.

"Baby-shit yellow," she said. "He gets pissed when I say that. . . ."

Tobin hit the brakes. His heart raced like a little engine in his chest, so fast he could almost hear it. The veins in his temples pulsed, and his mouth went blotter dry.

He watched Mona Falco handcuffing Henry, as photographers snapped pictures, leading him from his mustard-colored Explorer, identical to the one in the photographs sent by LL. His son wore blue jeans, white sneakers, and a blue Nike jacket. The same as the details in his column. Special Agent in Charge Luke Cox wore plastic gloves and carried the RPG-7 rocket launcher from Henry's car.

Reporters and photographers from rival newspapers clogged the street. A helicopter from a local TV station hovered overhead. More TV news crews shot handheld footage of the arrest.

All the neighbors were out on their stoops, gaping at the spectacle. Julie was in her robe, frantic, screaming at the agents and the cops, flashing her own police shield. She focused her invective at Mona Falco.

Laurie screamed, "Holy shit!"

Tobin nosed into a hydrant, threw the gear into PARK, and leapt out of the Lexus and ran to the arrest scene.

"You goddamned bitch," Julie screamed. "That's my son you're messing with!"

Another policewoman stood between Julie and Mona Falco, restraining her. A bevy of uniformed cops pushed the reporters and photographers back from the arrest scene.

"Mom, relax," Henry said, slurry. " 'S all right. This's a load of bullshit."

Henry's eyes were bleary, his face imprinted with seat-cushion designs as if he'd slept all night in his car where it was parked a few houses down from Julie's house.

Tobin and Laurie rushed to the scene. Print and TV reporters recognized Tobin and mobbed him, asking him for comments.

"I have no idea what's going on myself," Tobin said, pushing past them.

Mona Falco turned to Julie, holding up a copy of Tobin's column, illustrated with the photo sequence of a hooded man firing a missile from inside the car and the mustard-colored Explorer racing away.

"Don't blame me, Julie," Falco said. "His own father implicated him."

Tobin stopped behind Julie. Laurie embraced her. Julie swiped the newspaper from Falco's hands, scanned it, and turned to Tobin. As photographers snapped pictures and reporters scribbled notes and TV cameramen shot tape, Julie smacked Tobin across the face with the newspaper. Laurie wrapped her arms around her mother.

"How could you do this?" Julie asked, rattling the newspaper at Tobin.

Henry said, "Fuck she talking about, Pop?"

Laurie glanced at the newspaper in her mother's hands, and then she glared at Tobin, gazed to Henry, and squeezed her distraught mother. She glowered back at Tobin and said, "Oh, my God, Dad, what did you do?"

A stoic Cox chewed gum, put the now bagged and tagged rocket launcher in the trunk of his car, and stared at Tobin, who approached Henry.

Cox nodded for the cops to push the press back even farther from the arrest scene. Tobin knew that this time Cox had probably alerted the press, everyone but the *Examiner*, about the arrest. And Cox was wielding the power of the press this time.

Tobin said, "Henry, I promise, I'll take care of this. . . ."

"The fuck is happening? What did *you* do, Pop?"

"Don't make any statements until I get a lawyer."

"Statements about what? I didn't do anything. I went to cover a tip and I . . . and I . . . and I don't rem—"

"Quiet. Just be quiet."

Tobin couldn't hold his kid's dazed stare. He caught Mona Falco staring at him, in a pitying sort of way. The woman who was at the center of his wrecked marriage was now making the official collar of his son for the firebombing of a mosque.

"Henry Tobin Junior, you are under arrest for the arson of the Al-Koei Mosque and for the attempted murder of Nahira Shakoor," Mona Falco said in a low, labored voice. "You have the right to remain silent. If you wave that right, everything you say can and will be used against you in a court of law. You have the right to an attorney. . . ."

"Mom, I swear. . . ."

Mona Falco continued reading his rights from a Miranda warning card.

"Do like your father says," Julie said. "Dummy up. Wait for a lawyer."

Tobin scanned the faces of the crowd. He recognized most of the stunned neighbors. But also saw several gaping strangers. One guy in his fifties stood out—jet black hair that looked like a wig or a bad dye job, and matching beard, a Mets hat pulled low over his dark sunglasses, hands jammed into the pockets of a Mets jacket. Tobin thought he'd seen him somewhere before. But he couldn't pinpoint when or where. There was just something familiar about him. Like an imprint. *Wait,* Tobin thought. *That guy was outside the* Examiner *building yesterday, outside the ambulance.*

The man stared back. Cox broke the moment, saying, "We gotta take him. And we need to know who sent you these pictures."

"Stop that guy," Tobin said, pointing at the black-haired man nearing Avenue U.

"For what?"

"I think I saw him yesterday outside the newspaper. . . ."

"Yeah, and?"

"Why would he be at both places?"

"Maybe he has a Metro Card? Even if you're right, what's the point?"

Tobin had nothing to add. Cox chewed his gum. But he didn't smirk. He took a deep breath and said, "For what it's worth, I have no hard feeling toward you. If someone was on my kid's ass, I'd probably write what you wrote if I had a newspaper column. But then I felt sorry for that American Taliban kid's father, too. The Unabomber's brother is the nicest guy in the world. So, I don't blame you for the actions of your kid. I feel for you. Don't let your imagination run away on you. Get your kid a good lawyer. And give us the photographer who sent you those pictures. Now's no time for throwing up shield laws. Your kid's in a bad jam. The best thing to do for him is *co-op-er-ate.*"

"You cooperated by making sure the press was here for this."

Cox chewed his gum. "Who, me?"

Tobin didn't answer. Henry stared at him from inside the police car, his face as innocent as the day he started first grade. Now he needed a shave, and he was facing twenty-five years to life.

Falco eyed Tobin, shrugged, and mouthed the word, "Sorry."

She climbed into the police car that whisked away, lights flashing. The helicopter overhead banked and followed. Cox and Danvers trailed in an unmarked FBI car.

Laurie rushed Julie toward the yellow house, and Tobin followed. As he crossed the street, Tobin noticed the black-haired man with the Mets hat turning the corner onto Avenue U, looking back once.

He shouted Julie's and Laurie's names, but by the time he reached the brick stoop, the freed press separated Tobin from his ex-wife and daughter. Julie and Laurie hurried into the house. Tobin looked into the thicket of familiar faces of his trade and spotted Dani Larsen, microphone in her hand. He heard a dozen questions at once, most of them asking if his column had really fingered his own son for the mosque bombing. One reporter asked if authorities were investigating whether or not his son had manufactured many of his previous front-page exclusive stories, including the bombing of a synagogue.

Tobin said, "My son, Henry, is innocent. Otherwise, no comment."

Tobin retreated to his car and inched through the crowd of reporters driving toward downtown Brooklyn. His cell phone rang. He clicked it on and said, "Hello."

"How's it feel, Hank?"

"How's what feel?"

"Losing your kid."

"How'd this happen?"

"Same way it happened to me."

"What the hell are you talking about?"

"Ten years ago, I lost my kid. An innocent kid, it turns out, which only makes it worse."

"How?"

"Because of a Hank Tobin column."

"What the hell are you talking about?"

"Get ready. It gets worse."

"You contacted my kid last night, didn't you?"

"If you knew him, if you'd ever taken the time it takes to really be a father, you could have stopped it. You could have protected him. But you were too busy with your column and your bimbos and your fame and your money. Too busy being Hank Tobin to spend any time with your kid. So now he's gone."

"Who *are* you?"

"I'm just a guy from your rotten past who you violated, whose soul you

robbed. Just a guy who's back to tell you there are consequences for doing bad things like that, for big shots taking advantage of little people. One of the little people you love to say you champion. One of the little ones you stepped on and climbed over and manipulated to make yourself rich and famous and a big shot. How big do you feel right now, Hank?"

"I'm gonna find you, pal."

"You might just find yourself instead."

The phone went dead.

TWELVE

Henry said, "Pop, what the hell did you do to me?"

Tobin shifted in the plastic seat in the visiting room in the Brooklyn House of Detention on Atlantic Avenue and Adams Street, one block from the heart of the city's Arab Muslim stronghold. Outside Arab protestors chanted about the mosque bomber who was housed in the jailhouse. Jews from the Sinai Torah Temple in Midwood demanded that Henry Tobin also be charged with the bombing of their synagogue. Henry's lawyer, Steve Clancy, whom Tobin had hired to defend his son, stared out the window at the protestors and the media herd, jingling change in his gray suit pants pocket.

"I went with a blind source," Tobin said.

"My source?" Henry asked.

Tobin nodded, didn't want it to be taped. He glanced at the heavyset female corrections officer who stood by the door like an oak armoire, staring at Henry, who wore ankle and wrist chains.

Steve Clancy, his hair as white as whipped cream, said, "Forget, for a moment, what's already gone down. Focus on what we do next. These photos look bad, but they don't show your face. The rocket launcher is the killer. They still have to prove Henry fired it, but it's pretty damning evidence. Like the rifle in the D.C. sniper's car."

"What about the SUV?" Tobin asked.

"It doesn't show a license plate. DMV says there are 14,843 yellow Explorers in the state, 6,286 in the city. But you have a front-page bylined story in the *Globe* this morning that says you were there at the mosque. That, I gotta say, doesn't help. But still I could try to raise reasonable doubt

105

that another late-model, mustard-colored Explorer drove by and fired the grenade."

"So we're going straight not guilty?"

"What kind of question is that, Pop?" Henry said. "I didn't bomb a mosque! I went to cover a story and woke up in handcuffs. I don't even remember filing a story."

"It came from your e-mail address," Clancy said.

"Next thing I know they're stripping me out of my clothes," Henry said. "Searching my body for needle marks. Making me put on this orange jumpsuit, scraping my hands and under my nails, fingerprinting me, photographing me, taking blood, and throwing me in a cell."

"Ink and alcohol don't mix, kid," Tobin said, reaching to grab Henry.

"No touching, yo," the guard said. "Once more, you're gone."

Clancy pulled up a plastic chair, spun it, sat backward on it, leaned close to Henry and Tobin, and said, "They're checking for blowback on the clothes and your hands. I ordered the blood tests to check for a booze level and drugs because maybe I can use that later in a diminished-capacity defense, in case the not guilty trial balloon doesn't fly. Maybe temporary insanity. I asked for a rush job on the tests. My guess, after they test the rocket launcher, by the time they finish adding charges, they'll charge you with bombing the Midwood synagogue, too. Tell me your recollection again."

"Like I already told you, I was at the ballpark with the old man when I got a call from the same source who'd been feeding me leads for the last two months," Henry said. "The guy, he calls himself LL, he tells me there might be something going down at the Al-Koei Mosque at nine-thirty—"

"The call was about eight-forty P.M.," said Tobin. "I was with him."

"What'd he tell you?" Clancy asked.

"The guy told me what to wear," Henry said. "He said he knew I had white Nike sneakers, a blue hooded Nike jacket, jeans. He said he'd seen me wear them before. He told me to bring my portable laptop with built-in modem because I might want to file from the scene. He told me to be at the mosque at 9:30, and he would recognize me from where he'd be hiding. I went straight home. I live in the basement pad of my mom's house. I changed, grabbed my laptop, and raced right over to the mosque on Forest Avenue. It was dark. It was quiet. It was deserted. Then I heard someone call my name. Then I don't remember anything else."

"He orchestrated what you should wear?" Clancy asked. "And what time you should be there? Sounds like a set up. I asked to have your body searched for needle marks. They found nothing. Could someone have spiked your drink at the ballpark?"

"You mean like roofies?" Henry asked. "Rohypnol, the date-rape drug they dose college chicks with? On *me?*"

"Possible," said Tobin. "The beer guy. The sweeper. People behind us. An usher. Henry sat on the aisle. Anyone passing by could have spiked any one of his six beers."

"Rohypnol takes about thirty minutes to hammer a teenage girl," Clancy said. "Figure forty-five minutes to an hour on a grown man like you. One of the side effects is amnesia. That's why most rape victims who get dosed can't ID their rapists."

"Why would he do it?" Henry said. "This is a guy who gave me tips; I busted them out on page one. Other big papers, even the *New York Times,* picked up and ran with them. TV and radio, national network news followed my stories from our little upstart paper. Why would a guy who gave me such reliable stuff turn on me like that?"

"It's an old con," said Clancy. "On a Monday, you borrow a hundred bucks from a mark, promising to pay him back on Friday. He's hesitant, but figures, what the hell, it's only a C-note. You pay him back on Thursday, a day early, with a $10 bonus. On Monday you tell him you got the shorts again, ask if you can borrow two hundred. The mark figures you were good for it last time, paid him back a day early, plus an extra ten spot, so he gives it to you. This time you pay him back on a Wednesday, two days early, and throw in an extra $20, as a token of appreciation. This time you wait two weeks and you go to the guy and say you really need a quick thousand, your kid is in a jam and you need to wire him money in Cancun, where he got popped in bar brawl. You'll pay him back on Friday, with an extra $50 for him. The guy figures you're good for it so he loans you the grand. Last time he ever sees you. This guy, this LL, this source, he lured you in until he could set you up."

"And used me to do it," Tobin said.

"So this crazy tipster lures you there," Clancy says, pacing the room, trying to make sense of it all. "You zonk out from the Rohypnol. He jumps in your car, pulls you into the passenger seat, gets in the driver's seat, leans over you and fires the rocket launcher out the passenger window, and speeds away. Then he files a prewritten story with your byline, from your computer. And has an accomplice snapping pictures at the same time. Who then sends them to your father. Then he drives you home in your Explorer, puts you back behind the wheel, and leaves the rocket launcher in the car."

"Holy shit," Henry said.

"Sounds far-fetched," Tobin said.

"Yeah, but it's actually simple if given enough preparation," Clancy said. "The genius of it is that it seems too elaborate to be true. So selling it to a jury is gonna be like selling pork to a Muslim. Unless we find a guy to point a finger at. In the O.J. case Johnny Cochran had a complicated scenario, but he could point at Mark Fuhrman and the other L.A. detectives. I can't point at a ghost, some blind source."

Tobin didn't tell them that LL claimed he was getting even for something that Tobin had done to him a decade earlier. He didn't mention all of LL's other calls leading up to the one he went with. He didn't mention the fiftyish black-haired man with the Mets hat and shades who'd stood watching Henry's arrest like a guy who'd bought a ringside seat to a heavyweight championship fight. The same guy he'd noticed wearing aviator shades outside the *Examiner* after the anthrax hoax.

Tobin wanted to dig a little more before he revealed all of this. Before he got his kid even more pissed off at him. He'd confide in Clancy later, when there were no guards or microphones around.

The prison guard checked her watch and said, "Five minutes, gents. No way you making night court. But don't worry, we're putting him in PC."

"What's PC?" Henry asked, looking from the guard to Clancy to Tobin.

"Punk City," the guard said.

"Protective Custody," Clancy said.

"You won't be in general population," Tobin said. "It's safer."

"You mean I have to stay here all night?"

The guard stifled a closed-mouth laugh, a low scoffing giggle as she chewed gum and bebopped toward Henry, dangling a big ring of keys. Tobin knew she'd seen a thousand kids like Henry here, kids who thought they were all grown up until they discovered they didn't even know what manhood was until they lost it, rammed against a set of jail bars.

"After arraignment, the DA'll probably lateral this to the Feds," Clancy said. "Under the civil rights statute because it appears to be a hate crime or terrorist act. To be honest, kid, in the current antiterrorist climate I don't think you're gonna get bail."

"Oh, my God," Henry said, tears bulging in his young eyes. "I can't stay in cramped places. I have claustrophobia. Like Mom. I'll go buggy."

He turned to Tobin, the man-boy as vulnerable and scared as he'd ever seen him. He'd missed out on seeing his first shave and now his kid was facing life.

"Pop. You gotta get me out of here."

"I'll try my best for bail but don't get your hopes up, kid," Clancy said.

The guard led Henry toward the door. Tobin said, "I love you, Henry. I'll get you out. I promise."

The guard buzzed, inserted a key, and turned the lock. The steel door slid open. She stepped through with Henry. *It's like seeing my kid fed to a shark,* he thought. The steel door slammed, the sound echoing in Tobin's ears.

THIRTEEN

The first egg hit Tobin as he and Clancy exited onto Atlantic Avenue through the front door of the Brooklyn House of Detention. Then came a storm of tomatoes and more eggs. Clancy got smashed with an egg. Then two more. Tobin was pelted with tomatoes, bags of yogurt, humus, baba ghanoush. Tobin heard a cop in riot gear laugh and turn to another cop.

"Fuck 'em if they can't take a yolk," the first cop said, laughing.

"Sons a bitches!" Clancy shouted, shielding himself with his briefcase. Arab protestors screamed at Tobin. "Your son is a pig, Tobin!"

"You are a pig lawyer, Clancy!"

TV crews and press photographers advanced, getting the spectacle on film as reporters scribbled notes from the sidelines. When a bottle smashed near one of the riot cops, the police rushed the protestors. A shower of gravel rained from a rooftop across the street. Protestors pulled stones from their pockets, pelting the riot cops. Tobin and Clancy banged on the front door of the jailhouse. More stones skipped along the sidewalk at the entrance. A contingent of Jews Against Terror piled out of a yellow yeshiva van led by a short red-haired man named Rabbi Yitzak Cohn, yarmulkes pinned to their heads, and rushed at the Arab protestors, swinging clubs. The Arabs fought back, swinging protest signs, denouncing Tobin, the *Examiner,* the *Globe,* and Israel in the middle of Atlantic Avenue where the FBI claimed $20 million was raised for Al Qaeda in just one mosque.

The jostled press tried to record the pandemonium. Two cameramen fell as the protestors slugged it out. Riot cops on horseback galloped into the melee, panic shivering the crowd. Tear gas canisters exploded. Bleeding men and women fled in different directions across the busy intersection.

Traffic slammed to a halt. More police cars and an NYPD bus screeched to the scene, sirens and lights going. Riot-geared cops wearing gas masks charged into the fray carrying plastic shields and swinging clubs.

"Fuck all of yiz," Clancy shouted. "This is a nineteen-hundred-dollar Armani!"

Cops and corrections officers ushered Clancy and Tobin back into the jailhouse and rushed them through buzzing steel doors toward a back exit.

"I told you guys I wanted to leave this way in the first place," Clancy shouted. "You got a call from Winerib, didn't yiz? Telling you to feed us to the wolves? I'm filing a suit on this one. You knew those assholes were laying for us."

Out on Schermerhorn Street, Tobin and Clancy could still hear the police sirens and shouting from Atlantic Avenue. As they picked eggshells and tomato seeds off one another, Clancy said, "The 'Arab street' just formed a block association in Brooklyn."

"And the Israeli response," said Tobin. "I remember as a reporter for the Brooklyn College paper, in the 1970s, when the JDL bombed a restaurant called Tripoli right down on Atlantic Avenue. I also remember when crazy fucking Arabs opened up with machine guns on a yeshiva school bus coming off the Brooklyn Bridge. I think it's gonna get that kind of ugly again here in New York. I see a Friday night, rush hour, a game upstairs in the Garden, people running up from six subway lines, rushing for Amtrak and the Long Island Railroad trains to the sticks and the burbs, maybe a hundred thousand people in one concentrated spot, and here comes a guy who lost his entire family in a marketplace in Baghdad with a dirty bomb in a duffel bag walking into Penn Station. . . ."

"That's exactly why your kid isn't getting bail," Clancy said, picking off eggshells and tossing them to the ground, where pigeons the color of municipal buildings pecked at them. "Be prepared. The Feds, led by the one and only Abel Winerib, are gonna try to prove Henry torched the temple and the mosque, and use him as a sacrificial lamb to both sides to quiet these maniacs down. And you're paying for this suit. Look at these rat pigeons. They eat their own!"

"Who doesn't? And I'll pay whatever it takes to get Henry out of this joint. One of the shitheads they bust in that riot around the corner is gonna try to ice my kid inside. Probably the sole reason some of 'em wanna get busted, to get close enough to ice Henry. Steve, forget just PC, I want him in a twenty-four-hour lockdown cell. Alone."

"I'll do what I can. But you gotta tell me more of what the hell is going on here."

Tobin filled Clancy in on LL, about his ceaseless phone calls, and the guy in the black wig with the Mets cap whom he suspected might be him.

"He was friendly, like a crank fan, until after Henry got busted," Tobin said. "Then he gloated. I think this guy's been planning this for a long time, an elaborate revenge scenario for something I wrote years ago."

"You have to find this guy, Hank."

"I had the computer geeks at the *Examiner* trace the e-mail through the Internet server," Tobin said. "This guy logged on, using my personal e-mail address, and sent the pictures from a computer café to my *Examiner* e-mail address."

"Explain, I'm a bit of a Luddite," Clancy said, still picking debris from his suit. "I'm still trying to figure out why eggs have shells and tomatoes have skins."

"They have these ordinary cafés that are equipped with public computers. They work like pay phones. You use a credit card or pay a buck in cash for ten minutes access to the Internet. You log on. You type in your screen name. Then your password. Then for another buck you can scan in photos. Or other information. Then you type in an address to where you want to send it. Just like an envelope. And you hit the SEND button. And, poof, it goes into cyberspace. And the guy at the address on the other end opens it."

"I'm old and my VCR still blinks twelve twenty-four-seven so use baby blocks," Clancy said. "Somehow or the other, this guy, this LL, he knows your screen name and your secret encoder-ring password?"

"Yes. The same way you can get money out of someone's bank account if you know their PIN number."

"So if he knows your screen name and your password, he can send stuff to anyone and make it look like it came from you?"

"Yes."

"How does he know your password?"

"I don't know."

"He must know you."

"Maybe."

Clancy asked, "How do you steal passwords?"

"You can eavesdrop on someone mentioning it. A good hacker can program the computer to capture the first keys the previous user struck. But really, the easiest way, is to look over your shoulder at what keys you hit when you type it in."

"Another reporter? Some jealous hump?"

"Possibility."

"Wife? Kid? Maid?"

"At first I suspected the calls were from Henry himself. Obviously, they weren't. Julie would never do anything to hurt Henry. She'd never stoop to something like this. Never. I clean my own place. Hangover from my mother."

"Who gets close enough to look over your shoulder?"

"A number of people. I sit in the open newsroom."

"I defended a Russian hood once who stole telephone calling-card numbers."

"I remember. I did a column on it. Part of an identity-theft scam. They used camcorders with telephoto lenses to film people punching in their codes. Then they played the tape in slow motion and simply wrote down the numbers and sold them to people who ran up hundreds of thousands of dollars in international phone calls to places like Russia, Pakistan, Africa, and Asia. Jesus Christ, I fell for a scam I covered?"

Clancy said, "Ya think?"

"This guy knows his way around a camera. He sent me the pictures of the bombing, for chrissakes."

"Maybe it's a photographer at the paper. Any of them have a hair up his ass for you? You date one and never call her again?"

"I don't dip my nib in company ink."

"Square one," Clancy said. "So if Henry didn't write the story on the mosque, this LL could have, and if he also knew Henry's password, he could have sent it into the *Globe* from Henry's laptop and made it look like Henry wrote it?"

"Sure. All he'd have to do is write it first, have it on disc, load it into Henry's laptop, and send it straight to the *Globe*."

"You don't want Henry to do twenty-five years, find this LL."

Tobin nodded. "I intend to."

"Start with motivation, " Clancy said, wiping yolk on a hankie. "Why would someone do this, to you and your kid?"

"Like I said, something to do with an old column."

"Your enemy list is probably longer than Nixon's was. Maybe this is a setup. The work of a disgruntled fan. A jealous dame, or an envious coworker, some politician you ruined, a goldbricker you got fired from a city job."

"Or maybe a mad computer hacker who doesn't like my politics, especially on the Middle East. But I think it's more personal than that."

"Find this LL character, and maybe I can nip this in the bud. Before it goes to the grand jury. Before an indictment."

"How long do I have for that?"

"Less than a week before it goes to a grand jury or before the Feds exercise superceding jurisdiction. I didn't want to scare Henry. But believe me, Hank, we don't want this going to the Feds, especially after that column you did on them today. You called the whole Department of Justice a pack of rank amateurs and strong-arm Gestapo artists. That guy Abel Winerib, the Eastern District Federal Prosecutor you beat the shit out of for a month straight last year for nailing that cop you thought was innocent from the Brooklyn police brutality case . . ."

"Well, he got a new trial because of those columns."

"Exactly, but you made Abel Winerib look like a fucking monster. A mean, viscous, ambitious, power-abusing incompetent."

"He was more interested in a win than justice. He didn't mind jailing an innocent guy so long as he got a victory."

"Now I hear he's salivating for your kid's case. Believe me, we don't need a prosecutor with a personal motivation, a blood vendetta, going after Henry in this climate. You already got this top FBI task force agent, Cox, building the case against him. Together Cox and Winerib are gonna try to convince a jury that your kid invented or manufactured news, bombed a synagogue and a mosque, to get page-one bylines. And in doing so almost killed a woman and caused public hysteria, leading to riots like the one we just got egged in."

"If I produce LL, you think my kid has a shot?"

"I'll walk your kid if you bring me this guy."

He and Clancy said good-bye and Tobin started walking toward his car when Julie and Laurie rounded the corner. Julie glared at him. Laurie wouldn't look him in the eye.

"I saw Henry, with Clancy. He's gonna be fine," Tobin said.

"Don't you dare speak to me, Hank."

"Jesus Christ, Julie, he needs us both now. Please let me explain. . . ."

Julie brushed past him, walking to the rear door he'd just exited. Tobin followed, pleading with her as a photographer wearing a press card snapped pictures with a motor drive. Tobin turned to the photographer. "Come on, man, please!"

The photographer snapped away. "Sorry, Tobin, you and your family are news. Put the shoe on the other foot, man."

Tobin had invaded the privacy of more people than a grave snatcher in his day, and now he felt like a target in the crosshairs of a thousand assassins.

Laurie turned to her father as he pursued Julie. "Dad, take a hint, she doesn't want to talk to you," Laurie said.

The back door of the jail opened. Julie flashed her ID and entered with Laurie as the photographer continued to shoot pictures.

Tobin drove his Lexus through a barrage of press stationed outside his Manhattan apartment into the underground garage. He recognized Dani Larsen in the crowd. She'd slept with him in his apartment, in his bed, a few days before and now she was part of the media circus outside his building.

When he got inside and closed his apartment door, his phone was ringing. The caller ID said it was an anonymous call. He let the machine answer.

LL said, *"Pick up. I know you just got in."*

Tobin picked it up and said, "We need to talk in person."

"That's not possible, Hank."

"You wrote my kid's story, didn't you?"

"Open your e-mail."

Tobin sat at his desk and logged on, the RoadRunner Internet cable service popping open his e-mail and a photograph in two seconds. This was a shot of the mustard-colored Explorer rushing away from the burning mosque. This time, in the clear illumination of the flames, the license plate was perfectly visible. He checked his notebook where he'd written down Henry's license plate number. It matched the one in the e-mail photo.

Tobin's heart thudded because he knew this photograph alone could send his son away for life. He clicked to the next photo. This four-by-five-inch photo was of a man in a similar hooded outfit firing a shell into the

Sinai Torah Temple on Avenue L and Crosby Avenue in ninety-nine percent Orthodox Jewish Midwood. As clear as Exhibit A in the background
sat a mustard-colored Explorer.

"You see them?" LL asked.

"Yes." Tobin's voice was a squeak.

"You think your phone is tapped?"

"I don't know."

Tobin was silent, his heart racing faster.

"I can't make up my mind whether to send what I just sent you to the Post
or the News. *Or to hold on to this stuff for a while."*

"Name your price. I have a few million and—"

LL said, *"Don't insult me. This isn't about money."*

"What do you want from me?"

"What I want you can't give me back."

"What is it?"

"My innocent son, my ruined family."

"What happened to them?"

"Ask the man in the mirror, Hank."

"How? When? Where? Who are you? What exactly did I do to you?"

"You're the big shot Pulitzer Prize–winning reporter. You find out."

"Listen, if I hurt you, I'm sorry. But you're hurting my kid and—"

*"You stole my life, Hank. At heart you're a soulless thief. You sold your
soul for a column, Hank. And because you don't have a soul, you use your column to tear the souls out of other people's lives. But even when you walked
away from your wife and kids for pussy and fame, you still had a family.
There was always a chance of redemption with your kids, a glimmer of hope
with your wife. I didn't have that chance, that hope. You stole that away from
me, too. But now, now you'll know the pain and loss and agony I've known."*

"How do I make it better?"

"You don't. At noon on the twenty-ninth it will only get worse."

"Please, don't, we need to talk."

*"You need to, Hank. Not me. This is my turn to hold the power. Until I'm
gone at noon on the twenty-ninth. And then the power will go with me, and
you will inherit my pain."*

LL hung up. Tobin stared at the photo of his son's Explorer leaving the
scene of the flaming mosque. Then he stared at the photo of a mustard-
colored Explorer outside the Sinai Torah Temple in Midwood.

He walked to his window and peered down into the street where the press vans were parked and reporters, most of whom he knew on a first-name basis, waited for him to step outside so they could get fresh footage of his anguished face. As the sky turned a dark navy blue and the night-lights of New York ignited, he stared downtown through the hole in the skyline at Brooklyn. Somewhere over there his son sat in a solitary cell and his wife and daughter ached for Henry in the house Tobin still thought of as home.

Maybe all because of me, he thought.

FOURTEEN

"Everything before ninety-four is still in clip files," said Skip, the brilliant *Examiner* librarian who had a legendary photographic memory that spanned four of his five decades. "So you can't do just a simple CONTROL-F computer search. What exactly is it that you're looking for, Hank? Maybe I can help you?"

Clancy had warned Tobin to bring as few people as possible into the loop, so that the prosecution could never subpoena potentially damaging witnesses. He told Tobin to play his hand close to the vest. Not to trust a private investigator either. Those guys would love to use this trial to advertise, the way they did in the O.J. trial, leaking information to TV reporters. Clancy told Tobin that the only one he should trust with his son's life was himself. And his family.

Tobin had listened well. "Skip, I'm gonna go take out some files. I don't want you to have to know which ones, okay?"

"Tell you what. I'm going downstairs to get some coffee. Need any?"

"No, thanks. You're a prince."

"Hank, I'm really, really sorry about your son. He looked like he was going to be a great reporter."

Skip left and Tobin roamed the aisles, searching the hard-clip files once known as "the morgue," for the yellowed and crinkled old Hank Tobin columns going back eleven years.

He removed the envelopes dating back nine, ten, and eleven years. At three columns a week, it averaged 150 columns a year. He had to scan through about 450 columns in all, when he added in the extras he did on foreign assignments or on big breaking-news stories, searching for a guy who now called himself "LL."

He walked through the near-empty city room, with a skeleton crew working the "lobster shift," which got its name because they worked the same hours as lobster fishermen. He noticed a few reporters glance up at him, giving him awkward, embarrassed nods. Others avoided eye contact altogether. He felt like making a grand pronouncement. "MY KID IS INNOCENT!"

Instead, he took his clip files to his desk and started with the oldest ones first, some of them embarrassing in their light-weightiness, others not bad at all, some pretty damned good. Some were wretched, infested with adverbs, the prose so purple they might have been written with grape juice. And others underreported. Some were mindless thumb-sucking rants. He could see the whiskey stains in those columns. There were a few others where he reported out only one side of the story, and drew conclusions without giving the other side of a public battle its chance to respond.

"That's why we have letters to the editor," Tobin used to say to people who'd call after a Hank Tobin column hit them like a hand grenade at the breakfast table, leaving them publicly humiliated, their jobs doomed, their lives wrecked. As he sat reading through some of the columns, he felt deep shame because he didn't even remember writing them. *Stoned,* he thought. *Notes-on-a-cocktail-napkin columns. Outbursts dashed off in the back rooms of now-defunct saloons like the Lion's Head and Costello's and faxed in or dictated in a slurry rush to a copyboy.*

He groaned, sighed, and wiped his brow. This was like an alcoholic's intervention. The truth smacked him across the face. He realized others in the city room were watching him. He faked a smile, continued through the pile, didn't find anything about anyone whose name had the initials LL. He read one about a guy the media had nicknamed the "Vampire Landlord of Flatbush." *LL, for landlord,* he thought. *Maybe that's him.*

He skimmed the column and realized that he had gone to one of this "villain's" so-called hellholes to spend a night, expecting to report a building infested with roaches, rats, and gunslinging crackheads. But, as often happens, the reporting shattered his preconceptions. He hadn't found the deplorable conditions he'd expected. Instead he'd uncovered a collection of deadbeat tenants who'd conspired not to pay rent by concocting violations, abuses, and landlord harassment. As he read the column now, Tobin was kind of proud of it. He figured it was probably written when Julie had warned him he had better cool out and go on one of his periodic "wagons" because the booze was affecting his work and his family. Armed with sobriety, notebook, and look-see observations, he'd written a terrific column that ran against the herd.

A follow-up reminded him that his original column was offered at court as evidence for the defense. And helped the landlord walk. So this LL guy couldn't be the Vampire Landlord of Flatbush. *But maybe it was one of the deadbeat tenants,* he thought. He closed his eyes, tried to conjure their faces, but mostly women, single mothers, popped into his mind. None of them got arrested or imprisoned for their little scam. As he remembered it, none of them even got evicted. They just had to pay their back rent. People like that wouldn't wait ten years to bomb a mosque and frame his son because they had to pay rent.

He read through more columns. He could detect where he fell off the wagon about a month later. He flicked past a few thumb suckers. Shook his head at three clumsy, straight-opinion columns that were absent of irony, reporting, or wit. Groaned at a couple of nostalgia riffs. He labored through a batch of columns that read like an angry drunk venting at a bartender and knew they were probably written in desperation near deadline. They had a base appeal to a certain carnivorous, willfully ignorant segment of the readership. But reading them now, with the clear-eyed clarity of sobriety, they made Tobin want to crawl in a hole and do a little self-imposed solitary confinement. Or get drunk. They were written beneath his intelligence, pandering to the Joe Blow lunch-pail set, filled with swaggering macho bullshit, some of them sentimental and lousy with cynicism, or just goonish, the way certain radio numbskull talk-show hosts use the safety of the broadcast booth to act tough and mouth off.

"The mayor is the kind of punk who had his lunch money robbed off him in schoolyards. The Police Commissioner couldn't handcuff a Boy Scout with a Swiss Army knife, never mind control his own renegade cops. If either one of them has more than marshmallows in his pants, he'd meet me on the steps of that dirty Brooklyn precinct tomorrow at noon and let me see them haul in a few dirty cops. But they won't do that. This is an election year."

Christ, I made myself part of a story I had nothing to do with, he thought. *Just to make myself important.*

He moved on, skimming the columns for people's names, for anything that had the initials LL. Reading some of them was like reading the work of a stranger. Columns where he bragged about hangovers, nights in saloons, drinking with famous people, shameless name-dropping, and self-promotion. *I wish I could take half of them back,* he thought.

But half of them were pretty good, some very good. And that eased some of the pain.

After two hours he found a column about a ten-year-old firebombing in Gravesend, a tight-knit little neighborhood of one- and two-family homes sandwiched between Bensonhurst and Coney Island and Sheepshead Bay. He scanned the lead. He had only a vague, amorphous memory of it. He tossed it onto the dead pile. But before he picked up the next clip, some weird subliminal hook snagged his eye. He wasn't sure what it was about the last clip. He reached for it to scrutinize but was startled by Tracy Burns who spoke over his shoulder.

"You okay?"

He swiveled in his chair, faced her, and said, "No . . . yeah . . . no."

She wasn't high, but her faint perfume mingled with the dinner wine on her breath. She was allowed to have wine on her breath—it was after hours and she was the boss. Her dark pants suit fit nice around the narrow hips without trying to pass for twenty-five.

She leaned closer, ignoring the other reporters. She looked at the clip pile on his desk and said, "What're you searching for?"

"Answers. You're better off not knowing, Trace."

She nodded and whispered, "If you ever need someone to just talk to, call."

He nodded and sighed. "For what I did to my kid, I'm a fucking dog."

"It's not your fault, Hank."

"Yes it is."

"You went with what you thought was the truth. That's the gig."

"I went with a blind source. For a cheap page one."

"I okayed it."

"In the end, you let it be my call. I wrote it. My name was on it. I hung my own son. I'm a fucking loser. . . ."

Just saying the word triggered something in his head. Something his eye had just seen. The word "loser."

"Remember, anything you need, call."

"You're a queen."

Burns walked toward the exit. *Alone,* Tobin thought. *Always alone. Even when she's with someone, she seems so alone.*

Tobin glanced at the column on the top of the dead pile. Before it had landed, his eyes had caught a glimpse of a double L alliteration. One of the words was "lose," or "loser." He snatched up the column on the old fire-bombing. In the third graph there was a deep quote from a drunk whom Tobin had identified as "Lenny the Loser."

LL, he thought.

His heart raced. He held the column in trembling fingers and leaned back in his swivel chair and read it.

ATTACK MAKES US ALL LOSERS
BY HANK TOBIN

Everybody loses.

"My kid is a neighborhood hero," the man who called himself Lenny the Loser boasted to neighborhood pals in the Lucky Seven gin mill on Avenue X last night, as smoke from a racially fueled firebombing billowed past the front windows. "That's the last you'll see of those interlopers in our neighborhood."

"Lenny the Loser" was speaking of the suspect witnesses say wore a blue hooded sweatshirt, dungarees, and white sneakers, and who tossed a Molotov cocktail through the windows of Jimmy Hu's house on W. Second Place in Gravesend, Brooklyn last night.

Fortunately, no one was killed or injured in the race attack but not for lack of trying. One police source called this a "hate crime," coming out of the same poisoned mind-set as the infamous Howard Beach and Bensonhurst race attacks of the 80s. "We will get this perpetrator, and we will bring him to justice," said the police source.

I watched the Hu house sizzle and burn last night, flames scorching this immigrant family's American Dream to cinders of bigotry and hate. A white crowd gathered on the stoops and sidewalks, the flames mirroring in their eyes, as the sobbing Hu family stood in huddled shock behind a dozen police cars and fire engines. One of the Hu family, Debbie, 16, stood sobbing as she was comforted by her older, white boyfriend who draped a garishly tattooed arm over her shoulder and told her everything would be all right. "My family worked so hard and never bothered anybody," she said.

"I was in Desert Storm and as an American I'm outraged and embarrassed by this," said the boyfriend, who preferred not to give his name.

The smell of gasoline poisoned the Brooklyn night wind as smoke drifted toward a three-quarters moon in a clear, starry sky.

Firemen continued to fight the blaze that was swallowing Jimmy Hu's house like an appetizer.

Jimmy Hu is the breadwinner of this Vietnamese family that had come to America six years ago for a better life. The family worked round-the-clock in twelve-hour shifts at Hu's twenty-four-hour corner greengrocer. Two months ago the Hus had had the audacity to move onto this lily-white block, down the street from their store.

A little past nine the Molotov cocktail smashed through the second-floor window of the Hus' home that they purchased over the anonymous threats and objections of some xenophobic and racist neighbors. They had ignored the GOOK, GO HOME graffito on the front door and the unsigned letter warning them to move to a different neighborhood or, better still, "sail back home with the other boat people. Or face the consequences."

Unintimidated, Jimmy Hu bought his house anyway.

As police canvassed neighbors and firefighters fought the blaze, I went looking for a peek behind the soiled curtain of this tight-knit, white, working-class neighborhood. I bellied up to the bar in the Lucky Seven and ordered myself a big cold beer to wash the soot and the hate from my mouth. I glanced up at the Mets game on TV. They were losing. Again. So was everyone else in the Lucky Seven.

As I sipped my brew, I couldn't help overhearing a conversation bubbling like a witch's brew at the end of the bar. With the neon of a juke box and beer signs flashing on his stubbly white face and in his bleary blue eyes, the tall, lean man in his forties lit a Camel with a Zippo lighter emblazoned with a map of Vietnam. I told the bartender to give him a round on me. He did. Lenny the Loser lifted a shot glass of Four Roses whiskey, toasted me, and said thanks, belted it back John-Wayne-style, and followed it with a tap-beer chaser.

He wore a soiled green maintenance man's uniform, shivered, took a long drag on his smoke, and then the boilermaker caused his lips to percolate with poisoned bravado, as remarkably articulate as a Southern senator.

"Reminded me of Charlie charging out of the tunnels of Chu Lai," exclaimed the guy, who is known locally as Lenny the Loser. "My kid tossed the message through the ground-floor window and faster than the speed of light here came the whole interloping family screaming into the street, the parents jabbering in Vietnamese, the kids shouting in English taught in American public schools. The teenage girl yanked the little brother out. You don't want to see the kids die. Even in 'Nam we never wanted to see the children die. But they got the message, all right. Take the next slow boat home to Ho Chi Minh City. We might have lost the unwinnable war over there, but we also lost great young men. Many were my friends. And we don't need to be reminded by having the victors come here to throw our defeat and the tragic memories of those dead American GIs in our collective face. If American kids like my Billy have anything to say, we won't lose the new war here at home."

A couple of the others laughed at his liquor-fueled oratory. A few seemed shocked and horrified. Lenny the Loser noticed me listening. I bought him another round.

"You a cop?"

"No," I said.

"You ever go on the great Asian Vacation?"

"Too young at the time," I said, knowing he meant a tour of Vietnam.

The man nodded, lifted his shot glass with a hand the back of which had a tattoo of the letter "L," downed his whiskey, and said, "So was my Billy. But he did a little volunteering tonight."

The bartender intervened. "Leave the guy alone, Lenny," the bartender said, nudging Lenny the Loser away from me. I noticed that the back of the other hand also bore an "L" tattoo.

"No problem," I said. "Let him talk. He's articulate and has lots to say."

The bartender recognized me, grabbed Lenny the Loser's arm, and steered him further down the bar. The bartender told Lenny the Loser who I was and to dummy up.

Then the bartender said maybe Lenny the Loser had had enough to drink.

"F**k the gook interlopers," Lenny the Loser said, stumbling out the door. "My kid's a neighborhood hero. I'm proud of him. His kid sister Erin is proud of him. His mother might not approve, but he's made his father proud. I might be a loser, but my son is a winner."

The bartender leaned to me and said, "Don't pay attention to what Lenny says, guy. He ain't been right since he came home from 'Nam.

He imagines things. He dropped out of Brooklyn College but swears he has a master's degree. Sure, in Maintenance Engineering. He's a loser. The biggest thing he ever lost was his mind. We call him Lenny the Loser."

Whether this "Lenny the Loser's" kid was involved or not, yesterday all of Gravesend and the city were losers the moment that Molotov went through Jimmy Hu's window and burned a hole in the soul of New York.

You can put that on my tab, too.

Tobin had only a vague memory of the column. But he did remember that it was the story on which he'd first met Mona Falco. It clearly was written in a rush, probably phoned in from a corner phone booth to a copyboy on the desk. A sort of sidebar column to go with the main breaking-news story right on the Sports Final deadline. There were all kinds of things missing from the piece. Starting with Lenny the Loser's real name, the bartender's name, quotes from other customers, quotes from Jimmy Hu, or from neighbors. Tobin spoke to Jimmy Hu's daughter. And her boyfriend, who wouldn't give a name. He had a vague but nagging memory of that guy. He stood out. He was older than the young girl. If he was a veteran of the Gulf War, he was at least four years older than the daughter. And Tobin remembered that there was something about one of his tattoos. A name, or an incongruous image. But that was missing from the story, too. *Maybe I had an angle on the story and the fact got in the way of that slant,* he thought. *So I left it out.*

Funny how it nagged him right now. But that wasn't all that was missing.

He realized he'd manipulated Lenny the Loser, just fed him whiskey and quoted his drunker rants. He guessed that earlier he'd met Mona Falco at the scene. In fact, he remembered she gave him a fill on the background of the story. A history of racial vandalism. Threats. Now a firebombing. Falco had probably introduced him to Debbie Hu, who spoke perfect English, and Tobin dropped her quotes into the column.

The rest consisted of impressions—the moon, the stars, the wind—a piece of instant color, slapdashed from the scene, giving the reader a taste of the neighborhood and a quick knee-jerk point of view.

I was already drinking that night, he thought. He guessed he had already filed a different column and was probably at the Mariner's Inn or Charlie's on Avenue U, banging back a few and watching the Mets while

Julie was home helping the kids with homework and getting them ready for bed. He figured the city desk beeped him about the firebombing. And even though he was half-bagged, he probably raced over and filed something quick to sub the column he'd already written. He wouldn't have missed getting his two-cents about a story like this into the paper. *Ubiquitous Tobin,* he thought. *If it doesn't have a Tobin byline, it isn't news.*

He searched the clips for the columns he wrote following the one on Lenny the Loser and saw that they were datelined *Belfast.*

He'd left for Northern Ireland the next day and filed daily columns for five weeks on the historic peace initiative. If the story of the firebombing of Jimmy Hu's house had any legs—and he doubted it would have many because no one was killed or hurt—he didn't know about it. That story would have taken a backseat in his mind and the paper to Gerry Adams and the IRA cease-fire in Ulster

Tobin had the best Irish republican contacts of any New York paper. The *Examiner* broke him out on page one every day. Interviews with Gerry Adams, Martin McGuinness, IRA gunmen, Senator George Mitchell, who'd help broker the peace. And unionist leaders, low-level Protestant hard men, so-called war profiteers. And Long Kesh prisoners like Joe Doherty, and so-called rosary-bead republicans, who didn't want The Troubles to end and threatened the peace process with fractionalized fringe violence.

This had been the first foreign reporting Tobin had done as a columnist, and his exclusives had won him awards and a bonus and a raise from the *Examiner.* Caught up in the history in the making, the intricacies of the politics, the daily deadlines, Tobin had never given Jimmy Hu or some drunk named Lenny the Loser any more thought.

But here was the column now. Written when he was drinking about a ranting drunk. *Talk about the pot calling the kettle black,* he thought. He couldn't believe how irresponsible he'd been. These days, anyone with a whiff of booze on his breath while working would be suspended if not fired. Few columnists boasted about saloon exploits anymore. The wonderful and legendary New York saloon columns of Damon Runyon, O'Henry, John McNulty were now journalistic relics. Even Jimmy Breslin, who used to do beer and whiskey ads, didn't drink anymore. Guys with Runyonesque monikers like Lenny the Loser wouldn't be quoted in a newspaper column about a serious incident like a racial attack. You could still fly a name like that in a lighthearted piece of humor or satire. But when you were reporting a touchy story like a racially charged hate crime, you better get the names and the facts straight. And you better do it sober.

Tobin picked up the phone, called the library, and asked Skip to go for another cup of coffee. Skip said fine, and Tobin went back into the library and dug out the general news clips on the Jimmy Hu firebombing story.

He took them back to his desk. There were small stories for the two days following the firebombing, back on pages twenty-three and thirty-six. The next day, as he arrived in Belfast, police in Brooklyn arrested one Billy Kelly, twenty-two, an unemployed high school dropout, heavy-metal skinhead, billboarded with tattoos—including a swastika—for the firebombing of Jimmy Hu's house. Police traced the suspect through details made public by his father, Leonard Kelly, to *Examiner* columnist Hank Tobin.

Armed with a search warrant, Detective Mona Falco of the newly formed Hate Crime Unit searched the Kelly home and found a blue hooded sweatshirt that reeked of gasoline under Billy Kelly's bed. They also found a typewriter in Billy's room that matched the typeface of the threatening letter that had been sent to the Hu family.

Billy Kelly's only alibi was that he was stoned on beer and four Seconals at the time of the firebombing and couldn't remember if he'd done it or not.

As Tobin suspected, the story disappeared from the news after that. The only other mention was a news brief dated three weeks after the arrest when Billy Kelly's Legal Aid lawyer worked out a ten-year plea bargain for his client, who was being held on one million dollars bail and facing twenty-five years if he was found guilty at trial. The editors thought the story about this lone racist skinhead nut job was so inconsequential that the brief ran in the Brooklyn section crime blotter. The brief carried the byline of a young reporter named Phyllis Warsdale.

Tobin had no recollection of that part of the story, either. When he cross-checked with his columns, he realized he was still in Belfast. In those days, before all the newspapers were online, reporters on foreign assignment didn't keep up with local stories back home. They were too involved in the news they were covering.

Tobin had never really followed the firebombing of Jimmy Hu's house. It was a hate crime, but just a property-damage story, a mere footnote to the bigger race stories of his time. No one was killed. A local racist asshole kid was arrested and copped a plea. Even if someone had mentioned it to him, Tobin would have shrugged it off as a minor story. He was off covering a

major international event. And he was drinking. And between the headlines and the booze, small stories fell through the cracks.

The incident became a forgotten ink stain on the immense crime blotter of the big city. In the vernacular of the newspaper trade, a story like this
one, about a lone skell, without a larger conspiracy, no secret warren of
Klansmen, no chiseling politician, no sex appeal, simply had no legs and
was referred to as "a piece of shit."

Now this piece of shit had boomeranged through time.

Christ Almighty, he thought. *Was I that irresponsible? That reckless?
Interviewing a drunk when I was drunk? I helped a father drop a dime on
his own son in print.*

Tobin identified Lenny Kelly's lighter, his cigarette, and whiskey
brands, and his tattoos. He used Lenny Kelly's real first name, and nickname, and Billy Kelly's first name, and his sister Erin's. But maybe Billy was
innocent. Just had no alibi. Maybe he never had a chance because his father
was a drunk and a loser. Maybe Lenny Kelly had made up a wild story, and
after Billy Kelly was arrested, the family couldn't afford a good lawyer.
*Maybe Billy Kelly was railroaded because he was a young, dumb, zonked-out
skinhead,* Tobin thought, *and because I wrote about him.*

Tobin writhed in his chair, knowing he should have checked out all the
facts in the story before he went with it. For all he knew at the time he'd
filed it, this Lenny the Loser might not have even had a son named Billy.
And maybe Billy was out of town. Or had a rock-solid alibi. Maybe this
Lenny the Loser was just mouthing off, maybe it was just loud saloon brag-
gadocio. *Oh, man, what the fuck was I thinking,* he thought. *What the hell
have I done?*

He knew he was half-stewed and half-cocked when he wrote that column. But that was no excuse. That was like a drunk driver trying to blame
the whiskey for mowing down a family of four on the Belt Parkway. He
knew he had used his privileged, mighty space in a big, powerful daily
newspaper to bury a kid he had never met. A drunk had quoted a drunk in
the midst of a race crime, and this had forced a kid into a cage for ten years
of his life. In a traditional David and Goliath Hank Tobin column, the kid
would have been David and Tobin would have been the ruthless giant.

One graph in Warsdale's late-July story bothered Tobin most:

"After the ten-year sentence was announced, Billy Kelly's mother, Ilene
Kelly, wept uncontrollably in the courtroom. Billy Kelly was led from the

courtroom in handcuffs and leg irons, glaring at his teary-faced father, Leonard, who sat silent and alone as the door to the holding cells slammed on his son."

LL, Tobin thought. *The details he gave about his son that I printed in my column had him jailed. Now LL gave me those same details about* my son *and I've done the same horrible thing to Henry. I wrecked his family. Now it's his turn to wreck mine.*

FIFTEEN

Tobin called Julie's number. Laurie answered.

"Laurie, it's Dad, please let me talk to your mom," Tobin said.

"She won't talk to you."

"How do you know?"

"She told me to say so if this was you on the phone. The reporters call all day, all night. Your lousy friends. Like vultures, picking Henry's bones. What a creepy profession you're in. Flies on shit. All over our lawn, stoop, in cars, vans, helicopters buzzing, long-lens cameras, watching every time one of us goes to the store, interviewing neighbors, teachers, schoolmates. Every dick who Henry ever had a beef with is badmouthing him and the family on TV talk shows. Every goddamned station, Dad, TV and radio. It's all over the frigging web! Pigs in shit have more class than reporters."

"They're just doing their jobs," he said. "Like me . . ."

"They have zero scruples, no morals . . . no wonder you cheated on Mom. . . . It makes sense now. . . . Oh, God, I'm sorry, Dad, I shouldn't have said that."

"I know you're upset," he said, reeling from her words. "And, please, watch your language, you're my *daughter* and I'm still your *father* and—"

"Henry's facing life in jail. We're being portrayed as a family of terrorists, and you're worrying about whether we sound like the fucking Osbournes? Jesus Christ, get your fucking priorities straight, Dad!"

"I'll have your home number changed."

"Henry knows this one. Every time the phone rings, we keep hoping it'll be him. Dad, how the hell could you let all of this happen? How could you lead the cops to your own son?"

130

He heard his daughter collapse into tears. Tobin had no answers. "I'm sorry," he said. "I promise I'll get him out."

"You better."

"Please ask your mom to get on the phone."

Laurie placed the phone down, and Tobin heard her walk across the terra cotta tiles of the kitchen, onto the parquet hardwood floors of the living room. All familiar sounds of the place he once called home. He heard shuffling feet and the rattle of the phone.

Julie said, "Do you have good news for me, Hank?"

"No, I just wanted you to know we should be together on this. . . ."

Julie cradled the phone.

Tobin stopped at Old Navy, bought a change of clothes, and took Tracy Burns up on her offer to spend the night at her place. On the couch. Her sweet, sad smile was comforting. They were attracted to each other, but nothing would ever come of it because both knew even one fling might ruin a splendid relationship.

"I'm glad you came," she said, sitting on the suede couch with Tobin who sipped a club soda and stared at the ceiling. "I just wish you were *here.*"

"I'm sorry," he said. "All I can think of is my kid in a cage, with claustrophobia like his mother."

"Of course."

"Maybe I should take some time off from the column, Trace."

"Whatever you want. But if you want to write, write. With all the misinformation out there, no one can tell your family's side of the story better than you can. Like always, it's your call."

"I'm not making very good ones. Not with the column, not with women, not with my kids."

"The kids thing I have no advice for because I never had any," she said with a sigh. "But the women thing. Take it from an old broad who's been around the block a few times. I laugh at all these guys popping Viagra, hoping that will give them the upper hand with women. I'll let you in on a little girl-thing secret: Sometimes the most powerful weapon around a woman is a limp dick. Once we get you aroused, we can lead you around by *it.* Want to render a woman powerless in certain situations, every time you think hard, think limp instead."

Tobin laughed.

"I wish all my mistakes were as easily remedied," he said.

"Hank, we all make mistakes. We all do things we wish we could take back. Sometimes it's worse to do nothing than to do something you regret."

"You think?"

She pulled her legs up under her on the couch, her voice low and throaty. "Put it this way, guys, good ones, too, they proposed to me over the years. But I never married anyone because I was always afraid it wouldn't work. Not because of them. Because of *me.* I'm not sure I could have been faithful. I don't just love men, which I do. But I also really, really *like* them. I like *a lot* of them. I'm like Warren Beatty in *Shampoo,* but with a skirt. When I like a man, I just can't help it. Life's too short, and I just wanna like all of him. I want to sleep with him, sometimes just to get it out of the way. It's one of the great bennies of being a girl. If you're decent-looking, and you wanna bed a guy, he'll usually oblige."

Tobin laughed, "Yeah, we're real sweethearts that way."

"Which is a good thing, because once you get past that, with no demands, no strings attached, guys are better friends than chicks. Men meet me here. We make love before we go out for dinner. This way dinner tastes better. There's more laughs, more fun. And there are no games. No bullshit. The talk is clear, smart, honest, no tap dancing, no diversions, no secret agendas, no teenage mating rituals."

"Besides, screwing is better on an empty stomach."

She laughed. "So I was always afraid of picking just one apple off the cart. Plus, I saw other people I care about, including my mother, two sisters, and a lot of women friends, and men I really like, guys like you, go through painful, excruciating divorces."

"You have no idea how lucky you are to have missed all that."

"I used to think so, too. But, now, now that I have way more road behind me than ahead, I'm not so sure. I wish I would've at least *tried.* Sometimes the biggest mistake is avoiding mistakes. It's cowardly. And it has consequences worse than the mistakes would have had."

"Yeah?"

"Well, sure, because you never really *know,* do you? Maybe marriage would have been a mistake. But maybe not. Maybe I would've married the right guy if I went looking for that kind of guy. And if I didn't, well, at least I would've went down swinging."

"You have a point. But believe me, marriage, monogamy, divorce, weekend parenthood, all of that, is very hard work. A full-time job with endless overtime, seven days a week, no holidays or vacations. It's very complicated and never gets any easier."

"Yeah, but maybe I would have had a *kid*."

"Tell me about it. But the bigger the kids get, the bigger the problems."

"Someone to call me *'Mom.'* Sometimes I regret that. I don't mean to be corny or maudlin, here. But I think I was so afraid of being an unfaithful wife, a married cheater, a distracted working mother, that I cheated myself out of kids and a good man."

"But look at the pain it's causing me, right now, Trace. I miss my wife. I miss Julie. And when you have kids, you fly and crash with them. It's like having parallel lives you have to live, other deadlines and responsibilities to juggle in addition to your own screwed-up life. Then, if one of your kids gets hurt, or gets in trouble, like Henry right now, it hurts worse than your own pain and troubles. Believe me, right now, with Henry in jail because of me, I envy you."

"Nah. Bullshit. No, you don't."

"I'm hurting bad, Trace. In the soul. I ache for my kid. I'm dying in here."

"You should get Julie back. She's good for you."

It was odd being alone for the night in the apartment of an attractive woman who was as sexually desiring of him as he was of her, urging him to reunite with his wife. But Tracy Burns was no ordinary woman. In bed she was probably all woman, but at work and at heart she was all newspaper-*man*. Most of her adult life she'd thought and behaved like a guy, but now she ached and pined like a woman.

"Julie won't take me back," he said.

"You two need each other now. Something good will happen out of all this. Watch."

Tobin sat there staring at the ceiling, hoping she was right. He glanced at the pendulum of the grandfather clock that ticked and tocked Burns toward solitary old age: 3:18 A.M. He watched Burns stroke her hair, and thought of a day in Disneyworld when a caricaturist drew Henry as a boy of seven, his head ten times the size of his little running body. He remem-bered draping his arm over Julie's shoulder, laughing as Henry made faces for the unamused and sweaty sketch artist. As Burns stroked her hair, Tobin remembered stroking Julie's long dark hair that day in the Florida sunshine, the short blond spikes replaced by a natural mature mane, her head resting on his shoulder.

He saw a single tear fall from Tracy Burns's left eye and race down her pretty, aging face.

"You okay, Trace?"

"I'll be fifty in a month."

"You look spectacular. Forty."

"I know I asked you to come here so I could give *you* some support," she said. "And I know you're dying inside. But now all I want is to cry my stupid eyes out. Right now I need you to tell me everything's gonna be okay."

"I'm just happy to be with someone I can trust."

"It's kind of sad that it can never happen between me and you," she said, getting up from the couch. "But I have to say, the other day when you told me I looked good, it made me feel good, and sexy, and young."

"I imagine what it would be like with you all the time," he said. "It'll keep you beautiful, sexy, and young in my head forever."

She smiled and said, "Yeah?"

"Oh, yeah."

"I love you way too much to ever make love to you, Tobin."

"Is this where I'm supposed to think limp instead of hard?"

She laughed and nodded and said, "But right now, if me and you did get it on, I'd turn off the light and let you call me Julie. Good night, Hank."

Tracy Burns wiped her eyes, smiled, and walked to the bedroom. Alone.

"Good night, Julie," Tobin said.

SIXTEEN

Thursday, July 27

Burns was already gone when Tobin awakened a little before six A.M. He couldn't sleep well knowing his kid was spending the night in a steel drum. He pulled out his Palm Pilot and called up a home number for an ex–*Daily News* reporter who had moved on to the world of public relations a decade earlier because the money was better. These days he handled press for Local 32 BJ, which represented the maintenance men, superintendents, elevator operators, window washers, and doormen of the city's commercial buildings and apartment houses.

Devlin was already awake and dressed, sipping coffee. Tobin asked if he could meet Devlin at his office early. Devlin, who lived downtown in Battery Park City, said he'd be in by six-thirty. Tobin showered and dressed in the new Old Navy clothes. He left the dirty ones that Burns would send out to have cleaned. He combed his hair straight back and let it dry naturally, and ran the comb through his full beard to keep it from looking scruffy.

He drove straight downtown to Local 32 BJ, better known as the janitors' union, on the Avenue of the Americas near Canal Street, jammed the press parking pass in the window, and rode the elevator to the eighteenth floor. Anything higher in New York these days caused "plane-o-phobia."

"How are you so sure he's dead before looking in his file?" Tobin asked.

"Because I was one of the three people who attended Leonard Kelly's memorial mass," said John Devlin. Tobin averted his eyes, looking out the window into the bright morning sun. The last time he was in this office,

135

four years ago, interviewing Devlin about a doorman strike, the building shivered in the cool shadow of the Twin Towers. Now the room was as bright and warm as a solarium. Devlin clicked his mouse through a rank-and-file database, pausing to read sections, then scrolling on.

"What about his kid? Billy?"

"He had two kids," Devlin said. "Billy and a daughter, Erin."

"That's right."

"After Lenny Kelly died in the Trade Center on September 11, those kids had money coming to them. Life insurance and other union benefits. Neither one has claimed a dime yet."

"You sure he died? You said it was a memorial mass, not a funeral. They ever find a body?"

"No, but we know he reported to work that morning. He punched a time card on the ninety-sixth floor of the north tower at 8:31 A.M. that registered in an uptown central computer for National Maintenance Corp."

"That would have given him fifteen minutes before the first plane hit," Tobin said, stroking his beard. "He could have gotten out."

"What? You think an Irish maintenance man from Gravesend knew in advance that Al Qaeda maniacs were gonna crash jumbo jets into the towers? The axles break on your milk wagon, Hank? You drinking again?"

Tobin shot him a tough, icy glare and said, "You gonna help me or not?"

Devlin raised his hands. "Christ, Hank, just kidding. You AA guys, you should have a thirteenth step that says 'Get your fucking sense of humor back.'"

"Who were the other two people at the memorial? His kids?"

"No, aside from the priest and the altar boys, there was one die-hard old-timer sitting behind a hot broad who I figured was probably a coworker. Too young and beautiful to be a girlfriend. As a matter of fact . . ."

"Two mourners? Jesus Christ. He was that disliked?"

"Hey, excuse me, Hank, but I pitched his memorial as a column idea to you."

"I already did one about the window washer who used his squeegee to carve his way through a sheetrock wall to free five people from the elevator stuck on the fiftieth floor," Tobin said.

"But I got guys who died, too, Hank. I told you that if you were weary of writing cops and firemen, firemen and cops, cops and firemen, we had some 9/11 funerals, too. I told you there was one guy, name of Kelly, who might be buried without fanfare. I couldn't even get his kids to claim his life insurance. The Unknown Janitor. You didn't answer my call."

"I remember the message," Tobin said. "But you know how it was. I was inundated with stories. But you called me about *him?* About Lenny Kelly?"

"Yeah. I figured he was a Brooklyn boy, Irish, up your alley. Small world."

Tobin thought that Devlin had no idea how tiny it was. "Did you know the guy?"

"Nah," Devlin said. "But I asked around. People said he was a loner. Guys liked him okay. He was a fuck-up early in his career. But it looks like he straightened out. My bet, another 'Friend of Bill's.' "

Devlin was referring to Alcoholics Anonymous, founded by Bill W.

"He straightened out his act like ten years ago?"

Devlin scrolled down the screen, clicking the mouse. "More like eight or nine. He was suspended from the union for a while. He paid some fines, did some picket duty, took gigs no one else would take. I had to write a eulogy for him, talk to a few of the guys about him. What I could glean, solid guy, kept to himself. He was always willing to work weekends and holidays. He became Mister Reliable. Won a bunch of Worker of the Month awards. Worked tons of overtime. He'd always fill in for guys who wanted to take days off. He always put in for vacation replacement work. He worked all over the city, any building, any borough, day or night or weekends, and was qualified to do maintenance, janitorial, window washing, elevator operating. His main gig was maintenance in the Trade Center."

"Never tried for foreman, management, union office?"

"Nah. Just a good soldier, and a scholar. Guys say he never laughed. Never talked much. Every break, every lunch hour, he was busy reading or on a computer at the local computer cafe. He became a computer wizard. In the last nine years, using the GI Bill, he earned a B.A. in philosophy from Brooklyn College nights, and got a master's degree from Hunter. And he remained a freaking janitor. But I'll tell you how sad a life this guy had...."

Tobin thought about Lenny Kelly passing a decade reading Nietzsche, Sartre, and Kierkegaard, spending his free time on a computer at a computer cafe, like the one from which Tobin had received the photos of the mosque bombing. Devlin scrolled down through Lenny Kelly's file and said, "For the past nine years he worked every Christmas, every Thanksgiving, every Easter, every July Fourth. Even every *Father's Day*. The only holidays he ever took off were Memorial Day and Mother's Day. And he took off one personal day a year, no matter what—July twenty-ninth."

"For what? Birthday? Anniversary? What?" He stroked his beard, smoothing the moustache into the hairy chin as if stroking a pet.

"No idea."

Tobin thought of the Zippo lighter emblazoned with a map of Vietnam that he'd detailed in his old column. Kelly was a guy whose family had been torn apart by his son's arrest and imprisonment. His kids wouldn't even come to his memorial mass or accept his insurance money. Why would he take off on Father's Day, Christmas, or Thanksgiving? No one to celebrate with. The only day he took off was Memorial Day, probably to honor the guys he served with in Vietnam. And Mother's Day, which was pretty self-explanatory. And July twenty-ninth.

"His mother still alive?"

"Not according to the files. She wasn't a beneficiary, anyway."

"Wife?"

"Deceased."

"Since when?"

Devlin scrolled some more, typed in some data, and hit the SEND key. "She disappears from his health and life insurance nine years ago and change."

"Is there a cause of death?"

"No. We're a union. Not the coroner's office. Even if Kelly murdered her, we would've paid for a coffin. We paid three hundred and seventy-nine bucks toward the funeral. Then her name was removed as Leonard Kelly's life-insurance beneficiary and from the health insurance. Leaving just the two kids. But one of them was doing ten years for the state. One was away in college. Then Kelly was suspended for fucking up on the job, sleeping on duty, using a company computer, not paying dues, missing picket duty. He showed up at a union meeting with a full shitter on, cursed out the leadership. Not smart. Musta been on a doozy of a bender."

Lenny the Loser, Tobin thought. *Poor guy was off the deep end. His kid gets ten years. His wife throws a seven, heart attack, maybe. From stress. Or maybe she killed herself in grief. Then Lenny gets suspended from his own union. All because of a column I wrote when I was drinking. And so he waits and plans, and he gets even with me by doing to my kid what I did to his.*

"How was Lenny Kelly's health before he ... before September 11?"

"Those records are confidential, Hank."

"Not for a dead guy. You can't slander or break the confidence of a dead man. You're an old reporter, Dev, you know that. Pissing on graves is legal."

Devlin sighed, clicked through his computer. "You owe me two BJ columns if we go on strike before Christmas. Which looks like a lock. I mean we got some poor supers working in the Bronx still making like three hundred a week. Believe that?"

"One column," Tobin said. "Take your pick. And I write it as I see it."

"Put it this way," Devlin said, clicking on Lenny Kelly's medical file. "Lenny Kelly lived in the same house on W. Second Place in Gravesend until a year before he died. Then he had his mail transferred to a PO box. But before he died, Kelly spent a lot of his free time on the Upper East Side, Eighty-eighth and York."

"Memorial Sloan Kettering? The cancer hospital?"

Devlin nodded and said, "His insurance was maxed out, but he was on a liver wait list at Mount Sinai, anyway. Musta got desperate at the end because he even went to a Chinese herbalist and acupuncturist, but again, the insurance maxed out."

This guy has nothing to lose, Tobin thought. *If he faked his death, he won't even live long enough to pay for his crimes. He's immune, a walking statute of limitation.*

"You have addresses for the kids, Dev?"

"The last one I had for the son was for a rooming house in Kensington after he got out of Greenhaven Correctional six months ago," Devlin said. "The daughter, I have no idea. We sent out a letter to her last known address on E. Seventy-ninth Street, but it was returned. We took out a legal ad in the *News* and *Post*. No one came forward."

"What college did she go to?"

"Harvard."

"Harvard? She must've had a scholarship."

"I have no idea."

"You have a Social Security number for her?"

"Hank, you know better. I lose this gig, it isn't so easy to find another one."

"I'll owe you two columns. Plus I need a recent photo of Lenny Kelly."

Devlin rattled off the Social Security number that Tobin wrote in his Reporter's Notebook and also jotted the address of Billy Kelly's rooming house on Albermarle Road in Kensington. Devlin clicked a few more keystrokes and a photo ID of Lenny Kelly printed out. He walked to a file cabinet, poking through a stack of old union newspapers, found the one he was looking for, thumbed through it, and folded it open. Devlin handed the newspaper to Tobin, jamming a finger into the center of the photo of Lenny Kelly receiving a union citation. Stooped, gaunt, and pale with a bald head, Lenny Kelly was not smiling. He had not aged well. Tobin stared at the photo and the muddy memories of that night in the saloon bubbled up, vague and hazy, but he recalled a dark-haired man with a big, full, Irish-ham face, broad shoulders, barrel chest, arms like clubs. Time, sadness, cancer, radiation and chemotherapy had eaten him alive, inside out. *I ruined this poor bastard's life,* Tobin thought, the photo shaking in his hand.

"That's Lenny Kelly. Or was."

"Thanks, Dev."

Devlin walked around the desk to escort Tobin to the door. "You okay, Hank?"

"Not really but don't spread it around."

"How's your kid?"

"He didn't do this thing."

Devlin nodded. "What's Kelly got to do with all of this?"

"You don't want to know. Promise me you don't tell anyone I've been here."

"If I did, it'd cost me my job."

"People will try to barter with you for Tobin dirt."

Devlin pulled up his sleeves, baring his wrists. "I look suicidal to you? I'm gonna mess with the most powerful columnist in New York? But one thing bothers me."

Tobin shrugged, his body language urging Devlin to continue.

"I told you there was this beautiful broad at Kelly's memorial," Devlin said. "I told you I figured she was a coworker. Probably politically incorrect of me, but I figured she mighta been in our union because she was black. Light-skinned black chick, beautiful. She looked sort of familiar. Then I saw her again on TV two days ago."

"Doing what?"

"Escorting your son in handcuffs," Devlin said.

Mona Falco.

SEVENTEEN

Tobin pressed the elevator button, dialed the *Examiner* library, and asked Skip to find out a cause of death for one Ilene Kelly, who died about nine years ago, probably in Brooklyn. He also asked Skip to do a computer Finder Search on Erin Kelly, Harvard graduate, and gave him her last known address and Social Security number. In a matter of minutes this search engine could find almost anyone's home address in the country. Sometimes even unlisted home phone numbers, because it did a universal scan of databases that included cyber records for phone, cable, utilities, credit cards, insurance, marriage bureaus, coroner's lists, divorce courts, voter registration, real-estate tax records, pharmacies, libraries, criminal justice, and schools.

It was a sneaky reporter's tool. The way reporters reached people—even privacy freaks—at home in the middle of the night to inform them that a loved one was dead or arrested. And then asked for an obligatory reaction. The cliched misconception, of course, was that reporters took a morbid joy in asking things like, "Just for the record, how do you feel about your daughter being gang raped, murdered, and mutilated?"

No reporter, not even the cynical jaded ones who thought and talked like cops, liked that part of the job. No cop likes being the one to tell the family of their worst nightmare. There was never an easy way to do this work. It was unpleasant and upsetting, not unlike a doctor giving a terminal diagnosis. But it was part of the gig. So a reporter used the available tools. Your job was to find people, ask them questions, write down the answers, assemble the facts and reactions into a coherent narrative so that the reader could make order out of chaos in fifteen to twenty inches, a task that sometimes took a novelist four hundred pages. It was still a vital, noble craft.

This time Tobin was using the search tool to locate someone who might help make order of the upheaval in his own life. It would take more than twenty inches.

Tobin received a persistent call-interrupting beep as Skip told Tobin the search could take five minutes to locate an address for Erin Kelly. Tobin promised him his tickets for the next Mets-Yankees game. Tobin said good-bye and hit the flash key to switch over to the call-interrupt call. He stepped onto the elevator and pressed the lobby button at the same time. The doors closed and the elevator sank. The building had been rewired since September 11 in such a way that the cell phone worked in the shaft. The union was lobbying for all high-rise buildings to do the same, for the safety of their rank and file and all other residents and workers.

"Hello," Tobin said.

LL said, *"Up early today, Hank, huh?"*

"I know who you are, Lenny."

There was a long silence on the line.

"Lenny? Who's Lenny? I don't care if you're taping this. If you have half a brain you are."

"You're Lenny Kelly."

"Never heard of him."

"You want people to think you're dead."

"You're chasing your tail, Hank. But how does it feel? Let me tell you what you are gonna feel, in case you haven't gotten over the shock yet."

"How did your wife die?"

"Let's make this about you, Hank."

"Listen to me. . . ."

"No! This time you listen to me! I have the power here. You talk to me like that again, and I hang up, never call back, and I'll send the last photo directly to the Post. *If you have the tape going, I'm sure you won't want anyone to hear it now. Or they'll be asking what's on this other photo I have. But me and you know, don't we, Hank?"*

"Sorry."

"I'm sure you are. For yourself. For your son. For your wife. For your daughter. But I'm not so sure you're sorry for all the other people you've hurt over the years with your big, bad, all-powerful Hank Tobin column."

"I'm sorry for the column I wrote about you."

The line went silent for a long time. *"I have to hang up now. I'll call again when I get another phone. I will be changing the phone every time I call. So the minute you think it can be traced, think again."*

"Please don't hang up. I'm not recording you, I'm not tracing your calls."

LL laughed and said, *"How can you expect me to believe what you say when I can't believe a word you print?"*

"Look, I just need to see you. To talk to you. I need you to help my son."

"I know you do, Hank. I am the only man alive who can help him. And believe me, a part of me, the father in me, would like to do that. I actually feel sorry for you. Because, well, I've been there. However, now it's your turn. You are going to have to get used to the idea that you cannot just pick up the phone and hear your son's voice. You will not be able to take him to a ball game. You can't get together to have dinner. If you want to see him, men in suits must give their permission. Then men in uniforms will search you and monitor you and will forbid you from touching this young man who is your own flesh and blood. And who knows? Your son might not even want to see you. Might refuse your visit because you are the one he holds responsible for putting him there. But if he agrees to see you, the men in charge will tell you how long you can spend sitting on the other side of a Plexiglas window from the boy you brought into the world. They will tell you what you can and cannot talk about. They will tell you when it is time to say hello. When it is time to say good-bye. They will read all the words you write to him. They will own your son for most of the years you have left on Earth. All because of Hank Tobin and his wonderful column. Enjoy. Talk soon."

"Please, no, please don't hang up. I'm sorry. Please talk to me. Please let me meet with you. . . ."

But the line was dead.

EIGHTEEN

By the time Hank Tobin stepped off the elevator at 6:48 A.M., his phone rang again. It was Skip from the *Examiner* library. "According to the coroner's database, Ilene Kelly died of an accidental overdose of sleeping pills the same day her son was sentenced for the firebombing you wrote about," said Skip. "Erin Kelly, her daughter, married Barney Levine. The superrich real-estate mogul who is also a staunchly conservative Orthodox Jew. Supports all the conservative candidates. President of the biggest Jewish right-to-life organization in New York. Does all the gasbag shows, prolife, Zionist, owns a string of independent television stations, three skyscrapers, and a dozen luxury high-rise apartment houses in Manhattan plus an investment firm. Caused a mini-shitstorm a few years back when he married his *shiksa* accountant, a Harvard Business School grad and rising star exec at Christiansen Accounting located in the Chrysler Building. But the scandal was strictly Orthodox intramurals. It blew over when Erin Kelly converted to Judaism and agreed to raise their kid Jewish."

He gave Tobin the address of her townhouse, which Skip said a *Times* real-estate story claimed was worth $15 million.

Tobin drove directly to Erin Kelly Levine's W. Tenth Street townhouse. He sat for forty-five minutes with the air conditioner running, the only car parked on the south side of the street not in compliance with alternate-side-of-the-street parking rules. A Department of Sanitation street sweeper circled around him, the irked driver looking ready to write Tobin a summons until he saw the press pass in the window, shook his head, and kept going. With a forecast of ninety-nine degrees and seventy-five percent humidity with real-feel temperature of one hundred and six degrees, the city was starting to parboil.

Tobin switched on the *Imus in the Morning* radio show. A prerecorded spoof on the Hank Tobin family came on, imagining the whole Tobin family sitting around the dining room table making bombs and writing headlines to fit the targets. If the skit were about someone else, Tobin would have laughed aloud. But it was about his son, and him, and his ex-wife. He listened with a sort of out-of-body detachment.

Ten minutes later a garbage truck rumbled down the block, emptying trash barrels, swooping around him. A cop car cruised by and the driver waved for him to move until he saw the press pass and kept going.

Then Tobin saw a family of three exit the townhouse. Erin was in her late twenties, fair-skinned Irish pretty, frosted blond, swinging a briefcase and dressed in a navy pants suit that gave her an executive's bearing. Her daughter was a blond girl of maybe two or three, and her husband, Barney, was a thin, balding man wearing jogging shorts and a T-shirt and a yarmulke bobby-pinned to his head. A black woman, whom Tobin figured was the nanny, accompanied the husband and wife. She pushed the blond girl in the stroller. Tobin let them pass him. He checked the dashboard clock— 7:31 A.M. He climbed out of his car and followed the family three blocks at an anonymous distance. They paused in front of a synagogue. Erin and Barney went inside as the nanny waited outside with the child. Seven minutes later the couple exited, an elderly rabbi standing between them, an arm draped over each of their shoulders. They kissed as he gave them a parting blessing.

Tobin followed as the Levines continued walking together, as a tight-knit little family, until they entered the playground in Washington Square Park.

A dozen other working couples were there with their nannies, squeezing in early-morning time with their kids before rushing off to ten- and twelve-hour jobs in law firms, ad agencies, accounting firms, brokerage houses, and real-estate developers.

Barney Levine checked his watch, kissed Erin, and began jogging around the perimeter of Washington Square Park. Tobin watched the black nanny lead the child to the infant swings, strap her in, and push her. Erin sat on a park bench, opened her attaché case, removed a bottle of water, and cracked open a copy of the *Wall Street Journal*.

Tobin waited until Barney trotted off toward Lafayette Place, and he walked straight up to Erin, the bright morning sun at his back.

"I need your help," Tobin said, his voice calm and gentle.

"Sorry, I have no change," Erin said after a cursory glance up, her eyes returning to her newspaper.

"Your father has done something awful to my son."

Erin shielded her eyes from the sun with the newspaper and bolted upright, backing up. "I beg your pardon?"

"I know who you are. Your name is Erin Kelly. Your father's is Leonard Kelly. You have a brother named Billy Kelly who was sent to prison for ten years for arson."

She gazed around, as if for a cop, her husband, the nanny, anyone. "Who the hell are *you?*"

She lifted her sunglasses and looked at Hank Tobin. "Oh, my God . . ."

"I'm Hank Tobin, from the *Examiner.*"

"I know who you are, you rotten son of a bitch," she said. "You destroyed my family with the stroke of a pen."

"I want to talk to you about all that—"

"I am going to call a cop and have you arrested for stalking, harassment—"

"Please, I have a boy in a jail cell who was framed by your father."

She looked at him with utter disbelief, taking another step away from him, toward her child, as if she were dealing with a sociopath.

"My father? My father died on September 11. Maybe mental instability runs in your family, Mister Tobin. Your son firebombs synagogues and mosques for headlines, and you stalk me to a playground in the only time of the day I get to spend quality time with my daughter to tell me you think my dead father framed your sicko son?"

"He's not sick, he's—"

"Okay, look. If you don't leave me alone, I will have you arrested. I swear on my dead mother's grave. . . ." Erin Kelly Levine's lower lip trembled as if she'd developed a sudden palsy. She bit it to keep it from quaking. "My husband is a prominent—"

"I know he is. I know you're a successful businesswoman for Christiansen Accounting. I'm a reporter. But I'm also a father. I'm not here stalking you. I'm not here harassing you. I'm here as a father with a son in trouble. An innocent kid—"

"You okay, Misses Erin?" called the nanny, her voice heavy with Creole inflections.

"No, Fanny, I am *not* okay."

"Who that hairy man?" the nanny asked. "Want I should call a policeman?"

"I think Mister Hank Tobin was just leaving," Erin said, her eyes ablaze as she positioned herself between Tobin and the baby swings, a mother protecting her child, which Tobin admired.

"My son was framed as payback for the column I wrote ten years ago about your father and brother and the fire," Tobin said.

"That column destroyed my family," Erin said, tears in her eyes. "I lost a mother because of that column. My brother lost ten years of his life. Now my father's gone, too. But I have built a new family, Tobin. From scratch. On my own. And I'm warning you—stay away from me, stay away from my daughter, stay away from my husband, stay away from my family. Don't you dare mess with what's mine, or you'll be very sorry."

Initial maternal fear was now a white-hot rage in her inky dark eyes.

"I came here asking for help," Tobin said. "And I get threats. Get it straight, rich girl. I'm not afraid of you or your husband or his money. As far as I'm concerned you're still a working-class kid from Brooklyn, like my son. Like me. All your money and all your threats won't scare me, Erin. I got a kid facing fucking life! Which is worse than facing the time myself. That makes *me* someone *you* should worry about because I have absolutely nothing left to lose. We clear on that?"

Erin cowered, sensing that Tobin was not going to be bullied.

Her husband, Barney, trotted up, panting, sweating. His thin wiry body pumped from the morning run. He grabbed his wife's water, gulped, and said, "Problem?"

"He has one," Erin said.

"Which means you do, too, lady," Tobin said and left.

NINETEEN

As he drove downtown to the Brooklyn Battery Tunnel, Tobin dialed the home number for Billy Kelly to see if he was home. He heard a half-awake man answer. Tobin hung up. He knew Billy Kelly wouldn't be up and showered and dressed for at least an hour. So Tobin drove against rush-hour traffic, breezing through the tunnel and out along the Gowanus Expressway to the Belt Parkway, got off at Ocean Parkway, and made it to W. Second Place in Gravesend by 8:18 A.M. by the dashboard clock.

He wanted to take a fresh look at the Hus' house, which had been torched all those years ago, trying to jog old memories into consciousness.

The house had been rebuilt from scratch, with fine yellow brick and a pagoda-style roof. An Asian rock garden with a small gurgling waterfall promoted an incongruous sense of tranquility in the urban setting. Tobin didn't want to approach the Hus. Not yet. They had been victimized, and he didn't want to regurgitate their past horrors.

He parked the car, got out, and knocked on the door of the three-story apartment house across the street where the Kellys once lived. An Asian super answered the door. Tobin tried to extract from the man when Lenny Kelly had moved out from the second-floor apartment. Tobin showed the man his press card, and the man escorted him into the house and halfway down the cellar before Tobin realized the man thought he was from Con Edison and was there to read the meters. Tobin looked at the meter and left.

He circled the block and parked across the street from the little corner grocer that had expanded into a three-storefront superette. On the side where he was parked, Hu's Dry Cleaners and a Hu's Hardware did slim

morning business. Next door to the superette Tobin saw Asian men haul-
ing produce and fish from panel trucks into a restaurant called Madam
Hu's Golden Bowl.

A short, stocky white guy in his early thirties, whom Tobin made for
five-foot-four, smoke dangling from his lips, wearing a pointed chef's hat,
checked off each item on an inventory list. He had muscular arms that were
covered in garish tattoos, and he was handsome in a little Brooklyn tough-
guy kind of way. Handsome as it was, his was a face made for a mug shot or
a character actor playing nasty Irish hoods. *The kind of pretty bad-boy look
that made teenage girls go apeshit,* Tobin thought. *Early grapefruit-in-the-
face Cagney.*

The man's tattooed arms struck a flame of memory in Tobin's brain.
Who the hell is that guy, he wondered? Maybe he was an actor. Maybe he'd
seen him on a post office wall. Maybe he'd once seen him on page one of his
own newspaper.

Then he remembered the young, tattooed man who had stood with his
left arm around a sobbing Debbie Hu's shoulder the night her parents'
house burnt to the ground. He'd told Tobin he was a veteran of Desert
Storm. He wouldn't give a name. *It might be the same guy,* he thought.
Something about one of his tattoos nagged Tobin. But he couldn't remember what the hell it was.

Tobin parked the car again. He ran into Hu's superette, and even
though he didn't smoke, he bought a pack of Marlboros. He couldn't
believe they cost over seven bucks. The man behind the counter looked at
Tobin and then at the photo of him and his son Henry on the cover of the
Daily News.

Tobin knew the guy recognized him.

"He's innocent," Tobin said. The young Asian said nothing, just
blinked at him and the picture in the newspaper.

Tobin grabbed his change and left. He opened the pack of cigarettes,
put one in his mouth, and approached the guy with the chef's hat and muscular tattooed arms.

"Got a light?" Tobin asked.

"No problem."

The guy pulled out a Bic disposable as Tobin studied his left arm.
Tobin puffed on the cigarette and gagged and coughed.

"Nice morning," Tobin said.

" 'Nother day, 'nother dollar. Million days, million dollars."

The counter clerk from Hu's superette stepped out onto the sidewalk and shouted at the man with the tattoos in Vietnamese. As Tobin studied the tattoos on the guy's left arm, the little guy studied Tobin's face. And pointed.

"Yo! You're Hank Tobin."

"Yeah."

"The columnist?"

"Yeah . . ."

The little guy smiled and said, "No shit? Guess what?"

Tobin brightened and said, "What?"

"You suck. Take a fuckin' march, asshole. You and your scumbag kid that I hope maxes out. That fuckin' column you wrote about my wife ten years ago caused more fuckin' trouble in our lives than a fuckin' IRS audit. Took two years to get the insurance straightened out. If you woulda left it alone, it woulda went unsolved, nobody woulda given a shit. Nobody even woulda done time. It woulda been worked out amongst us. Instead you poked your big, fuckin' rummy nose in. You caused nothin' but trouble with that piece of shit column you write. So fuck you, hotshot."

"Fuck you, too, short change."

The little guy threw down his smoke, balled his fists, and took a step toward Tobin when a police radio car slithered by. Tobin noticed a lifetime of street radar ignite in the little guy's eyes. The only thing he feared was a badge.

Tobin knew he'd get nowhere in a hurry with the little guy, so when the cop car stopped for a light, he used the opportunity to cross back over to his car. He drove off as the little guy gave him a departing finger.

Another loyal reader, Tobin thought.

Tobin drove to the corner of McDonald Avenue and Avenue C in Kensington, Brooklyn, and parked with his rearview and side mirrors focused on the front door of the tenement where Billy Kelly lived. At 8:58 A.M. he called Billy again to be sure he was still home. He answered, wide awake this time, and Tobin made believe he was a telemarketer for a new cable system. Billy said, "No, thank you. TV is the devil's playground, but God bless, bro." And hung up.

Tobin sat for another eleven minutes. It was a crummy little corner of the city—grimy, shadowy, treeless, defined by roachy tenements, abandoned factories, and a defunct elevated-subway trestle. Weeds and litter strangled an old bocci ball court, a reminder that the Italian immigrants of the fifties and sixties and their first-generation American kids were long gone to Staten Island, Jersey, Long Island, and Florida.

Kids on idle summer vacation, most of them black and Hispanic and a few Middle Easterners, were already hanging out in front of the corner tenement. The girls skipped skillful Double Dutch, and the boys shot hoops through the bottom rung of a fire escape, dribbling around plump working women hurrying from the front doors toward the Church Avenue stop on the subway F line. The giggling girls eyed the boys.

Tobin looked again in his mirrors. No Billy Kelly. He turned on the *Imus in the Morning* radio program where they were still making Hank Tobin jokes. He punched the dial to the Curtis and Kuby show, and left-wing attorney Ron Kuby and right-wing Guardian Angel founder Curtis Sliwa were also parodying Hank Tobin and his son, Henry: "Hello, city desk? This is Henry Tobin Jr."

"Hey, Henry, what great scoop do you have for us today?"

"Hold the presses until I bum a light to blow up St. Patrick's Cathedral and get an exclusive from a pedophile priest."

Anger rose in Tobin. Then he tried to put it in perspective. If this were happening to someone else, he would probably have swept together the loose facts and constructed a scathing, venomous column about this ego-propelled kid, a cheap chip off his father's narcissistic block, and about the dysfunctional family that spawned him. He would have added a few dollops of pop Freudian "kid competing with the absentee father" psychobabble and called for a life sentence.

During celebrated crimes and trials, a columnist was like a second judge, an ADA, and an alternate juror. Other times a columnist rated the defense, offering advice and making predictions, like a sports pundit picking a prizefight or a horse race.

Tobin punched to the all-news radio. More Tobin news. He half-listened, as he watched Billy Kelly's front door. Then came a story about Rabbi Yitzak Cohn, head of a militant Jewish vigilante group called Jews Against Terror, from Queens, who said his members would be armed with shotguns and baseball bats and patrolling the streets of Brooklyn neighborhoods like Midwood in the aftermath of the bombing of the Sinai Torah Temple. Local Jewish politicians, community leaders, and clergy condemned Cohn and told him to stay away, that he was a meshuga, "a nut."

Then came details of the latest Palestinian suicide bombing. And another update on India and Pakistan exchanging heated words, which one of Tobin's readers had once said was like dueling newsstands or picking sides in a fight between Checker and Yellow cabbies—except nuclear. Then came more Tobin news, interviews with some of Henry's former NYU journalism classmates. One classmate said Henry Tobin Jr. was driven by insatiable ambition to the point where he dropped out of school while on the dean's list to see his byline in a big-city paper. Then came details of a four-day heat wave, with a forecast of heavy rain on the weekend.

Laurie is right, Tobin thought. *I am in a scummy business. I make my living off the misery of others. Sometimes I create that misery. . . .*

He turned on the classical music station as SUVs rolled past him, windows opened, rap music blaring, the bass line pounding so hard that it made the tip of his nose itch. One driver, a white guy wearing a do-rag, listening to Eminem, shot him a suspicious look.

"Five-O," he heard the white guy say, using black ghetto slang for police.

Tobin sat for almost a half hour with no sign of Billy Kelly, entering or leaving the corner tenement.

As Tobin sat watching, a police car pulled abreast, facing the opposite direction.

"Lost, pal?" asked the uniformed driver.

"Or looking to score?" asked his partner.

"I'm waiting for someone," Tobin said.

"Who?" asked the driver, studying Tobin's face, turning and whispering to his partner. Tobin thought he heard his name mumbled.

He didn't want to mention Billy Kelly's name. It would call for too much unneeded explanation to a uniformed cop. Tobin just wanted to tail Billy Kelly to see if he'd lead him to Lenny Kelly. He wouldn't make the same mistake he'd made with Erin. He wouldn't stop and confront this kid he'd helped send to the penitentiary for a decade of the only life he would ever live. Not yet.

Tobin flashed his press card. "I'm on assignment."

The cop driver asked to examine the press card. Tobin handed it to him. The two cops discussed it. One of them must have made a joke because they both laughed. Tobin drew a deep breath and caught a reflection in his side window of a white guy exiting the corner tenement. Dark hair, cleanly shaved, tattoos on his muscled arms, and dressed in jeans and sneakers and a collared black polo shirt. *Billy Kelly,* Tobin thought.

Billy half-glanced at the cop car hassling a motorist across the street, lit a cigarette, and walked north toward Church Avenue.

The driver handed the press card back to Tobin. "Any mosques or Jew temples go up in smoke in our sector today, we know you were around," the cop said.

"How's it feel, Tobin?" asked the cop in the passenger seat, leaning past his partner. Tobin remembered that LL had asked him the same question.

"How's what feel?" Tobin asked.

"You columnists like to rag on cops all the time. How's it feel now that it's your turn in the barrel? With a skelly kid in lockup, facing major time?"

Tobin said nothing, his eyes peering to the sideview mirror, following Billy Kelly as he walked toward Church Avenue.

"We done?" Tobin asked, staring at the driver cop's badge number and nameplate: OTIS. Tobin wrote both down, checked his watch, and recorded the time. Cops didn't like ordinary citizens writing down badge numbers and names. When a reporter did it, they became infuriated and nervous. Even if it didn't amount to anything, it put them on the radar screen and caused agita.

The cop pulled away without another word. Tobin jammed his parking pass in the window, climbed out of the car, and hurried after Billy Kelly, who turned right on Church Avenue.

Tobin followed Billy at a half-block distance as he entered a plain white-brick storefront. Tobin approached the door Billy Kelly entered. Stenciled on the steel door was the word: CLINIC. Tobin stood on the corner, watching people enter and leave. Many of them had the angular, collapsed faces of career junkies, clenched-jawed, sunken-eyed, wearing perpetual scowls that came with years of furtive, ever-foraging drug abuse. Most of the clients of this methadone clinic, men and women, had bad or missing teeth and walked with stooped postures, their unbending legs moving like men on stilts because of methadone-depleted calcium. Some were also fat because methadone caused sloth and mad sugar cravings.

Tobin crossed the street to wait and watch from a more discreet vantage. Twelve minutes later Billy Kelly exited, and he walked straight down Church Avenue. He popped in and out of every store, collecting what looked like old-fashioned charity cans, where customers donated loose coins from their change. He collected cans from a dozen stores in two blocks, placing them in a paper shopping bag. *Junkie scam,* Tobin thought.

Billy Kelly collected his final can in a Korean grocer, then poked through a display of flower bouquets, picked a mixed bunch, and entered. Tobin watched Billy pay the Korean with a bill he removed from his wallet, smiling as he made small talk and received his change, which he stuffed into one of the collection cans.

Tobin was confused. Billy Kelly did time for bombing the home of an Asian grocer and now he makes small talk and little jokes with one and collects charity cans from every store on Church Avenue?

He doesn't look like a guy consumed with hate, bigotry, or vengeance, Tobin thought. *LL believes so much in his son's innocence he's dedicated his life to getting even for his wrongful incarceration.*

Tobin ordinarily didn't believe in frame-ups unless there was extraordinary evidence. But this LL has showed how easy it was to frame Henry Jr., so why not give the same benefit of a doubt to LL's son, Billy? Because he'd never actually had a trial, Tobin was now ready to presume Billy Kelly's innocence, even if it was ten years too late.

Billy Kelly exited the Korean grocer. Tobin continued to shadow him from across the street. Billy glanced over his shoulder a few times, as if looking to see if he was being tailed. He never looked across the street. Few stalking victims ever do. An old homicide cop had taught Tobin the simple parallel-tail trick, which meant you tailed someone from the side, across the street, instead of from the obvious rear.

Kelly bought a paper at an Arab newsstand on the corner of McDonald and then turned right, carrying the flowers and the shopping bag filled with the charity cans. *Maybe he has a girlfriend,* Tobin thought. *The two of them'll probably rip open the cans, count the coins, sell their methadone, and go cop dope and boot up all afternoon.*

Then Tobin followed Billy Kelly as he veered a few blocks over to Immaculate Heart of Mary church, where he descended the basement steps. Tobin waited a few minutes and approached. A sign read: IHM SOUP KITCHEN AND FOOD PANTRY OPEN DAILY 8 A.M., 9:15 A.M., AND NOON TO 1:15 P.M. EVERYONE WELCOME.

Tobin bounded down the stairs and peered inside. The place was mobbed with homeless men and impoverished families, waiting on line to be served food by volunteers. He saw Billy Kelly hand the shopping bag with the charity cans to a portly priest. Tobin felt like a shitheel for assuming Billy Kelly was a petty thief. Then he saw Kelly tie on an apron, point to his watch, place his flowers on a shelf behind the serving counter, and begin ladling pancakes, scrambled eggs, hash browns, and toast to the hungry.

Junkies for Jesus, Tobin thought.

Tobin caught himself in midthought.

There you go again. Thinking like a cynical, arrogant columnist. Judging the poor bastard again. So, he's on the methadone program. So what?

Tobin thought: *What if the poor guy went to jail unjustly? If he did, maybe I helped put him there. After ten years, he comes out. Can't find a job. Lives in a rat hole. Mother's dead. So he starts shooting dope to make the pain go away. He feels bad. Feels guilt. Decides to clean up again, and he finds solace in methadone and Jesus. Who the hell am I to judge this poor guy? He's on methadone; I'm addicted to my own byline. I wish I could find Jesus or someone or something like him to help me kick my jones. To help me get my kid out of the jam I helped put him in.*

Tobin waited across the street until 9:15. Then Billy Kelly emerged from the church basement, carrying the flowers. Tobin followed him to the gates of Green Wood Cemetery on Fort Hamilton Parkway. *The flowers are for a grave,* Tobin thought.

Tobin straggled way back, keeping Billy Kelly in sight only as a faceless figure in the distance as he strolled the twisty paths and rolling hills of the massive necropolis where Revolutionary War rebels, Civil War heroes, sports and movie stars, famous gangsters and the judges who sentenced them to life terms and the electric chair were buried with the common citizens under the same big Brooklyn sky. Dozens of species of birds chirped and cawed and sang in the trees and hedges. Carp jumped in an iridescent lake, sending ripples to the shady shore. Widows tended the graves of their vanished men. A cortege wound through the green hillocks, bringing in the new dead.

Billy Kelly stopped at a marker on a small knoll just inside Fort Hamilton Parkway, across from a McDonald's, where kids played at an indoor playground, noshing breakfast burritos and Egg McMuffins. Next door motorists waited on line to have their cars washed at Brooklyn Car Wash. Billy Kelly placed his bouquet on a grave and bowed his head in prayer, hands clasped at his belt buckle. He didn't look like the kind of guy who would torch your house. *Did I destroy this poor guy's life?* Tobin wondered.

Tobin wanted to approach him, right there, in the cemetery, and tell him he was sorry. And ask him to help him clear Henry. But he couldn't do that. *This kid would probably spit in my face,* he thought. *I helped take ten years out of his life, and I come asking him for a favor?*

No, the best Tobin could hope for was tailing him and hoping he'd lead him to his father. To LL, to Lenny the Loser Kelly.

Tobin pretended to pray over the headstone of someone named Michael Cassidy who'd died a week before September 11. He wondered who he was, what his story had been, and if his kid had ever gotten jammed up. He read the epitaph on his wife's headstone, "Earth receive an honored guest." He thought that was from W. H. Auden about William Butler Yeats. He wasn't sure. Maybe it was the other way around. The guy's wife died thirty-two years before him. He wondered what the guy did for three decades without his wife, his mind reeling. Then he heard the screeching of a car. The honking of a bus and a truck. He heard squealing tires and loud horns and people screaming and metal crunching and glass shattering.

Down the hillock on Fort Hamilton Parkway a three-vehicle collision twisted the roadway into a wicked steel pretzel, like a piece of grotesque op art. A city bus driver was collapsed on his blaring horn. People screamed. Families rushed out of McDonald's, mothers shielding their children's eyes from the horror. One bloodied man—his face sheared like a peeled grape—climbed through a shattered, crimson windshield onto the mangled hood of his truck, steam shooting up at him from a severed hose. The man could not see and walked aimlessly, a lost soul groping for something to touch. As people screamed, he walked right off the six-foot-high hood, landing on his face. Screams mixed with the blaring horn followed by moans and wails and the urgent shouting of immigrant men racing from the car wash, carrying tools and towels.

Tobin held his Reporter's Notebook in his hand, scribbling notes as he rushed down from the hillock toward the eight-foot picket fence. There was no escape. The nearest gate was at the far end of the graveyard where he'd entered. The immigrants evacuated passengers from the bus, dazed, disoriented, crying, hollering, a few bloodied. No one could open the doors of the silver Honda Accord that resembled a ball of crumpled aluminum foil, blood leaking from its center.

Cemetery workers rushed down the incline to gape, offering tools through the steel-fence bars to the immigrants who were trying to free the man from the Honda. Behind him women gasped and people from the funeral gathered to gape, a priest starting a rosary on the hillock above the carnage. Tobin thought about how all these people who lived in the terror age, watching the skies, fearful of swarthy men carrying suspicious parcels, worrying about where the next terrorist attack would happen, never saw this coming. *Just another human accident,* he thought. One driver trying to overtake another, someone running a red light or a stop sign or acting out an outburst of road rage. He scribbled notes, out of habit, looking for new ways to write death and tragedy. Unless he wrote it as a column, as a counterpoint to death by terror, a car accident in Brooklyn would never make an inch of news in the *Examiner.* Unless one of the dead or wounded was a celebrity or one of the drivers was a drunken cop. He knew he would never write it.

"Oh, my God, man," said the voice behind him. "You see what happened, bro?"

Tobin took notes, and without looking up, he said, "Not really, I was up there when I heard it and . . ."

Then he turned and looked into Billy Kelly's eyes.

Billy's pupils were pinpricked by the synthetic Methadone opiate. His false teeth were state issue, like Chiclets set in hot pink wax, and he smelled like three-dollar cologne. Tobin's heart thumped, adrenaline rocketed through his veins. Sizzling blue arcs of human hate crackled between them in the sun.

Tobin had felt the heat and anger and scorn of many people over the years. It came with the column. But this was different. Billy Kelly stared at Tobin for so long and with such venom, his veiny eyes never blinking, that Tobin felt an eerie tingle on his skin. It was like looking at the face of a demon that haunted Tobin's own tormented soul. Hank Tobin the man saw in Billy Kelly's face all the rotten, miserable, self-centered, and plain mean things that Hank Tobin the columnist had ever done wrong to all the people in his writing life. All manifested in this one Halloween mask of hate and anger and vengeance.

"Hey . . ." Tobin said. He couldn't find any words to follow.

Billy Kelly backed away, clutching the crucifix of the rosary that dangled around his neck. Tattoos of Jesus and the Blessed Virgin now covered the old swastika tattoo. Tobin sensed that Billy was not afraid of him. Not afraid of Hank Tobin. No, there was something darker in the way he retreated, walking backward up the hill, clutching his crucifix, big arms bulging, neck veins popping, that said Billy Kelly was most afraid of what he might do to Hank Tobin. In front of all these witnesses. If he did not get away from him. Fast. And there was something else he seemed to be backing away from, fleeing from. Tobin thought Billy Kelly was also running from himself, or at least from the Billy Kelly he used to be, before the fire, before jail, before he found Jesus in the joint. Jailhouse Jesus freaks rarely found the Gentle Redeemer waiting for them when they came home. But the devil was always waiting, pitchfork, hypodermic needle, or gun and knife in hand, ready to take whatever was left of your soul. Billy Kelly saw Satan in the guise of Hank Tobin, and he was getting as far away from him as possible.

The cemetery security patrol arrived on scooters and in a Bronco Jeep, gaping down at the accident. The sirens of approaching emergency vehicles split the afternoon as the crowd swelled and traffic snarled on Fort Hamilton Parkway.

"Billy . . . we need to talk," Tobin shouted.

Billy Kelly just kept backing up the hill. He stared down at Tobin for a long sweaty moment, framed against the police cars and fire trucks and ambulances converging on the awful scene beyond the gates. A mother squirrel hopped by Tobin followed by a baby squirrel. Tobin glanced at baby following mother up a tree, an image of life amid the death. When Tobin looked back to Billy Kelly, he was gone.

Tobin pushed through the crowd, scrambled up the hill, but by the time he reached the top, Billy Kelly was nowhere to be seen.

Tobin walked away from the accident to the gravesite where he had seen Billy Kelly stop and pray. He looked down at the markers. One was for his mother, Ilene Kelly. The other was for Leonard Kelly.

The flowers were on Lenny Kelly's grave.

TWENTY

Tobin stood at the back of the 10:30 A.M. Staten Island–bound ferry, breaking pieces off a soft pretzel and casting them onto the foamy wake that spilled toward the wounded skyline of Manhattan.

Seagulls swept down, snatching the soggy dough from the roiled harbor as Mona Falco plugged another quarter into the coin-operated telescope and peered off toward Lady Liberty. The FBI had issued an orange-level terrorist alert, and traffic was snarled on the Brooklyn Bridge where cops did spot checks, a little citizen-approved ethnic profiling, pulling over swarthy men driving rented trucks. These traffic jams had become part of the new New York. Truck drivers and businessmen alike now carried piss bottles in their vehicles, and used hands-free cell-phone devices hooked to compact computer notebooks to conduct business while sitting in traffic.

Against Steve Clancy's advice, Tobin had called Falco at One Police Plaza and asked if there was somewhere they could speak privately. She suggested they both catch the 10:30 ferry. She said it was probably a good place to meet, away from the bottom feeders of his craft. As he fed the birds and she spied through the telescope, Tobin asked Falco if she remembered Lenny Kelly and his son, Billy. She had a complete recollection of the case because it had won her a promotion.

"I'm awaiting reassignment. Today might just be a very big day in my career. And I owe my career to that column of yours about Billy Kelly. It's the one that got me the attention of the brass."

"Then your career might be built on sand," Tobin said.

"Why?"

Tobin was not yet certain Billy was innocent. But his father, Lenny Kelly, was. So certain that he'd gone to extraordinary ends to get even for what he believed was Tobin's role in his son's wrongful imprisonment. If Lenny Kelly so firmly believed his son was innocent, Tobin was going to give him at least the benefit of the doubt, even if it was ten years late.

"First, do you believe my son did this mosque arson? And all the other nonsense they're accusing him of?"

"I'm not sure."

"Good, that means you're not convinced. Why?"

"Because he's your kid. I know you didn't raise a bigot. Still, kids develop hate in the street, too. But my feeling is that if he did do this, it wasn't out of hate. It was for a cheap headline and the whole thing backfired."

"What if I told you I think Lenny Kelly was behind this?"

She looked from the telescope to Tobin. "I'd say you were crazy."

"Why?"

"Lenny Kelly's dead."

"You went to his memorial mass, but they never found his body," Tobin said, leaning on the railing, gazing at the docks of Brooklyn, following the waterfront from Red Hook to Bay Ridge as the ferry plowed through the harbor, passing groaning tugs that pushed big tankers through the Narrows and out toward the open sea. He couldn't get used to the Twin Towers being missing.

"How do you know I went to Kelly's memorial mass?" Falco asked.

"I'm a reporter. Why'd you go?"

"Not sure," she said, shrugging. "Maybe because he was part of a milestone case in my career. Maybe because I always sort of felt sorry for Lenny Kelly."

"Why'd you feel sorry for him? He raised a bigoted kid who torched an Asian family's house because they were yellow, people of color, no? That's what you and the DA said at the time."

"And you. No one said it louder than Hank Tobin," she said, gulping harbor wind and drubbing her lips in frustration. "Me? I was young and hungry on that bust. Proud. I really wanted a trial. I wanted to take the stand. To sit firm and composed and unflinching through a wicked cross-examination by a hotshot defense lawyer, like Clancy. I wanted a sketch artist to draw me, make me look pretty and tough, and put me in the *Daily News* and the *Examiner*. I wanted to play my part in a big-city courtroom melodrama. I wanted to watch the DA build an airtight case, present all my circumstantial evidence, make a brilliant summation to the jury, quoting my unshakable testimony, and hear a jury foreman announce a guilty verdict. I wanted the press to swarm around me, like they swarm around you now. Instead, Billy Kelly, the poor, dumb, mixed-up kid copped a ten-year plea with a fresh-out-of-law-school Legal Aid lawyer. And all I could do was watch a mother collapse, a father disintegrate before my eyes. The Asian family didn't even show up for the plea. It put me on an upward career path, but it always felt sort of unfinished to me."

"It was," Tobin said. "It's being finished now. Henry is the third act."

Falco looked at him for a long time. "I'm not following."

"Henry is being framed for what happened to another man's son ten years ago."

"By Billy Kelly?"

"No, I don't think so."

"Who, then? You saying you think Lenny Kelly is alive?"

"No one ever collected his life insurance," Tobin said.

He was being careful with the information he divulged. He didn't want to tell Mona Falco about the phone calls from LL until he was certain he could fully trust her. He was working it like he worked some stories, from around the edges before he revealed his hand.

"What about his kids?" Mona asked.

"You tell me," Tobin said. "I tried talking to them. They blew me off."

Mona clamped her hands behind her neck, thrust her chest out, shoulders back, and groaned. "You're asking me to punch holes in my own case," she said. "Which I would if I thought you were on the money. But this sounds wacky, Hank. Besides, Henry's case is going to be Federal fast and—"

"You still have clout."

"This case is being played on page one of every paper in town. Besides, I'm up for a transfer to the Task Force, Hank. Orders are supposed to be approved today. How many ranking black-female NYPD Task Force supervisors did you ever run into? I do a year on the Joint Terrorist Task Force in this climate, and I could make Inspector. Because of this case, Cox has asked NYPD to assign me to the Task Force ASAP. I can become the highest-ranking minority woman in the PD. And now you're asking me to undermine Cox? And my transfer?"

"What're you saying, Mona? You don't wanna rock the boat because you're more interested in promotions than the learning the truth?"

She looked at Tobin, cocked her head, and scoffed at him. "Don't give me the sanctimonious *truth* routine, Hank. You've played fast and loose with *'the truth'* yourself over the years. I remember, in your drinking days, when you used to quote from some John Wayne movie, *The Man Who Shot Liberty Valance,* if I remember right. 'When the facts get in the way of the myth, print the myth.' From what you're telling me, maybe you printed the myth instead of the facts in the original Kelly column. And now you want me to find those facts from a long-closed case for you."

"I'm asking for your help, Mona."

She was silent for a long moment as the ferry's engine was cut, bringing an eerie silence to the watery center of the loudest metropolis on the planet, except for the swish of the water and the hungry yapping of the gulls. The big boat drifted toward the Staten Island dock. "I've been asking you for a god-damned courtesy call, a lousy date on some lonesome Tuesday or Thursday night, for so long it makes me feel like a panhandler as I push forty," she said. "And now you want my help? I fell in love with you, Hank. And then you walked away from me. That hurt. It still hurts. And now you want me to hurt my own career to help you because your kid is jammed up?"

"You and me both know the reason I avoid you."

"Yeah, because I'm the little Jemima that busted up you and your precious wife," she said.

"Don't you dare play fucking race roulette with me, Mona. I'm appealing to you as a friend. As a woman. An officer of the law. I'm sorry. I guess I was wrong."

He stepped past her, toward his car parked in the auto hold of the ferry. Mona Falco grabbed his arm and led him to the other railing, facing Staten Island.

"If this was someone else, you'd understand what you were asking," she said. "But because this is about you and your kid you're not focusing on reality, Hank."

"Nothing's more real than my kid facing life."

"You made Cox look like an asshole. In person. In print. In front of me. In front of his peers. In front of his bosses. The President of the United States of America probably read your column about Cox. He probably jotted the scarlet letter 'A' for 'asshole' next to poor Cox's name. You messed with Cox's career path. He's on a personal crusade to nail your son. I would help you if I could, Hank. When it goes Federal, even if I'm on the Task Force, I can't."

"Why?"

"Because if you believe Lenny Kelly is alive and that he framed your son because you used his own words to finger his son in print, that's a whole other amazingly complicated investigation."

"That's what cops do. Good detectives investigate."

"We'd need to bring in the NYPD Cold Case Squad, find old witnesses, if they're alive, find Kelly, if he's really still alive. Then, assuming for argument's sake that you're correct about all this, to establish motive for this phantasmagoric conspiracy, we'd have to prove that Kelly set up Henry to get even with you for your role in his son's arrest and incarceration. Then the Brooklyn DA would have to be willing to say his office might have made a mistake on an old hate crime, which means suggesting that the real culprit has been free all this time, and the statute of limitation has passed."

"That's been done before."

"Yeah, but usually only when someone else exposes the injustice. NYPD and the Brooklyn DA's office would never go out of their way to find Kelly, just so they can exonerate his son, Billy. So that Billy can then sue the ass off the city and state for false arrest and a coerced plea bargain, like the guys in the Central Park jogger case. This Assistant District Attorney who prosecuted this case is dead. But it's the same District Attorney as ten years ago, too. He's a career politician. You think he wants to be made a fool of? He doesn't want this on his record when he runs for reelection or higher office. Then they'd have to find the victims and explain that they never found the real guy who tried to kill them when the house burned down."

"So what?"

"So it's political suicide! He'd have to admit his office made a rush-to-judgment false arrest ten years ago. And another one now, with your son. He'd look like a Keystone Kop. They'd have to piece your theory together. But first they'd have to believe this was all plausible or possible. And it would cost NYPD a fortune in manpower in a city that is ten billion in the hole. They won't pay for an investigation like that when they believe, and the public believes, that they already have a win-win trophy collar in Hank Tobin's son."

"They have to know I'll never rest."

"Hank, you have used this Mayor for target practice. You nicknamed the PC 'Commissioner Clouseau.' The Feds, the entire Justice Department, hate you. You think any of them would trade in convicting Hank

Tobin's son to exculpate the kid of some old rummy who had seven-and-a-half-minutes of page-ten fame ten years ago? On a wild theory for which you have absolutely no proof?"

"What if I prove Lenny Kelly is alive? I've been getting phone calls from a strange guy—"

"Does he claim to be Lenny Kelly?"

"No."

"Have you met him?"

"No, but he's the guy who sent me the photos and gave me the description of Henry—"

"You know where to find him?"

"No."

"Come on, Hank. Even for the sake of argument this anonymous caller is Lenny Kelly. What of it? He didn't fake his death to run from criminal charges, back taxes, alimony, or child support. I know because I checked. When he died, he left a clean house. Even his rent and bills were paid up. He didn't take any loans he'd never repay. Didn't run up his credit cards. You'd have to prove he committed these elaborate crimes and framed your son. I could never, ever sell that story to my bosses. And Cox would laugh me out of his office. I'm sorry, Hank. I don't think I could help you even if I wanted to."

"Why wouldn't you want to?"

"Because, I think you're so close to this you can't see how crazy your story sounds. I think that if you go this route, it'll make it worse for your kid. I was you, I'd have Clancy hiring the best shrinks in town to get your kid off on an insanity defense. Or work on the best plea bargain he can hammer out. If you go this route, if you cost the city and state a fortune, if you go to trial on a not-guilty defense and blow trial, you are going to help send your kid away for so long that you will probably die of old age or a broken heart, whichever comes first, while he's inside."

"Right now you're still the head of the NYPD Hate Crime Unit. My kid is a victim of a hate crime, Mona. He's paying for the hate another man has for me. But you're too jaded by the job and personal experience to see that. You think all hate has to be racial, ethnic, gender based."

"Oh, *really?*" she said. "Then you have no idea how much I hate myself for ever falling in love with you."

As the boat docked and the deck hands fastened it to the greasy berth with long mechanical hooks, Mona Falco walked to her car and climbed in.

Tobin did the same. They exchanged a parting glance through their car windows. Falco exited first. Tobin followed her off the ferry onto Staten Island. As she approached the first red traffic light in the neighborhood of St. George, Falco slapped her magnetic cherry light onto the roof of her black Crown Victoria and blew through the light. Tobin waited two minutes for it to turn green. Then he took Bay Street straight up to the Verrazano Bridge and sped back toward Brooklyn.

His cell phone rang. It was Clancy. "Two things: Henry's story definitely was filed from his own laptop. Second, the test on the blowback came back. His hands were clean as a nun's knickers. But there was residue from the rocket launcher all over his jacket."

"Sure, Kelly fired it," Tobin said, "and then put the jacket on Henry."

"The way the prosecution is gonna paint it is that Henry was stoned on beer and pills," Clancy said. "He wore gloves when he fired the rocket launcher. Then to cover his tracks, he threw away the gloves somewhere along the way. Then after he drove home, he passed out in his car until the cops read your description of the car and shooter and found him with the weapon and the blowback on his clothes."

"So what are you saying?" Tobin asked, his heart pounding, dread cascading through him.

"I'm saying that unless you find this Lenny Kelly guy and get him to fess up to framing Henry, we better start looking at an insanity defense."

For the first time in four years, Hank Tobin went looking for a liquor store.

TWENTY-ONE

Tobin ran through the Marine Park playground, watching the old parkie wearing the white wig and beard race the Department of Parks truck out the exit onto Avenue R. The truck made a left and sped down the avenue and whipped another left up toward Avenue U when Tobin gave up the useless chase.

He realized he had probably just come face-to-face with LL, with Lenny the Loser, with the "deceased" Lenny Kelly, who had looked him in the eyes and gloated as he watched Tobin writhe in pain over the framing of his son.

He's probably been tailing me all morning, Tobin thought. *Who the hell looks for a Parks Department truck? Probably knows some guy who went on vacation, grabbed his keys, uniform, a broom, and a pick and a shovel. Slapped on a Halloween-store disguise and a different pair of shades. One day a black wig and aviator glasses. Next day a white wig and beard and dark, wraparound shades. Tomorrow a red-haired disguise with horn-rimmed glasses. A dead man can become anyone.*

Tobin saw the mothers in the playground gaping at this bearded man clutching a pint bottle wrapped in a brown paper bag who had been chasing a parkie truck through the park. He realized he looked like a deranged nut. One mother lifted the cell phone, tapped three digits, and put it to her ear as if she were calling for police help.

Tobin looked at the bottle of Stolichnaya. He gripped the cap between his thumb and forefinger again, ready to twist.

Then he thought of Henry in his cell. Henry needed him now more than ever.

The same way that more than ever he knew he needed Julie's help. He tossed the bottle of booze in a trash can and hurried to his car parked on Avenue U and drove the three blocks to Julie's house, shouldered through the reporters, mumbling "No comment, yet," climbed the stoop, and rang the bell.

When Julie answered, Tobin said, "I have nowhere else to turn."

Julie stood in the doorway, hands jammed in the back pockets of her snug old jeans, looking past Tobin to the gathered reporters staked out on the lawn and sitting on their vehicles parked up and down E. Thirty-eighth Street. Cameramen shot tape, some of it feeding live all-news-all-the-time cable stations.

"Hank, give us a bite, will ya," shouted one reporter.

"Something," said another.

"Anything," said a third. "Recite the ABCs, sing 'Twinkle Star'. . . ."

"How about giving me and my family a fucking break?" Tobin said, then he took a deep breath, held up his hands. "Sorry, guys. It's hard on this side of the press card."

He glanced at Julie and indicated with his eyes that he had to talk to the reporters. She nodded approval.

"Off the record, first, okay?" The reporters nodded, grumbled that it was okay. "I gotta ask you guys to pull back, move to the corner, and I'll give you something whenever there's something to say. Otherwise I'll say nothing. If I get my balls busted, you'll get yours busted by your editors and producers because I won't say anything. The other ground rule is you talk to the lawyer or me. Leave my wife . . . um, ex-wife, Julie, and my daughter, Laurie, alone."

Tobin and the reporters hammered out a collective agreement to give the family some breathing room so long as they got some kind of sound bites and some fresh updates and pictures every day. But the reporters warned that when a major new development arose in the case, they would need some kind of comment, clarification, or family response. Tobin agreed. Then Tobin gave them a sound bite.

"My family stands together, one thousand percent behind my son, Henry," Tobin said. "He's innocent, and we're confident he will be exonerated. I ask that the press, the judicial system, and the public keep an open mind. There are other darker things going on here that I cannot yet discuss that will come to light later. That's all our lawyer will let me say for now. Thank you."

This sent a flutter through the press. Tobin turned back to Julie. She eyed him and the press who swarmed closer, asking for him to be more specific about these "other darker things."

Julie said nothing, just swung the door open wider, and Tobin entered the house. For the sake of the cameras, Julie clutched Tobin's arm as she closed the door.

"I don't want you here," she said, moving into the living room furnished with the leather couches he'd bought fifteen years before.

"I don't care," he said. "I need you."

"Dream on, hotshot—"

"Stop with the bullshit, Julie. I don't mean I need you, *need* you. I need your help so that *we* can help Henry."

"What the hell can I do?"

"The PD and the FBI have their minds made up that Henry did this."

"You believe he didn't?"

"Yes. That's just not our kid—"

"Excuse me, I believe he's innocent, too. But how the hell would *you* know? You hardly know *our* kid anymore. Let me show the great Hank Tobin who his son, Henry, is."

She grabbed his hand. Her hand was small and strong, and she yanked him across the room with a wicked little tug, stronger than most men of her size and weight.

She unlocked the door leading to the basement and led Tobin down the stairs to the apartment where Henry lived alone, paying monthly rent to his mother. Tobin stopped on the bottom step. Julie walked ahead, switched on the overhead track lights. Tobin glanced around the room and felt lousiness rise like dirty steam in his veins, flushing his face, leaking through his pores, hissing in his ears.

The whole apartment had been tossed by the Feds, searched and dusted and torn apart. Books were missing from shelves. Julie said that bags and boxes of potential evidence—files, notebooks, bank statements, Rolodex, phone records—had been carted away, but Tobin was only half-listening. Henry's computer table was bare; Julie said something about it being confiscated. Drawers had been dumped out, closets gutted, couch cushions ripped open, mattresses slit.

But Tobin gaped past all of that, oblivious to the grotesque violation, ignored the aftermath of the savage evidence hunt. Instead he gazed around at the walls of Henry Tobin Jr.'s apartment.

One wall was decorated with scores of photos of Tobin and Henry, father and son, taken at Henry's consecutive birthday parties over the years. They covered a time span of seventeen years. There were no birthday photos in the last four years since the divorce.

Another wall displayed every single one of Hank Tobin's book jackets, mounted and framed, many from foreign editions. Framed posters from bookstore windows and subway-car advertisements.

Another wall was a celebration of Hank Tobin's journalism awards—Meyer Berger, three Polk Awards, several AP awards, and his two Pulitzer certificates. Henry had also framed incremental "softball" columns his father wrote about home life with his son, Henry, over the years. Stories about Henry's first day of school, Little League, grammar school graduation, and entering high school.

A fourth wall displayed framed 8-by-10-inch photographs of his father with some of the major players in the city and the nation and the world—politicians, sports legends, movie stars, literary titans, famous artists.

"To say he worships you is the understatement of the new millennium," Julie said. "Everything here but a holy-water fount with your icon to genuflect and bless himself with as he enters and leaves. I don't get it. It's a shrine to Hank Tobin, absentee father. Way to go, ace."

"Go ahead, get it out, beat the shit out me," Tobin said, sagging against the banister. "Say all the nasty stuff you want. About what a lousy, self-absorbed, neglectful, piss-poor father I've been. I'm not gonna argue with you."

"Good. Because you'd lose."

"I know."

"You are a lousy, selfish, piss-poor piece of . . ."

She stopped in midsentence as she looked at Tobin, his face as resigned as a guilty man searching for redemption in the rifle barrels of a firing squad.

"You okay?"

"No."

"Me neither," she said.

"I know."

She nudged him up the stairs, back into the living room.

"Want a drink? Soda, coffee . . ."

"Water."

"We use tap."

He laughed and said, "Fine."

"You can sit down," she said, moving toward the kitchen as he entered the living room. "You paid for the furniture."

He sat in his old leather recliner, reached down to the left side, and yanked the stick lever that made the footrest pop up. He'd bounced both his kids on his knee in this chair, often dozed off in this chair when he came home from work and the post-deadline saloons. He'd even made love to Julie in this chair dozens of times when they got the kids asleep upstairs.

He looked around the living room. It had been repainted. The rug was new. Everything else was the same. For the first time in days he felt a frail sense of safety.

Julie walked back into the living room, paused, harumphed, handed him his water, and said, "You're in *my* chair."

Tobin pushed himself to get up. She nudged him back down. "It's okay," she said. "I just wanted you to know that we both know it."

"Duly noted, *Ms.* Capone."

He gulped the water as Julie sat on a coffee table, staring at him. Old familiar ticks, knocks, squeaks, and groans of the living, breathing house caused the kind of homesickness no amount of money or penthouse amenities could ever cure.

"You look wiped out," Tobin said.

"I'm fine. Okay, I let you in. Talk to me. What are these 'dark things'?"

He got up from the chair, walked to the entertainment center, turned on the radio, and dialed the volume up loud to an oldies rock station. Rod Stewart was singing "Do Ya Think I'm Sexy." Julie walked to him, her perplexed face begging explanation. He walked closer to her, both of them leaning against the mantel, just feet from one of the crackling stereo speakers. He whispered in her ear, smelling the soft Opium perfume rising from her long elegant neck, blending with the old familiar soapy scents.

"If the Feds were in the house, they might've left behind bugs," he said, his voice low and grave.

"You think?"

"On this case, without a doubt. Ditto the phones, yours and Henry's."

Standing so close he could feel her body heat and hear the nervous rumblings of her stomach, he filled her in about the anonymous crank calls from this guy LL, about how he was also Henry's source, and about how he faked his own death on September 11. The Rod Stewart song cross-faded into John Lennon singing "Imagine," as Tobin told Julie about how this source also sent him the dramatic photos by computer. And about how he and Tracy Burns decided to go with them but that ultimately it was his call. He also told her about the photo not yet released to the press, the ace in the hole, which was the picture of Henry's Explorer fleeing the scene with the license plate clearly visible. And the other photo of a mustard-colored Explorer at the Sinai Torah Temple firebombing.

She said, "You think this guy set up Henry?"

"Yes."

"Why, Hank?"

He told her all about tracking down the guy's name from going through the old columns. He didn't tell her Lenny Kelly's name yet. He wanted to focus her anger on what Kelly was doing to their son before he told her his name. Tobin just told Julie that Kelly was a disgruntled interviewee whose kid was sent to the can because of a column Tobin wrote ten years ago. And that this man, as deranged as he was, believed his kid was innocent.

"Sounds like he wanted you to know who he was," she said.

"He did. Now he wants me to try to find him. A game of cat and mouse while Henry goes through arrest, trial, maybe conviction, and jail. But this guy's officially a dead man, a memorial mass was said for him. There's insurance money waiting to be claimed. The scary truth is that he's a dead man walking. He has liver cancer."

"Oh, Jesus . . . How long does he have?"

"With the liver, it can be any day."

"So you're saying this guy, this vengeful son of a bitch you wrote about ten years ago, has come back to haunt you? And he framed Henry to get even with you for what you wrote in your column that hurt his son, his family? And he might fucking *die* before we can get him to clear Henry?"

"Yes. That's about it."

"And the cops and the Feds won't pursue this?"

"Correct," he said, explaining that Cox and the Feds hated him, as did the NYPD commissioner and the Brooklyn DA, because of ferocious Hank Tobin columns.

"You've burned more bridges over the years than General Sherman," she said.

"I know."

"One of them to your family."

They stood staring at each other for a long, wordless moment as the Lennon song ended and an ad for an antihistamine came on, proclaiming more side effects than arsenic. "I'm afraid to ask the next question because you obviously left out this detail on purpose," she said.

"Shoot."

"Careful I don't take that literally."

"C'mon, Jule. . . ."

"Okay, so what's the name of this guy, this bastard who set up our baby?"

"Lenny Kelly," he said. "Son's name Billy Kelly."

She closed her eyes, old betrayal boiling in her, collapsing her face and popping the veins in her neck and temples. She wheedled her fingers. Her lower lip trembled. He wanted to kiss her lips to stop the quivering. He touched her shoulder. She shrugged him off. She swallowed, hard, sipped some water. Tears gelled in her faded blue eyes.

"The firebombing case in Gravesend?"

He nodded.

"The case where you met Mona Falco," she said, her face as hopeless as an unanswered prayer.

"Coincidence, Jule . . ."

She fiddled with objects on the mantel, lifted a family portrait taken on the day Henry graduated from grammar school. She placed it facedown. "I'll tell you what's not a coincidence, Hank. I remember a young police-woman you met at a murder crime scene once. You helped her secure the scene, got a license plate number, in exchange for details for a story. That young female cop eventually slept with you, fell in love with you, and par-layed that help from Hank Tobin into a gold shield, and a life as a homicide detective, and a wife, and a mother."

Linda Rondstadt came on the radio, singing "Blue Bayou."

"Julie, for Christ's sake, stop, please stop. . . ."

"Then there was another female cop," she said, her voice rising. "Also young. And she took the details from Hank Tobin to make a big case. And slept with him. And she parlayed all that into a great career as a hate-crime-unit detective, a mistress, and a home wrecker."

"That's bullshit. But go ahead, let *them* know how united we stand."

"This bimbo got so big she personally locked up our son. And, I hear on the blue tom-toms, she's parlaying it into becoming an inspector, the top NYPD cop on the JTTF. That's not a coincidence, Hank. That's unforgiv-able. Mona Falco is connected to all the worst days of this family's brief and miserable history. But I can't blame just her. Home wreckers always need an 'inside' accomplice. Someone to open the front door and let her in. That someone was you, Hank."

Rondstadt sang, "I'm coming back someday/come what may/to blue bayou. . . ."

Tobin raked his fingers through his hair, leaned forward, and looked Julie in her damaged blue eyes. "That's your version, Jule," he said. "I could bring up that the guy who brings you flowers now is your old homicide partner. I could ask when that romance started, how many years ago. But I won't because I didn't come here to accuse you or defend myself. I came here because we have to defend Henry."

Julie took a deep breath, cleared her throat, and gathered her scattered composure. She walked to him, looked him square in the eyes.

"Have you talked to marvelous Mona about all of this? She put the fucking cuffs on our son. Did you tell *her* that he was set up? By some nut from the past? From a case she cashed in on with details you supplied?"

"Yes. I told her."

"When?"

"Today, a few hours ago."

"I won't ask if this was before or after you fucked her. Just tell me what she said."

"I didn't sleep with her."

"I don't fucking care!"

"Good, I don't care about Moog. About his old late-night phone calls, his beeper messages, the fucking flowers."

Julie looked at him, narrowing her eyes.

"What did Mona Falco say?"

"She said it was gonna be a Federal case now."

Julie walked to a wall closet, pulled down a strong box, and opened it with a key on her key chain. Tobin made the music even louder and followed her.

"And you say the Feds won't pursue this either," she said, a strong, cold confidence bolstering her voice as she opened the strong box and pulled out a 9mm automatic and a .25 pistol. "Okay, fuck it, then."

Tobin looked at her handling the 9mm and .25-caliber pistols with the dispatch of a trained professional, checking the slides and the barrels, making sure all the workings were oiled and clean.

"Cox and the Federal prosecutor are gonna use Henry to get even with me," Tobin said. "Even if someone wanted to do me a favor, no one could.

No one is gonna touch this. Too high profile. Too sensitive. Too political. This case is under the national microscope. It will proceed through the system on greased rails."

"And if we go public, Lenny Kelly'll send the other photos to the DA and the papers?"

"Right," Tobin said.

"So we have to find this Lenny Kelly," she said, slamming in clips.

"You really think we're gonna need those?"

"This guy blows up synagogues and mosques and frames our son for doing it," Julie said. "When I find him, if he doesn't confess, on tape, loud and clear, he is going to learn that the most dangerous place in the world is the distance he put between this mother and her child."

"That's if we find him," Tobin said.

"Just remember we're working together as the mother and the father of our son," she said, strapping a holster on the middle of the belt of her blue jeans so that it would fit into the hollow of her back. "Not as man and wife. Not even as pals, Hank. It took me a long time to fall out of love with you. Like beating a chronic illness. Stopping the loving was hard. But I stopped *liking* you the day you done me wrong. So this is not a reunion or reconciliation here. Just call it an alliance. Once we do what we have to do to help our kid, it's sayonara all over again. I don't ever let anyone hurt me twice. Understand?"

"Yep."

"Good, then we'll leave through the back door," she said, jamming the .25 in her front pants pocket and the 9mm in the rear holster, and letting her loose polo shirt fall over it. "Me and Laurie have been hopping over the backyard fence into the Coogan's yard and leaving up their alley. I have a rental car with tinted windows and Jersey plates parked on the next street so that no one will know it's us."

"Where the hell are we going? Where do we start?"

"What was your old line about never finding stories in the newsroom? Same was true with squad rooms. Well, we won't find any answers sitting in here."

He followed his ex-wife out the back door, watching her move in swift, confident strides in the snug, faded jeans like a woman on a mission, like a cop on a hunt, like a mother defending her young.

Man, what a cute behind, he thought.

TWENTY-TWO

They stood on the sidewalk across the busy four lanes of Coney Island Avenue from the scorched and boarded-up mosque near the corner of Forest Avenue. Tobin held the photos he received from LL in his hands. Julie stood next to him, glancing down and trying to determine the angles from which they were shot. Julie held a disposable camera she purchased from a corner Arab deli up to her eye, trying to match the framing through the viewfinder.

"Dig yourself," Tobin said. "Don't let the press or the cops make us."

"You're the one they'll pin," Julie said. "Gotta shave your beard. It's your calling card. Nobody recognizes me."

"I haven't shaved for fifteen years."

"I rest my case. You're a millionaire. Splurge for a goddamned razor."

They inched along Coney Island Avenue from one tenement storefront to the next, protected from view by parked vans, trucks, and SUVs.

Across the busy avenue a gathering of cops, reporters, and curious onlookers stood behind the yellow crime-scene tape. Fire marshals hauled out evidence. Photographers made pictures. Local Arabs stopped, held out their arms, palms up, mumbling small prayers before moving on.

Tobin spotted Phyllis Warsdale from the *Examiner* interviewing a fire marshal. Dani Larsen conversed off-camera with Vinny Hunt, the action-hero-handsome NYPD Intelligence Division captain who had cornered Tobin in the men's room of Elaine's. Because he was in Intelligence, Vinny was in plain clothes. But the big cop's fidgety body language told Tobin that Dani Larsen's beauty and celebrity defused him, like a bomb with a wet fuse. *Beautiful women can reduce big strong men to piles of tapioca,*

Tobin thought. Vinny kept rubbing one eye as he spoke to her, having a hard time looking directly at Dani, laughing in bursts, straightening his tie, shifting his weight from one foot to the other. As Vinny stepped backward, Dani Larsen followed, moving closer, like a fighter cutting off the ring. Until he leaned against her news truck.

As Julie studied angles through the little camera, Tobin watched Dani pursue Vinny, the mouse cornering the cat. Dani grabbed his big bicep for support as she laughed. *She'd done that to me,* Tobin thought. Same kind of touchy-feely tactile moves, at some premiere party for a shitty but expensive movie. Sultry, tenacious, sweet.

Watching a woman he'd bedded stalking another man, Tobin felt a worm of jealousy wiggle through him. A disquieting reminder that Tobin could so easily be replaced by another man. By a younger, bigger, better-looking man. Proof of his own mortality was evidence that there was life after Hank Tobin. And here he was, with Julie, the woman and wife he'd chased and won and lost and chased again, searching for clues to get their kid out of jail. *Life's nutty,* he thought. *It's all folly. You chase, seduce, hunt, track, connive and swindle, lie and cheat, and always it can only lead to a dead end. I threw my family away for cheap celebrity, fake powerful friends, beautiful women I never tried to make an emotional connection with, for self-aggrandizement, for money, and for prestige. But they were all cheap trappings, like an overabundance of garland and lights and decorations that hid a scrawny Christmas tree. Instead of being a loyal husband, devoted father, and good person, I aspired instead to be the most congratulated, award-winning, and recognized newspaper columnist in New York. I let the mask become the man.*

Tobin now realized that if he ever had one urgent, worthwhile mission as a man, as a *father,* in his dead-end life, it was getting Henry out of this jam, to give him back his life.

"Here," Julie said, grabbing the photos from Tobin, holding them up to her face, and matching the perspective through the camera viewfinder. "They were shot from just about here."

"You sure?"

She backed up, getting more perspective, until her spine was against the pane-glass window of a storefront. "I'm not Scavullo, but I'm not Helen Keller, either," she said.

Tobin took the small camera and matched it against the photos sent by LL.

"Pretty close."

"Looks like it might've been shot through glass," she said.

They turned and looked at the storefront window behind them. The window was covered in yellowed Islamic newspapers, with Arabic-script stories Tobin could not decipher. He recognized photos of Osama bin Laden, Saddam Hussein, George W. Bush, Donald Rumsfeld, Attorney General John Ashcroft, and Richard Reid the shoe bomber. There were some older newspapers with photos of the September 11 attack on the World Trade Center and the bombing of Baghdad.

"Creepy," Julie said.

They stepped into the doorway of the storefront only to find a pad-locked accordion gate covering the shut front door. They entered the tenement vestibule. Tobin rang the bell marked SUPER. Tenements gave Tobin the shudders. They reminded him of childhood, loud drunks, banging doors, breaking glass, cold mornings, and the omnipresent suffocating smell of the hungry roach.

"Buildings like this, in neighborhoods like this, this is where the Al Qaeda cells nest," Julie said, hooking a thumb north over her shoulder. "Muhammad Atta, that fucking dead-eyed swine, lived for a while a mile from here on Twelfth Street in Park Slope. And that big, red-headed Egyptian—Ibrahim Elgabrowny—the one who was convicted for the 1993 Trade Center bombing lived about ten blocks down on Prospect Park South West. Number seventy . . ."

"I know," Tobin said. "The reason *you* know it is because *I* wrote about it in my column. I interviewed his American-born wife, Helen, in the street. She was from Pennsylvania. Not a bad looking piece of . . . chick, either. . . ."

"You can't help yourself," Julie said, ringing the super's bell again. "You're always putting your hind paw in your mouth."

"Elgabrowny sent his kids to PS 154, right around the corner from where he lived in the drowsy little neighborhood of Windsor Terrace. He lived his life like anyone else. He was a carpenter. I interviewed neighbors who hired him to put up new kitchen cabinets, hang doors, and lay floors. . . ."

"They should make him build his own coffin," Julie said.

"Elgabrowny's cousin El Sayed A Nosair supplied the gun used to assassinate Meir Kahane. . . ."

"Didn't the NYPD DTs find files in his Jersey apartment that linked him to the Trade Center attack of 1993?"

"That's right," Tobin said, "and they also found information all about a group called Al Qaeda that was founded by Osama bin Laden in 1988. But the Feds seized the files from NYPD. A lot of those guys went to *this* mosque, and other ones in Brooklyn that are affiliated to the blind sheik, Abdel-Rahman. But the Feds never connected the dots. The same guy, Khalid Mohammad, conceived both Trade Center attacks, but the Feds should have known that back then. The Feds dropped the ball. These terrorists aren't hard to find. They don't hide out in shacks in the mountains like the Unabomber. They hide in plain sight, driving cabs, hanging kitchen cabinets, waiting tables, sending their kids to public schools. . . ."

"Taking flying lessons where they're not interested in knowing how to take off or land . . ."

". . . and living in dumps like this, waiting to blow themselves and innocent citizens to smithereens so they can get to paradise."

"And they bust our Henry," Julie said, ringing the super's bell once more.

"That's why there's no protection. They live amongst us. And since the war in Iraq, there's a whole new set of young Arab terrorists and suicide bombers looking for jihad revenge. And I don't give a rat's ass how much they shook up the FBI. The real name of the place is CYA, for Cover Your Ass, and that's why they won't even try to find out who really bombed this mosque. And now the Feds see our kid in the same light as those mutts," Tobin said.

"Worse, the public thinks those maniacs at least did it for Allah or politics," Julie said. "Listen to the news, the cable ghouls, they're saying Henry did this for ambition, money, ego. They are calling him a war-profiteer, cashing in on other people's misery for exclusive bylines under sensational headlines, Hank. They're making our kid look like a monster."

"They're not ghouls, Julie, they're reporters reporting the news," Tobin said. "It's just our turn to be on this side of the story."

The super, a short rotund man in his forties, walked down the gloomy ground-floor hallway, wearing a sleeveless T-shirt, shorts, and flip-flops. Plaintive Arabic music filtered from upstairs. Someone was cooking lamb with pungent spices. Loud keys clanged on a large ring dangling from the super's belt loop. He peered through the glass panel of the door at Tobin and Julie, shielding his eyes from the light that spilled through the transom. Tobin turned his face toward the street door. Julie flashed a disarming smile with her dazzling white teeth.

"Let me do the talking," Julie said.

As the super swung open the inside door, the smell of incense also wafted on the stale air. It mixed with the cooking food and the stench of futile bug spray and the molting cockroaches that bred for decades, sometimes as long as a century, deep inside the dark walls, behind the old furring strips and wet plaster. Tobin was nauseated. New York tenements had their own necrosmell of the dead and dying roach the way forests smelled of pine and mint and loamy life.

"Hello? No. Sorry, no apartment," the super said.

"What about the store?" Julie said. "Is it for rent?"

"Sometimes."

She smiled and said, "How about now?"

"Almost the prayer time."

"Listen . . . what did you say your name was?"

"Fuad."

Julie looked at Tobin and then back at Fuad. "Whadda you mean 'for what'?"

Fuad seemed confused and said, "My name, call me Fuad, please."

Tobin smiled, stifled a chuckle. Julie glared at him and turned back to Fuad. "Sorry, Fuad. My misunderstanding. Look, just let us have a quick peek inside that store."

"We don't want the cooking on premises because of the fires and maybe mices. What do you want store for renting for?"

Julie drew a blank, said, "Well, um—"

"Italian ices," Tobin said, fast. "We want to put in an Uncle Louie G's Italian ice store. Best Italian ices in New York."

Fuad stepped into the vestibule now, into the bright daylight that spilled through the dusty transom. He studied Tobin's face. Fuad's jaw dropped. Tobin knew Fuad had made him and turned away.

"No vacants," Fuad said.

Before he could slam the inside door, Julie pinched an inch of Fuad's dark chest hair between her left thumb and forefinger, pulled him closer to her, and pushed a facsimile of her old gold detective shield into his face with the other hand. "Open the fucking store, Fuad."

Tobin knew that most retired cops carried copies of their old shields, reduced in size by one-sixteenth of an inch, and used them to badge their way out of traffic tickets. Civilians never knew the difference when a retired cop flashed a fake shield, especially when accompanied by a legal ex-cop's pistol.

"I already speak to other polices." Fuad stared at the police shield and then at Tobin. Hate blistered his eyes. "You having the warrant?"

"I don't needing the warrant to rent a store, Fuad. You just told me the store was for rent. You don't open the door, I figure you're discriminating along racial lines. Which might be okay in parts of the United Arab Emirates, but it's a crime in the United States of America. We clear on that, Fuad? I hope so. Because if not, once we have you in custody, we'll run you through every computer and database on the planet: Interpol, Scotland Yard, FBI, CIA, INS, Mossad, in front of every lineup from here to Tel Aviv to Sudan to Bali. And then I'll do the same with all your family, until we find some way of getting you fitted for an orange jumpsuit designed by my Uncle Sammy. You been in New York long enough to understand any of that, Fuad?"

Fuad answered with coal eyes and a jingle of his keys. He stepped into the street. Tobin glanced across the street to the crowded crime scene and was thankful for the human bustle, heavy traffic, and parked SUVs on Coney Island Avenue that provided them with a certain degree of cover and misdirection.

Some passersby, most of them Arabs, gazed at Tobin. A few did double takes. A Mister Softee truck jingled up the street, playing the old familiar song from Tobin's youth. "The creamiest, dreamiest soft ice cream/You get from Mister Softee...."

A young boy, about eight or nine, raced up to Fuad. "Yo, Papa, ice cream man, ice cream," he said, his accent as Brooklyn as the trees of Prospect Park, dirty hand out for change.

Fuad barked a long string of sentences in Arabic, harsh, urgent, incomprehensible to Tobin and Julie. The boy looked up at Julie and then Tobin and backed away. And sprinted down Coney Island Avenue.

"What did you say to him?" Julie asked.

"No ice cream before *Zuhr*, the noon prayer time."

"Five very long words," she said.

Fuad stepped into the doorway, unlocked the gate, and opened the Medeco lock on the front door. He swung the door open.

"Okay, go, look store."

Fuad tried to exit past them, but Julie nudged him inside. "Show us around, Fuad," she said. "Give us the two-cent tour."

Julie and Fuad walked through the empty storefront, a dreary affair in need of new Sheetrock walls and a new floor. Dust covered everything—old chairs, a decrepit store counter, a dingy showcase, a few old tables. Ancient iron radiators sat like indestructible relics of the last century. Tobin sneezed as he gazed up at exposed hot-water risers and overhead plumbing criss-crossing the crumbling walls and saggy ceilings. When Fuad switched on the overhead fluorescent lights, a dozen roaches zigged and zagged for holes and crevices.

"Okay, so how much do you pay me to take it," Julie asked, leading Fuad to the tiny bathroom in the rear, where incessant water gurgled in a broken toilet tank.

"Huh?" asked Fuad. "Fifteen hundred for one month, you paying to me."

Tobin walked to a raised platform that served as a three-foot-deep display counter under the pane-glass window facing the street. He studied the newspapers on the window. Tobin knew newsprint. Most of his life's work was printed on it. He knew that no matter what language was printed on them, newspapers yellowed fast, especially when exposed directly to the sun like these papers taped to a window. One sheet in the very center of the window was newer than the other sheets, a linen-beige instead of a jaundiced yellow like the others. In July in New York it couldn't have been there more than a few days.

Tobin heard voices out on the sidewalk but paid little attention. Probably more reporters and gaping citizens who flocked to crime scenes like sports fans. He tilted his eyes directly down from the newest sheet of newspaper to the window seat. Directly under the newest page were three round dots, the size of quarters, imprinted in the heavy dust.

Tobin called to Julie. She told Fuad to stay put, strode to Tobin, and took a look at the three impressions in the dust.

"Tripod," Tobin said, also telling her about the fresh sheet of newspaper on the window, the place through which the long camera lens probably pointed. Tobin and Julie spoke in whispers, glancing at Fuad who stood in the rear of the store, checking his watch, jingling change in his short pants pockets.

"With an automatic timer, digital camera, Lenny Kelly might not have needed an accomplice?" Julie said.

"Especially if Lenny Kelly knew exactly when and where the bombing would take place and synchronized the camera timer," Tobin said. "He called Henry on his cell phone when we were at the ballpark. He told Henry to meet him at the mosque at a precise time. Henry also said he had to go home and change first. Kelly told Henry what to wear. Stuff he knew he already owned from months of surveillance. So that Kelly could wear duplicate clothes. Remember, he planned this for ten fucking years."

"So you figure Henry meets Kelly a block away?" Julie asked.

"Yeah. Henry is already half in the bag from beer. Then the Rohypnol slipped into his beer at the ballpark hits him. He zonks out. Kelly throws Henry into his own Explorer."

"Then Lenny Kelly himself, or using an accomplice wearing identical clothes to Henry, in the dark of night, drives to the mosque at a precise time. He double-parks exactly where he planned, so that the camera in here on the tripod would be clicking away at that same time, on that very target."

Tobin nodded, excited, angry, his voice rising. "He gets out of the Explorer. . . ."

Julie waved for him to lower his voice, glancing over at Fuad.

Tobin whispered, "Kelly, dressed like Henry, leans across him and fires the goddamned round into the mosque, all as the camera clicks away. Then he speeds away. The camera clicks on it as it flees. Even gets a shot of the plate number. He must've practiced and rehearsed it all week from right here until he knew exactly how to do it, like an actor hitting his chalk marks on a sound stage."

Julie took a deep breath, exhaled, and said, "Then Kelly, this son of a bitching bastard, drives Henry's Explorer straight to our, um, *my* block and parks it. He yanks Henry into the driver's seat and switches jackets. Then he calmly walks to his own car, maybe parked on the next block or around the corner . . ."

"Then Kelly drives back here," Tobin said, "and probably retrieved the digital camera while I stood across the street at the fire! Watching me. Laughing. And then a few hours later he e-mails me the pictures. And to my everlasting shame, I went with them on page one. Jesus Christ, Jule. . . ."

"Praying time, *Zuhr,* please!" Fuad shouted.

"In a minute, Fuad." She looked at Tobin, who looked like he would get sick. "You okay?"

"No. I don't know if I ever will be."

"Stop feeling sorry for yourself," she said. "I hate a man who cries in his beer."

Her words stung. But Tobin nodded. *She was right,* he thought.

"Sorry," he said.

"I've learned that word is useless," she said, steering back on topic.

"Okay, so after the pictures appeared in the morning paper, a cop car spotted the Explorer on my block. He saw Henry was wearing the same get-up as the bomber in the photos, and sat on him until Cox and Mona Falco could come and cuff him. And find the rocket launcher."

"I'm positive that's what happened," Tobin said.

"But nobody's gonna connect those three dots the way we just did," she said. "Or believe it when we show them how. These people couldn't connect the dots to save three thousand people, you think they'll do it to save one kid, who happens to be the son of a columnist who ranks in the top ten on their Most Hated list?"

"Which brings us back to finding Lenny Kelly."

"Before the prick dies," she said.

More voices babbled from the sidewalk outside, people speaking in Arabic.

Julie looked Tobin in the eyes, nodded, and turned back to Fuad. "Hey, Fuad, have any other cops been in this store?" she asked.

Fuad didn't answer. "Okay," she said, reaching behind her for her handcuffs. "Let's do this in a cell with no prayer mats."

"One cop look around, say nothing, and leave," Fuad blurted.

"You know his name?"

Fuad shook his head.

"Who was the last person to rent this store? Who'd you rent it to?"

Fuad shrugged. Julie swung the handcuffs. "For one week he pay to me five hundred dollar," Fuad said, rubbing his fingers together. "Please . . . I don't even telling the landlord. Cash, he paying to me. I like the paying cash."

"Everybody likes the paying cash, Fuad," she said. "You didn't ask him why he wanted it for just one week?"

"He say he wanted to taking the pictures of his girlfriend," Fuad said, smiling in an embarrassed way.

"Did he come with a woman?" Tobin asked.

Fuad spat at Tobin's feet and said, "I not talk to him."

"Fuck you, Fuad," Tobin said.

"Tell me, Fuad," Julie said, making a "cool it" face at Tobin.

"I never see a woman."

Julie took the photograph of Lenny Kelly from Tobin and showed it to Fuad. "This the man?"

Fuad looked at it, scrunching his face.

"He might be connected to the mosque bombing, Fuad," Julie said.

Fuad's eyes opened wide, terror seizing him. He fell against the wall, plaster bits falling out of the ceiling. He grabbed his forehead. "Please, not to say that. Not to say I rented to man who helping bombing my mosque."

He bowed, palms up, saying an Arabic prayer. Julie shook his shoulder. "Fuad, sorry to interrupt, buddy, but is this him?"

Fuad glanced at the photo, sweat breaking on his brow, like a condemned man. "Not so sure," he said. "Man I rent store to have the black hair, like me, and the big beard, dark glasses. He wearing the gloves all the time. Saying about allergic skin."

"What kind of gloves?"

Fuad pantomimed a golf swing. "How do you saying it?"

"Forget dusting," Julie said. "There won't be any prints with golf gloves."

"Rent the store," Tobin said.

"What?"

"This way if the cops want to come back in, they'll need a warrant and have to show it to me," Tobin said. "I'll put a new padlock on it."

Tobin handed Julie a wad of cash as car horns exploded in a tone-deaf symphony outside on Coney Island Avenue. "He won't take it from me. We should secure this place. No matter what, we should secure the scene. We have Fuad over a barrel. If he doesn't cooperate with us, we can threaten to tell his landlord he rented the store on the side for personal cash. We can also threaten to tell his fellow mosque congregants that he rented this place to one of the bombers."

She looked at Tobin, half-shrugged, grabbed the cash. "It's your dime," she said and led Fuad off to the rear of the store. Julie haggled with Fuad. He shook his head, pointing at Tobin. She spoke some more, waving a finger in his face, counting out hundred-dollar bills until he nodded and took the cash. By the time she walked back to Tobin, she had the keys to the store and handed Tobin some change.

"Got it for a month," she said. "Eighteen hundred. He threw the roaches in free."

"Let's lock it up and find Lenny Kelly," he said.

TWENTY-THREE

When they stepped into the street, Fuad slammed the automatic-locking door behind him. He padlocked the gate, handed Julie the keys, bowed his head, and made a sharp left into his vestibule. He said nothing.

Julie pulled on a pair of sunglasses, turned, and said, "Holy shit."

"Literally."

Tobin fell back against the gate as he stared out at a hushed crowd of several thousand on Coney Island Avenue. Horn-honking traffic was at a standstill. Uniformed cops negotiated with several young, hard-looking Arab men to break up the show of force. Every set of eyes was on Tobin and Julie.

Tobin said, "This is not good."

"Fuad musta told the kid who you were, and he spread the news."

One young man, wearing a hand-knitted skullcap, jeans and sneakers, muscles rippling in his nut-brown arms, walked toward Tobin. "Your son bombs our mosque and you have the audacity to come here?" he said, fists balling. "To further desecrate us?"

"My son is innocent," Tobin said.

"Our—"

"Shut up, Julie." She recoiled, amazed Tobin would talk to her like that.

"Your son's a swine," the Arab said. "Which means he's a son of a swine."

The Arab's words hurt, the way he knew his words had hurt so many people over the years. "My son is not a swine," Tobin said. "He wouldn't do something like that."

Tobin pointed at the charred mosque, another symbol of the crazed new century.

An angry murmur shivered through the crowd. "You come to write

185

more of your garbage, to make more money off our suffering?" asked the young Arab, moving closer to Tobin. "A woman suffers in a burn unit, and you dare to come here, to where she lived and prayed and dreamed? Where we live with ashes?"

"A poet," Julie mumbled.

"What did you say, lady?" asked the Arab. "That woman in the hospital happens to be my sister. You addressing me?"

"No, I am," Tobin said, glaring at Julie. "I'm sorry about your sister. But my kid is innocent. He's no red-neck racist. Like me, he was born in Brooklyn."

"So was I," said the Arab. "So was my sister. So let's settle this Brooklyn style!"

The Arab's punch landed high on Tobin's head. Tobin thought he heard his brains slosh. Tiny sparkles spun before his eyes. Tobin counterpunched, a right hand flush on the Arab's cheekbone. He staggered ten feet backward and fell into the arms of friends. A unified warble rose from the crowd. Five men moved toward Tobin. Julie pulled out her 9mm in a single motion, squatted into an NYPD-trained shooting stance.

"Don't," she said.

A dozen uniformed cops, led by Vinny Hunt, rushed to the sidewalk. Photographers snapped photos. A news crew rolled tape. The ululating crowd grew frenzied, people thrusting hands in the air, warbling, shouting, chanting, and stamping feet. Vinny Hunt lifted the young Arab off the ground then pulled out a pair of handcuffs.

Tobin said, "Don't, Vinny, please. . . ."

"Don't?" Vinny said, incredulous. "This fuck hit you first. I saw it. Assault, Discon, Inciting to riot . . ."

Tobin said, "It was a misunderstanding."

A disappointed Vinny Hunt shoved the young Arab into the crowd like a man pushing open a hollow door. Phyllis Warsdale sidled up to Tobin in the confusion. "Call me later," she said. "I have a few things to tell you. About the judge."

Tobin looked at her, startled, his head spinning.

Vinny Hunt grabbed Tobin's arm and said, "Don't be running around fucking with these people. These guys are from a group called Umma. They're a PD-sanctioned citizens patrol. But there are splinter groups that'd kill you just for being your son's father. Am I making myself clear? I told you, you need help, you call me."

"Thanks, I might need it."

"I also might need some help from you on another matter. . . ."

"Sure," Tobin said.

Abrupt silence fell as the Imam that he'd seen the night of the bombing parted the angry crowd. He made a sweeping gesture, uttered a simple Arabic command, and in unison the people knelt, facing Mecca. Horn-blaring traffic gridlocked in both directions.

"We'll talk another time," Vinny said.

The Imam approached Tobin and Julie, saying, "This is not respectful. Please don't cause us any more trouble."

"My son didn't burn your mosque," Julie said.

"I suggest you pray for him," the Imam said. "Elsewhere."

Vinny nodded agreement and motioned for Tobin to leave. The Imam turned and joined his praying flock on his knees.

Dani Larsen approached Tobin and Julie as they departed, her cameraman several feet behind, shooting tape. "Hank, . . . can we . . . you and your ex?" Dani asked, her microphone at her side.

"Not a good time," Tobin said.

"You for real, honey?" Julie asked Dani. "I know who you are. All about you two."

Dani looked at Tobin who shook his head, and she gave up the chase.

"Oh, we wouldn't have to go into all of that," Dani said. "That's history, anyway. I'd like to focus on how this has affected the family. . . ."

Tobin closed his eyes in dread as Julie quickened her pace.

"This is like a fucking hallucination," Julie said, storming ahead, mumbling to herself. "My kid's in jail. We almost get killed by a mob of crazy Muhammads. I almost fire my gun at a real live human for the first time in my life. And the Dairy Queen *weatherchick* my ex is boinking wants an interview with *me*?"

Tobin followed, listening to Julie vent, and caught up with her just as they turned the corner onto the side street where she'd parked the rented car.

"Julie, Christ sakes, she's doing her job. And I'm not boinking her . . . anymore."

Julie stopped dead in her tracks as she saw Mona Falco and Agent Cox standing by the parked Taurus rental.

"Marvelous," Julie said. "The gang's all here. Or should I say the gang bang."

"Well, if it isn't Nick and Nora Tobin, the unhappily married crime-fighting couple," Cox said, chewing his gum. Danvers stood beside him, quiet as deep space, looking from Cox to Tobin. Mona Falco wore dark shades, avoiding eye contact, but making her look rough-trade sexy.

The low murmur of praying Muslims hummed in the afternoon air. Horns bleated, irate motorists screaming in a dozen foreign languages from Coney Island Avenue.

"Why don't you go spindle another skyjacker memo, Cox?" Tobin said.

"That's my car you're blocking," Julie said.

"I know," Cox said, smiling. "Detective Falco was just telling me about your theory about your son being set up by a crank caller. That true?"

Julie walked closer to Mona, sniffed. Unintimidated, Mona stared back at her through the dark glasses. They reminded Tobin of two fighters doing a stare down as the ref gave prefight instructions.

"Yeah, it's true," Tobin said to Cox, watching the sweaty, crackling, wordless dynamic between Julie and Mona.

"Now that wouldn't be the same crank caller you told us about the other day when you called in an anthrax scare, would it be?" Cox asked.

"Matter of fact, yes," Tobin said, watching Julie remove her sunglasses to stare at Mona.

"So your theory is that a dead man set up your son?"

"He isn't dead. He—"

"No, he's just touring with Elvis," Cox said.

"Why don't *you* investigate it, Detective Falco," Julie said.

Mona took off her dark glasses and stared right back into Julie's eyes. "It's no longer just my case to call," Falco said.

"You never seemed to mind pushing your nose into places it didn't belong before," Julie said.

"I only go where I'm assigned or invited," Mona said.

"That's correct," Cox said. "As of this morning, your son Henry's case was officially handed over to the U.S. Attorney's office of the Eastern District under the civil-rights violations statute. But as a newly recruited member of the Joint Task Force, Detective Falco will remain involved, under my command as Chief Agent in Charge. I respect her ideas and advice."

"And what's your advice, Detective Falco?" Julie asked.

"My advice to you is to remember that I'm a ranking member of NYPD and that you are *retired,*" she said. "If you get mixed up in incidents like the one that just occurred around the corner, pulling your weapon on unarmed civilians, especially after you were heard calling them by racial code words, well that would fall under the category of a hate crime. Because you are a former Member of Service, I will give you some wiggle room this time."

Julie smiled, stepped another foot closer to Mona Falco, their noses almost touching. "Did you say 'wiggle room'? Funny, how you found lots of *that* in bed wiggling my husband, ho girl."

Mona Falco stood up straight, glared down into the shorter Julie's blue eyes. "That could be interpreted as another racial code word, Ms. Tobin."

Julie held up a finger for Tobin to butt out. Cox stopped chewing his gum, narrowing his gaze on Mona Falco. Danvers seemed embarrassed.

". . . The name is Capone."

"How fitting . . ."

". . . Yes it is, baby. Siciliana. Which probably means I have as much of the African tar brush in me as you have, *sistah*. In a DNA lab and in my NYPD personnel file, we'd both be labeled eggplant parmigiana, *capise*, yo? So don't you fucking dare try running me over with your soul train. There's so much white trash in you that you went shoplifting for a man in my marriage."

Cox, lips pursed into a bud of anger, looked at Falco for a reply. Danvers glanced at him, and the silent Fed walked in a tight, silent circle.

Mona took a deep breath, puffed her cheeks, looked at Cox and then Julie, and said, "You ever consider it might have been the other way around, Julie?"

Julie blinked at her and glared at Tobin. "You two deserve each other," Julie said and climbed into her car. Tobin opened the passenger door.

"Hey, Tobin," Cox said. "Dump the column. Stick with fiction."

Tobin looked once more at Mona Falco, who nodded to him with saddened eyes as the prayers and the horns continued from Coney Island Avenue. She shrugged, and he climbed into the front seat of the Taurus, next to Julie.

Julie's tires squealed from the parking spot.

TWENTY-FOUR

They raced in silence through the Brooklyn streets, out Coney Island Avenue, Julie honking around buses and double-parked cars, cutting off other motorists, and then ripping a mad right through a red light on Avenue M. An oncoming Jeep Cherokee, with the green-signal right of way, fishtailed to a halt. The bearded driver, wearing a yarmulke, leaned on his horn and launched his head out his window, screaming, "You dumb fucking asshole!"

"You almost killed that poor bastard," Tobin shouted.

"Fuck him, and fuck you. Twice."

"Oh, okay. Ditto. So where we going?"

"Fucking crazy, wanna come?"

"Already there. About you."

"Oh, man, shove that line of happy horseshit right up your—"

"Soon as you strap on the gun and carry the badge, you start talking and acting like a guy. You pick fights, blow through red lights, curse like a mob wiretap."

"Go f—" She banged the heel of her right hand off the steering wheel. "How the fuck could you f— oh, man, with *her.* . . ."

"Forget her, concentrate on Henry."

"Henry's the *only* reason you're in this car with me."

They sped toward Ocean Parkway, where she yanked a left out toward Coney Island. Tobin told her about his brief meeting with Billy Kelly in the cemetery and some more about the phone calls from LL.

Then, changing the subject, Tobin said, "I didn't know you had African blood in you."

190

"I only confirmed it after we split. Why does it matter, Mister Knee-jerk Liberal?"

"It doesn't now. But in those thin early years, when the dough was short, it mighta helped get the kids some affirmative action grants."

"You really are a piece of shit."

"Matter of fact, you could have used it to climb ranks in the PD," Tobin said. "A twofer. Minority woman—"

"I got where I got on merit," she said. "Brains and balls. Not as a 'guinea nig,' which is what my Italian uncles used to call me. I only thought they were teasing me."

"Think maybe we should tell the kids?"

"I did."

"And?"

"They tap danced and applied for basketball scholarships."

"That's not funny."

"They're white kids from Marine Park. They didn't believe me. My Sicilian grampa who told me about it is dead. What difference does it make?"

Julie snatched up her cell phone and hit a speed-dial number.

"Who you calling?"

"None of your business. You wanna read my mail, too?"

"Hey, baby, it's me," she said into the phone.

Jealousy tightened Tobin's chest, his heart surging, and his breathing labored. An HJV attack.

"I need your inside help, PD access," Julie said.

Moog, Tobin thought. *She's talking to this Moog asshole. In front of me. Probably in spite. To get even for Mona.*

"Yeah, check with probation. See what you can learn about William, aka Billy, Kelly, released six months ago for a hate-crime arson," she said. "Last known address . . ."

She looked at Tobin for help. He flipped through his Reporter's Notebook and read it to her. She repeated it into the cell phone. The air in the car was close. Sweat blotted the back of his shirt.

"Doesn't the goddamned air conditioner work in this car," Tobin said, hoping Moog could hear him as he fiddled with the control knobs on the dash.

"I owe you something very special for this one," Julie said into the phone, smiling and blowing through another red light, causing two cars to almost collide as she made a right onto Avenue X.

"Jesus Christ! Watch where you're going, for Christ sakes!" Tobin shouted, certain Moog would hear him this time.

"Oh, nobody special. I'll tell you later," she said into the phone. "Same here, honey. We'll talk when I'm alone. . . . See what you can find out for me. . . . I will. . . . Yeah, you too, babe."

Tobin couldn't take anymore. He whipped out his own cell phone and dialed a number written on a sheet of paper he pulled from his pocket.

"Hi, hon, it's Hanky," he said.

Phyllis Warsdale said, *"Who?"*

"I'm calling, just like I promised, baby."

"Is this Hank Tobin? Because if it is, I guess you know that I don't let anyone call me 'hon' or 'baby.' "

"I know that, sweetheart," Tobin said. "You asked me to call."

"I'll assume you're doing this because there's someone else there, and you don't want that person or persons to know who it is you're talking to. Correct?"

"Oh, *yeah,* baby."

"This is almost obscene," Warsdale said, laughing.

"What are you gonna give me?"

"Remember you gave me the name of that guy Lou Barratta who runs the *goomatta* cheater hotel near the airport?"

"Yeah?"

"He thinks Koutros is an honest judge who's being set up."

"Why?"

"Something to do with a ten-year sentence he gave somebody ten years ago in Brooklyn. I went through all his old sentences from ten years ago, and the only thing that looked close was a case involving a kid who firebombed a house in Gravesend. A skinhead named Billy Kelly. I wrote a few briefs on the sentencing, but all the stories refer to the original column you wrote about it. This was back before we had computer databases. When I went to check your column, you had it out of the library. Before I order a warehouse search for an old copy, can I get a copy of that column?"

"I'll call you later, sweetcheeks," Tobin said. "Really I will. Promise."

He hung up, thinking: *Is LL framing Koutros, too?*

"Okay, call me on the cell later," Julie said into her cell phone and clicked off. She made a fast swerve to the curb and parked in front of a hydrant. Tobin looked to his right and saw they were parked in front of the Lucky Seven tavern. The second letter "e" was missing from Seven.

"Let's go, Tonto," she said as she got out of the car. Tobin climbed out of the Taurus and followed his ex-wife into the gloomy saloon where he had met Leonard Kelly, aka Lenny the Loser, ten years earlier.

TWENTY-FIVE

Tobin looked around the barroom, the smell of cigarette smoke and sour beer strangling what little air penetrated as people entered and left. In the half-gloom he tried to remember where everything had been a decade before. When his pupils adjusted to the low light, he realized he didn't have to dig deep. Everything looked the same. The only things that had been updated were the jukebox and the pay phones, both part of the new century. Almost everything else—beer signs, dropped-ceiling lighting, backless stools, pay pool table, mirrored bar back, old-fashioned silver cash registers—was as Tobin remembered it. Of course, he'd been drinking that night, so the details were vague. The Lucky Seven looked like a hundred other neighborhood saloons he'd gotten plastered in over the years while covering a hundred other booze-fueled columns.

Even the fat bartender looked familiar. He remembered that the guy had one of those incongruous Brooklyn nicknames like Skinny or Slim. He was a little fatter, hair a little grayer, a few deeper ravines in his face, but Tobin was sure he was the same guy who'd served Tobin and Lenny Kelly on the night that the Hu family's home burnt to the ground a few blocks away.

"Classy," Julie said, looking around and crinkling her nose. "This where you romanced Mona?"

"Stop."

They walked to the bar. Five men, two of them big husky guys in their thirties who looked like they lived on the three Basic Brooklyn B's—beer, burgers, and butts—and three old-timers, sat several stools apart like wide-

194

gapped teeth at the bar. ESPN was showing highlights from yesterday's ball games. The fat bartender got up off a stool at the end of the bar when Tobin and Julie approached.

He nodded at Julie. He stared at Tobin, recognition inflaming his eyes.

"Bottle of bud," Julie said. "No glass."

"Buy everyone else in the place a drink," Tobin said, creasing a $50 bill and tenting it on the bar.

The fat bartender stared Tobin in the eyes and moved down the bar in a wordless shuffle, refilling beers, building highballs, and pouring boiler-makers for the two husky guys. "Thanks," he heard one old-timer with a Jets cap say.

" 'Bout time, Bones," said another old-timer wearing a Cyclones cap.

Bones, Tobin thought. *That was his name.*

Bones the bartender finished serving the drinks, nodding toward Tobin, to indicate that the drink was on him. Bones walked back up to Tobin and took the fifty off the wood.

"How about one for yourself?" Tobin asked.

Bones looked Tobin straight in the eye again, reached for the top shelf, and poured himself a double Hennessey cognac, the most expensive drink in the Lucky Seven. Bones belted it back in a single, almost defiant, gulp.

"I'll have a cranberry and club soda," Tobin said.

Bones ignored his request, walked to the register, and tallied the drinks, punching in the price of each one into the old-fashioned register, including Julie's and his own and banged the TOTAL button. He speared the $50 bill into the register, counted out the change, and slapped nine dollars on the bar in front of Tobin.

"Where's my drink?" Tobin asked.

"We don't serve Hank Tobin in here."

Julie cracked up laughing, smacked her hand on the wet bar, and took a gulp of her beer. "My kind of place," she said.

"No offense to you, hon," Bones said. "But last time I served this bum, a friend of mine's son served ten years."

"It's why I'm here," Tobin said. "Maybe try to right a wrong, if I did him wrong."

"Kinda late, pal," Bones said. "Lenny Kelly died in the Trade Center. His kid did all his time already. Can't undo either one."

The old-timer with the Jets cap sat mute at the bar, hovering over his beer. The one wearing the Cyclones hat moved down the bar. He stopped in front of Tobin, baring nicotine-stained teeth, put on his thick glasses, and said, "You really Hank Tobin?"

Tobin smiled, extended his hand, and said, "Yeah, pleased to meet—"

"Here's your fuckin' drink back, scumbag," said the old-timer, throwing his cocktail into Tobin's face. Tobin balled his fists, and the two husky patrons moved toward him like a wrestling tag team. Behind the bar Bones lifted a small club, slapping it against a bag of ice cubes.

Julie slugged her beer, clicked her gold badge on the bar top, and placed her holstered gun on her lap, like knitting.

"One at a time. I don't give a shit if you kick his ass out the door and up and down Avenue X," Julie said. "But I'll shoot the first son of a bitch who piles on."

Tobin blinked at her through booze-stung eyes, his nose and beard dripping. She grabbed Bones's damp bar rag and tossed it to Tobin. He blotted his shirt and reached for some cocktail napkins, decorated with little cartoons of barfly bimbos with torpedo tits and asses like shelves, to wipe his face.

"Nice napkins, Bones," Julie said, lifting the one under her beer. "Saks?"

"No, by the box," Bones said, baffled.

No one moved on Tobin. He blinked his eyes. "Come on, Jule, let's get out of here," he said.

"You can go if you want," Julie said. "I came to ask some questions and get some answers. My kid is in the can for something he didn't do and maybe some of these fellas can help. Maybe not. But I owe it to our kid to at least try."

"Like I sez, got no beef with you, lady," Bones said, looking Julie in the eyes. "But maybe yuse two're gettin' a taste of your own medicine."

"Oh yeah?" Julie said, sipping her beer. "How do you figure that, Bones?"

Tobin grabbed more cocktail napkins and dried his wet beard, glaring at the old man with the Cyclones cap and the big guys who had put their beer balls on simmer at the sight of Julie's badge and gun.

"Your husband put Lenny Kelly's kid in the can," Bones said. "Now it's kinda poetic your kid's in the can."

"Poetic?"

"Yeah."

The big guys grumbled beery, phlegmy agreement.

"The way I see it, this asshole, who I divorced since, wrote a column that might've gotten Kelly's kid in a jam," Julie said. "But I certainly didn't write it. I didn't arrest Billy Kelly. I didn't testify against him. I sat at home that night, doing homework with my two kids, while this clown was out getting his load on and taking notes for his column on napkins like these."

"You're a real sweetheart, Jule. . . ."

"You had your say in here ten years ago, Hank. It's my turn this afternoon."

"Let the lady talk," Bones said.

"So he came in here the night of that fire," Julie said. "And what?"

"And so he oiled poor Lenny with booze, buying him drink after drink until the poor guy spilled his guts, foamin' at the mouth," Bones said. "I remember clear as a bell because I was cold sober. Lenny was lit, your ex here was in his cups, too."

"How unusual," Julie said.

Tobin felt uneasy, blanks from a boozy old night being filled in for him like a paint-by-numbers brush.

"Lenny was bullshittin', as usual," Bones said. "Then I told him it was a reporter in from the *Examiner*. He told Tobin there that he knew who the hero was that firebombed the gook's house. Tobin was antsy, buying drinks, bitin' at the bit to hear who did it. Lenny asked, distinctly, because it made me nervous, 'Is this off the record?' Tobin said, 'Absolutely.' "

"I don't remember that," Tobin said, sweat springing from his pores, but a vague recollection began to emerge from the swampy past.

"Oh, that's the way it went down," Bones said, pointing down the bar. "I can produce two guys who were here that night who heard it, too."

"I heard you say 'off the record' loud and clear, asshole," the husky guy said from four stools away.

"Me, too," said the second husky guy.

Julie glared at Tobin, who swallowed a knot of dread and took a deep breath. "Go on, Bones," she said.

"Then Lenny started embellishin'. To make himself look like a big shot. He bragged about his kid bein' the one who torched the chink's house. His kid was such a drugged-out, skinhead loser that Lenny was always tryin' to paint him as a neighborhood hero. But he wasn't thinking clear about the ramifications, the consequences of saying all this shit to a stranger. Especially a stranger with a fucking newspaper column. I tried to stop him. I said, 'Lenny, dummy up with that bullshit story. You're just blowing smoke.' But Lenny kept pouring out the line of shit, enjoying his own story, and Tobin made notes. I kept asking Tobin why he was making notes if it was off the record. He told me to mind my own business. I knew this was just Lenny the Loser's act. But your husband there . . ."

"Ex," Julie said, holding up her bare wedding hand and sipping her beer.

"Yeah, okay, your 'ex' got Lenny as stewed as a bowl of prunes. Lenny didn't stop his bullshit braggin' about his kid torchin' the gook's house for an hour. Then your ex left me a ten-dollar tip and printed every drunken thing Lenny said in the goddamned mornin' paper," Bones said. "And it got his kid locked up. It destroyed that family. Mother killed herself, daughter took off and never come back. Billy went to the joint, and Lenny died a little every day 'til he went down in the Towers. And, so, yeah, I think it's poetic your kid gets jammed up so your ex knows what it musta felt like to be Lenny."

Tobin stood there, as if he'd been de-panted in public, exposed for one of the worst violations of journalistic ethics. The booze had bent the needle on his professional and moral compass, and he'd quoted the poor son of a bitch word for word about his own kid. Which helped lead to ten long years in jail.

Julie sipped her beer and said, "You got any kids, Bones?"

"Two daughters."

"See 'em much?"

"Holidays and like that. They're married, kids a their own. Connecticut, Tom's River, Jersey, like that."

"You ever been in trouble, Bones?"

"I had scrapes."

"I won't pull your yellow sheet, but what if somebody made your kids pay for your sins? Had to do the time for your crimes?"

Bones went silent. "Well, I never hurt nobody the way Tobin over here hurt the Kellys. But I get what you're getting at. Anyone wants to get even with me, get even with me, not my kids. Yeah."

"Don't blame my son for the sins of his father," Julie said.

"I hear ya," said one of the husky guys, cocking his head, taking a gulp of beer, and lighting an unfiltered butt in violation of the new no-smoking law.

"Yeah," said the other, blowing out a stream of smoke, picking a piece of tobacco off the tip of his tongue. "It's Tobin's who's the doozebag."

"Watch your language, broad in the place," said the old-timer with the Cyclones cap. The one with the Jets cap sat silent, staring straight into the mirror of the back bar as if he were expecting someone to step out of it.

"The day Hank Tobin wrote that column my son, Henry, was eleven years old," Julie said. "He was still in grammar school in St. Edmund's. He played Little League for Amity. What the fuck did he have to do with my ex-husband's column? Excuse *my* language."

Bones made a monkey face, shrugging. "I guess, ya know, not much."

"What would you say if I told you that I think Lenny Kelly is still alive?" said Julie. "And that he set my kid up to get even with my ex?"

"Say you're fulla shit," said one of the big guys.

"Why, you see him dead?" asked Tobin, who was still woozy from learning how far he'd gone over the journalistic line.

"No, but . . . hey, no one's talkin' to you, shithead," said the husky guy with red hair.

"You want me, I'm still here, if that's what it takes to get some answers about Kelly," Tobin said, flapping his arms. "But the fact is, not one of you who say you were Lenny Kelly's friends went to his memorial mass. How come?"

Silence fell on the barroom like a smog of old neighborhood guilt.

"How come, Bones? You won't serve my ex a drink, but you're ready to club him," Julie said, then turned to the husky guys. "You guys are ready to tune him up all because of what he did to poor Lenny Kelly, too. But not one of you went to his memorial mass? What's up with all that?"

"Well, . . . Lenny went a little nuts," Bones said.

"Yeah?" Julie said.

"He stopped talkin' to people," Bones said. "Lenny blamed me for lettin' Hank Tobin get him shit-faced. Said I was lookin' for cheap publicity for my joint, so I let Tobin take advantage of him. Said I got him smashed and let him fly with the mouth, which gave Tobin the column that got his kid the dime upstate."

"Then he blamed the whole neighborhood for not helpin' him out when his kid got jammed up," said the husky guy who was drinking plain beer.

"But the kid, Billy, he was a fuckin' nut anyways," said the second one, his arms covered with tattoos that looked like they were inked by the same guy who drew the cocktail napkins.

"Billy was a skinhead, drugs, alla that shit," Bones said. "We figured he prolly did torch the gook's house. If one of us woulda put up our house for bail, he woulda prolly skipped, lammed to Ireland or somethin'. If we raised money for a fancy lawyer, he was gonna get convicted anyways because he looked guilty, sure as shit goes through a goose."

"That fire hurt alla us around here for a long time," said the old-timer with the stained teeth. "Made real-estate values fall. Made us all look like this was some kinda Klan country. Scared the lib'ril yuppies from Park Slope and the Heights from buyin' here."

"Meanwhile, the chinks that got firebombed?" Bones said. "They made out like bandits. They turned a Chinese fire drill into a lottery. They took the insurance money and expanded the deli into a supermarket, opened a restaurant next door, a dry cleaners, hardware, and newsstand all on the same block. The Kellys wind up in jail, dead or dying, and the gooks wind up with a Ding Dong dynasty on Avenue X. Their daughter even married a local white kid, name of Freddie Buckles, with little kids I call the McGooks. Fuckin' spoiled brats in two languages."

The little guy with the tattoos and the chef's hat, thought Tobin, recounting the run-in with the guy outside Madam Hu's Golden Bowl that morning. *What the hell was the tattoo I saw on his arm the night of the fire?*

"Tobin here mighta delivered the news that was supposed to be off the record," said one of the husky guys. "But we all believed the kid delivered the Molotov."

"So now you think it's poetry that *my* kid faces time for something he *didn't* do?" Julie said.

Bones and the others in the bar looked at each other. Tobin walked closer to the guys at the bar. They still weren't fans.

"Look, I'm not asking any of you to like me," Tobin said. "I'm not proud about what I did. But I got a kid in a cage. I'm standing here, not as a newspaper columnist or any of that two-bit celebrity shit you see in the gossip pages, but as a man. As a father, a guy from Brooklyn. Like the rest of you. If you know anything about how we could find Lenny Kelly, if you've seen him since September 11, I'm asking you, as men, as *fathers,* please don't make my kid pay for my fuck-ups. It just isn't right."

"Why don't you write like that in your bullshit column?" asked the guy with the Cyclones cap. *"On* the record?"

"I'll drink to that," Julie said, sipping her beer, staring at the faces of the men. The old-timer with the Jets cap, who'd been silent through the entire exchange, drained his beer and exited the bar, throwing a panel of light across the booze-ravaged faces of the men in the Lucky Seven. There was something vivid in the smoke-strangled air that told Tobin that these men were torn between doing the right thing for an innocent kid and a fretting mother, and being rats. In Brooklyn there was no lower life-form than a squealer, a two-legged rat, like Sammy the Bull Gravano, who dimed on John Gotti. Plus they had some weird kind of unspoken debt of guilt to repay to Lenny Kelly. It was an inexplicable "neighborhood" thing, a cock-eyed code of street honor that said you stood behind one of your own, even when he was a fucking monster.

"Have a great summer, guys," Julie said and moved for the door.

Tobin paused, hoping someone would yell, "Wait!" No one did. He left. The door whipped closed behind him like a trap. Julie's cell phone rang. She glanced at the caller ID and answered it, "Hi, baby."

Moog, Tobin thought. *Fucking Moog. Was this guy banging Julie when I was still married to her?*

Tobin felt the HJV rise in him again, scorching through his veins like a lethal injection, zooming in fast on the heart. He watched Julie listen on her cell phone. "Later, honey, I promise. I'll tell you where and when, okay?" she said in a hushed, soothing voice, flicking a smile, and nodding. "You, too, baby."

"We have our ducks in a row here?" Tobin asked. "Priorities straight?"

"Put it this way, Tobin. My priorities take priority over yours."

Tobin noticed a parking ticket on Julie's rented Taurus.

"Red-letter day," she said.

"I'll pay it."

"I don't need your charity."

"Thanks for not letting them kick the shit out of me."

"I should've. At least then I would've accomplished something positive."

The old-timer in the Jets cap who'd remained silent through the barroom encounter stood under the canopy of the next-door newsstand in front of a big sidewalk-display magazine and newspaper rack. He paid the Pakistani newsie for a copy of the *Daily News* bearing a headline about India and Pakistan on another nuclear brink over Kashmir. A skyline on the *Daily News* plugged a story about the fractured Tobin family.

"Lenny Kelly goes to the same Chinaman on Avenue U for cancer herbs as me," said the old-timer in the Jets caps, pronouncing the "h" in herbs. "Name's Dr. Chan."

Julie glanced at him. "You saw him? You saw *Kelly?*"

"Don't look at me," the old-timer said. "Browse the rack. We never talked."

Julie and Tobin scanned the magazine rack. Julie grabbed a copy of *In Style*. Tobin thumbed through a boxing magazine. Both pretended to read as they listened to the man in the Jets cap. "When was the last time you saw Lenny Kelly?" Tobin asked.

"Two weeks ago," the old-timer said. "I'm Bob, by the way."

"You certain it was him, Bob?" Julie asked.

"He wore a black wig and a bullshit beard, but it was Lenny Kelly," Bob said.

"How are you so sure? He say hello? He use his real name? What?"

"None of that there," Bob said. "But see, Lenny has a letter 'L' tattooed on the back of each hand."

"That's right. For Lenny the Loser," Tobin said. "It's in my old column."

Julie glared at him, shaking her head.

"Actually, he liked to call himself Lucky Lenny," Bob said, "because he had the best wife and kids in the world. The rest of us called him Lenny the Loser."

"So you saw him?"

Bob said, "In Chan's office, he wore gloves. But when he was leavin', the receptionist gave him an appointment card. He dropped it. He couldn't pick it up with his gloves on. He took one off, by instinct, to pick it up. He had a Band-Aid on the back of his hand. But it flopped off. And I was sitting in the reception area, and I seen the 'L' on the back of his hand. I didn't say nothin.' I figured he had his share of sorrows. Like me, he's dying, or he wouldn't a been there. Chan's office is like a waiting room to the grave. And I figure, so maybe crazy Lenny faked his death so he could leave his kid a few bucks insurance. I did a few insurance jobs on cars in my day, too. But if he framed your kid, all bets are off. I ain't going to my grave knowing I coulda helped an innocent kid out of the can."

Tobin stared at the boxing magazine, at a picture of Mike Tyson on his back on the canvas. "You're a prince," Tobin said.

"Thanks," Julie said.

"I just don't want nobody to know I'm telling you this because, well . . . because I'd sort of would like a few of the guys to show up at my funeral mass, ya know?"

"This Chan, the herbalist," Tobin said. "He have a first name?"

The old-timer laughed. "Sorry for laughing. His name is Charles. I'm dying and my life's in the hands of Charlie fucking Chan."

"Well," Tobin said, "you might've just helped save my number-one son."

TWENTY-SIX

Tobin couldn't stop rubbing his smooth face as he stared at Julie's short, blond, spiky hair. His hair hadn't been this short since he first met Julie twenty-three years ago. The black hair dye and the clean shave took a decade off his appearance. Julie had also made Tobin take out his contact lenses and put on a pair of blue-tinted prescription glasses. And she'd gone to the Ace King Laundry on Avenue U, picked up Henry's laundry, and made Tobin change out of the designer suit and tie into a pair of his son's jeans and open-necked polo shirt. She made him replace the Botticelli loafers with a new pair of sneakers purchased in a local sporting goods store.

"At least some people might not recognize you now," she said.

They exited the Rossi Hair Salon on Eighty-sixth Street looking at each other. *She looks twenty-one,* Tobin thought. *Well, thirty-one, anyway.*

She smiled at him in an embarrassed way and said, *"What?"*

"You look the same as the day I stole your bikini top."

"Get lost," she said, shoving him. "I'm an aging hag."

She stared at him, grinned, cocking her head like a puppy the way she used to when he first met her.

"I feel like a shorn sheep," he said. "How do I look?"

She shrugged, as if memories exploded in her head. "Like someone I used to know."

"Who?"

"Never mind."

"The guy you fell in love with?"

"Don't flatter yourself, dickweed."

She walked to her rental car. He watched her swagger across the Brook-

204

lyn sidewalk, admiring her wasp-thin waist, narrow hips, and round rump in tight, faded jeans, all topped with the new, short, blond pixie hair. He wanted to leap on her. If he hadn't already done it, he might have fallen in love with Julie Capone. There and then.

She turned to him as she climbed into the Taurus. "You look good, Hank."

The wizened old-woman receptionist in Dr. Chan's Acupuncturist and Chinese Herbalist on Avenue U near Nostrand Avenue said the doctor was running a little late. The glass door of the office was covered with stickers indicating that Dr. Chan took medical insurance from every one of the major HMOs, including the one from the *Examiner*. The waiting room was filled with people who grimaced in pain, sat coughing in phlegmy fits, some in wheelchairs or on walkers, obese or emaciated, pale or greenish and bald from chemotherapy that had not killed the tumors that were killing them. And so they came here, hoping for secret herbal cures from the mysterious Orient and for acupuncture relief from the chronic pain of cancer.

Julie dangled the gold badge, and the receptionist said that they should come back in an hour when the doctor was in.

Tobin suggested they grab a sandwich at the Brennan and Carr roast-beef sandwich restaurant on the next corner. The service was lightning fast, and they sold the best roast-beef sandwich on the planet. Tobin entered, gazing around the modest and immaculate bare-brick-and-exposed-beams eatery. It hadn't changed much in twenty-five years. He walked to a specific corner table overlooking the parking lot. As they crossed the room, none of the neighborhood people recognized either one of them. It was a good sign. Tobin accidentally bumped into a table where an Asian man sat reading the *Daily News* sports section, scoffing a pair of bloody roast-beef sandwiches with sides of onion rings and fries and a large Coke. He gabbed on a cell phone.

"I want ten dimes on the Mets, three dimes on the Diamondbacks and, for chrissakes, Downtown, I need a better line on the Braves. . . ."

"Sorry," Tobin said, to which the Asian man grunted, shifted on his chair, chomped a bloody bite of roast beef, and continued arguing with his bookie as he turned the page to the baseball box scores.

Tobin recognized a half-dozen faces in the room. No one said hello to him. "I think the Clark Kent disguise actually might work," he said, sitting down at the corner table.

"No one's seen your real face in fifteen years."

"Been keeping count, huh?"

"Sure. It's when the guy I met, fell in love with, and married got swallowed by his alter ego, the columnist. A woman, especially a wife, she notices those little things."

"What're you having?" He studied the wall-mounted menu that consisted of about a dozen, basic, top-quality fast-food items.

"I don't eat cop food anymore," Julie said. "Red meat slows me down."

"So do forty-three birthday candles. Have the chicken."

"Up yours."

The stoic, sixtyish waitress sidled up to the table on black-gummed shoes, pulled a pencil out of a graying hair bun and an order pad out of a soiled apron, and said, "Ready?"

"Bowl of Manhattan chowder, please," Julie said.

Tobin ordered the dipped roast beef on a roll with fries, and they each ordered Diet Cokes. The waitress nodded, scribbled the orders, and hurried off toward the loud kitchen. Tobin and Julie sat across from each other for a long, silent, awkward moment, the first time they'd broken bread in years.

"Chan's looks like the last-chance saloon of medicine," said Julie. "Like going to Lourdes."

"There must be something to it," said Tobin. "A billion Chinese can't be wrong."

"I guess. But looking at all those poor people just sitting there. . . ."

"You realize where we're sitting?"

"Yeah," she said, scraping her chair a few inches away from him. "Too close."

"No, this is the table where we sat on our first date."

"God, guys aren't supposed to remember girlie things like that."

"I kissed you right out there in the parking lot."

"Oh, sweet Jesus . . ."

"I grabbed your ass."

"At least that's guy talk."

"In the car I copped a feel of your . . ."

The waitress brought the sodas and the soup. Julie smirked as the waitress placed down napkins and silverware.

"You were saying?" Julie said, daring Tobin the way she used to on dates.

"I was just saying we sat here on our first date. We kissed in the parking lot. I grabbed your buns against the fender of your Volks, and once I got you in the car, I cupped your jugs for the first time." Julie dropped her head in embarrassment.

"Romantic," the waitress said, striding away.

"You always loved to embarrass me," she said.

"You were a good sport."

"You were a great boyfriend," she said, drumming her fork on the laminated tabletop, staring at him. "But a shitty husband, Hank."

He reached across the table and touched her hand. She hit the back of his hand with the sharp prongs of the steel fork. "Don't."

"Fork you, too."

She dropped the fork, sighed, and grabbed his hand and said, "Listen to me, Hank, listen good. Don't confuse the way I *feel* with the way I *think*, okay? Right now, with my firstborn in danger, I feel vulnerable. I *feel* like I need you—need you more than ever. But I still *think* you're a miserable bastard. You might look good, you might say and do all the right things right now. But I know what you *are*. Don't take advantage of me. Please."

"You're right, I'm no good and—"

"And don't try the self-effacing bullshit routine on me either," she said, gripping his hand harder, leaning forward, pulling him closer. "It won't work. Besides, that's even more sissified than the romantic nostalgia ass-kiss act."

Their faces just inches apart, she looked ready to kiss him. Her cell phone rang.

The moment was fractured. She looked at the caller ID, half-turned in her chair, and spoke into the phone. "Hi, honey."

I'll break this Moog's fucking nose, Tobin thought, his HJV flaring again, rage rushing in a geyser to the roof of his skull, rapid-boiling his brains.

"I promise, I'll call you in a little while, just be patient," Julie said into the phone. "Of course I do. You, too. Bye."

Julie snapped closed her phone. She stared across at Tobin.

"You okay, Tobin?"

He nodded. She reached out and patted his hand.

The waitress arrived with the food, and said, "You guys want this to go? The Golden Gate has short-stay rates."

Julie let go of Tobin's hand and ate her soup. Tobin devoured his sandwich and fries. Then he stopped eating, took a slug of soda, looked Julie in
the eyes, and said, "You banging Moog?"

"None of your goddamned business."

"Is, too."

"How you figure?"

"I want you back, Julie."

Julie looked Tobin in the eyes, an unblinking stare.

"Get me my son back," Julie said.

Chan said, "Very funny thing."

"What's funny?" Tobin said.

"You second guy named ah Henry Tobin Senior I meet from *Examiner*
newspaper."

"Maybe my son . . ."

"No, man older than ah you," Chan said.

They were in Chan's inner office, where dark bamboo shades covered
the big windows, and soft ambient light from Chinese lamps with rice-
paper shades with prints of women bathing in a waterfall promoted a sense
of tranquility. Candy-colored fish swam through a six-foot-long tank that
cast an aqua-green hue over the uncluttered room. Delicate Asian wind-
chime music played from unseen speakers.

"How much older?" Tobin said.

"Maybe ah ten year. Same number on insurance card, too. He wear
gloves alla time."

"He ever take the gloves off?" Julie asked.

"Only when I do acupuncture on ah fingertips."

"Did he have tattoos on the back of his hands?"

"Maybe. Don't know. He always wear big ah Band-Aids on back of
hands."

"Lenny Kelly," Julie said.

"Not name he use ah with me—Lenny Kelly."

"What name does he use with you?'

"Told you already—Hen-ry To-bin Senior."

"That's my name."

"I know, you say that already, too," Chan said, fiddling with his computer keyboard. "That why so funny. His insurance card say he from the,

ah, *Examiner* newspaper, too. I never pay attention to name of company if insurance approved, I treat patient."

Julie walked around the counter and looked over Chan's shoulder at the screen. "He's using your insurance card, Hank," she said. "Same Social Security number."

"You remember my Social Security number, Jule? I'm touched."

"I also remember jingles for Drano and Raid," she said.

Coincidences and LL's unexplained knowledge of Tobin's personal information started to make sense and click together for Tobin. "The guy is impersonating me," Tobin said. "If he has my Social Security number, there's no limit to what he can do with it in the computer age."

"This is called a crime, Charlie Chan," said Julie.

Tobin showed Chan a photograph of Leonard Kelly and asked if he could recognize him.

"Man I examine wear ah black wig and black beard," Chan said. "Much more ah skinny than that. Can't say same man for sure. He let me take off wig for meridian pressure points on bald scalp."

"You have any kind of DNA samples here?" Julie asked. "A biopsy? Hair? Something like that?"

"No," Chan said. "I sterilize the acupuncture needles after each ah use. I don't do biopsies. His hair gone from chemotherapy."

"I can have you busted for insurance fraud, Charlie," Julie said.

"Hey, I run a clean business here, man," Chan said. "This guy asked us to send all his bills care of the *Examiner*."

All at once Charles Chan was speaking perfect Mandarin English. Gone was the fractured syntax of a Mott Street waiter just smuggled off a "snakehead" ship. Julie and Tobin looked at each other, their eyes sharing a knowing moment.

"He make ah co-pay in cash," said Chan, returning to his impersonation of Henry Lee, the famed forensics expert from the O.J. Simpson case who became the fodder of a thousand jokes on the comedy circuit. "I treat man who berry sick."

"I never saw these bills," Tobin said.

"Like ninety percent of people, you probably not ah scrutinize your itemized HMO statements," Chan said, going in and out of the pidgin English.

Tobin knew Chan was right about that point. If he ever received the bills or records of them from the HMO, he probably shit-canned them without opening them. "Okay, so tell me what's wrong with me?" Tobin asked.

"I can't discuss. . . ."

"He's asking you to read him his own file," Julie said. "Believe me, Charlie, you don't want insurance adjusters down here. This is Henry Tobin Senior of the New York *Examiner*. Tell him what's in his fucking file."

Chan shrugged and scanned the chart for Henry Tobin Senior.

"You came to me first time ah six month ago," he said. "Your cancer started with hepatitis C. Left untreated for many years. Maybe from giving yourself tattoos in juvenile jail when troubled kid. Dirty needles. Maybe from heroin needle in Vietnam. Then lifetime of drinking alcohol block more *chi,* closing many meridians. Caused many problems until hepatitis C liver cause so much blockage of *chi* that you get cirrhosis and then that block even more *chi* and close more meridians, and it become eventually the tumors of the liver. Berry bad. But Chinese herbs used to treat liver cancer for two thousand years. . . ."

"What the hell is *chi?*" Julie asked, her face that of a skeptical cop interrogating a suspect. "Meridians? What is this mumbo jumbo, Charlie?"

"*Chi* is the life force that keep us alive, the blood and all the fluids of the body combined are the *chi.* It circulate to keep us healthy and happy with inner music every twenty-four hour. It travel through the fourteen meridians of the body, or energy life-force channels, from the top of head to tips of fingers to tips of toes. When you unlock these meridians with acupuncture, acupressure massage, Chinese herbs, you unblock meridians to let the *chi* flow. Healthy person have healthy, balanced flow of *chi,* which keep blood and body fluid circulating and fight disease. Block the *chi* and you can call an undertaker."

"So what about Lenny Kelly . . . Henry Tobin?"

"His cancer from severe energy imbalance," Dr. Chan said. "His *chi* became imbalanced when meridians get blocked by external and internal forces. Stress, unhappiness, sorrow are internal forces. Dirty needles, hepatitis C, alcohol, bad food, too much sugar, tobacco, red meat. All bad external forces. Together they block flow of *chi* in most of his fourteen meridians."

Tobin looked at Julie for approval and then he leaned his face an inch from the doctor's.

"Okay, Charlie, so how many ah meridians and how much *chi* did you ah clog with those two roast-beef sandwiches, the onion rings, the fries, and the ah Coke over in Brennan and Carr at lunch?" Tobin asked. "I heard you calling in your bets to your ah bookie. In better English than ah William Safire's."

Charles Chan looked at Tobin and smiled. "Okay, so arrest me, dude," he said. "I'm second generation Chinese American. My real name is David Chan but my middle name is Charles. This is America. I figured I could cash in on you round eyes by calling myself by a name none of you would ever forget—Charlie Chan. Cary Grant's real name was Archibald Leach. Anybody bust his balls? Whadda you want me to call myself? Richard Kimball?"

"I don't give a rat's ass if you call yourself Hop Sing," Julie said. "We just want some real answers."

"You a legit herbalist?" Tobin asked.

Chan piled his diplomas and certificates on the countertop. "My grandfather was *the* top herbalist and acupuncturist in Chinatown for years," he said. "My older sister took over his business. I figured Brooklyn now has two Chinatowns, one here on Avenue U and another one in Sunset Park. Plus, I figured I could attract a lot of the round eyes. But you guys, you come to a guy like me, you want me to call you 'Grasshopper' and speak like Sidney Toler. But I help people, I save lives, man. The name might be bullshit. The herbs and treatments are legit."

"So the roast beef and fries and rings and Coke are okay?"

"I'm thirty-two," Chan said. "I run five miles a day. I go to the gym. I do yoga. So every once in a while I can pig out. But do it every day for years and you throw the balance of your *yin* and *yang* off, get sick and die."

"Sounds like a bad marriage," Julie said.

Tobin and Julie looked at each other.

"Same thing, if the *yin* and *yang* are no good, the marriage dies."

"What about the man pretending to be me?" Tobin asked.

"When he came to me, he already had chemo, radiation, interferon. So I made a diagnosis based on the Eight Principles, which are really four sets of polar categories. . . ."

"Jesus Christ, just the hard news headlines, Doc," Julie said. "Not the whole edition."

"Let him finish," Tobin said. "God is always in the details."

"So I look at the *yin* and *yang*, the cold and heat, the deficiency and excess, and the interior and exterior," Chan said. "The texture and color of his tongue alone told me he was at Stage Four cancer. His pulse told me his *chi* was completely off balance. I put him on a diet of whole grains, beans, and fresh vegetables, but no raw food. Too cold. Everything must be cooked. No citrus, no shellfish."

"How about Molotov cocktails, were they okay?" Julie asked.

"I am not following," Chan said, then jabbed his finger into Tobin's name on the computer screen. "Oh, wait a minute. You're *Hank* Tobin? The columnist? Hank is short for Henry in English, for some unfathomable reason. You're the Henry Hank Tobin Senior with the kid, Junior, who bombed the mosque?"

"He's accused of it," Julie said. "He didn't do it."

"You know, I never put the Henry Tobin Senior together with Hank Tobin. I read the *Times,* the *Daily News,* no offense. But I've seen your column and your picture on the TV. But, matter of fact, you don't look like Hank Tobin, either. You another impersonator? One Henry Tobin wears a fake beard, man. The other Henry Tobin shaves his real beard? I got two guys named Henry Tobin Senior, neither one looks like him. Talk about imbalanced *yin* and *yang,* man."

"Never mind," Tobin said. "Tell me about the guy who's impersonating me."

"Well, I prescribed Jianpi Wenshen recipe, which is an antiviral treatment," Chan said. "He made some minor progress. Then, of course I gave him tang kuei—"

"Of course," Julie said. "I mean, who the hell wouldn't?"

"Exactly," said Chan. "Then Fu Zhen therapy. Including astragalus, ligustrum, ginseng, codonopsism atractylodes, and gangoderm. They all help immunity and the T-cell count. And kelp and pokeroot to dissolve tumors. I gave him a whole host of other herbs for the pain and *chi,* or energy flow. It's very complicated. I prescribed eighteen different herbs. They helped clear a lot of the toxins and germs and waste from his body. His *chi* was backed up like a clogged slop sink. See, man, when that happens the *chi* has nowhere to go and instead the trapped *chi* grows into tumors. I give him a regime of *chi gong* and after a few weeks your alter ego got his appetite back. He had more energy."

"Remission?" asked Tobin.

"Well, not exactly. But the *chi gong* sure helped."

"Doesn't it always?" Julie said. "Especially with soy sauce."

"Your *chi* is fine, lady, but your *yin* and *yang* are haywire. I have some herbs that could help."

"My *yin* and *yang* can't be as off kilter as your insurance and your fraud," said Julie.

"What's *chi gong?*" Tobin asked, shooting Julie a fierce look. "Soup?"

"It's a three-thousand-year-old Zen exercise that combines the slow, writhing, symmetrical movements of tai chi with meditation, relaxation, and patterned breathing. I made Mister Tobin concentrate on his *dan tian*—"

"Who the hell is *Dan Tian?*" Julie asked.

"It's means 'vital center,' " said Chan. "Located two inches below the belly button. This is the Grand Central terminal of the *chi* in your body. All the energy trains leave from there and travel through the fourteen meridians, or life-force channel tracks, to the distant points of the body. When you concentrate on your *dan tian* and do your *chi gong* exercises, you manipulate and distribute the vital energy or *chi* through the body and inner-healing begins. It balances the *yin* and *yang,* improves circulation and emotional and mental health. It's not bullshit. It's the real deal, man. It works."

Tobin said, "Look, Doctor Chan, no disrespect, this is all very fascinating, but did this save your patient's life? This guy who's impersonating me?"

"He came to me so deep into Stage Four liver cancer that I couldn't save him."

"How long?" Tobin said.

Julie groaned and said, "Please, Hank, don't do your 'How long is a Chinaman's name?' joke."

Chan smiled and said, "Everyone knows that one, man. How Long *is* the Chinaman's name. It's a statement, not a question. Hardy-har-har. Everyone makes fun of my name, too. But it's good for business."

"How long?" Tobin asked again, dead serious. "How long does this man who called himself Tobin have to live, Dr. Chan?"

"I don't think I'll see him again," Chan said, scrolling the computer file. "I mean he might have one or two months to live. But he said all he needed was enough herbs for pain and energy to last until July 29."

"That sends up signals like saying you don't want to know how to take off or land, just how to fly the plane," Julie says. "It sounds like a suicide date to me."

Tobin knew that was the day Lenny Kelly always took off from work. But he didn't know what the significance was.

"Can he get around?"

"If he takes the herbs, he can endure the pain and get enough *chi* to move around and function a few hours a day. Then one day the tumors will grow so big that all the meridians will be clogged, and the *chi* will have nowhere to flow inside of him and so it will just flow out of him, and his body will stop being alive."

"We're talking what? Weeks? Days?" Tobin asked.

"Yeah, after his herbs run out, maybe a week. Tops two."

"What's his address?" Julie asked.

"Care of the *Examiner*," Chan said.

"But did he mention to you where he lived?" Julie asked.

"No. But I told him if he could, he should stay near the water to help the flow of the *chi*," Chan said. "Like the tides, the *chi* changes every twenty-four hours."

"So he lives near the water?" Julie said.

"He always had the salty smell of the sea on him," Chan said.

"You mean like he lives on a boat?"

"Maybe. Or near the beach. When I would massage him or insert the acupuncture needles in his toes to alleviate the pain, I always had to clean the sand from between his toes with the alcohol wipes. He must do his *chi gong* exercises on the beach. I told him to do that whenever he could. *Chi gong* near the sea in the clean, fresh sea air is the ideal. The flow of the sea helps the flow of the *chi*."

"He's a poet, too," Julie said. "Right up there with Johnny Cochran."

"Thank you, Dr. Chan," said Tobin.

"If this guy calls or shows up again, call me, will ya?" Julie asked, handing him a card with her various numbers.

"Sure," Chan said.

"You keep this meeting confidential until I say otherwise," Tobin said, "and I won't report the false claims to my HMO, which I hate anyway. We clear on that? You never saw me. Never talked to me. You don't know Hank Tobin has a shave and a haircut. We clear on all that, Charlie Chan?"

"Never, ah, see honorable self before in life," Chan said.

As they left Chan's office, Julie was still confused.

"Why would Lenny Kelly do it?" Julie asked. "Doesn't he have his own insurance at the janitor's union?"

"Devlin, the union PR guy, told me Kelly maxed out his insurance at

Sloan Kettering on conventional treatments. Besides, once he faked his own death, his insurance was cancelled. So the brazen son of a bitch used mine. He wants me to know he's taken over my life, has his hand up my shirt, that he's in control, playing me like a puppet."

"Okay," Julie said. "So how'd he get access to your information?"

"He's a janitor," Tobin said, approaching the rented Taurus parked in the Brennan and Carr lot. "He worked everywhere. Including the *Examiner*, and the *Globe*, and Cyclones stadium. He was the guy sweeping up peanut shells the night Henry and me went to the game. That's how he slipped the Rohypnol in Henry's beer. No one ever pays attention to the janitor. At the *Examiner*, he comes in at night, after deadline, and he has access to all the offices. Passkeys to all the security rooms. Where passwords and codes are kept. Or he might've set up a small camera to tape me punching in my password on the computer keyboard. He could have just looked over my shoulder as I typed it in when he was emptying trash. I never paid any of the janitors any mind. Nobody does. They're invisible. Even when he 'died' on September 11 and the same PR guy, Devlin, pitched me a story about the unknown janitor, to my everlasting shame, I ignored the column idea."

They stopped by the Taurus, looking at each other in their new, youthful haircuts and dye jobs, trying to make sense of the situation.

"But meanwhile, Lenny Kelly was compiling everything there was to know about you—and Henry," said Julie. "He learned Henry's computer password the same way he knew yours. And you figure Lenny Kelly used it to send in Henry's copy that this son of a bitch had prewritten before the bomb even went off in the mosque?"

"That's right."

"He sent Mona Falco a prepaid ticket to Cannes. He set up that cheese-cake photo with Mona in the background—"

"Stop there! *That* I'm not buying."

"He wanted to hurt our marriage, Jule, our family, the way I wrecked his."

"Don't try tap dancing me with your *yin* and *yang* routine, Tobin."

She blinked in the bright sun, trying to make sense of the data that was hurtling at her like an information overload. And then Hank Tobin kissed Julie Capone on the lips. She didn't hesitate or resist; her lips parted, and he kissed her deeper. Even as angst twisted in his guts, as his mind seared with images of Henry sitting in a pissy cell, he felt a surge of basic goodness in the simple act of kissing Julie. He felt like he'd won a small battle in a raging war. He took any minor triumph where he could find it. It offered hope. It gave him energy. As if blocked *chi* had just been set loose in all fourteen of his meridians, throbbing in his toes and his fingertips, to the top of his head.

He knew that she felt his arousal.

"Stop," she said, pulling away. "I'm not ready for this."

"I was just about to grab your ass."

"Do that and I'll knee you in the balls."

"Talk about blocking a life-force channel."

"Get in the car, assbag."

He climbed in, still feeling charged from the one brief kiss.

"Why'd we waste our time with this Chinese guy?" she said, buckling on her seatbelt and firing the engine. "He told us nothing."

"I dunno. Now we're looking for a guy who does hula-hoop exercises, gazes at his navel, and who might live by the sea. We also learned that he's running out of time, fast. Which means that so is any chance of getting him to exonerate Henry."

They looked at each other, two divided parents who loved the same child with equal passion. Which had, for at least this brief time, brought them back together.

She eased the Taurus out of the lot.

"Thanks," she said.

"For what?"

"Lunch."

"Don't be ridiculous."

"And for loving Henry as much as I do."

"Julie, I . . ." He welled with emotion and chose not to finish the sentence for fear of losing his composure. He looked out the window, watching his native Brooklyn whip past. Nothing looked better than home when you're in trouble.

She reached across and touched his mouth, soft sexy fingers drubbing his lower lip. "Thanks for the kiss, too. You still do it pretty good."

"There's no one else I'd rather—"

"But don't do it again," she said. "In fact, maybe we better split up and cover more ground."

"I don't want to split up."

But they did.

TWENTY-SEVEN

Judge Nicolas Koutros said, "I don't know what you're talking about, Hank."

"You never heard from a guy who calls himself LL?"

Tobin could see a scribble of panic in the old judge's eyes.

"No!"

It was a few minutes before four P.M. The two men who shared a terrible secret sat at a small table in the rear of the Boulevard Coffee Shop two blocks down from the Queens Supreme Courthouse, after Koutros and his lawyers spent a day of motions and legal haggling in the judge's bribery case. Defendants and their mostly minority and poor white families ate lunch here. Not even Legal Aid attorneys would dine here, never mind a judge. That's why Tobin picked it, so that no one would recognize him or Nick Koutros.

Julie had taken the Taurus into Manhattan to see Erin Kelly Levine, who worked at a high-profile accounting firm in the Chrysler Building on Forty-second Street and Lexington Avenue. "I want to talk to her mother-to-mother," Erin had said. "I never did anything to her."

Tobin took a car service straight out to Queens, leaving his car parked outside Julie's house on E. Thirty-eighth Street in Marine Park, where the media thought they were both huddling.

Tobin had called Lou Barratta, the old Democratic-machine politico fixer, and asked him to set up an "off the record" meeting with the judge to discuss some details in his case. Koutros agreed to meet Tobin, but with great reluctance, and an absolute journalistic vow of confidentiality and promise that he not write about him. He didn't want Tobin to quote a word. But he also didn't want a columnist of Tobin's clout pissed off at him. He didn't need the added heat. So they sat down for coffee. Tobin was sure there was another reason. Koutros had to know that Tobin had a common enemy in Lenny Kelly.

"Let me refresh your memory, Nick," Tobin said. "Remember a kid named Billy Kelly? Ten years ago, Brooklyn, an arson on an Asian family's home in Gravesend."

"There were so many cases—"

"Stop bullshitting me, Nick. Billy's father, Lenny Kelly, is doing to you what he's doing to my kid, isn't he?"

"I don't know what you're talking about, Hank. I have enough problems. . . ."

Koutros pushed himself up to leave. Tobin took another sip of his coffee and said, "He has something more on you, doesn't he, Nick? A document? A photo? Some definitive piece of evidence, a smoking gun, that will sink you, guarantee your conviction. He calls you all the time. E-mails you. Mind-fucks you. Keeps you awake nights. Plays with your sanity. Knows all your moves. Threatens your family."

Tobin looked at Koutros, whose mouth looped into a tight little letter "O," his eyelashes fluttering. "I have to go."

Koutros turned to leave. Tobin said, "I just came from his doctor. He might only have days to live."

Koutros turned, his doomed, defenseless eyes like a baby seal's before the final swing of the club. He grasped the edge of the table for support, causing Tobin's coffee to lap over the edge of his mug and splatter on the Formica table. The disgraced judge collapsed onto his chair with a boneless thud, as if all his collective lifelong guilt had landed with him.

"He's the only one who can clear me," Koutros said, the words peeling slowly from his sticky white tongue as if they'd been pasted there.

"Same with my son. What does he have on you?"

"I'd rather not say."

"Did he go after your marriage?"

"Yes, that's finished."

"Photos? E-mails to the wife?"

Koutros nodded. "He followed me. I have no idea how he got into my computer, inside my girlfriend's apartment, her bedroom, where we—"

"She live in a Manhattan high-rise?"

Koutros nodded.

"He was probably a fill-in custodian, maintenance man, doorman," Tobin said. "He probably filled in for someone on their sick day, holiday, or on vacation time, went in under the pretense of fixing a leak, and planted a simple five-hundred-dollar, digital, pinhole, spy camera in a smoke detector, thermostat, or phone jack in her bedroom. My bet, an audio bug, too. You can buy this stuff over the counter in one of those spy stores. The same way they busted poor Frank Gifford boffing the airline stewardess in the hotel room. Gizmos people use to catch nannies abusing their kids, or employees pissing in the boss's Mr. Coffee pot, or quack chiropractors cheating insurance companies. Then, during one of your rolls in the hay with your lady friend, the digital images and voices transmitted live straight to Lenny Kelly's personal computer where they were recorded. And then he just e-mailed a few frames back to you. Am I right?"

Koutros nodded again, bowing his head in shame. "He knows everything about me. My marriage has been dead for years. Claire let herself go—obesity, pills, booze. She lies around the house all day, eating, drinking, watching TV, sleeping. Waking up to more pills, more booze, more junk food, more TV. An obese, aging zombie. I begged her to get help. My daughters and I did an intervention. We put her in a rehab for substance abuse and eating disorders. She up and left. I'm a man, Hank. She refused to even try to be the woman I once loved and married. She gave up. She was dragging me deep into old age and the grave—"

"Please, you don't have to tell me all this. I'm the wrong guy to confess to about failing at husbandry."

"I was a good husband. A good father. A very good judge. A good guy. But I am still a *man*. What can I say? I had needs, desires, and I found another woman. That's my crime in life. To that I plead guilty. Nothing else. I have no idea how this man has done all of this to me."

"But you do know why?"

"I sentenced his son."

"Did you ever use your girlfriend's computer to go online, check your e-mails, do your banking from her place?"

"As a matter of fact, yes. I used her PC many times. But I always used my own AOL account, with my own private password."

"Lenny Kelly probably installed one of those computer-cop programs onto her hard drive without her even knowing it. One that made a duplicate of every keystroke you made online. Every web site you visited. It basically carbon copies everything you do on a computer. Parents use them to monitor what their kids do online. Kelly did that to you. He also probably picked up your passwords and banking PIN numbers with the camera focused on the keyboard. It's pretty simple. All he has to do is play the film in slow motion and see what keys you hit to open your web server, then your PIN numbers. Once you have access to someone's apartment and their personal computer, you have access to their private lives, all their secrets."

Koutros shook his head and said, "I feel so violated, like such a patsy, such a fool."

"Hey, don't feel bad," Tobin said. "I did a column a while back about a seventeen-year-old kid in Vienna, I think his name was Hirsch, yeah, Marcus Hirsch. This kid was able to lie on his bed in his bedroom in Vienna with his laptop and hack into top secret files in the Pentagon! Another guy was able to tap into CIA antiterrorist satellite-camera feeds. These days, hacking into your computer is like picking a luggage lock. Nothing and no one is safe. ESP between Siamese twins isn't hacker-proof anymore."

"Oh, my God," Koutros said. "Then he told me he would e-mail my correspondence with my girlfriend to my daughters. My daughters love their mother. They worship and adore their mother. They have children of their own now. Beautiful grandchildren. I adore my daughters and my grandkids. But my daughters would disown me for betraying their mother. Especially now, in a time of her life when she's clearly losing her . . . grip."

"So, Kelly's blackmailing you?"

"He doesn't ask for money. Never asked me to fix a case."

"No, he wants you to pay with your soul and your freedom," Tobin said.

"I thought Kelly was bluffing about having that stuff, the correspondence between me and my girlfriend. There are some very unflattering comments in there about my wife. Things my daughters would never forgive me for thinking, never mind writing to my mistress. Or saying to her while naked in bed. I wrote some of the e-mails to my girlfriend in fits of anger at my wife. I made verbal promises to my girlfriend, in bed, made plans to place my wife in a conservatorship so I could get a divorce and marry again without losing everything."

"LL's withholding it, just to keep you twisting in the wind. Same with me. He has something, something manufactured, on my kid, too."

"My girlfriend, she's younger than my daughters, for chrissakes," Koutros said, loosening his tie as if it were a hangman's noose. "They'd never understand. If I weren't in trouble on the bribe case, they wouldn't even be talking to me because of the affair. But if they read the e-mails, and saw me talking on videotape, *naked,* with a naked woman, having *sex,* betraying and degrading their mother, they would condemn me forever. Disown me. Christ Almighty, Hank, I never planned it this way, never went looking for another woman. My girlfriend was my law clerk—attractive, smart, talented, single, and sober. She looked up to me. When my wife refused my advances, this sexy young woman came on to me. I refused to give up on life, just become old and worthless. I needed to show that I still mattered. That I was still relevant as a *man*—"

"I'm not interested in your love life, Nick."

"Thank you. This is mortifying."

"But when you refused to be bullied or extorted, LL sent a few of the tamer photos to your wife, didn't he? And a few selective e-mails that confirmed you were having an affair?"

"This happened to you, too?"

"Similar. But that's the least of my problems right now. I have an innocent kid sitting in the can."

"I'm so sorry for you. In some ways that's worse than it happening to you."

"I'd swap places with him this instant if I could."

"I can't imagine what I'd do if Kelly had gone after one of my daughters. . . ."

"First, Kelly destroyed your marriage and mine, because he blames us for destroying his. Then he set you up on criminal charges, like he did my son."

"Somehow he made computer transfer deposits into my accounts from the accounts of two defendants who appeared in my court. In one case, I dismissed an indictment against the head of a private sanitation company on an illegal-search technicality, a Fourth Amendment breach. In the case of the second defendant, a fuel-oil company with offices in those new towers in Long Island City, the DA indicted the CEO for selling tax-free home-heating oil as diesel and pocketed the sales tax on millions of gallons. The detectives said he made a voluntary confession. But one cop admitted he asked for a lawyer, and they never let him call one. I threw out the confession. Without the confession, he was acquitted. But, Jesus Christ, Hank, I never made any deals. I ruled on the law. I never solicited or accepted any bribes in my life."

"But they made deposits into your account?"

"Without my knowledge, these two guys, defendants who appeared before me and walked, made computer transfer deposits into my savings account, which I almost never check. Then one day two DA cops burst into my chambers. They present me with deposit transaction records, totaling four-measly-thousand bucks, which made me look like a low-rent, two-bit, cheap, greedy, corrupt judge. I'm sixty-four years old, Hank. I'm gonna risk my freedom for four fucking grand?"

Tobin sipped his coffee. Koutros had the bewildered, defeated look of a man who had been victimized, like a tourist blowing all the travelers checks at a rigged Times Square three-card-monte game. The same look that Henry wore on his young face when Mona Falco snapped handcuffs on his wrists.

"Kelly got their computer information the same way he got yours and mine," Tobin said. "Posing as a janitor. He cleaned their offices, probably at night, and stole their secrets. Identity theft, but not for profit. For revenge. These two guys who made the deposits charged with bribery yet?"

"Both have previous criminal records. They were given the choice between standing trial on the bribery charges or immunity if they agreed to testify against me! Even though they must have sworn they were duped, who'd believe them? I wouldn't if I were sitting at a bench trial. So they took the immunity and will swear to whatever the hell the DA wants them to swear to. I've seen it happen a zillion times. Now the DA has physical evidence and witness testimony against me. Anyone who reaches out to them will be charged with witness tampering. I have only my word. No one is going to believe me. I'm a dirty-judge trophy bust."

"Like Hank Tobin's kid," Tobin said. "And only one guy can clear you."

"Right."

"Leonard Kelly."

"Yes. And he's officially dead. Even my own lawyers look at me like I'm an asshole when I tell them this story. Like their intelligence is insulted that I would even try to run this load of horseshit past them. They're pressuring me to cut a deal, into throwing myself on the mercy of the court. And these are the best lawyers who've ever appeared in front of me."

"The way Billy Kelly's Legal Aid lawyers pressured him."

Koutros nodded, closing his tired eyes. "I cannot go to jail," he said in a soft voice. "I will be mutilated, savaged in there. I will not go to jail."

Tobin glanced at him and then noticed a man peering into the restaurant from the street, his face obscured by the handlettered lunch-special signs taped to the window. All Tobin could see was a mop of jet-black hair. And maybe a beard. He couldn't really tell. *Paranoid,* he thought. Every time he noticed someone with black hair and a beard in a city of eight million he thought it was Lenny Kelly.

"We're both in the same sinking boat, Nick," Tobin said, glancing back at Koutros. "There could come a time when we need to support each other's story."

Koutros looked at Tobin for a long, terrified moment. "You want me to align myself with your kid, who's charged with bombing a synagogue and a mosque? I'm facing bribery and now I should join forces with a terrorist? Are you fucking nuts?"

"I'm the only one who believes you, Nick. The only one who knows you're telling the truth."

"Even if I did step out in public with you, Kelly would send everything else he has to my daughters. And other manufactured evidence he has against me in the criminal case. My lady friend is keeping her distance. She's afraid of being indicted as a co-conspirator as my law clerk. She'll be subpoenaed. I'm sure I've already lost her, too. Then I'd lose my freedom. The only thing I'd have left in the world to keep me sane is the love of my daughters and grandkids. If Kelly sends them the e-mails he threatens to send, I'd lose the love of my children, too. I'd be denied access to my grandchildren. I can't help you, Hank. We might be in this together. But we go down as individuals."

"Then what the hell are you going to do?"

"For the sake of my daughters, and myself, I'm gonna do what Kelly says."

Tobin said, "You won't fight him? What if he dies before he clears you?"

"As he said to me, 'You sat with the fate of my son's life in your hands. Now I sit with the fate of your life in mine.' This time he's the judge. I'm the skell. I'll do what he says. I pray he shows me the mercy I didn't show his kid. To be honest, I was never so sure that Billy Kelly torched that house."

"Why?" Tobin said, fearing confirmation of his own doubts. "The cops found the gasoline in his house, on his clothes. He fit the description. His father, Lenny Kelly himself, bragged about it."

"None of those allegations were ever proved as facts in a courtroom,"

Koutros said. "From what I know, Billy Kelly copped a plea because he was so stoned he was never sure if he torched the Hu house or not. He was afraid of blowing trial, risking twenty-five years. Besides, we both know now how easy it is to make an innocent man look guilty, don't we, Hank?"

"Did you ever reach out to the kid? To Billy Kelly?"

Koutros looked at Tobin. "You mean you haven't spoken to him yet?"

"I tried, today, but he wouldn't talk to me. He ran away. He's living in a Brooklyn boarding house."

"Then you don't know?"

"Know what?"

"I first started getting these phone calls from LL last year. I figured out it was Leonard Kelly from your old column. When I figured out who he was, I went to see Billy Kelly in jail. I wanted to see if he had computer access, if he was the one behind all the calls and e-mails. He didn't have access to a computer. He couldn't have done all this to me. I wanted to find out if his father ever visited him in jail. Lenny tried to visit Billy twice, early on in his sentence, and both times the kid refused to see him. Then I learned from his records that he was beaten and stabbed by a black Muslim sect called the Five Percenters in jail four months after he got to Elmira. The Aryan nation tried to take him under their wing. He joined them at first. But I guess he realized just how nutty they were. A priest convinced him to break away from them. They broke one of his arms. He survived both attacks. Tough kid."

"Oh, Jesus . . ."

"Three years ago he was diagnosed with hepatitis C, which could be deadly if not properly treated."

Tobin was silent, absorbing what he was hearing. His benign guilt metastasized into malignant dread, rampaging through him like the cancer that was killing Lenny Kelly. "Which means Billy Kelly copped a plea to a slow death sentence."

"Did he contract it in jail?" Tobin asked, guilt rising in him.

"I assume he did. When they brought him into the visiting room in Green Haven where they transferred him, I asked him questions about that and his father. The only thing he said was the rosary. He didn't answer a single question. Just decades of the rosary. I asked him what he was praying for. You know what he said? He said two words. He said, '*You*, motherfucker.' "

"What did you say?"

"I asked why he was praying for me. And he said, 'Because you sinned.' He gave me the creeps. Fact is, right now, I could use his prayers. In Billy Kelly's mind I was the sinner."

"Especially in his father's mind. And now we're at his mercy."

"Every day I wake up, I just can't believe it. Good luck, Hank."

He watched Koutros walk out of the coffee shop, head bowed.

Tobin was going to be early for his six o'clock appointment with Julie outside the Chrysler Building where she had gone to see Erin Kelly. He left a five-dollar bill under his coffee mug and hurried after the judge. He stopped him on Queens Boulevard. "Nick, did his sister, Erin, ever visit Billy in the joint?"

"I checked that, too. No. Besides the two times he turned away his father, I was the only other visitor he had in ten very long years. The kid is a total sad-sack case."

Tobin noticed a tall, thin man with jet-black hair and a beard standing in profile at a bus stop across the six lanes of Queens Boulevard. His eye then whipped to another thin, bearded, white-haired man stepping out of a taxi. Then Tobin looked back at the first man, but a bus pulled into the stop obscuring his view. He looked back at the white-haired man who'd exited the taxi and saw him jaywalk across the busy boulevard.

"You look as distracted as I am," Koutros said.

"Good luck," Tobin said.

"This has nothing to do with luck, Hank. This is a stacked deck."

"I'll be in touch."

"Don't be so sure."

Tobin nodded and hurried for the subway to meet Julie, turning twice, looking to see if a man in a black or white wig and beard was following him.

TWENTY-EIGHT

Tobin exited the subway at Grand Central and hurried east toward Lexington Avenue. He checked his watch, saw that he was still forty minutes early for Julie. He hoped she was all right. Tobin glanced at the Chrysler Building, which he knew was 1,046 feet tall to the very tip of its helmetlike vertex. He'd done a couple of columns on the Chrysler Building over the years, including one on its evacuation plans after the World Trade Center attacks. They stunk. They were old-fashioned fire drills. Tobin had written that if an attack similar to the Trade Center hit the Chrysler Building or Empire State Building, the world would see a repeat of hundreds of high-floor workers choosing a final, breezy leap into oblivion over an agonizing death by flames.

Then the street crowd gasped. Everyone seemed to look up at once. Including Tobin.

Thousands of people now gazed skyward, shielding their eyes from the sizzling sun. Great screams, shrieks, and "Ooos" and "Ahhhhhs" erupted from the crowd. Tobin visored his eyes with his notebook and craned up at the Chrysler Building. A businessman on a ledge!

Ready to leap.

From a very high floor, maybe seventy stories up.

As workers evacuated the building, the drama on the ledge continued. People in the street wept and embraced, praying that he didn't leap.

Tobin searched the crowd for Julie and gazed back up at the man on the precipice.

"Don't jump," an Emergency Service cop shouted through a bullhorn.

The man wavered on the ledge. Then the businessman jumped.

226

Screams deafened the street.

The man soared earthward in free fall, his tie trailing behind him. It was all too reminiscent of the sad leapers off the World Trade Center. Tobin's stomach flopped.

And then a great big red, white, and blue parachute popped open, emblazoned with an advertisement TERROR CHUTES INC. 1-800-555-4500. The jumper was sucked back upward into the azure sky over the teeming city streets. A man and woman near Tobin collapsed in legless twirls.

The skydiver manipulated the chute with a poetic grace, a midair urban ballet aiming for the painted gridlock box of the Forty-second Street and Lexington Avenue intersection, exploiting a new way to cash in on the terror age.

Cops halted all traffic and cleared pedestrians out of the way.

As the man descended, Tobin yanked a notebook from his rear pocket, scribbled notes, and thought again of Julie. Because of her claustrophobia, she had probably taken the stairs up to and down from Erin Kelly's office on the thirty-second floor. It was how Julie stayed in such phenomenal shape.

Watching the skydiver float to earth, Tobin's cell phone rang.

LL said, *"Hey, Hank."*

"Oh . . . hello."

"I lost track of you today after our tête-à-tête in the playground. But it's funny. When I caught up with a certain man of the law on Queens Boulevard here, he was having a coffee with a man I didn't recognize at first. But then the more I looked at him, especially the way he walked and gesticulated, I realized that this was someone I knew. Someone I had studied for the past ten years. Amazing what a shave and a haircut and a little hair dye can do to change the way a man looks. You look much younger, Hank. More like your son."

That LL had picked up his trail when he met with Koutros on Queens Boulevard was not good news. But it meant Lenny Kelly didn't know that he and Julie had gone to the Lucky Seven or Charlie Chan's.

The skydiver landed safely in a nimble trot. The crowd exploded into cheers, applause, whistles, and chants. Police surrounded the handsome yuppie, cut loose his parachute, handcuffed him, and rushed him toward a waiting police van.

"Yes, I spoke with the judge," Tobin said. "I contacted him. I suspected you might be behind his problem. I tried picking his brain. He wouldn't tell me anything. He's a broken man. He's very frightened."

"He should be. I'm perturbed at you, as well."

"Why?"

"Stay away from my son. You've hurt him enough. He has nothing to do with this. Leave him to Jesus."

Tobin felt exposed, as if trapped in a glass ant farm, with Lenny Kelly watching him burrow every tunnel, all his moves. Creepy. Like what it must be like to have a tenacious cop poking into your life. Or a reporter. And thanks to Lenny Kelly, Tobin now had both of them in his life as well. He had to be more cautious. Smarter. More observant. Lenny Kelly, cops, Feds, reporters all watched him.

"You followed me following him?"

"Yes."

"Then you know where he put the flowers."

Tobin searched for Julie amid the throngs rushing out of the Chrysler Building. He didn't see her. Firefighters rushed in. Citizens pushed out.

"No, I was too far away to see what he did with the flowers. I was busy watching you. And that accident on Fort Hamilton Parkway. That was terrible. . . ."

"Yes, it was. All unnecessary waste of human life is terrible."

"Tell me about it."

"You're trying to waste my son's life."

"You wasted my son's."

"Punish me, not my son."

"Both is better. Believe me, it saddens me. I don't relish human suffering. At best it's bittersweet. But it is necessary to balance the yin and yang. I can't let all this psychic anger, cosmic hate, bad energy have nowhere to flow. It has to have a meridian to pass through. I am just channeling what you began. I'm passing your bad chi, *your bad karma, and your bad energy back to where it came from. A perfect symmetry."*

"Kinda like Zen and the art of revenge, huh?"

"I like that," LL said, laughing in an ironic way. *"But the word 'revenge' is too strong. It's balance, Hank, like the scales of justice. Except you are exempt from regular laws. So it must be handled this way."*

Tobin continued to search the steady stream of people for Julie. No sign of her.

"Do you think your son would agree with what you're doing?"

"Maybe not. So where did he place the flowers?"

"He placed them on your grave, Lenny."

LL fell silent.

"Lenny? Who's Lenny?"

Tobin knew that Kelly was discrediting the tape as any kind of evidence. His scrambled voice was already a robotic drone. Kelly was making sure that if Tobin was taping him, it would be useless generic babble.

"He placed the flowers on your grave, which must mean he still loved you before you died. Still loves you in so-called death."

Another long silence. *"You are in no position to toy with my emotions, Hank."*

"I'm telling you the truth," Tobin said.

"Fathers always find out too late how much their kids mean to them and vice versa," LL said, sighing with a wheeze of regret. *"Look at you, Hank. What would you do right now to get the last four years with your son back?"*

"Listen to me, we both still have a chance to salvage our relationships with our sons. Don't squander the last chance, Lenny. Please—"

"Stop calling me that."

"I'm sorry."

"Me, too. Part of me hates seeing your pain because it evokes my own. But it's too late for me. I made too many decisions. I have to live and die by them."

"No you don't, man. Please, meet me, look me in the eyes, tell me what it is you want me to do to make up for what I did to your son. Talk to me as a man, as a father. You still have some time—"

"What do you mean by that?"

"I know you're sick."

"I know you're still madly in love with your wife."

"I don't care who knows that. Like you, I made some bad choices."

"Yes, you have. In fact, you should have chosen the Lexington Avenue exit from Grand Central like I did, Hank. If you had, you would have gotten out earlier. Like I did. See, I figured if you followed my son this morning and now you were getting off the Number 7 Train at Grand Central, it must mean you were going to harass his sister. So I exited at Lexington Avenue to wait and watch. I was going to anonymously call and warn her that Hank Tobin was coming to harass her. But if you had chosen the Lexington Avenue exit like me, you would have seen your ex-wife leaving the building. She looks so cute in her new blond cut. I had to do a double take. She looks like she does in the photo of her you keep on your bedroom bureau."

He's been in my apartment, too, Tobin thought. *Probably while I was out of town, on assignment, went in posing as a maintenance man.*

"You saw Julie?" Tobin said, still searching for her in the crowd.

He had someone watching his daughter, Erin, Tobin thought. *That person probably saw Julie approach Erin. And followed her. This guy doesn't have to be in two places at once. He has people working with him. Cox. Or Mona Falco. Or Moog . . .*

"I guess she was here to try to see Billy's sister, huh?" LL said. *"She'll get nowhere with her. But I applaud the both of you for your tenacity and your ingenuity, even if it is in vain."*

"Did you see where Julie went?"

"Yes, I followed her north, to Sixty-ninth Street and Park, the Italian Consulate. She stopped in there, picked up an envelope. Now she's at the Starbucks a half-block away, the one with the outdoor tables."

"She's there now?" Tobin asked, convinced that LL had to have an accomplice.

LL laughed. *"I'm looking at her as I speak, sitting at a sidewalk table. . . ."*

"Is she with your daughter?" Tobin asked as he crossed Forty-second Street and double-timed it uptown along Third Avenue through the crowd.

"She's not alone. Come see for yourself. I don't like to spoil surprises."

"Can I see you? Please, just let me talk to you, man to man."

"We already did. But I promise, I'll be seeing you, Hank. Nice try. Bye."

"Wait!"

LL clicked off.

TWENTY-NINE

Tobin paid the cabbie and exited the taxi on Sixty-ninth Street and Lexington Avenue. He gazed around, looking for the man in the black wig and beard. He didn't see him. Nor did he see anyone who looked like a grayer or balder version of the photograph he carried of Leonard Kelly.

He saw the Italian flag flapping from the consulate and wondered why Julie had gone there. He searched the area for the Starbucks cafe and slid on a pair of Ray-Ban shades to dim the sun that reflected off the storefront windows. He stepped sideways into the shade of a Korean greengrocer's awning and squinted.

He saw Starbucks. Then he saw her.

Julie.

At a sidewalk table, under a wide umbrella. The blond pixie haircut. The angular cheekbones. The flab-free jawline. The long elegant neck. The tiny little diamond earrings. Her right hand stretched across the small, round table. Gripping the big, hairy hand of a man too large for the chair he sat in. Holding hands with her boyfriend.

Moog.

Tobin stopped breathing. The roast beef, the fries, the Coke, and the coffee all rose in him like a fermenting mash. The human jealousy virus rumbled through him in a general, lousy malaise.

Tobin walked to the sidewalk table; Julie's back was toward him. She didn't see him coming. Zach Moog did. The big man glanced at Tobin. Then back at Julie, massaging her hand, smiling, saying, "I'm doing what I can do, Julie. Maybe you need to get outta town a few days, up my place, the Poconos, to think and make plans for Henry."

Tobin stared down at him, at his hand on the hand on which he'd once

231

slid a wedding band, the hand of the woman who'd once told him, "I do," for life. Moog glared up at him. Didn't recognize the dark-haired, closely shaved, bespectacled Tobin.

"Got a problem, ace?"

"Yeah, you, deuce."

Julie spun in her chair, astonished, withdrawing her small hand from Moog's. Moog pushed himself up from the chair, tipping it backward, jostling the paper cups on the table.

"Take a walk, asshole, before I give you a good smack," Moog said.

"Hank, what the hell are you doing *here?*" Julie said, checking her silver Coach watch. "How'd you know? . . . I'm not supposed to meet you for twenty-five minutes down on Forty-second. . . ."

"You okay?" Tobin asked her.

"Who's this comedian?" Moog asked. *"Another* guy named Hank?"

"My hus—ex, same Hank."

Moog studied him, laughed. "Shit, I was just gonna knock you out, Tobin."

"You were gonna *try,*" Tobin said.

Moog laughed. "You couldn't beat a bongo, Tobin. You might be tough in print. But don't have street delusions. . . ."

"Spell it," Tobin said.

"What?"

"Spell 'delusions.' "

Moog looked at Julie, who seemed just a tiny bit pleased to have two men ready to rumble over her.

Moog said, "Okay, f-u-c-k y-o-u."

"You should be commissioner," Tobin said.

Moog waved a finger in Julie's face and shoved Tobin at the same time. "I'm gonna hurt this wimp, Julie, you don't shut his smart mouth for hi—"

Tobin had spent the past ten years repeating a mantra that had guided him across the yellow brick road of the Brooklyn Bridge into the Oz of Manhattan. Into respectability, as a player on the New York stage, a stroller of the Rialto, an important name on every party A-list in New York. The simple mantra was, "Whenever you think Brooklyn tough, think Manhattan smarter."

That little credo had made him what he was today—rich, famous, important, respected. Crossing the bridge had also made him an absentee father, divorced, with a family in ruins and a kid facing life. *Real smart,* he thought. So this time when he thought tough, he said fuck smart, and thought tougher.

He knew the instant he threw the punch that it came all the way from the Brooklyn street, across the storied bridge, and straight uptown on an express track. He planted his left leg, launched the right uppercut fast and sure, and detonated it onto Moog's jaw. Moog staggered backward. He was as big as any man Tobin had ever hit in his life, and Moog crunched on top of a plastic table, splattering iced cafe lattes onto the laps of two hand-holding gay men who leapt to their feet, soiled and furious.

"You big, gaping, fucking asshole!" shouted the taller of the two gay men, dashing what was left of his iced latte into Moog's dumbfounded face.

"Sowwy," Moog said, his mouth short-circuited from his brain.

"Sorry my ass! You started it! I saw you push that guy and jab your finger into that woman's face. You colossal asshole! Now I have to run home and change before my interview. Goddamn it!"

Tobin looked at Julie and said, "He had it coming. . . ."

"You're an asshole, too. I have a son in the slammer and Laurel and Hardy helping me."

Julie stormed off toward Lexington Avenue. Tobin looked at Moog.

"You spelled 'delusions' wrong," Tobin said.

"Fuck you," Moog said.

Tobin chased Julie down to crowded Lexington Avenue to the Taurus parked at a no-parking area. She took the ticket off the windshield.

Tobin climbed in, buckled himself into the seat.

"Don't talk to me," Julie said, trying to control her anger.

Julie raced down Second Avenue toward Thirty-fourth Street.

"First you wreck our marriage," she said, breaking the silence.

"I thought you didn't want to talk. . . ."

"I don't want to hear *you* talk."

"Me neither. I'd rather listen to you."

"Then you ruin your relationship with the kids."

He was about to speak but caught himself, and sank lower in the seat.

"Then some drunken, irresponsible, poisoned, old column leads to our son getting locked up," she said. "And then when I meet with my ex-partner . . ."

"Boyfriend . . ."

". . . Who was giving me inside stuff from NYPD on this whole awful mess, you come along and insult him and *assault* him."

Tobin didn't say anything, but just watched her run a red light at Thirty-fourth Street and blow through a yellow light onto the downtown FDR Drive. He rubbed his right fist, which throbbed with a sweet pain, like a sexual afterglow.

"Don't you have anything to say?"

"You told me to shut up!"

"What kind of a pussy you turning into? You let a woman shut you up? You never let me shut you up before. That what these upscale, yuppie, Manhattan bimbos do to you? Put you in your place, like you're some kind of second-tier Brooklyn goon who can only talk when he's given permission? They make you sit down to pee, Tobin? So you don't get their designer bowl-seats wet? Grow your fucking balls back, Hank! This is me, Julie! Fight me and I'll know you're fighting for Henry."

"I just hit that big fuck for you."

"Yeah?"

"I didn't like the way he put his finger in your face."

She pressed harder on the accelerator, as if the thought of Hank Tobin fighting for her honor raced her blood. She weaved in and out of traffic.

"Thanks," she said.

"My pleasure," he said, shaking his pulsating hand.

"Moog is gonna be pissed at me."

"What do you give a shit?"

"He's a nice guy."

"Your boyfriend is a horse's ass."

"He's not really my boyfriend boyfriend. Laurie would say I'm 'talking' to him. Why am I even talking to *you* about this?"

"To make me fucking nuts."

"Moog's gonna help me try to find Lenny Kelly."

"He better find an icepack first."

"Moog doesn't know what Kelly looks like."

"Moog couldn't find his balls if they weren't in a bag. He didn't even recognize me. Lenny Kelly called me to tell me you two were together at the Italian consulate and then Starbucks. Neither you nor Sherlock Moog noticed him."

She looked at him to see if he was kidding. She realized he wasn't.

"Lenny Kelly followed us?"

"Yes. What the hell were you doing in the Italian consulate?"

"Research. I have a guy in vital statistics checking on some genealogy for me. I used him once before on an extradition case, searching for a mob perp who fled to Italy."

"What kind of research you doing now?"

"Family tree. He'll have it soon."

"In the middle of all of this you're doing a family tree? Jesus Christ, Jule, did you at least see Erin Kelly Levine?"

"For about forty-five seconds. She said she lost contact with her family after the fire ten years ago. She said she visited her brother regularly in prison over the years. But lost contact with her father. She says she has no doubt he's dead. But that she doesn't want a dime of his insurance money. She doesn't need it. Her husband's worth a few bil. She's good for high six figures. In fact her husband is negotiating to buy the firm. Then she'd be CEO. How ya like them golden apples? She's as cool as a pool, but when I brought up her mother, she literally broke into a sweat and folded her arms across her chest, as if trying to hold herself together. The kind of body lingo that always tells me there's something she's hiding. Just a hunch. But no way is this yuppie lady behind Henry's case. It's like it would be *beneath* her. You get the sense that Brooklyn is a faraway nation, on the other side of the globe, a place that she emigrated from. That her family died there."

"She's lying about at least one thing."

"What?"

Tobin filled Julie in on the meeting with Koutros, how he was being set up like Henry was set up, with Kelly gaining access into people's lives using his janitorial guise. Without betraying the sordid details, he told her that Lenny Kelly had dirty pictures and tapes and e-mails that would make his daughters hate him forever.

He wondered if Kelly had similar pictures of Julie with Moog. "Oh, God," he moaned.

"What?"

"Nothing," he said.

"The judge is a cheating dirtbag, too, isn't he?" Julie said. "It's a mental illness with men. God gave guys this wonderfully useful gift called the dick, but by the time you reach middle age, it causes mental illness in ninety-two percent of the species. It makes almost every one of you dirty swines self-destruct. You chase your dicks in circles, searching for the fountain of youth, and wind up screwing yourselves. So it's not really a bribery case he's involved in. He literally fucked himself, didn't he?"

"He'd plead guilty with an explanation to that. But one thing he was absolutely certain about was that no one but the father ever tried to visit Billy Kelly in jail over ten years. And he turned him away. Erin, the little sister, never visited."

As she plunged into the gloom of the small tunnel leading from the FDR to the Brooklyn Battery Tunnel, Julie drew a dreadful breath, held it, bit her lower lip, and let it out in a slow measured stream. "Oh, man, how's all that make you feel?"

He half-shrugged, widened his eyes. "What's done's done."

"That's what skells say. 'I can't un-ring the bell, so give me five years probation for killing five people in Wendy's.' It's lame, Hank. It's not good enough."

"What do you suggest I do, Julie? *What?*"

Julie turned right toward the tunnel, a few blocks south of Ground Zero, where the rebuilding had begun, passing city cops and state troopers positioned at the mouth of the Brooklyn-bound tube. One uniformed cop questioned a swarthy-looking man as his partner searched a plumbing-supply truck. The nervous Arab smoked a cigarette and answered questions, humiliated as a car pulsating with rap and filled with shouting young Italian-looking teenagers passed.

"Die you fuckin' camel jockey mudda fucker," shouted one, poking his head through the red Camaro sunroof.

"Your mother blows goats, you dirty dune coon," screamed a second kid with short hair and no sideburns, wearing a gold crucifix.

The Arab watched them disappear into the tunnel. *That's one way to recruit new fanatics to jihad,* Tobin thought.

Julie looked at Tobin and said, "The old Hank Tobin, the guy I married, he wouldn't need to ask that question."

Tobin fell quiet for the entire ride through the tunnel.

"What are you thinking about?" she asked, exiting onto the Gowanus Expressway.

"You."

"What about me?"

"The idea of you and Moog. . . . Never mind."

"You have any useful ideas?" she asked.

Tobin's cell phone rang.

Steve Clancy, the lawyer, said, "You better get to the federal lock-up right away. Henry's been hurt."

THIRTY

Henry lay in the prison hospital bed, one arm in a sling, the other handcuffed to the steel headboard. Bandages swathed his face. Gauze covered one eye.

"I'm okay, stop making a big deal out of it, Mom."

"They broke your goddamned arm and slashed your face," Julie said.

"Superficial wounds, Mom," Henry Jr. said. "I won't look like Al Capone."

Tobin looked at the deputy warden named Quentin, who stood with Steve Clancy near the gray steel door of the Brooklyn Federal prison hospital room, where a uniformed hack stood with his arms dangling at his sides, like a gunslinger ready to draw.

"How the hell . . . how did this happen?" Tobin asked Quentin.

"During the transfer," Quentin said. "He was in a holding pen while we processed him into the system and—"

"With other prisoners?" Tobin asked.

"Of course, with other prisoners. Your son is an adult. He's been insisting he go into general population. He doesn't want protective custody or isolation. We thought protective custody was the correct status. We made sure there were no Middle Eastern prisoners near him. But we can't keep track of everyone who converts to Islam in here. He was assaulted by three prisoners, all members of the Nation of Islam. We're trying to determine if any of them are connected to any of the designated terrorist groups like Al Qaeda."

"So the Nation of Islam rules the federal jails instead of the nation of the United States?" Tobin said.

Clancy clarified, "Mister Tobin doesn't mean to be sarcastic. He's distraught over his son's assault."

Tobin knew Clancy was right. He took a deep breath, careful not to offend the man in charge of his son's incarceration. "Sorry . . ."

"Your son is suspected of blowing up a mosque," Quentin said, never raising his voice. "If we had radical Jewish prisoners in this jail, we'd worry about them, too, because your son is also suspected of torching a synagogue. We do the best we can under the circumstances. This is an unfortunate incident that we hope will not be repeated. But be advised, one of his attackers has already told us that there is a *fatwa,* a holy contract, out on your son's life, Mister Tobin."

The word ricocheted around Tobin's brain like an assassin's bullet. He looked at Henry Jr. He was about the same age as most of the suicide bombers in Gaza.

Julie drifted over from the bed and said, *"Fatwa!* Like they had on Salman Rushdie? For chrissakes. That's a worldwide Islamic bounty on his head. Any Muslim who kills him is guaranteed a cash reward and paradise."

"Correct," Quentin said. "So now we have no choice but to put your son into isolation, twenty-four-hour lockdown. For his own safety."

"I already made a renewed plea for bail," Clancy said. "Denied. They want to transfer Henry to another state ASAP. I'm fighting that until he's at least grand juried."

"Can I spend a few minutes alone with him?" Tobin asked.

Quentin looked peeved and checked his watch. "I'll make an exception this one time because of the assault. But get it straight. Your son is accused of very serious crimes. He will get no special privileges. He is just another prisoner to us. You can have three minutes with him. You, or your wife. Take your pick."

Tobin made a facial plea to Julie. "I'll wait in the car," she said, blowing a kiss to Henry Jr. and telling him she loved him and not to despair. Julie left with Steve Clancy and Quentin.

Tobin approached Henry Jr.

"Keep a three-foot distance, sir," said the guard, stepping toward Tobin. "No touching."

"Can we have a little privacy here?" Tobin asked.

"There is no privacy in jail, Pop," Henry Jr. said.

"Thank you," the guard said, standing at the foot of the bed.

"How'd the Yanks do today?" Henry Jr. asked.

"Lost."

"Figures," Henry said, faking a laugh. "Mom okay?"

"She's strong. Hell of a woman."

"Ha. Too bad you didn't figure that out sooner. So what's the deal?"

"We're looking at stuff," he said, eyeballing the guard, tugging his ear.

"Me, too. *Life*."

"That's not gonna happen."

Tobin saw a plump, pregnant cockroach, like the ones that ruled his tenement childhood, crawling up the headboard of the bed. Tobin pulled a tissue from his pocket, reached out, and nabbed the roach in the tissue, crackling it between his thumb and forefinger.

"Stand the fuck back!" shouted the guard.

"Killing a roach, man," Tobin said, showing it to the guard.

"Just stand back three feet!"

"Okay," Tobin said, balling the roachy tissue in his fist. He realized that all his work, effort, luck, success, maneuvers, all his life's plans for success and dreams for his kids had come to this. His assaulted son chained to a bed that was crawling with roaches. The same roaches that inspired Tobin's climb to the top of his craft. He had never so much climbed to a destination as he scaled higher and higher away from the tenement roach that was the ultimate symbol of single-parent childhood squalor.

"Any sign of this guy you're looking for?" Henry said, his one useful eye popping from the guard to his father.

"Getting closer."

"That's what you always told editors when you had nothing. Me, too. I learned it from you."

"I want you to know that I know you're in here because of something I did. Something I wrote a long time ago. Not something you did."

"Remember the day you taught me to ride a bike, Pop?"

"Sure. Never forget."

"In Marine Park. You took off the training wheels. You let me go. You promised me that if I fell you'd be right there."

Tobin nodded and said, "You fell."

"You picked me up and made me do it again. And I fell again. And again. And again. And you picked me up every time."

"Then you just started pedaling, and you didn't fall anymore," Tobin said to Henry Jr.

Henry Jr. nodded. "Because I knew you'd be there in case I fell."

He thought immediately of Lenny Kelly, dressed as a white-haired parkie, talking about standing behind his son, Billy, on the baby swings to catch him if he fell.

"I remember."

"Pop, I need you to pick me up again. I need you to pick me up and get me the hell out of here, Pop. There're people in here who wanna kill me for Allah. For something I didn't do. I'm scared. Pick me up, Pop."

Tobin stood staring down at his injured, chained son.

"Time," said the guard. "Let's go, sir."

Tobin hesitated.

"I said *time,* sir. Don't make me say it again."

"Can I hug my son, please."

"No, sir."

"I'll pick you up, Henry. I promise I'll pick you up," Tobin said as the guard escorted him out of the room and slid shut the steel door with a deafening slam.

THIRTY-ONE

"How the hell can you eat at a time like this?" Julie asked as the waiter slid a platter of chicken and shrimp with broccoli in front of Tobin.

Julie sipped green tea. Madam Hu's Golden Bowl in Gravesend, around the corner from the site of the ten-year-old arson, filled up fast with diners. Couples on dates, Asian families with children, and old ladies wearing flowered summer hats that Tobin figured you could only purchase if you showed your half-fare card with a Brooklyn address. Customers sipped umbrella-shaded drinks, soft Asian Muzak tinkled from unseen speakers, and waitresses and waiters and busboys worked the tables of the popular upscale restaurant.

"Must be good, Chinese people eat here," Tobin said, checking his watch. It was 6:41 P.M. Dinner rush in Brooklyn started about 6:15 P.M. because most people liked to eat fast and race home in time to see their favorite TV shows.

"I could never understand that logic," Julie said. "That mean Chinese should flock to McDonald's because so many Americans eat there? Can't Chinese pick bad restaurants? I mean, if you told me it's great because Chinese gangsters eat here, maybe I'd believe you. . . ."

"You made your point," Tobin said, shoveling up florets of broccoli, sliced breast of chicken, and plump fresh shrimp in a perfect brown sauce with just a baby's teeth bite of hot spice. "Food's great. But I didn't come here to eat."

"You could have fooled me, Hank," she said, sipping her tea. "Henry's in a shit hole, carved up like a Butterball, chained like a mutt, probably eat-

241

ing snotted-in gruel made by *fatwa* fanatics who wanna poison him, and you're chowing down on the Madam Hu's Chef's Delight."

Tobin chopsticked another mouthful, sipped his Diet Coke, reached in his back pants pocket, and pulled out the balled tissue with which he'd killed the pregnant roach on his son's prison hospital headboard. Careful that no one was looking, Tobin peeled open the tissue and shook the roach into the middle of his beautiful plate of food.

"You're a fucking *animal*," Julie said, recoiling, ramming her cloth napkin against her mouth.

Tobin signaled for the waiter. The waiter hurried to the table. "Yes?" asked the waiter.

Tobin pointed at the roach and the football-shaped roach egg dangling from her undercarriage and said, "I'd like to see the owner and the chef, please."

The waiter's eyes widened, looked both ways at other diners, and reached for the plate. Tobin held on to the plate and waved a finger. "Bring the owner and the chef out to me, please."

The waiter banged through the swinging doors into the loud kitchen. Tobin heard shouting in English and Chinese and Vietnamese. Julie turned her face away from the dead, pregnant roach, still covering her mouth with the cloth napkin.

"You could have just asked to talk to them, sans roach," Julie said.

"Nothing like having people on the defensive," Tobin said. "The best weapon in ambush journalism is embarrassing physical evidence."

"Your same shit ethics got us into this mess."

"Cheap shot."

"I know. But I meant it."

The kitchen doors swung open and a tall, slender, twenty-something Asian woman who carried herself with an elegant gait approached Tobin's table followed by a white man in his thirties who wore a chef's hat on his head. The same guy Tobin had the run-in with in the morning. His arms were covered in tattoos like almost everyone else in this corner of Brooklyn, as if people exchanged tattoo gift certificates for Christmas. Tobin adjusted his glasses, rubbed his smooth chin, and patted his dark hair. The little guy didn't recognize him.

"Good evening, lady and sir, I am Debbie Hu-Buckles," she whispered. "I'm the owner. This is my husband, Fred, also our chef. I understand there has been an unfortunate unpleasantry."

"Lemme see that plate," Buckles said, leaning over the table, reaching for Tobin's dish. His tattooed arms resembled a couple of graffitied subway cars from the 1980s. "I prepared that dish myself. Our place is spotless, pal. We got no cock-a-roaches here. We eat here. Our kids eat here. I got a guy cleans here like he was saying a High Mass. Immaculate! We change the earl four times a week. We lay boric acid. We get the exterminator twice a month. . . ."

Tobin hadn't heard anyone call oil "earl" since he moved to Manhattan.

"Freddie," said Debbie Hu. "Let me handle this. . . ."

"This's the oldest scam in the book," Buckles said. "Four A.M., after last call, all-night Greek greasy-spoon, the old roach-a-dope in the hash browns routine might work. Not here. . . ."

Debbie Hu elbowed him, whispering, "Be quiet, Fred."

Tobin continued to stare at Fred's left arm, remembering him draping it over the shoulder of sixteen-year-old Debbie Hu as they stood on the street watching her family's house burn to the ground a decade before.

Tobin cocked his head sideways, staring at Buckles's left arm, as if searching in the blue-and-red collage of tattoos for a certain one. His arm was a cluttered, overlapping mess. The retired Catholic in Tobin imagined that Fred Buckles's arm looked just like his soul, blemished with a lifetime of indelible, unforgivable sins. Tattoos of naked strippers, ballerinas with bare asses hanging out, a prepubescent Coppertone girl being mounted by her little dog. A devil clutching a pitchfork with one hand, his crotch with the other. Mickey Mouse copulating with Minnie Mouse. Archie engaged in a ménage-à-trois with Betty and Veronica. A mermaid performing oral sex on Neptune. More vulgar tattoos of Woody Woodpecker, Goldilocks, Little Red Riding Hood, Popeye and Olive Oyl.

Happy childhood, Tobin thought.

And scattered in with the skillful, professional, and colorful tattoos were the crude self-inflicted ones that always read like a portable rap sheet. Guys in jail often gave themselves tattoos to pass the idle cell time. Winding thread around the shaft of a sewing needle, they dipped it in India ink and jabbed their own skin in a patient and painful game of connect the dots. The faded blue-gray names of at least a half-dozen of Fred Buckles's old girlfriends—including Cookie, Lulu, Maria—were buried in the frantic tapestry of his left arm. Tobin kept searching the arm for the one name he vaguely remembered, more an impression than a memory. Like a joker in a deck. A "what's-wrong-with-this-picture" imprint that still nagged him all these years later. One of those stubborn details that at first glance mean nothing but later speak volumes. And yet he only knew that there was a detail, couldn't remember exactly what it was. Just that it was a name that didn't fit.

Hundreds of other tattoos had been added in the years since, like an illustrated ledger of one very disturbed man's evolution. But Buckles's arm kept moving, up and down in frustration, also showing off his rippling biceps, triceps, and powerful forearm that were wired with cables of pronounced vein. The sleeve of his white T-shirt also covered the top half of his arm.

Buckles noticed Tobin staring at his arm and said, "Wanna take a pitcher? My father-in-law sells Kodak disposables next door."

Three of the Hu children rushed out of the kitchen, the oldest a gorgeous Eurasian girl of about ten. Followed by a boy who couldn't have been more than a year younger and another girl about five.

"Ma, we wanna go hang," said the eldest.

"Ixnay, now am-scray inside," Buckles yelled, with a hooked thumb, using the pig Latin for "no, scram."

"Come on, old man," the oldest kid said. "Can't we even hang on the stoop?"

"No," Buckles said. "Am I talkin' Greek? The world's filled with freaks."

"I'll be with you in a minute, Lily," Debbie Hu said to her daughter. The disappointed kids pushed back through the swinging doors.

Debbie Hu noticed patrons on line at the front door watching the commotion at the table. Other diners turned to ogle and gape.

"We will certainly replace the dish," Debbie Hu said. "And give you a gift certificate for a future meal."

Buckles said, "Joint's spotless."

Debbie Hu waved for Fred Buckles to be quiet, a dismissive gesture that angered her husband.

"Actually we were just in the neighborhood because we were taking a walk down memory lane," Tobin said. "We were both around the corner one night about ten years ago when there was a big fire. . . ."

Debbie Hu looked at Tobin, blinking several times. "Long time ago," she said.

"I bet her that this restaurant was owned by the same people who got burned out back then," Tobin said, nodding toward Julie, who kept the napkin over her mouth, staring at the roach. "You were the family whose house was burned, no?"

"My parents still own the rebuilt house and the store," Debbie Hu said. "They expanded. When my husband came back from chef school, we opened this restaurant."

Tobin continued to focus on Fred Buckles's left arm. Buckles became self-conscious and folded his powerful arms across his chest.

"Look, we're sorry about the whatchimyacallit in your dish," Fred said. "But as you can see, we're busy. My wife made a more than generous offer and I'd like—"

"I apologize for my husband's abruptness," Debbie said.

"Chefs are temperamental," Tobin said.

"Whadda you, a shrink, pal?"

"Look, I don't want a replacement meal. I just need some answers."

Debbie and Fred looked baffled. "You INS?" Fred asked. "This a touch or what? Putting the arm on me? I passed four straight health inspections. You wanna check greencards, Social Security numbers, for mouse shit, skinned cats? Peking pigeon and sweet and sour Dobermans? Be my guest, pal."

"Be quiet, Fred."

Tobin smiled and said, "Did you know Billy Kelly well, Debbie?"

Freed Buckles squinted, his breath a little short, holding up his hands as if for protection. He assessed the situation, glancing from Julie to Tobin. He looked harder at Tobin's face, as if there was something familiar about him. Buckles scratched his head.

"Billy Kelly?" Debbie Hu said. "Is that what this is about?"

"Sort of," Tobin said.

"Get to the point, pal," Buckles said, leaning closer to Tobin's face, his breath heavy with tobacco and beer. "You come in here, roach-a-dope me, asking about a ten-year-old arson. Talking Billy Kelly. For what? The fuck is this?"

"That fire is still smoldering," Tobin said.

"Talk English, not fortune-cookie riddles," Buckles said, clutching Tobin's shoulder with a tight, strong fist. "Or I'll break your fuckin' hips and send you home on a dolly."

Tobin said, "Take your hand off my shoulder, elf. Or I'll take this roach for a stroll around your store. Then I'll make you fucking eat it."

"You threatening me?" Buckles said.

Julie took the napkin from her mouth, flapped open her wallet to reveal the gold shield, and said, "No, I am. For threatening him. And assaulting him."

Buckles recoiled from the badge like a vampire from a crucifix.

"Oh, come on, man," Buckles said.

"Please," Debbie Hu whispered. "Please, we've done nothing wrong. This is our life. Please. We work hard. We have children."

"I see my PO religiously," Buckles said, low and seething. "I work my ass off here. I support my kids. I pay my taxes. I'm clean as a Yankee bean. You want a piss sample? Take one right now. You won't find anything stronger than One-A-Days and Bud. They might be rewriting laws for terrorists, but you can't just come in here and bust my fuckin' balls for piss and giggles."

"Wanna see?" Julie said, opening her pocketbook wide enough to reveal the gun and handcuffs. "Just an arrest violates your parole."

Debbie glared at Buckles. He deflated as fast as a punctured tire.

"Can we at least talk in the back room?" Debbie Hu asked, faking a polite smile for show in front of the other customers. "We have customers. . . ."

"How about outside, on the corner?" said Tobin, standing and leaving a $50 bill for the waiter. Buckles noticed the gesture. He lifted the fifty and held it up to a rice-paper lamp, studied both sides, and rolled it between his fingers, checking for ink.

"Fred!" Debbie Hu said as Buckles dropped a cloth napkin on top of the dish with the dead roach and placed a glass on top of the fifty-dollar bill. He snapped his finger for a waiter to clean it up. The waiter hurried over.

On the corner Tobin, Julie, Debbie Hu, and Fred Buckles stood outside Hu's Superette and stared down the block at the house that had been torched a decade earlier. Buckles lit an unfiltered Pall Mall with his disposable lighter, spit out a fleck of tobacco, and said, "What'd you say your name was?"

"Capone," said Julie. "Detective Julie Capone."

"From what? You guys from cold case?"

"Yeah," she lied.

"Billy Kelly done his time," Buckles said. "Found Jesus. Why you still busting his balls?"

"Maybe he didn't do what everyone says he did," Julie said.

Buckles looked concerned, took a heavy drag on his smoke, and blew out a heavy gray stream, adding a few smoke rings. He had jail tattooed all over his behavior. "That's a closed case, not a cold case, guys," Buckles said, looping his left arm over his wife's shoulder the way Tobin had seen him do it that night of the fire, the tattoos now illuminated in the sun the way they were that night by flames.

"They caught Billy with the gasoline-stained clothes, the gasoline, the same typewriter that was used to send the racist letters to my family," said Debbie Hu.

"But he never even had a trial," Tobin said.

Now in the bright sun, with Buckles's left arm stretched across his wife's shoulder, the sleeve of his shirt riding up to the shoulder, Tobin found what he'd been looking for. On the underside of his left arm, lost between Mickey banging Minnie and the mermaid going down on Neptune, Tobin spotted the tattoo that had nagged his shrouded memory. The legend was hand-dotted inside a lopsided, self-drawn, old blue heart, with one of Cupid's bent arrows piercing it.

Tobin said, "Just for the record, did the arresting officer at the time ask you how long you two had been dating?"

Debbie looked at Fred and said, "No, I don't think so. . . ."

"Well, how long had you been dating?" Tobin asked.

Debbie said, "A few months, but—"

"What the hell does it matter?" Fred said. "We been married almost nine years now."

"How old is your oldest daughter, Lily?" Tobin asked.

"She'll be ten next month—"

"You didn't answer my question," Fred Buckles said. "What difference does it make how long we were dating when Billy Kelly torched her parents' house?"

"No particular reason," Tobin said, reaching over and pinching the tattoo on Buckles's arm where the legend in the old faded heart read: *Fred&Erin4-Ever.* "But how long was that after you broke up with Erin Kelly?"

Julie's eyes popped, looked at Tobin. Debbie glared at the old tattoo, currents of old jealousy igniting her eyes.

"What kind of teeny-bopper bullshit question is that?" Buckles asked, pulling his arm free, rubbing the old telltale tattoo. "So I dated Erin for a little while before I dated Debbie. What of it? I haven't laid eyes on her since the fire."

"Oh, nothing," Tobin said. "I just thought it was funny that you once dated the sister of the guy who did ten years for torching your new girlfriend's house. Who you were forced to marry. But it's probably just a coincidence."

Debbie stared at her husband like some old buried truth was clawing to break free.

"Forced to marry?" Debbie asked.

"What did you say your name was?" Buckles asked Tobin.

Tobin said, "I didn't say."

"I didn't see your badge."

"I didn't show one."

"Yo, I got nothing more to say to yuse two," Buckles said. "You wanna ask me anything else, I'll call my lawyer. I'll roll the dice with my PO."

"What are you implying, here? Are you saying you think my husband burned my parents' house?" Debbie asked.

"Stop talkin' to them," Buckles said.

"I never said that," Tobin said.

"Inside," Buckles said, grabbing Debbie's arm. She yanked herself free as Tobin led Julie to the Taurus. Climbing into the passenger seat, Tobin saw Debbie and Fred Buckles exchanging heated words, not all of them audible. But three of the words were loud and clear: "Fucking Erin Kelly."

THIRTY-TWO

Julie parked the Taurus on E. Thirty-seventh Street, and they sneaked through the alley next to Julie's rear-neighbor's house and entered Julie's house through the back door like a pair of burglars. Tobin was alarmed to hear the buzz of the press in front of the house again.

"Something must have happened," he said. "The reporters are back out front. There must be a new development. . . ."

Inside, their nineteen-year-old daughter sat with her head on the kitchen table, sobbing into her arms. Her blouse was dotted with blood.

"Baby doll, you okay?" Tobin said.

Laurie said, "I can't take it anymore."

Julie ran to her, crouched, lifted Laurie's head from her arms. Scratches covered her face and a clump of her lustrous dark hair had been ripped from the back of her scalp, leaving a sore raspberry of bright blood.

"I have to dodge reporters to get in and out of my house again," she said, her frazzled voice bordering hysteria. "I'm at a party on the beach down at Kingsborough between classes. The news comes on the radio saying my brother's been attacked in jail. I hear two girls from school, dirty Arab bitches, gloating, goofing, laughing about it, saying Henry got what he deserved. I stuck up for him. And we wound up in a big fucking fight."

"It's okay," Julie said, hugging her daughter, then holding her at arm's length. "You stuck up for your brother. You took some lumps. Lemme get some peroxide."

Julie hurried to the bathroom. Tobin took a seat at the table, next to his daughter. He brushed the hair from her eyes and assessed her scratched-up face.

249

"Henry's gonna be okay, baby doll," Tobin said.

"You sure? I heard they tried to stab him. These sick Arab fucks."

"He's fine," Tobin said. "And they weren't Arabs. Easy on that kind of talk."

"They said they were Islamics," Laurie said.

"Jailhouse Muslims," Julie said, returning with the peroxide, dabbing Laurie's face. "Most convert for protection and better food."

"Whatever, Arabs, Islamics," Laurie said. "Sicko, psycho, fundamentalist fucks! I fought two Arab bitches and then I come home, and I don't have the key for the back door. And your asshole 'journalist' pals are out front taking pictures of me all beat up. I feel like throwing some fucking bombs of my own. I'd start by throwing one onto the front lawn to blow up all your creepy, demented reporter pals. Then I wouldn't mind blowing up a few fucking mosques myself."

"Hey," Tobin said. "Knock it off. Now! Watch your filthy mouth and your loose tongue. People can go to jail for just *saying* stuff like that these days. Don't think there aren't bugs in this house. You're saying angry, ignorant, reckless things."

"Look who's talking! Maybe Mom was right about you. I always gave you the benefit of the doubt, Dad. Maybe you made a mistake. You're human. But maybe I was wrong. You cheat on Mom, wreck the family, take a hike, and now you think you have some kind of moral authority around here all of a sudden? You walk out the door when I'm a kid, and you come home like a white knight when there's trouble? Trouble you started with your bullshit column! And try to tell *me* how to fucking think? No way, old man! BOMB THE FUCKING SHIT OUTTA THESE ARAB FUCKS! There, I said it."

"Terrific," Tobin said. "Intelligent talk like that, maybe they'll let you transfer to a four-year school."

"Hank, bad time for Fred McMurray lectures."

Laurie said, "What's he doing here anyway, Mom? Shouldn't he be home in his penthouse banging an intern?"

"Hey," Julie said, putting a finger into Laurie's face. "That's over the line, lady! I'll wash out your friggin' mouth with my fist, you talk to your father like that again, understand? I don't give a shit how pissed off you are. We're all pissed off. All upset. Stop feeling sorry for yourself. Don't you dare think the whole world's on Laurie's shoulders. We all hurt. The whole family hurts."

Laurie stood up from the table. "Some fucking family," she said. "The Tobins. Twenty-four-hours-a-day cable, headlines, talk shows, radio, the net. We're so proud of the name that my mother and father are incognito, chasing their vanished eighties youth. Pathetic. The Tobin name is a fucking curse."

Laurie stormed toward the back door, grabbing a key from a wall ring.

"Where you going?"

"I'm sleeping over Megan's. She's blessed with a normal family. Then maybe I'll join the army to kill these fucks. And become a hero like Jessica Lynch."

Same mindset as the Arab kids who flock to jihad, Tobin thought.

She exited through the rear of the house, slamming the door behind her.

Tobin and Julie looked at each other. There was an unspoken sadness and a general shame of failure, of letting their children down.

There is no greater human defeat.

"Thanks for sticking up for me," Tobin said.

"This isn't how it should be, Hank," Julie said. "Mother defending father from beat-up daughter, son in a jailhouse hospital bed with a contract on his head. Bombarded from outside. Fighting each other. What's left of our beautiful little family is being destroyed, Hank."

He clung to one straw of hope in that statement, her use of the word "our," as if somewhere deep in her heart she still considered him family

He walked to her, put his arms around her. "Maybe I should stay here tonight," he said, kissing the top of her pixie-blond head.

Julie was rigid and cold, devoid of affection. "Nah," she said. "That ain't gonna happen, Hank."

He let go of her. Nodded. Abashed.

"You can take the Taurus," she said, tossing him her keys.

"See ya tomorrow," he said and left through the back door.

And felt like he was abandoning what was left of his family all over again.

THIRTY-THREE

Tobin drove down Bedford Avenue, the longest street in Brooklyn, his eyes weary, his right hand pulsating from punching Moog, his stomach grumping, wishing he'd eaten more of the Chinese. He steered toward the distant, undefeatable glow of the New York skyline and realized, as he stopped for a red light and looked up at the street sign of the cross street, that he was on the corner of Avenue L in Midwood. Just three blocks from the Sinai Torah Temple that Henry Jr. was suspected of firebombing a month before.

LL had sent Tobin an e-mail photo of a man in a hooded outfit identical to the one Henry was wearing when arrested, firing upon the temple. A mustard-colored Explorer dominated the photograph. Tobin reached in his stack of four-by-five-inch computer-printout photos, chose that incriminating shot, and drove straight to the synagogue through the silent, deserted streets of the residential neighborhood, which were shadowy with lush leafy summer trees that wavered in the thin night breeze.

He knew police patrols and the NYPD-approved civilian Shomrim patrol cruised the area. Tobin had done a column on Shomrim once, an unarmed neighborhood watch group equipped with red cherry lights, sirens, spotlights, handcuffs, walkie-talkies, and a sophisticated block-watcher and radio-dispatch network. But some of the more zealous members had been accused of overstepping their power, stopping and frisking black kids, and on occasion even assaulting minority civilians. Other members of Shomrim used their police toys as a license to speed, run red lights, and double-park. Many members of the black community resented them and believed that cheap politicians in City Hall handed out these police credentials to members of Shomrim in exchange for the powerful Brooklyn Jewish–voting bloc.

But even Tobin had to agree that this civilian patrol was a welcome presence in these jittery times, especially in a neighborhood where a temple had been torched. And after it was revealed that those responsible for the 1993 World Trade Center bombing had first considered attacking Jewish neighborhoods in Brooklyn, before doing the math and deciding that they could kill more Jews in the Twin Towers. After witnessing the handiwork of what a nail bomb could do to a morning bus in Jerusalem, Tobin shivered thinking of a similar bomb on an Avenue J or Thirteenth Avenue bus on a busy Sunday shopping day. It would tear a hole through the soul and psyche of his city.

Tobin waited for a dark van with tinted windows to pass him. Then a station wagon turned left, creeping past. Two more dark vans passed each other on Bedford Avenue, each one honking three times, as if in greeting. Then the intersection became still. Not a car or person on the street. Lampposts hummed. The traffic light turned green. Tobin made a right and parked the car at a hydrant across from the Sinai Torah Temple.

He walked to the front of the charred temple, which was already under reconstruction. Palming the small paper photo in his left hand, he tried to duplicate the framing with the viewfinder of the disposable camera—as Julie had across from the mosque. Tobin backed up across Avenue L to Crosby, until the vantage point of the photo came into approximate perspective. He turned. He was standing on the northeast corner of L and Crosby Avenue, in front of an abandoned store with glass wax covering the windows. One three-inch circle of glass wax had been wiped clean. *Large enough for a camera lens,* he thought.

Tobin leaned his face against the glass, closed one eye, peered into the charcoal darkness of the empty store, and knew the photo had been shot from inside.

Then he heard squealing tires.

Shouting.

Doors opening.

Doors slamming.

Feet shuffling.

Men shouting. In Yiddish. In English. He looked up into blinding light. Three unmarked vans and a Pontiac station wagon faced him from different points of the intersection. One mounting the sidewalk. High beams blinding him. Tobin heard a baseball bat rattle to the ground. Then a shell clacking into a shotgun. Tobin crushed the computer-paper photograph into a tight little ball in his fist, pretended to cough, and buried it in the gully beneath his tongue.

Four men held shotguns; three others had baseball bats. All of them wore yarmulkes.

"Frisk the bastard," said an unarmed bantam of a man with a bright copper beard that looked like exposed electrical cable. His Israeli accent was thick, and he was the one in charge.

"Fuck you doing?" Tobin shouted, his words garbled with the paper under his tongue. No way was he letting these nuts find the photo. *That* photo.

A large bearded man with a black yarmulke buried the barrel of a shotgun under Tobin's chin. He grabbed the disposable camera from Tobin's hand. "Shut the fuck up."

Two other burly men in dark jackets spun Tobin and shoved him ten feet down Crosby Avenue, pinned him against a brick wall, frisked him, checking his balls, his belt, the soles of his shoes.

"I am Rabbi Yitzak Cohn from JAT."

"What the hell is JAT?"

"Jews Against Terror, sir."

The looney tune from Queens, Tobin thought. *The one from the mini riot outside the jail.*

Tobin asked, "Then why the hell are you terrorizing me?"

Cohn slapped Tobin across the face. Fear and rage boiled Tobin's brain in its own juices. "Who the fuck do you think you are?" Tobin said.

"Why were you taking pictures of our temple?" Cohn asked, eyes shifting like a casino pit boss's. Rabbi Cohn had a detached, metallic voice like an operator on a telephonic-information tree. Tobin had zero doubt that this little man would kill him without a detectable rise in his pulse rate.

Tobin hesitated. He didn't want to tell him that he was Hank Tobin, father of Henry Tobin Jr., the young man accused of torching the temple. "I was . . . curious."

"Curious? Okay, kill him, fellas. Leave his body as a message to others who come into good Jewish neighborhoods with bad intentions. Hurry. We have a community to protect."

The little man turned and walked toward the station wagon. One of his gunsels pumped his shotgun.

"Wait!" Tobin screamed. "You guys fucking nuts? Okay, look, I'm Hank—"

Before he could finish the sentence, police cars descended on the scene from four directions, penning the area. A helicopter hovered, its brilliant high-intensity spotlight turning the Brooklyn night to day. Other cars skidded to the scene, with bearded men from the legitimate NYPD-supported Shomrim neighborhood patrol piling out, chasing and tackling the armed Jewish vigilantes.

Rabbi Cohn raced twenty yards down the block, leapt, grabbed the lower rung of a fire escape, and scaled it like a gymnast. An overweight cop tried to pursue him but dropped from the ladder and a young, fitter cop scaled after the militant rabbi. By the time he got to the first floor, the little man had scrambled to the tenement roof.

The chase was on.

Tobin ran twenty yards in the opposite direction, trying to get distance, perspective. Trying to get his eyes and his mind around the situation, panic bubbling in his veins.

Tobin's heart raced.

He tried to swallow. He didn't have enough saliva. He yanked out his notebook, making hasty, furious, big scrawly notes. His one instinctive reaction, his offense and defense. His weapon—a *pen*. His bullets—*words*. On paper.

Cops shouted for the Shomrim members to "get lost," that they would handle it. The Shomrim patrol leader shouted at handcuffed JAT guys. "You disgrace us!" screamed the Shomrim leader, built like a brown bear.

"Cowards," shouted the JAT guy who'd held the shotgun on Tobin, struggling with police. "Do nothings! Lambs! Professional victims. Never again!"

Two, big, pink-faced cops folded him into the back of a squad car.

Tobin watched in disbelief, then he felt someone gazing over his shoulder as he scribbled his frantic notes to keep from collapsing. He turned with a start, breathless.

Captain Vinny Hunt said, "You keep getting yourself in jams, Hank."

Tobin was surprised he recognized him.

"Sorry, after that stunt on Coney Island Avenue today, I tailed you for a few hours. Saw you and your ex get your new hairdos. . . ."

"I . . . they . . . I was just . . . these maniacs were going to *kill* me. . . ."

"Nah, these JAT brats're mostly all talk," Hunt said. "The shotguns are all unloaded or loaded with blanks. Between you and me, the guy with the gun to your neck was my deep-cover guy. Cohn has more loose screws than a hardware store. But he's a stunt-meister. Wants cheap publicity. Wants people to think he's the new Meir Kahane. He's about as dangerous as Woody Allen, but he's capable of causing a riot. We've been watching him. And sure as shit he picked you because you were at the wrong place at the right time. I want this nut in the can so if you give us a statement, I'll book him for assault, unlawful imprisonment, menacing—"

"You want a statement from me? Under the circumstances? Across the street from the temple my kid is suspected of torching?"

"Hank, Cohn's a loose canon, but you keep poking your nose where it don't belong, one of these crazy fucks is gonna pop you. They're determined to start a street war with the New York Arabs. I'm also watching that other Arab group you messed with earlier, Umma. They're mostly law abiding and work with us, the Arabic version of Shomrim. But they have a radical fringe, too, and they're just itching for one of these meshuggeneh Jews to waste one of them so they can call open season on all Jews. Then you'll start seeing suicide belts. I don't need you in the middle of this shit, understand?"

"As a journalist I have the right to investigate anything I want," Tobin said. "My press card says I can cross police lines."

"Me and my guys at the Intelligence Division have spent months tracking these Looney Tunes on both sides of Coney Island Avenue, radical Jews and Arabs, and then in one day I find you almost causing two incidents. What gives, Hank? We tailed you today. You on a suicide mission of your own or what?"

"Why were you following me?"

"I had to. You and your wife gave us probable cause. Besides, we got pressure from the Joint Task Force to keep an eye on you. I don't take them serious, but I go through the motions, so I can keep an eye on them."

"My kid's been framed, Vinny."

"Walk with me," Hunt said. "And maybe you better talk to me. Can we do this off the record?"

"Yeah, in fact I want it that way, too."

"Don't play me, Hank. I got Jimbo's death in the mix here."

"I got a kid facing life. Don't play with me."

As his detectives and uniformed cops rounded up the JAT members, Vinny Hunt took Tobin for a walk-and-talk around the block. Tobin told him as much as he thought he could trust him with, even off the record. He didn't tell Vinny about Chan, the herbalist, or the other damaging photos that Lenny Kelly kept as an ace in the hole. Or his evolving theories on what had actually happened at that arson a decade earlier. But he told

Vinny Hunt that no one wanted to believe him about Kelly being alive, not Cox, not Mona Falco, not even Kelly's own son and daughter.

"Now I understand why you're sniffing around that old arson," Vinny said. "That's the one where Mona Falco made her bones."

"Yeah, where I met her."

"Now she's with the Joint Task Force assholes," Hunt said.

"You don't sound like you're too fond of them."

"I hold them personally responsible for Jimbo's death and twenty-eight hundred others."

"How?"

"The FBI blew the whole terrorist investigation from the beginning," Hunt said. "I was a new detective working in the Seventeenth Squad right after crazy Kahane was killed in 1990. The head of the squad was a guy named Eddie Norris. Day after Kahane was killed there was a big meeting on the thirteenth floor of One Police Plaza. The head of NYPD detectives was there. The top New York FBI guys were also there. Michael Daly wrote a column about all this in the *Daily News*."

"I remember, but refresh my memory. . . ."

"Top brass asked if the guy they busted for killing Kahane in the midtown hotel ballroom, El Sayed A Nosair—"

"He had an address on Prospect Park Southwest."

"That's right. Anyway, PD brass asks if he acted alone. I remember Norris saying, 'Absolutely not. We have two other people we think are involved.' There were two other Arabs in Nosair's apartment when Norris and the rest of us in our squad got a warrant to search it. Cab drivers, what else? Both admitted being outside the hotel where Kahane was whacked. We carted two filing cabinets worth of documents, written in Arabic, from Nosair's apartment to our squad room at the Seventeenth Precinct."

"What did the chief of detectives say to Norris?"

"He said, 'You handle the Kahane murder. They'll handle the conspiracy.' "

"Meaning the FBI?" Tobin asked.

"Yep. And the Feds said, 'We have no evidence to indicate anyone else was involved.' We left. Eddie Norris was fuming. But not as pissed off as he was when the Feds showed up and carted away the two filing cabinets of papers. All they did was sit on them for three years before they had it translated."

"What were in the cabinets?"

"Only a bomb manual, military training guides, and an assassination list. Oh, and photos of New York landmarks including the World Trade Center. One document bore the name of a new organization formed by a big, skinny fuck named Osama bin Laden called Al Qaeda. There was a handwritten sermon from the blind Sheik Omar Abdel-Rahman calling on his congregants to attack America and quote, 'blow up its edifices.' Unquote. It also later turned out that the FBI had a phone intercept in 1990 of the blind Sheik Rahman speaking to our friend Nosair about 'attacking big buildings, attack skyscrapers.' This is all public record now, thanks to Daly's column in the *Daily News*. They had all this shit for three years. Then on February 26, 1993, came the first bombing of the trade center. One of the bombers was one of the two cab drivers from Nosair's apartment that the FBI ignored in 1990. They didn't even share the information with the CIA, because of their idiotic rivalry. Eight years later these clowns still couldn't connect the dots before September 11."

"Jesus Christ," Tobin said.

"Hey, Jimbo didn't have to *die*. If those guys had done their jobs the way they were supposed to back then, maybe Jimbo and twenty-eight hundred other people would be alive today. And what really pisses me off now is that one of the FBI agents who blew the original case now runs the goddamned Joint Task Force."

"Luke Cox?"

Hunt nodded. "But we have a former CIA guy running the seven-hundred-member NYPD Intelligence Division now. As you might expect, he has no use for the FBI. So the JTTF works more hand in hand with the new NYPD Counterterrorism Bureau."

"It's like law enforcement Scrabble," Tobin said.

"But notice that the Counterterrorism Bureau has the word 'bureau' in their name, because they are essentially in bed with the FBI. But I run the field operations of the Intelligence Division like it's more than a job, Hank. For me it's family business. We investigate loonies like this Rabbi Cohn in our city. And all kinds of foreigners. And scary Arabs. Since Iraq, the whole world hates us more than ever. And the place the crazies'll probably aim that hate is New York. We have guys and gals who speak Pashtun, Urdu, Arabic, Fujianese. Every dialect you can think of. And I think we should have had your kid's case under our purview. But Mona Falco was just a little too eager to make it a hate-crime case for herself, before getting promoted to the Counterterrosim Bureau, working with JTTF."

"I'm getting confused," Tobin said.

"The NYPD has two separate units working in the war on terrorism," Hunt said. "The one I work for has very little affiliation with the NYPD/FBI Joint Terrorism Task Force. The unit Mona Falco just joined, the Counter-terrorism Bureau, is part of the task force. And even more eager to lateral your son's case to the Feds. It's like she didn't want to let go of Henry Tobin Jr. At first I thought it was because she wanted to dump the case because you and Mona had reignited your old fling."

"You knew about that?"

"Who didn't? But then I realized she was involved with someone else. And that you were chasing your wife. Even over someone as perfect as Dani Larsen."

"Are there any secrets left in life?"

"No. We can find out anything about anyone. And what I found out about Mona Falco is that she wants to be the first female commissioner. Between you and me, because I don't trust the Feds, my unit keeps a very close eye on what the JTTF does. And especially what it *doesn't* do. So I have a full plate."

"I understand. But don't you think we'd all be a little better off if, instead of investigating each other, NYPD spying on the FBI, and vice versa, that everyone worked together against the same common enemy?"

"That would make too much sense," Hunt said. "And, look, Hank, sorry but I don't think I can get anyone in the brass to launch an official investigation into all these things you're saying. But I wanna believe you, Hank. Even though I know someone with a kid in the can will do and say just about anything to get him out. But considering Cox and Falco are involved, and refuse to listen to you, I'll give you the benefit of a doubt. Come to me with some hard evidence—and not some bullshit mechanical voice on the phone—and I'll look into it. I'll give you some of what little spare time I have if you will do me a favor."

"Name it."

"You really done with Dani Larsen?"

"Yeah. We were never really serious. She deserves better than me. She's a terrific chick and talented reporter."

Hunt smiled, rubbed his eye in that boyish way of his, and said, "Will you, ya know, tell her what a wonderful guy I am? Use the magic Hank Tobin words. Sell her on me."

"I don't think I'll have to sell too hard. But it'll be my pleasure to play matchmaker. Can you do something for me overnight?"

"I'll try."

"Can you pull up the rap sheet on a guy named Fred Buckles, white guy, works as a chef at Madam Hu's Golden Bowl, probably born and raised in Brooklyn."

"Good restaurant. Fred Buckles. Name sounds familiar. I'll pull his sheet."

By the time they had circled the block, Rabbi Cohn was in handcuffs in the back of a detective car. Four others were in custody.

Hunt leaned close to Tobin and said, "Not for nothing, but you oughta keep your daughter from talking too loud about bombs."

Tobin knew Julie's house was bugged, but Hunt shocked him with his verification.

"Yeah?"

"I was you, I'd get an exterminator, and spray the house," Vinny said. "Specially around the stand-up lamp in the living room. Follow me?"

Tobin nodded.

"Hey, by the way," Hunt said. "Did you bring that asshole Moog into the loop on all of this stuff you're telling me?"

"Not really," Tobin said, and then remembered Julie talking to him on the cell phone on the drive to the Lucky Seven tavern. "Julie used to be his partner and asked him to run a few things down."

"Oh, that explains it then."

"Explains what?"

"I mean it should be pretty clear to you, Hank. Who do you think planted the bug in your wife's house? Who else has access, Hank? Moog is back with his wife, has a full-time mistress on the job, who I hear might be Mona Falco. . . ."

"Moog and Falco," Tobin said. *Holy shit. It explains everything.*

"That's the skinny, and now it's pretty obvious to me this runaround lowlife is fucking around on his wife and his mistress by trying to get in your ex-wife's pants, too. That's if he isn't already, no offense."

"What's your vibe on that?" Tobin asked, his head spinning. "You think so?"

"You really wanna know, Hank?"

"Yeah, I really wanna know. You think Moog and Julie are getting it on?"

"Why else would he be over Julie's house right now?" Vinny Hunt asked, checking his watch. "He showed up right after you left."

THIRTY-FOUR

Tobin drove right back to Julie's block, the human jealousy virus pulsing in his veins. Moog's Jeep Cherokee was parked in Julie's driveway. The press still hung around but kept their distance by the corner gas station as promised. Tobin slouched in the Taurus for the better part of an hour and finally he saw Julie's front door open. She kissed Moog good night on the stoop.

Tobin felt like he'd been knifed.

Then he'd followed Moog on the westbound Belt Parkway to Bay Ridge, careful to tail the savvy cop in a different lane, several car lengths behind. Then he trailed Moog on surface streets to a slate-roofed, two-story red-brick home on Colonial Road in Bay Ridge where a little wooden sign hung from the mailbox: THE MOOGS.

Moog passed two bicycles chained to a standpipe as he eased down the driveway to the two-car garage, where a basketball hoop was affixed above the mechanical door. Tobin parked under a leafy tree across the street, in a deep pool of shadow. He cut his lights and engine. He watched the remote-activated garage door yawn open. Tobin's heart raced when Moog's headlights illuminated the second car in the garage.

A brand-new mustard-colored Explorer.

Tobin drove home in a weary, hazy stupor.

Of the half-dozen reporters and three photographers who stood outside his Manhattan apartment building, not one recognized Tobin with his shave, haircut, dye job, glasses, jeans, and sneakers. Most of the reporters just glanced at him and kept gabbing amongst themselves. Waiting for news to fall off the back of a truck.

Tobin rode the elevator to the penthouse. He ached in his body and in his heart. His brain swelled with unprocessed information. Tobin's heart thumped from seeing Moog with Julie and seeing a mustard-colored Explorer in Moog's garage. He was too tired to process the raw data as the elevator rose in the high-rise shaft toward his penthouse apartment. As soon as the doors opened, he smelled a familiar perfume.

"Isn't this like old times," Mona Falco said, one leg draped over the arm of an oversized armchair, her tight pants accentuating her crotch. "You even look like old times, Hank."

Tobin gazed at her, dropped his keys in a silver bowl by the door. Mona Falco wore spaghetti-strap sandals and a tailored, dark pants suit with tight white blouse, her lips pouted in a confident sexy half-smile. *Come-bite-me-till-I-bleed lips,* Tobin thought.

"Warrant?"

"I wish I could get one for your heart, Hank."

"I'm a hurting man right now, Mona. I'm weary and wounded, and I need sleep. I assume you have a warrant and forced management to open the door. That's hardly the key to a man's heart."

Outside the big windows the countless lights of New York burned like eternal votive candles, each one keeping someone with a broken promise in his life awake at night. Tobin had promised himself to make Mona Falco a part of his past, in order to have a future with Julie. But no matter how hard he huffed and puffed, Mona Falco was a trick candle he couldn't blow out.

"Yeah, I got a Republican judge to sign a paper, but that's a formality now," Falco said, waving a warrant. "We indict defense attorneys, judges, and politicians theses days. We hold suspects without charges. We even search for dirt in Martha Stewart's laundry hamper, Hank. Reporters still enjoy a shield these days. But the First Amendment is being amended. The Fourth Amendment is a Stairmaster. So Cox made me get a warrant on you. The judge wouldn't give me one for your newspaper-office computer. But we will be taking the one out of here, Hank."

"Will be taking?"

"Cox doesn't know I got the warrant yet. I thought I'd come see you first. As a courtesy. You know I care about you, Hank. I don't want you to get in any more trouble. My advice, bring the laptop to the office. It'll be off-limits there."

Tobin was wary. Why was this ambitious woman who arrested his son being so good to him? Why would she help him hide evidence? Warn him about a coming warrant search? Maybe he was looking a gift horse in the pretty mouth. Maybe she still cared about him. He was too tired, too drained to even try to figure it all out.

"I have nothing to hide," he said, knowing that he had the e-mails from LL on his hard drive. Especially the one with his son's license plate number and the other one of the mustard-colored Explorer outside of the Sinai Torah Temple.

"You never know how the Feds might interpret stuff, Hank," Mona said. "But when one kid gets busted, and a second one is heard talking dangerous stuff . . ."

Tobin's voice rose as he said, "You talking about my daughter, Laurie?"

He controlled himself. Tobin couldn't let Mona know that he knew about the bug in Julie's lamp. Planted by Moog. He needed to listen more and talk less. Like when he was still a reporter, before he became a columnist.

"Yeah, she was in some fight at school," Mona said. "They say Laurie got nasty and physical with a couple of Moroccan girls on Kingsborough Community College beach."

"Kids in a schoolyard . . ."

"She might be daddy's little girl but under the law she's an adult, Hank. She's nineteen. And it's not a high school schoolyard, either. A college campus. I hear the school is considering terminating her."

He lost his composure again. "Oh, what bullshit! Kids on college campuses in the sixties made fucking bombs, plotted to overthrow the government, took over buildings. Give me a break, Mona."

"Hate talk leads to hate crimes, Hank."

"Speech is still protected."

"Not when it's connected to an assault," Mona Falco said. "Way I hear it your kid threw the first punch. That's assault in this state. If witnesses corroborate the victim's account that Laurie called her a 'sand nigger,' that's a felony hate crime, and you could have two kids in the can. If the state doesn't prefer charges, the Feds might. Cox might say the victim's civil rights were violated. Her arrest won't look good for Henry's case. If we find bad stuff, your lawyer is gonna own this condo, Hank."

Tobin's heart raced. He took a deep breath, felt light-headed and clammy. *Signs of a heart attack,* he thought. *Also a sign of fear. Which means defeat.* He needed to get a grip. Mona Falco had the upper hand. *Think on your feet.*

He inhaled a deep breath, walked to the kitchen, pulled a tall glass of cold water from his Brita filter tank, took a long drink, and laughed. His heart slowed. He shifted the cold glass from hand to hand, cooling his sweaty palms. He walked to the big window peering out at the night city, his city, the biggest bull's-eye on the planet, and yawned.

"I'm not worried about it, Mona," he said. "I believe in the law. I learned some things today that give me complete confidence that Henry will be home soon."

His back to Mona Falco, Tobin sipped his cold water, pretending to stare out at the vulnerable city but studied Mona's reflection in the night glass. She toyed with the warrant, her small fingers skipping over its mighty edges, jerking her head left and then right, earrings clicking.

"Really?" Mona said. "Not worried at least a little bit?"

She rose from the armchair and strutted toward him, shoulders back, breasts pushed out, playing with the warrant.

Falco learned early in her career that her two best police tools were her race and her disarming beauty. He'd always thought that when dealing with the bureaucracy and her career, Mona exploited the race card. *This time she's playing the sex card,* Tobin thought.

She'd always made prisoners, especially men, want to tell her everything as if a confession would lead to pillow talk. She worked on it, too. Honed it into a craft and a science. The vacuum-packed pants that split her vagina. The half-buttoned blouse. Those luscious lips. Whether she was grilling a white-trash skinhead, a gangsta homey, or a skirt-chasing yuppie, these feminine attributes were more effective interrogation tools than the rubber hose and the head-thumping Yellow Pages.

But this time Mona Falco's walk across the room was a little too affected, an unsure prance. Tobin figured she was a little too curious. Bordering on nervous.

"Absolutely," he said. "Jeez, the city looks so calm tonight. It looks like, well, like September 10."

"There's always a calm before a storm."

"Yeah, but New York has a great chin," Tobin said.

"You always loved boxing metaphors, Hank."

"Boxing is life, Mona. Life is a brawl. But what most people don't realize is that boxing is ninety-percent mental. The smartest fighter usually wins. He does that by waiting for the other, dumber fighter to make a mistake. And then boom. You always get knocked out by the punch you don't see coming."

"You always thought you were smarter than your opponents, Hank."

"Ah, see that would be arrogance. Arrogant fighters always end up getting beaten by second-rate fighters. Tyson got arrogant with Buster Douglas, underestimated him, trained in Tokyo on geisha girls and champagne, and got knocked out. Lennox Lewis was so arrogant he got starched by journeymen like Hassim Rahman and Oliver McCall."

"Tyson and Lewis I know about. I don't even know who any of those other fighters are."

"Ah ha," Tobin said. "There's a lesson in there for you, Mona. Be afraid of what you don't know, like the punch you don't see coming."

"Is there something I should know, Hank?"

She was standing right behind him, the smell of her perfume as strong as original sin, the tempting heat of her body radiating on his back like a candygram from hell. She searched the reflection in the glass for his eyes. He knew she was trying to capture his attention. But instead he stared southeast across the cityscape and fixed his eyes upon the golden vertex of the Chrysler Building, then tilted his eyes down, counting the floors backward from the seventy-seventh floor.

"There's lots you should know, Mona."

"Tell me."

He felt the warrant trace down his spine, like a stripper's feather, as light and devious as a white lie to a virgin.

"I can't, Mona."

Her hot breath pebbled the flesh on the nape of his neck as she stared over his shoulder into the glass, the warrant gliding over his belt and down over his ass and in between his legs. The folded warrant rubbed the inside of his thighs and then ever so lightly touched the underside of his privates. A taunting tickle, then, "Why can't you, Hank? I came here to warn you that Cox will be here in the morning with this paper. Why can't you?"

She rubbed the warrant with a firmer thrust now. He became aroused. But this time he thought of Tracy Burns's line, "Sometimes a man's strongest weapon around a woman is a limp dick." *Less really is more, here,* he thought.

"I can't, Mona, because you're the woman who snapped handcuffs on the wrists of my only son."

He gulped a long drink of ice water and kept counting backward until his eyes affixed on the thirty-second floor of the Chrysler Building, where he knew Erin Kelly had some other secrets he needed to learn.

"Better me than someone else," she said.

"You really think so? Mona, you don't get it. You might have come and given me a warning, but you work for Cox. The man who wants to put my son away for life."

The man whom Tobin was beginning to suspect was in cahoots with Lenny Kelly. Or taking information from him and using it against the Tobin family. He suspected that Lenny Kelly fed Cox the information that got poor Judge Nick Koutros indicted. Mona was too ambitious not to please Cox in the end.

"I treated Henry with dignity," she said. "Loose cuffs, got him something hot to eat, a clean cell, candy, something to read. He wasn't treated like a skell, Hank. No in-your-face, under-the-lamp, sleep-deprived interrogations without a lawyer. I did that for you, Hank."

Tobin kept staring at the thirty-second floor of the Chrysler Building. "And for that you want me to tell you what I learned? Even though you said you didn't believe me about Lenny Kelly and didn't think anyone else would?"

Mona continued to rub the warrant between his legs and now brushed her breasts against his back, still searching for his eyes in the reflection. "I don't want to be made a fool of on my new job, Hank."

"My kid's facing life, and I should worry about your standing in your new job?"

"Help me and I'll help you."

"How?"

"Maybe I can make the arrest of your daughter never happen."

Tobin reached down between his legs and grabbed the warrant. Mona Falco wouldn't let go. He tugged it, and her hand came with it between his legs, palming his privates, and pressing her breasts against his back. He refused to allow himself to grow in her hand like some human Chia Pet.

Instead of thinking hard, he thought of things that would keep him limp and powerful. He stared at the thirty-second floor of the Chrysler Building, forming questions for Erin Kelly. He imagined his beaten, wounded son chained to a bed. He flashed on Julie kissing Moog good-bye and the mustard-colored Explorer in his garage. And as Mona Falco kneaded him, he took a final drink of icy water and turned to her, warrant in hand, flaccid and strong.

He looked into Mona's skittery eyes. "Should I consider myself *served*, Mona?"

Mona Falco stared at him, and for the first time, he thought he saw a tiny broken vessel of fear in her perfect pale gray eyes.

"You just fucked *her*, didn't you? That's why—"

"She has another man for that."

"Really? Who's that?"

"Zach Moog."

Mona Falco rocked back on her heels. Tobin grabbed her arm to steady her. She pulled herself free and snatched the warrant from his hand.

"I'll be back," she said, stepping onto the private elevator.

"You were never here."

The elevator door smacked shut.

THIRTY-FIVE

Friday, July 28

First light awakened Tobin at 5:30 A.M. He showered, dressed in jeans and sneakers, hurried downstairs with his laptop, and locked it in the trunk of the Taurus.

Back upstairs Tobin called Bernie Zachbar and told him that if he wanted a quick phone interview, he should have Dani Larsen call him by seven. Zachbar protested, told him he was in TV news, not radio or print. Tobin didn't want to explain about his changed appearance and said he wouldn't go on camera because he looked and felt like shit. Tobin said he felt obligated to Zachbar, but if he didn't want the interview, he'd call New York One. "I want the fucking interview," Zachbar said.

Then Tobin called Steve Clancy, told him about the warrant, and asked that he come and monitor the search. Clancy said he'd be there at 8:30 A.M.

Dani Larsen called on time, setting up ground rules. She couldn't let her relationship with him interfere with the questions she asked. He told her he respected her for that and told her to fire away. Dani Larsen asked him some personal questions about himself and Julie. Tobin said they were divorced but united in their commitment to their son. Dani flung a few tough ones about his son being assaulted and the rumor that his daughter had gotten into a fight at school.

Tobin gave direct answers, from the gut and the heart, proclaiming his son's innocence and saying he believed the incident with his daughter was just unfortunate fallout from his son's predicament. Tobin refused to answer any questions about legal strategies but talked mostly about what it felt like to be on this side of a big story.

When they were finished with enough for an eight-minute spot that would play over a still photo of his column logo, and after he asked that they go off-the-record, Tobin searched for a way to pitch Dani Larsen on the subject of Vinny Hunt.

"As you can see, I was the wrong guy for you," Tobin said.

"You sure do have a lot of baggage, Hank. Designer luggage, but still lots of it. But, hey, I have no regrets. I'm a big girl. I've had worse flings in my search for Mister Half-Right."

"You sure?"

"Listen, if you think I don't know you helped get me this gig, then you must think I'm too stupid to have it."

"Okay, so I made a call. But you're doing a great job."

"I'll try to make you look . . . *human.*"

"As opposed to what?"

They laughed and Tobin said, "Listen, I wanted to talk to you about something else—"

"Can I ask you a favor first? I know you're preoccupied with your own personal horrors, and I know you called Bernie to get me this promotion. You give me exclusives. So I know it's incredibly selfish and presumptuous of me, but can I ask one more favor? This probably isn't ethical, either. But I don't know how else or where else to go about this."

"Sure, ask. What?"

"It's awkward because, well, because me and you had a thing-a-ma-fling, but I know you're mature enough for me to ask."

"*What?*"

"You know that big, gorgeous cop?"

"Vinny Hunt?"

"Yeah. You think there's any backdoor way you can, ya know, find out if he's interested in, like, ya know, *me,* or anything? So I don't make a complete ass of myself. Where I come from, a girl still doesn't ask out a guy. I tried sending him signals, batted my eyes, touched his arms, pouted my lips, used everything but FedEx, but Vinny's bashful to the point of rigor mortis. Which I kinda like in a big, handsome lug like him. But I don't know the scoop on him."

"He's single, straight, and he's head over two-left-feet nuts about you."

"*Really?* How the hell do you know?"

"Guy thing. But if I get him to call you, Dani, promise you won't play cat-and-mouse games."

"Games, I have to play. I'm a *woman.* But I won't say 'no' to a date. And tell him to make it simple. I know what cops make. Honest ones, anyway."

"He's a captain. He can afford dinner."

As soon as he hung up with Dani, he called Vinny Hunt and got his voice mail and left his cell-phone number.

About ten minutes later, his doorbell rang and Tobin answered. Mona Falco wore a conservative skirt suit with low heels and her relaxed nappy hair pulled tight on her skull. The more of her face you saw the more beautiful she became. But she wore dark glasses that shielded her eyes from Tobin's stare, like portable police barricades.

Cox and Danvers stood behind her as Mona presented Tobin with a copy of the same warrant she'd rubbed between his legs the night before. It still didn't arouse him.

"We have a premises search warrant," she said, her voice as flat as cheap champagne.

Cox stepped into the penthouse and looked around, chomping his gum, gazing at the expensive paintings, opulent furnishings, and the ceiling-to-floor bookcases that covered one whole long wall.

"Nice," Cox said, popping a small bubble. "Nothing I like better than giving a penthouse a cheap toss."

Tobin knew there were two ways of doing this. He could be polite, hoping to win Cox into his corner to curry favors with a man who held strings in his son's life. But he didn't think that had any value because Cox wasn't ever letting go of this trophy bust. So Tobin decided to taunt Cox, the way Muhammad Ali ridiculed and mind-fucked George Foreman until the big man made mistakes. Tobin wanted to cause a chasm between Mona Falco and Cox. He knew Cox was sweet on her and thought the best way to wobble his knees was to play off that chink in his male armor.

"Thanks," Tobin said. "Be my guest. You helped pay for it."

"Oh, yeah?"

"Yeah, I made out like a Most-Wanted-List bandit writing about the astounding incompetence of your organization," Tobin said. "Keep up the shit work, baby, and I'll never miss any meals."

"Your kid won't either," Cox said. "Federal pens serve three squares a day."

"He'll be home soon."

"Oh, yeah?"

Five plastic-gloved men from the JTTF search team entered behind them.

"I think so," Tobin said.

"My guess is your other kid'll be arrested within forty-eight hours," Cox said. "That'll be two in the can. And if we get lucky here, we can make it a family-plan vacation to Club Fed."

Tobin felt a swoon in his guts but smiled. "That'd make it an even better book when we all walk," Tobin said. "And you'll be the leading federal fuck-up. Probably pay me three times what your pension will be. If they ever give it to you. Never know, you might wind up eating my son's three daily squares."

The search team fanned out in the apartment. Mona Falco remained mostly silent. He still couldn't understand why she had tipped him to the search. She didn't want Cox to find something that was on his hard drive. Something that he told her about. He figured she was probably already conniving to seize it later, on her own, with her own warrant, to win brownie points with Cox after his warrant proved fruitless.

"Have a seat," Cox said. "This could take hours."

The private elevator whined to Tobin's floor again, and his doorbell rang.

Tobin walked toward the elevator to answer it, stopped in front of Cox, looked him in the eyes, sniffed him, made a revolted face, and said, "Actually I have a million things to do. But make yourself at home. Plenty of coffee in the pot, take whatever you want from the fridge. And listen up, you smell like you gotta use the toilet, so be a sport and flush, will ya?"

Cox stared right back into Tobin's eyes, chewing his wad of gum like he was searching it for pearls. "You're not afraid of us planting anything, huh?"

Tobin sniffed Cox again, like a bloodhound, and said, "A free word of dating advice and mating etiquette, Cox: Did you know that chewing gum can make you fart like an elk? The air you swallow when you chew gets trapped in your large intestine and works its way down the colon, and the more you chew gum, especially when you're *talking* shit, the more you fart. You really oughta have more respect for the lady, man. It's plain to see you're nuts about Mona here, and that she knows it, and she'll exploit that obvious weakness to climb to the top of the JTTF class."

"That's just not true," Mona said.

Tobin nodded and said, "Oh, come on, Mona. Sure it is. But if you wanna score with *her*, Cox, the way she scores on *you*, you gotta stop the farting around the lady, man. Women always smell it on your clothes."

Cox stopped chewing. Tobin thought he saw a corner of Mona Falco's seductive mouth tug in a private smile. Danvers turned his back on the scene, pretending to search a bookcase. In the reflection of a polished bronze plaque of an Associated Press Award hanging next to the bookcase, Tobin could have sworn he saw Danvers grin. A fast one.

"You won't laugh when your own words hang you, Tobin, the way they hung your son," Cox said.

Tobin absorbed the body blow. Kept smiling. A humiliated Cox couldn't look at Mona Falco or any of the others who'd listened to Tobin. For a fleeting second, Tobin almost felt sorry for Cox. That passed fast.

"But to answer your question, *Cox*, no, I'm not worried about you planting anything," Tobin said, pulling open the elevator door to reveal Steve Clancy and a half-dozen young paralegal associates from his law firm entering his apartment, carrying small video cameras. Clancy pointed to various JTTF searchers, and his paralegals fanned out, shadowing and taping each searcher.

One paralegal pointed his video camera at Cox. He rammed his hand over the lens.

"Hands off," Clancy said. "We have every right."

Cox pulled his hand away, anger, frustration, and embarrassment jumbling together in his broad face. Mona Falco stood with her hands behind her, shoulders back, as silent and proper as a cadet. Tobin watched Danvers, who seemed to watch everything. He never uttered a word.

Tobin handed Clancy the warrant. Clancy perused it. "This is limited to my client's computer, files, and anything in plain sight," Clancy said. "Tell your guys they can look for files, discs, and communications between father and son. And the computer. Nothing else. Stay out of closets, drawers, and other concealed spaces."

Tobin pulled Clancy out onto the terrace and told the sharp-minded lawyer about the bug in Julie's house, put there by her old partner, Zach Moog.

Then he told him about tailing Moog and spotting the mustard-colored Explorer in his garage.

"What unit in NYPD does this Moog character work for?" Clancy asked.

Tobin was embarrassed to say he didn't know. Clancy told him to find out. And told him that in the meantime he should tell Julie about it but leave it where it was as a great way of sending out misinformation. "If they don't know that you know it's there, that's *your* bug," Clancy said.

Tobin nodded. He went back into his apartment, winked at Mona Falco, sniffed Cox once more, nodded to a silent Danvers, and left.

THIRTY-SIX

Twelve minutes later Tobin paced the sienna-colored onyx, blue marble, and inlaid-steel lobby floors of the Chrysler Building, waiting for Julie, staring up at the Edward Trumbull mural of the actual workers constructing this magnificent monument to the Art Deco style. His cell phone rang. He searched his pockets for the phone. Stragglers, late for work, rushed to the thirty-two elevators to join the other 15,000 people who earned their living in what Tobin had declared in his column many times was the most beautiful building in New York City, and on which he prided himself as something of an expert.

The cell-phone caller ID told him it was Vinny Hunt calling him back. And logic told him that if there was a warrant for his apartment, his phone was tapped. Tobin told Vinny, without mentioning his name, that he'd call him right back. He hung up and walked to a public phone near an open door marked SECURITY. Inside underpaid square-badge guards watched security monitors where they could see what was happening in each of the thirty-two elevators. Tobin called Vinny and told him that Dani Larsen was expecting a call from him. The big, handsome cop stuttered, asking Tobin what he should say to Dani. He told Tobin he never dated a celebrity before. He asked where he should take her.

The two security guards broke up laughing as they watched an elegant yuppie woman alone on an express elevator pick free a wedgie and fix the pads in her bra before stepping off the lift as busty miss-prim-and-proper.

"Oh, man oh man, check out the hooters on the babe in number twenty-seven," said one square badge, pointing to a big-breasted woman

Tobin smiled, turned his back on the open door revealing the security

274

monitors, and suggested that Vinny Hunt take Dani Larsen for hot dogs and fries at Nathan's in Coney Island. And beers and peanuts at a ball game at Cyclones stadium. And drinks afterward in Peggy O'Neil's downstairs. And a stroll on the boardwalk and rides on the Wonder Wheel and the Cyclone. "If you win her one of those big-assed kewpie dolls at the rifle range, she'll have to invite you to carry it upstairs for her when you drive her home," Tobin said.

"You're a genius, Hank," Vinny said.

Then Vinny asked if he was sure, that maybe Tobin should make him a reservation in Elaine's.

"She wants a date with *you*, Vinny," Tobin said. "Be *you*. She's tired of blowhard Manhattan phonies. Like me."

Vinny Hunt laughed and listened to some more advice. Tobin told him that Dani came from working-class Scranton, Pennsylvania, roots and that she would probably be intrigued and engrossed by what Vinny did for a living. Tobin knew that he was giving away Vinny as a future source. After the first date, Dani Larsen would always get first dibs on all the best stories coming out of the NYPD Intelligence Division. *But what the hell,* he thought. *They were meant for each other. Somebody should be happy in this miserable life.*

Besides, Tobin wasn't thinking about the future. He needed Vinny Hunt's help right now on the biggest story of his life. The story of his family.

"How can I ever repay you?" Vinny Hunt said.

"Oh, man, you're gonna be sorry you ever asked me that."

"No, I won't. You're fixing me up with the girl of my dreams and now I get to help you take on the scumbag Feds who coulda prevented Jimbo's death. Tell me what you need, Hank."

"First, did you pull the rap sheet on that Fred Buckles guy I asked you about?"

"Oh, yeah, I almost forgot," Vinny said, as Tobin heard the rustling and crinkling of paper from the other end of the line. "He has a long, dirty sheet. Drugs, scams, burglary. And four statutory rape arrests. A pedophile. Guy loves banging young broads bareback. He has seven kids by five mothers."

"Jeez, he missed his calling. He shoulda been a priest."

"He only did time on that stat-rape charge once. Once he got out of trouble by enlisting in the service. He went to Kuwait. The other times the charges were dropped when he agreed to marry the girls. Then he'd divorce them. Or they had abortions. Or miscarriages. Which means he probably beat a few babies out of young girls. Real fuckin' belly crawler. But looks like he straightened out for a while. Married to the Hu girl, Debbie, a long time. Three kids. He got busted two years ago running cigarettes up from down south with a sixteen-year-old chick. They tried to get her to flip on him. She wouldn't. He was probably dicking her, but all they got him on was the cigarette smuggling. He's on parole. A real skelly, skanky, low-life mutt. An odor comes up off the printout."

Tobin asked the names of Buckles's parole officer and some of the girls he knocked up and wrote them all down in his Reporter's Notebook. Hunt told him that none of them could be used for publication because they were minors at the time. Tobin assured him that no reputable newspaper would print the names of rape victims, no matter what their ages.

"I need you to find out something else for me," Tobin said, at the public phone. "First about my daughter, Laurie."

"What about her?" Vinny asked.

Tobin told him about the fight at her college campus and Mona Falco suggesting there'd be a possible arrest for hate crime. Tobin asked Vinny to find out who the two girls were she fought with and to see if the deck was being stacked against her by Mona Falco, or Cox, or anyone else inside the PD. He told him that Falco said Laurie threw the first punch and called the kid a "sand nigger." Tobin needed to know if it was true.

"I also need you to pull an old file for me," Tobin said.

"On what?"

"That arson ten years ago," Tobin said, giving him all the details of the Billy Kelly case, about how Fred Buckles was dating Debbie Hu at the time, probably had her knocked up.

Vinny said he'd get on both things right away and asked for some more coaching on how to talk to Dani Larsen.

Tobin gave him some last-minute tips on how to be himself. "And stop sticking your finger into the corner of your eye and looking away when Dani's talking to you," Tobin said. "Look a chick in the eyes, Vinny. Women love a guy that looks them right in the eyes. They think that's ballsy and honest and sexy."

And then Tobin spotted Julie enter the lobby dressed in black tights and a red belly shirt, white designer sneakers, and a small handbag on a shoulder strap that he knew contained her badge, .25-caliber pistol, pepper spray, and handcuffs. Julie badged her way past security and grabbed a

brochure for the Chrysler Building being handed out to tourists by a uniformed Chrysler Building worker. She shoved the brochure in her bag with
the badge wallet and searched the lobby for Tobin.

Tobin thanked Vinny Hunt, wished him good luck with Dani, and
hung up and approached Julie. He refused to look her in the eye. He nodded to the elevator bank that went from floors twenty-five through fifty.

"Sorry I'm late," Julie said.

"Okay."

"I'm gonna walk up."

"No time."

"Why?"

"Lots to do."

"You know I have claustrophobia and I—"

"Deal with it."

"Who's writing your friggin' lines today? Clint Eastwood?"

The elevator door popped open. She moved toward the stairs. Tobin
grabbed her buff arm and dragged her into the elevator. He hit the thirty-
second floor. The dazzling Art Deco doors, paneled with eight different
kinds of wood from all over the world, slammed shut. Julie looked around,
trapped. She seemed to melt into the Art Deco façade as the lift rocketed
skyward in a windy, gut-sinking whoosh.

Julie clutched Hank's arm, and mumbled, "Oh, my God, I am heartily
sorry for having offended Thee. . . ."

The elevator slowed as it neared the thirty-second floor.

"You've offended more than Him," Hank said, snapping his arm free of
her clutch. "Starting with yourself."

"The hell you talking about? What's your problem?"

The doors popped open. Julie rushed off.

"Never again will I step on one of them. . . . Come on, this way."

They walked to the end of the hall and through a glass door bearing the
legend: CHRISTIANSEN ACCOUNTING. Tobin crossed the plush,
burnished-wood waiting room to a large window, facing west on Forty-
second Street, that ran like a spine to the cool, blue Hudson River. The
bright-eyed Hispanic receptionist looked up from her pulsating phones
and said, "May I help you?"

"I'm back," Julie said, unfolding her gold shield. "Please tell Mrs.
Levine the pain-in-the-ass cop from yesterday is here again."

"I'm afraid Mrs. Levine is at a meeting and can't be dis—"

Julie put her hands on the counter, leaned toward the receptionist, and said, "Get her out, honey, or I'm going in. Simple."

As the receptionist rousted Erin Kelly Levine, Tobin felt Julie turning to stare at him. He gazed down at Forty-second Street where a scrimmage of humanity seemed to be jamming in as much life as it could before something terrible happened.

Julie walked up next to him and said, "What, you're pissed off I asked you to leave last night?"

"Nope."

"You expected after spending one day together after four years I should rip off my clothes and ask you to hop in the sack with me?"

"Nope."

"Why the attitude? Someone else beat you out for another Pulitzer?"

"Nope."

"Hey, ya know, fuck *you,* okay."

"Better than fucking Moog, like you did last night, while your son's in a hospital bed—"

"What? What the hell are you talk—"

Erin Kelly said, "Excuse me, Detective Capone, but this is really starting to piss me the hell off. I told you yesterday I had nothing to say to you. . . ."

Tobin turned from the window and looked at her. "Don't you dare talk to her like that, you spoiled rich brat," Tobin said.

Erin Kelly Levine stepped back. Astounded. "Who the hell are *you?*" she asked.

"You stop to pray with the rabbi in the synagogue with your devout husband on the way to the park this morning, again?"

Erin Kelly Levine looked violated, wrapped her arms around herself, as if for protection, and whispered, "What is going on here? This is way too creepy. . . ."

Tobin asked, "How many months pregnant were you with Fred Buckles's baby when Debbie Hu's house went up in smoke, Erin?"

It was a wild guess, coming off the floor like an overhand fastball. He was hoping she'd swing at it.

Julie was as speechless as Erin was, looking from Tobin back to Erin and to Tobin again. Tobin saw muscles in Erin's face sag and crumple like tiles falling out of a mosaic. Her eyes had a waxy faraway stare like someone gazing through the smoked-glass windows of purgatory.

"I . . . don't . . . know . . . what you're talking . . . who you're—"

"Bullshit," Tobin said, startling Erin and the receptionist. "You know exactly what and who I'm talking about, baby. The question is does your husband know about the abortion you had as a kid? Bad enough he married a white-trash shiksa whose brother was a swastika-sporting skinhead who did ten years for a racial hate crime. Orthodox Jew who marries a shiksa is bad enough. But when he reads in the newspaper that he married a shiksa who had an abortion, a baby killer—"

"Please," Erin said, pushing open the door, and leading Tobin and Julie into the hallway, near the elevators.

"Why are you here snooping into my life?" Erin asked, her fragile voice crackling like the envelope of a bad-news telegram. "Why are you bringing up things that are dead and buried?"

"Dead and buried? You mean like that fetus you made with Fred Buckles?"

Julie's eyes narrowed, signaled for Tobin to calm down. He didn't.

Erin cupped her hands over her ears. "Stop it!"

"Boy or girl, Erin? The fetus?"

"Stop!"

"Dead and buried," Tobin said. "Like ten years of your brother's life?"

Erin turned to Julie, appealing to her, her voice as plaintive as a graveyard prayer, "Please make him stop."

"Hank, maybe—"

"Dead and buried," Tobin said. "Like your mother who killed herself, Erin?"

Erin slinked to the floor, weeping. Julie put a finger in the air.

"That's it. Cool it, Hank."

" 'Cool it' my Irish ass. I got a son cooling it in the can because this spoiled rich bitch's crazy father faked his death and wants to get even with me for helping to send Billy Kelly to prison for ten years. But we know there's way more to it, don't we, Erin? That little weasel, Fred Buckles, the father of your dead baby, tried getting rid of Debbie Hu, who was also knocked up, by tossing a Molotov. When that didn't work, he framed your brother, didn't he? And you let it happen because you were in love with that dirty bag of dog shit. I might be missing a few pieces, but that's the story, isn't it?"

"No!" Erin shouted. "You have it wrong."

"Where the hell is your freak of a father?" Tobin shouted. "He's the only one who can clear my son's name, and your father is planning on ending his own miserable life tomorrow. When he goes, so will any chance of me saving my son. I need you to tell me where to find this fucking monster."

"Help us, Erin, please," Julie said. "I'm begging you. I don't care what you or anyone else did ten years ago. Help me help my son."

"My father is dead!"

"No, he's fucking not!" Tobin shouted.

"He's alive, Erin," Julie said. "Help us find him."

"Leave me alone! None of that—any of that—is *my* life anymore. Get out of here! Get away from me! I made a new life. Stay out of it. Stay away from me and my new family! You're not allowed in. Stay away!"

Tobin slammed his fist against the elevator button. Erin Kelly Levine sat on the floor, wailing big, loud, body-wracking sobs. The receptionist and two men in suits ran out of Christiansen Accounting, followed by a beefy security guard.

"The hell goin' down here, man?" asked the security guard, holding a walkie-talkie, making a move toward Tobin.

Julie dangled her gold shield. "It's okay, we're through for now."

The elevator arrived with the bang of a bell. "I'll be in touch, Erin," Tobin said. "You better think about all of this. I will be back."

"Enough," Julie said.

"Screw you, too," Tobin said stepping onto the elevator and hitting the lobby button. "You and Moog—"

"Who the hell do you think you're talking to?" Julie said, storming onto the elevator after him. Julie froze, turned to exit. The doors snapped shut. And the elevator plunged in the shaft like it was dropped from a great height.

"Jesus, Joseph, and Mary help me," Julie said, flattening herself against the back wall, gazing around the elevator. She shut her eyes and said, "Oh, my God, I am heartily sorry for having offended Thee, and I detest all my sins—"

"Shut up," Tobin said.

"Who the f—"

Then: BOOM!

The elevator jammed. It clanked to an abrupt stop. In the shaft. Between floors. Banging against walls. Knocking. Clacking. Swaying. The motor died with a soft sigh. The lights flickered. Silence.

"Oh . . . my . . . God . . . Almighty . . . help . . . us. . . ." Julie said, eyes popped.

"Actually, an Otis repairman would be better right now."

Tobin pushed the lobby button. Nothing. The lights flickered. Silence. Faraway shouting. More silence. Swaying. Cables rattling. Chains. Tobin hit the emergency button. Nothing. He climbed up on the handrailing and searched for an escape hatch to the roof of the elevator. Everything was sealed. Nothing budged. He pounded on the ceiling. The sounds echoed in the huge shaft like an indoor slot canyon.

"You have a knife?" Tobin asked.

"Keys and a gun and a metal badge."

He jumped down from the handrail and his hard landing made the elevator rock and sway and clang in the shaft. Julie screamed. He tried prying open the doors. The old steel doors wouldn't budge. Julie crawled on hands and knees and tried pulling one door her way while Tobin pulled the other. It opened far enough for them to see the number twenty-seven written on a greasy brick wall. Between floors. Then the doors snapped shut. Useless.

Tobin used his penthouse key to pry open the switch panel on the Otis control panel. He flicked an ON/OFF button. Nothing happened. He looked at the camera mounted in the upper corner of the elevator. He spoke into what he thought was a microphone. No response. He waved at the camera, screaming "Help!"

Julie joined in. For the next six minutes they banged, shouted, and screamed for help. Their only response was their own echoes. After ten minutes, they stopped shouting. Silence. Dangling. Floating. As if lost in deep space.

Tobin looked at Julie, crouched in a fetal ball in a corner, terrified. She had never looked more gorgeous. Or vulnerable. Or sexy. "This could take a few days," he said.

"Don't play with me, Hank," she said. "This isn't funny! Some sicko might've planted a—"

"Nah," Tobin said, yawning, checking his watch.

Julie took out the Chrysler Building brochure she'd been handed in the lobby. She glanced at it with trembling fingers.

"You know when this building that's gonna kill us was built?" Julie asked.

"Nineteen twenty-eight," he said. "Finished in 1930. And we're not gonna die. We're stuck in an elevator. Happens in my building a few times a month."

"It's the eighteenth tallest building in the world," Julie said.

"It was designed by William Van Alen, stands 1,046 feet and 77 stories high, and was the world's tallest building for a few months before the Empire State Building was finished in 1930," he said, hoping the trivia would take death off Julie's mind.

"Of course the great *Hank Tobin* would know all that," she said, glancing at the brochure. "But did you know that when we go down, 20,961 tons of structural steel will be coming down on top of us, Hank? And 391,881 rivets; 3,826,000 bricks; of which 1,735,000 are white; 1,863,000 are common; with the rest being black and gray. . . ."

"Talk about hitting the bricks."

"Plus 446,000 tiles; 794,000 pieces of partition block; 3,862 windows; 2,788 doors; 200 flights of stairs; two-fifths of a mile of aluminum railings; 35 miles of pipes; 15 miles of brass strip for jointing terrazzo floors; 10,000 electric light bulbs; 750 miles of electric conductor wire—"

"Julie, you're giving me a fucking headache. . . ."

". . . and 52,000 square feet of exterior marble; 112,000 square feet of marble wainscot; 3,200,000 square feet of painted surface; and at least one ex-wife who never stopped loving her miserable asswipe of a husband."

"I love you, too, Julie."

Then the lights went off.

She whispered, "Hank . . ."

"I'm here, Jule. What, you thought I caught a crosstown bus?"

"Hank?

"What?"

He felt Julie groping in the dark.

"Hank?"

"What, Jule?"

"Hold me, Hank, please. Hold me."

He grabbed her in his arms. Her strong, tight little body trembled in his hands.

"We're gonna die, Hank."

"In thirty or forty years, Jule."

"No, something's happened. And we have no way of knowing what it was. People are probably running out of the building, down the 200 flights of stairs, out the three exits. Erin Kelly is probably racing right past us now. And we're trapped, Hank. We're gonna die, Hank. I said an Act of Contrition for you, too, because I know you don't remember the words."

"Jeez, I feel better already."

"How can you be sarcastic with God, for chrissakes?"

"We have the same twisted sense of humor."

Then he smelled the first wisp of smoke.

"Smell it, Hank?"

"You're so hot in those tights that you're smoldering. Better take 'em off."

She grabbed him tighter. "I'm glad I'm with you, Hank."

"Ditto, Jule." He draped his arm over her shoulder, letting his hand brush against her right breast. She cupped his hand over her breast, and he started to get aroused.

"No one is gonna help Henry now, Hank. Without us, he's got no chance."

"We'll get out, Jule." He began unbuttoning her blouse, rubbing her exposed flat belly.

Her hands groped, finding his face with her soft trembling hands, and guided it to her face. She kissed him, softly at first.

He kissed her deeper, massaging her bare breast, fully aroused now. She kissed him harder, reaching for his belt buckle.

"I need to know something," she said. "Before . . ."

"Anything," he said.

"Mona Falco . . ."

"Once. In Ireland. Drunk. And I couldn't get it up. As God is my witness."

"You're an agnostic. Swear on the kids."

"I swear on the kids."

"Make love to me," she whispered, pulling off her blouse.

"First *I* have a question," he said.

"*What,*" she said, peeling off her tights. "Guys are supposed to screw *first* and ask questions *later.*"

"Moog?"

"*Never!* There were a few others, *after* the divorce. One-nighters after three dates. I'm human and I won't lie. Men you never knew or ever will. They meant nothing. Couldn't hold your jock. I never, ever cheated on you when we were married, Hank. I never stopped loving you after we were divorced."

The elevator swayed as she embraced him.

"I don't care about the others. But not even last night with Moog?"

"He came to warn me that Laurie might be getting arrested for the fight in school," she said, the smell of the smoke stronger now. "He tried to get it on with me. . . ." She placed Tobin's large hands on her bare breasts, the nipples hard and pronounced with fear. Her breasts were magnificent, better than he remembered them, soft and firm and on fire. The perfect breasts that bobbed in the waters of Coney Island on that long ago summer day when he'd stolen her bikini top and asked her to be his wife. The breasts that made young, riled men applaud and cheer and chant, "Tits! Tits! Tits!" She cupped her hands over his hands on her perfect breasts. "Moog never even got this far," she said.

Tobin was erect now and hungry for his wife. And so Julie kissed him, shoved him onto his back on the elevator floor, fumbled in the sweaty dark, and straddled him, about to spindle herself upon him. Tobin felt her dangling breasts brush across his cheek.

"I love you, Hank," she said, guiding him, about to let him enter her.

"I love you, Julie."

Then the lights came on.

And the elevator growled. Groaned. And swayed. And the motor kicked over. And the lift whined and rattled and plunged at terrifying speed into the deep black hole.

"Sweet . . . Mother . . . of . . . Jesus!" Julie shouted.

"Are you guys okay in elevator number twenty-four?" came a mechanical voice over a hidden speaker. "We had a temporary mechanical failure, but we're okay now."

Julie leapt to her feet, staggered naked across the Art Deco elevator, scrambling for her tights and her blouse, trying to get the tights over her tied sneakers and tripping and falling to all fours as she dressed, revealing all of her beautiful self to Tobin.

Tobin almost caught himself in his zipper when he couldn't take his eyes off the breathtaking and naked Julie. She pulled on her blouse. Tobin stared at her hard, ripped belly.

Then all at once the elevator hit a cushion of soft air and slowed.

Julie looked at Tobin, gasped, "We alive?"

"Balls-achingly so, I'm afraid."

The doors burst open.

Applause echoed through the lobby. People whistled, hooted, cheered. Julie stepped off, astonished. The maroon-jacketed head of security, wearing a red nametag that said MILLS approached. "Thank God you're all right," Mills said. "An elevator generator blew, and it took us longer than we expected to get the auxiliary going because there was a small electrical fire. Please accept our profound apologies."

"Couldn't you people hear us?" Julie asked.

"We could see and hear you fine on the camera, before the lights went out," Mills said. "Then we lost the video. But the audio stayed on. So we knew you were all right. Would you like medical treatment, there's an ambulance waiting?"

Hank shook his head, no. "Jule?"

"Nah," she said.

People approached and shook their hands as they walked for the Forty-second Street exit. Then something Mills said occurred to Tobin.

"Wait, come with me," he said, leading Julie to the door where he'd seen the security people watching the yuppie pick her wedgie earlier.

"What?" Julie asked.

Tobin half-smiled as he steered Julie toward the security office. The door was open, as it had been earlier. A group of male guards gathered around the monitor panel where thirty-two small screens showed what was happening in each elevator.

They were watching a replay of the tape from elevator number twenty-four on a monitor.

"You could play racquetball off that hard little behind, man," Tobin heard one guard say.

"Them titties are *fine,* too," said another.

"Hit slo-mo, and freeze-frame, man," said another.

A square-badge guard rewound the tape and played it in slow motion. Tobin and Julie peered in when the screen was dark.

"Watch this shot as the lights come on, man," the guard said.

Tobin looked over Julie's shoulder as the screen filled with light. He saw Julie straddling Tobin on screen.

Tobin looked at Julie watching the men watch her as she leapt to her feet. Tits-ass-naked! Her eyes widened like an electroshock patient's.

Julie pulled her badge and .25-caliber pistol from her purse. She elbowed her way to the monitor. "You filthy pigs!"

"Hey, man, it's the babe!"

"You fine, shorty."

Julie lunged at the guy at the control panel.

"Gimme that fucking tape," Julie said. Tobin smiled.

"Can't do that, lady, belongs to management and . . ."

Julie dug the gun into his crotch. "I'll blow off your balls."

The guard hit the EJECT button. Handed Julie the tape.

Julie grabbed it and hurried across the lobby.

"Someone once described this lobby as 'Jazz Age poetry set in marble and steel,' " Tobin said. "They could have been talking about you."

"Pigs! You let them talk about me like that?"

"They didn't say one thing about you I disagreed with."

"That supposed to be a compliment?" she asked, hurrying for the Forty-second Street door.

"They liked what they saw. Me, too."

"Those horn dogs were ogling me? And you didn't say one word."

"I don't blame them."

"Men are truly twisted."

"Yeah, but you're the one wearing your blouse inside out."

Julie stopped, looked down, saw that her blouse and tights were wrong-side out, and shrieked. "You son of a bitch!"

"I want a copy of that video," he said and banged through the front doors and into Forty-second Street, trailed by a mortified Julie.

"Not on your life."

"I'm the co-star, so why not?"

"Because what I said and what almost happened in that elevator don't count," she said, jaywalking toward the ticketed Taurus parked across the street.

"Oh, yeah? Why not?"

"Because they were said under duress. Under the threat of death."

"But they were your true feelings," he said, tossing her the car keys as he climbed in the passenger seat. "You *laid* yourself, um, *bare,* my darling wife."

"Temporary fucking insanity," she said, snatching the ticket from under the wiper. "My darling *ex.*"

THIRTY-SEVEN

Tobin made Julie stop at the *Examiner* building, where he spent three minutes trying to convince a security guard that he was Hank Tobin. Upstairs, no one in the city room recognized him at first. Not Tammy Kwon, not Skip the librarian, not any of the copy editors.

Tracy Burns did.

She smiled and said, "Your makeover makes me feel like your great-aunt."

He asked Tracy Burns to lock his laptop in her drawer. There were maybe a half-dozen people out of 6.2 billion people on Planet Earth whom he trusted. Burns was one of them. With his heart and his soul and his copy and his secrets.

"You okay, Trace?"

"Whatever problems I have, they don't add up to a hill of Bogart's beans compared to yours," she said.

Tobin noticed circles under her intelligent eyes. "You need to talk?"

"I have a paper to get out," she said. "Nothing stops that. It's like trying to stop the Mississippi. Maybe later."

"I'll call."

"You gonna write a column for tomorrow?"

"Can you hold my spot in case I do?"

"Sure. You can always be replaced with a vodka ad."

"You're a queen."

"Anything else you need?" she asked.

"Yeah, I need to borrow your cell phone."

"I won't even ask why," Burns said, handing him her phone.

*   *   *

Julie let herself out on E. Thirty-seventh Street, saying she was going to sneak through her neighbor's yard into her house, change, and go try to isolate Debbie Hu to talk to her on her own. Without Fred Buckles around.

Tobin gave Julie Tracy Burns's cell-phone number. He told her to borrow one from Coogan, her backyard neighbor, and call him in two hours. It was now almost 11 A.M. Julie said that wouldn't be a problem.

Tobin waited outside Immaculate Heart of Mary food pantry and soup kitchen until he saw Billy Kelly emerge. He'd peeked in through the windows and saw him feeding the poor and the hungry. But he didn't want to make a scene inside. He waited until the lunch feeding was over. He watched poor people, white, black, Hispanic, Arabic, many immigrants, probably illegals, leaving the pantry carrying shopping bags filled with canned food, powdered milk, and rice.

They were the city few ever saw. The kinds of people Hank Tobin used to write about when he first got the column. Before he became a player and a pundit, remarking on national and global issues, or riffing off local headlines.

When Billy Kelly reached the top of the church steps, Tobin figured it was a safe place to approach this younger guy with the unholy jail muscles.

"Morning," Tobin said.

"Morning," Billy said. "You a member of the parish?"

"No."

"I volunteer with the pantry, soup kitchen," Billy said. "You hungry?"

"I look underfed?"

"Be surprised how many people're out of work since September 11," Billy said.

"Sad."

"A hundred and thirty thousand New Yorkers lost their jobs," Billy said. "And that's just the documented people. Tens of thousands more, poor undocumented people, also lost their jobs. We feed a tiny number of them and their children. We do clothing drives. Give job counseling. Help with résumé writing. So don't be embarrassed. A lot of well-dressed, educated people like you started showing up after the extended unemployment benefits ran out. People have to eat, man. They have to feed their kids. Sometimes you gotta put your pride in your pocket. You got kids?"

"Yeah, actually that's why I'm here."

"No problem, food we have," Billy said, his enthusiasm, humanity, and generosity making Tobin feel edgy, nervous, and ill. "Maybe I can't wangle a small emergency loan outta Father Fanning, or a Metro Card to help you look for work. . . ."

"I'm not looking for that, I'm . . ."

Billy Kelly was on a roll, and Tobin knew that was probably the Methadone buzzing in his brain, producing a motor-mouthed, synthetic-opiate euphoria that was standard among guys on "the program."

"Look, I work nights, porter, washing dishes, like that," Billy Kelly said. "But I only have myself to support. I have free time so I spend it here. Maybe I can get you a gig working weekends."

"Helping others, huh?"

"Well, it's the Christian thing to do. I don't think it's corny. When I rediscovered Jesus Christ, I rediscovered my humanity, bro."

"Charity, helping thy neighbor, forgiveness, redemption, like that?"

"You goofin' on me, bro?"

"No. No way. I admire what you're doing."

Billy stared at Tobin, like he was trying to place the face. Tobin was wearing the tinted shades and had shaved again that morning.

"Yeah, well, I work especially hard on forgiveness," he said. "Lots of prayer, novenas, Stations of the Cross. My pastor, Father Fanning, he explains that in order to forgive others, you must forgive yourself first. I'm wrestling with it, man. But Jesus will show the way. I also do some recruiting for the parish. Are you looking to volunteer, do a little work for the Lord, bro?"

"Actually I was looking for some help, an old-fashioned Christian help-ing hand, and some charity and a whole lot of forgiveness."

"You jammed up with the law or something, bro?" Billy asked. " 'Cause if you are, I know a little about that there. I know some legal coun-selors. Maybe we should get Father Fanning involved. What you tell him is a secret if you do it in a confessional, bro. It's like testifying with immunity. And you go in the Lord's witness program. Come hang out on Serenity Beach, Bay Twenty-two in Coney Island, where all the people from AA and NA and GA and other twelve-step programs, and people trying to get in touch with their souls go every day, to try to make amends with the world and the Lord and loved ones in their lives. You'll find you're not alone. Then go back to the church, find solace, light a candle in your darkest hours. I swear to you it works, bro."

"No, I don't need the help of Father Fanning or the Lord right now. I need more than Serenity Beach, or whatever you call it, or a votive candle. I need *your* help, Billy."

Billy Kelly looked at him, the savvy ex-con cracking through the religious shell.

"You know my name, bro? I know you? You do a bit? We cell somewhere?"

"Our paths have crossed."

"Yo, I want mysteries, bro, I'll read the Loaves and the Fishes. What's your game? Who're you? You the man? Yo, I don't owe the state one fu . . . one stinking day. I did every day of my bit so don't you come around here crushing my stones. . . ."

"I need you to help me get my son out of jail."

Billy jerked his head back and forward like a chicken. "I cell with him or something? Was he in my Green Haven Bible class? Which joint? What's his name?"

"Henry Tobin Junior. I'm Hank Tobin."

Tobin saw the tattoo of Jesus that covered the old swastika on Billy Kelly's right forearm ripple with ten godless years of jail yard, iron-pumping muscle as he clenched his fist, each finger from thumb to pinkie tattooed with one letter that spelled out J-E-S-U-S.

Billy squeezed shut his eyes, pointed up the street.

"Leave, bro."

"I can't," Tobin said, waiting for the assault. "I need your help."

Billy clutched the crucifix dangling around his neck, as if for strength. Anger rippled under the skin of the young man's face. Throbbing thick veins climbed his bull neck like blue beanstalks. The big man began to shake, a motorized quaking like someone had plugged in an attachable cord.

"Listen to me, Hank Tobin. Even Jesus had his limits. You're worse than the moneychangers in the temple, bro. You are a wrecker of people's lives. You are a messenger from Satan. You're *e*-vil, man. You sent me and my whole family to hell. But I'm not in hell anymore. I'm preparing myself for Heaven. Jesus lives in my soul now. Jesus won't let you keep me from Heaven. Jesus will stop me from doing what the anger in my heart wants me to do to you. I will not let you condemn me twice. I spent ten long years scouring my brain for a scrap of memory about torching that house. I came up with *nothing*. Know why? I don't think I ever did it. I don't think I woulda been arrested if it wasn't for that column you wrote, quoting my drunken father. I was a kid in a hellhole, on a million dollars bond, facing twenty-five years. So I copped to ten years. But I don't think I deserved a day."

"Maybe I was wrong back then for quoting your father off the record," Tobin said. "Maybe I wrote a reckless column. Maybe it helped ruin your life. Maybe you are innocent. But my son had no hand in it. Now your father has framed him for things he did not do, and my kid faces the rest of his life in jail. I'm not looking for redemption for myself, Billy. I'm asking you to help me save my son, who's paying for my sins."

Billy Kelly opened his wallet, took out the old, yellowed Hank Tobin column, the one that put him in jail and gave Mona Falco a career. It was neatly folded and held together with Scotch tape.

"I've been waiting for this for so long," Billy Kelly said. "I used to lie awake at night staring at this column that was pasted to my cell wall. In the early years, every night I thought of a new way of getting even with you. I thought of slow deaths, torture, castration, burning you to death. Locking you in a cell and starving you to death. It was how I passed the time. Some guys jerked off, counted sheep, smoked cigarettes, and shot bad dope. I lay awake each night thinking of a zillion different ways to kill Hank Tobin when I got out of jail."

"I can understand—"

"No, you can't. I'd read about you in gossip columns and seen you on TV talk shows selling books or pontificating about the political scene, big, wise, man-of-the-people pundit, man. And I would pump iron, add new weight-plates every month, build bigger muscles, and think of one day getting out, finding you, and making you eat every column you'd ever written. Mashing them into your mealy mouth and making you chew and swallow all your phony words, every period, comma, and question mark, until you choked to death on your own rotten words."

"Go ahead, blame me, but Jesus Christ don't—"

"Jesus is the only one who could have saved me," Billy Kelly said. "Lucky you. For in turn he saved you from me. I fully intended killing you within the first week of my release. But, lucky you, I found Jesus. A friend of mine inside who was dying of AIDS discovered the Lord, and it gave him a special divinity, a cleanliness, a halo of dignity even in the hellhole where we were caged like animals. He asked me to pray with him every night as he was dying, and as we prayed, I felt His light enter my soul. I went to prison Bible class, and I discovered a deeper and more profound wealth than you will ever know, Hank Tobin."

"I'm sure you have but please—"

"I won't bore you with my own salvation. Suffice it to say that I live in peace and go in dignity. I already been to hell in this life; I don't want to go back in the next one."

"I'm asking you to help save my kid from the same hell, not me."

"Hey, asshole, I don't have enough forgiveness for *myself* yet to even come close to forgiving *you*. I didn't even *forgive* my own father. And now it's too late. And I find that unforgivable. I can't forgive myself for not forgiving him before he died. And so if you're selling me some bullshit story that my dead father is alive and that he framed your precious little boy for those awful attacks on houses of worship, you've come to the wrong guy, man. If I never had it in me to forgive my own father, you think I'm ever gonna forgive you? No way, pal."

Billy Kelly ripped the old Hank Tobin column into little bits and tossed them in Tobin's face.

"See, just me doing that instead of stuffing them down your lousy throat means I'm on the right road to salvation," said Billy Kelly. "You wrecked my life, my mother's life, I lost my sister, and my father died alone, and nuts from what I hear, before I ever had the decency to forgive him for blabbing to you that night ten years ago. And if I don't kill you for it, it means Jesus is alive in my heart and soul. But I don't forgive you, bro."

"You won't help me?"

"Like I said, I have work to do on my Christian soldier act," Billy Kelly said. "It'd take a sign straight from Jesus for me to ever help you. So the short answer is, FUCK YOU! God forgive me, but I hope your kid dies in the joint."

Tobin watched Billy Kelly bless himself, kiss his crucifix, and walk off with the flowers for his father's grave.

THIRTY-EIGHT

The cell phone that Tobin borrowed from Tracy Burns rang. He looked at the caller ID, saw it was a 718 area code, and figured it was for him. It was Julie saying she'd borrowed her neighbor's cell phone. She said she would be meeting Debbie Hu at one o'clock at Astroland in Coney Island, where she was taking her kids on the rides. Julie learned from Debbie that Buckles was on his way to the Bush Terminal wholesale meat-and-produce markets on the Brooklyn waterfront to buy stuff for the Hu family supermarket and the restaurant.

Tobin knew that Bush Terminal was just twenty blocks from the headquarters of NYPD Intelligence Division at the Brooklyn Army Terminal, on the Brooklyn piers. Smack in the middle of those two places was the Brooklyn Federal Detention Center, where his son Henry lay chained to a sick bed with a jailhouse *fatwa* on his head.

Tobin's hand still hurt from punching Moog. And he didn't feel like rolling in the gutters with a young, tough jailbird like Fred Buckles, so he called Vinny Hunt and asked him to meet him at the markets.

Ten minutes later Vinny did. Alone. He left his driver back at headquarters.

Tobin jumped in Vinny's black Crown Victoria and told the big cop that he believed that Buckles, who liked impregnating young girls, had probably thrown the Molotov through Debbie Hu's window ten years before, an incident that sent Billy Kelly to jail, and inspired Lenny Kelly to frame Tobin's son.

"In the immortal words of Archie Bunker," Tobin said, " 'Revenge is the best way to get even.' "

"You do understand that the statute of limitation has expired on this," Vinny said.

"I just want Buckles to admit it. I want Lenny Kelly to know there is someone else with underlying blame here. That this guy also knocked up his daughter, Erin. That somehow we *all* got the story wrong. If this nut calls me again, I just want to try to make him come to his senses before it's too late. Before he goes to his own grave. I only have until tomorrow, Vinny."

Tobin and Vinny cruised through the sweltering truck-clogged market, where shouting men jockeyed hi-los laden with skids of fruit, vegetables, poultry, and meat. Sweaty, overweight, immigrant men grunted handcarts piled with ice-dripping crates and boxes through this cobblestoned labyrinth of alleyways and warehouses and loading docks, loading them into vans with the names of restaurants, butchers, supermarkets, and grocery stores, many of them men of Middle Eastern descent. Most of the greengrocers were Asian, stamping their selections with their store brands.

Not so much as a baby's breath of wind blew off the stagnant harbor.

The market was the bruised city in microcosm—native Brooklynites, immigrants of every stripe, loan sharks, and bookmakers, honest toil and dirty swindles, food, cops and gangsters, dreams, nightmares, and money—all clogged into ten square blocks by the most famous harbor on Earth, in plain view of Lady Liberty and the disfigured Manhattan skyline.

Tobin knew there was a titty-bar named Wild Wild West two blocks away and whatever the working stiffs didn't drop there on sweaty lap dances, they brought home to the wife and kids, or mailed home south of the border or overseas.

"We got guys planted here," Vinny said. "Looking for shakedowns, kickbacks, and smuggling scams. Some of it old-fashioned wise-guy shit. Some to raise money for organizations like Hezbolah in Lebanon, which is a pipeline to Al Qaeda. Guys have to give cash kickbacks or go on some Imam's or sheik's Allah-akbar shitlist."

Bored Federal Government meat inspectors and itchy-fingered political-machine patronage kibitzers from the City Department of Health oversaw this market, which supplied most of the meat and produce that reached the tables of three million Brooklynites every day. Rabbis blessed food to make it kosher. Imams blessed other food and declared it Halal. No one went home empty-handed.

Vinny grabbed Fred Buckles at Liberty Wholesale Meats, where the little tattooed man pounded his Madam Hu's Golden Bowl beet-juice stamp on two sides of beef, three pork loins, and three boxes of chickens he'd hand-selected for his wife's upscale—by Brooklyn standards—restaurant.

"Get in the car," Vinny said, flashing his captain's badge and ID.

"Captain?" Buckles said, incredulous, sweat drooling down his wanted-poster-handsome face. "Intelligence Division, man? The fuck I do? I didn't do nothin'. You listenin' to this guy? I'm workin' here. I got a family to support. Gimme a break, boss."

Tobin climbed in the front seat next to Vinny. Buckles plopped in the back without having to bend his head, jittery, fidgeting. Vinny drove the black Crown Victoria along Second Avenue, made a right just before the jail, and rolled out onto an abandoned, rotting wood-piling pier. He and Tobin climbed out.

Buckles got out of the backseat looking like a schoolboy going to detention.

"Too hot to waste time," Vinny said. "Bullshit me and one phone call to your parole officer becomes five more years of hard time."

"Wait a minute—"

"I didn't say you could talk, yet," Vinny said, raising a finger, his voice as quiet and final as the whisper of a dorsal fin. "Be quiet until I say 'talk,' or I make the call right now, and I'll have you charged like the next Jose Padilla, as an enemy combatant with no charge. Maybe forever. I'll say you were heard talking to one of the Iraqis or Qaedas on our watchlist in the market about carrying a dirty bomb into Penn Station or LaGuardia. That's all I need. Talk. An anonymous Atlantic Avenue source. I can make the call, Fred."

Tobin looked at Vinny, happy he wasn't working against him. Vinny held the cell phone in his hand. The sun baked down on the old pier that jutted into the harbor like a gangplank to Brooklyn's murky past. Coast Guard vessels and NYPD harbor-unit boats patrolled the waters. Sweat blotted Tobin's shirt, and he saw buttons of sweat form in rows on Buckles's high forehead. Buckles's eyes showed fear. There was no interrogation lamp in the world worse than a windless, 103-degree New York City high-noon sun.

Buckles nodded. Humble. Vinny pulled out Buckles's rap sheet from his inside jacket pocket and rattled it like an X ray of his life.

"Okay, little man, I see you still like young girls," Vinny said. "Had one with you when you got arrested smuggling cigarettes up from down south. You know they busted a couple of Arabs smuggling cigarettes and sending the money to Hezbolah? Maybe I can make the connection to you."

"C'mon, man, I was muling untaxed butts with a coupla gindaloons from Bath Beach," Buckles said. "These guys were so low-level they wouldn't let them valet-park a capo's Caddy at a Jew lawyer's funeral."

"But you know I could make them reopen the case to make sure you weren't connected to the Hezbolah guys."

"You guys can make shit smell like soap and vice versa, you want to," Buckles said. "I know that. I look dumb?"

"You were also with a sixteen-year-old girl, huh?" Vinny said.

"Listen, man, I was a dog when I was younger, I admit that," he said. "But that kid I got pinched with on the cigarette-run rap, she was my *daughter*, man."

Tobin and Vinny looked at each other.

"Daughter?" Tobin said.

"I'm thirty-two," he said. "I had my first kid when I was sixteen. Her mother was fourteen when she gave birth. But my wife, Debbie, man, she gets superjealous if I have anything to do with any of my other kids from other women. I had a daughter who moved down to South Carolina. When I went on the cigarette job, to bail out the restaurant because Debbie's father lost a bundle on the stock market after September 11—Enron, Tyco, ImClone, WorldCom—name it, he rode it down. The restaurant got strapped, couldn't meet all our bills. So I heard about this cigarette run. The price up here just went past seven bucks a pack. I figured I could score and say hello to my daughter at the same time, and when we got pinched, I didn't want them to pinch her so I said I picked her up hitchhiking, and they let her go. That's all that was. I'm still a dog, but I'm trying to work on my pedigree papers, here, if you get my drift, for the sake of my kids. But nobody wants to put redemption on the fuckin' menu in America anymore. The whole country is one big perp walk."

"So you don't deny knocking up young chicks when you were young?" Tobin said.

"Of course not. But I didn't do it with grammar school kids. . . ."

"No, you waited until they were in junior high," Tobin said.

Buckles looked at Vinny, pointed at Tobin, and said, "Who is this guy? He never shows ID. He just yaps."

"You don't ask the questions," Vinny said. "You answer them."

"Okay, boss."

"Go back ten years."

"Again with this fire? Sorry, I meant that as a statement, a rhetorical question. See, I learned vocabulary. I grew up. I evolved. When I was young, I was *real* young, meaning emotionally immature, see? I kept on banging young girls because I was immature, psychologically stunted, developmentally arrested. I was criminally arrested so many times, and spent so much time in institutions as a kid, that the shrinks tell me I was socially and emotionally arrested. I didn't know how to rap to chicks my own age. So I always went after younger ones. I could talk to *them,* sometimes even be their intellectual superiors."

"We don't need a psychological profile, Fred, we need answers about the fire," Tobin said, the sun squinting his eyes, broiling the nape of his neck.

"When I got home from Desert Storm, I was nineteen," he said. "Two years later I knocked up two chicks. Debbie was sixteen. Erin was seventeen. What, neither one of you guys ever went with a chick five or six years younger than you?"

Tobin ran his hand through his sweaty hair, knowing he had fifteen years on Dani Larsen.

"Yeah," Vinny said. "But when you're sixteen and the girl's eleven, it's a little different."

"I never did that!" Buckles said. "In fact seventeen is legal in New York. Some states sixteen is legal. So it ain't like I'm some fucking monster. I was a dog, not a monster, all right? That's another rhetorical question, please."

Tobin said, "Did you torch Debbie Hu's house to try to kill her because she was pregnant and the family was threatening to have you arrested for statutory rape?"

"You fucking nuts? Sorry! No fucking way. Here's a family with money and property and a family business who wants *me,* dead-end Freddie Buckles, as a son-in-law, with a promise of some kind of future. You think I'm throwing a fucking gasoline bomb at that? Let me rephrase, your honor. This was my meal ticket. I couldn't wait to marry Debbie Hu. She was beautiful, hot, young—yes, like I liked them—and sweet. And devoted. She looked up to me, like I was smart, like I was important, like I was in charge. You know how that makes a five-foot-four, emotionally arrested twenty-two-year-old jailbird feel? Like fucking Thor, man. Nobody had ever shown me so much love and respect and honor. Debbie was so jealous of other women coming near me she never let me out of her sight. I strutted that shit, man."

"So you weren't forced into marrying her?"

"Come on, man, I just told neighborhood people that to save face, so I didn't look pussy-whipped," Buckles said. "Brooklyn street-shit. Fact is I never had a real family. My old man is still doing life for killing my mother when I was eight because she burned his favorite Hawaiian shirt with a cigarette when she was drunk. Three days later he came home from the saloon still pissed off about the shirt and stabbed her to death in her drunken sleep. I seen it, too. Me, I was raised in reform schools, foster homes, jail, and the army. The Hus offered me a family and their beautiful daughter. If I didn't love her and them, I wouldn'ta stuck around the last ten years and banged out two other kids, went to Chink cooking school, and then to jail trying to raise money for the family on a hair-brained cigarette-smuggling scheme. Between you and me, I didn't get pinched until the tenth run so I did make some money outta the scam. But not one penny went in my arm or up my nose. It all went to pay bills and save the business. I owed them, man. The Hus are my family."

Vinny looked at Tobin, blew out a long stream of breath, sucked for oxygen from the pasty air, and wiped his brow. Tobin was having the same trouble with Buckles's story. Seasoned cops and reporters develop a built-in polygraph that tells them ninety-nine percent of the time when someone is lying. In the glare of the scalding sun, Buckles's story had the distinct ring and smell of truth.

"You didn't light that fire?" Tobin asked.

"Absolutely not."

"Not even for the insurance?" Vinny said, wiping his brow with a clean hankie. "The statute has run out. You can tell us, Freddie."

"No, square business, no."

"You think Billy Kelly set it?"

Fred Buckles stared off toward Staten Island.

"No, I never thought so," he said. "That's why when he got out, I gave him a job washing dishes. I believe in redemption. I had a hard time convincing the Hus, but they went along with it. They love me like a son."

"Billy Kelly works for you?" Tobin said, remembering Billy telling him that he worked nights as a dishwasher and porter.

"Sure, law against that? Sorry, rhetorical. Rephrase: no law against that."

"If you don't think he torched your in-laws' house ten years ago, who did then?"

"First of all, all I could give you would be an educated guess. And, like you sez, the statute's run out. But here's where I draw the line. I never was and never ever will be a rat."

Vinny looked at Tobin and half-shrugged.

"Take a hike," Vinny said.

Buckles walked down the pier. Tobin checked his watch. He had to meet Julie, who was meeting with Debbie Hu, the jealous young girl who was starting to look like the prime suspect for starting that old fire.

THIRTY-NINE

Before going back to Intelligence Division headquarters, Vinny Hunt helped get Tobin a fast three-minute visit with his son at the nearby jail.

"Hey, Pop."

"We're making progress," Tobin said.

"How's Mom?"

"Tough as nails."

"Laurie?"

"Fine."

"No, she's not," Henry Jr. said, shifting in the bed, the handcuffs straining on his wrist, in clear discomfort and pain. "That FBI guy Cox was here. Telling me that Laurie's going down next, for a fucking hate crime! That maybe if I just took a plea they wouldn't arrest Laurie. That true, she might get arrested, too, Pop? You can't let them do that to my kid sister. They're only going after her because of me. And they went after me because of you . . . sorry. I didn't mean that. Maybe I should just . . ."

"You're not pleading to anything," Tobin said. "And don't be sorry. It's true that they're going after both my kids to get even with me. For that I'm the one who's sorry, Henry. Sorrier than I've ever been in my life."

Tobin stepped closer to his son.

"Step back, please, Mister Tobin," said the female guard.

Tobin stopped, frustrated, impotent, furious. He concentrated on his *dan tian,* the Zen center of his body below his navel, trying to get the *chi* flowing through his meridians. And wondered where Lenny Kelly was doing his *chi gong* exercises, as he prepared himself for his excursion tour of eternity.

"You okay, Pop?"

Tobin felt the tension run out of him like water down a drain. "Fine, Henry," Tobin said.

"Less than a minute, Mister Tobin," the guard announced.

Tobin didn't let her ruffle him.

"Henry, I've failed you as a father and as a friend," Tobin said. "I can't redo those years. I can't undo the mistakes. I can only promise you that I will get you out of here. And when I do, I'm gonna be asking you to help me be a better man, a better friend, and a better father."

Henry lay still, fumbling for words. "Pop, man, I—"

"Almost time," the guard said.

"Last question, Henry," Tobin said. "Answer fast. The night you covered the synagogue bombing. When did you get there?"

"About twelve minutes after the firebombing," Henry said. "Fire trucks were already there. I was the first reporter."

"Were there any cops there?"

"Yes."

"Recognize any?"

"Yeah, Cox. And that guy mom dates, Zach Moog."

"Okay, time, Mister Tobin," the guard said.

As the guard led Tobin out of the prison hospital room, Henry called to him. "Love ya, Pop."

Those three beautiful words from his son, words he had never heard Henry utter as a man, made Tobin feel all the more guilt-ridden.

Tobin met Julie at two P.M. in front of Gregory and Paul's fast-food stand on the Coney Island boardwalk, with a big silver rocket ship on the roof bearing the name ASTROLAND. Julie ate a shish kabob.

She was dressed in tight, white denim shorts, sneakers, and a red halter-top that revealed the rippling legs and flat, cubed belly. With the blond pixie haircut and tiny rectangular sunglasses, she looked more like a college student on summer vacation than a forty-three-year-old mother looking to free her imprisoned child. Tobin eyed her up and down and could see the outline of her badge-wallet in her pants.

"Where's your gun?"

"Left it in the Taurus earlier," she said. "Too hot to carry it."

Tobin considered a dozen littleneck clams but then had second thoughts. He was afraid of getting sick. He ordered a corn on the cob, fig-uring anything in boiling water would be safe, even here in the Poor Man's Purgatory where his mother took him as a kid on those rare occasions when some horny big-spender left her a $20 tip in the all-night Tip Top diner. He always loved the salty Coney air because it scoured the stench of the tenement roaches from his nostrils.

Julie nodded toward Debbie Hu, who waved at her two younger kids on the tame kiddie helicopter ride while her ten-year-old rode the rollicking water flume. Hurdy-gurdy music echoed through the crowded amusement park, sweaty mothers standing on long lines with whiney kids, young lovers spinning on heart-stopping rides, hawkers beckoning the crowd with hip-hop spiels under the white-hot sun. A sea wind blew in off the Atlantic.

"Debbie says she'll talk but didn't want anyone to overhear," Julie said. "Asked that we wait till her kids went swimming."

Tobin nodded, skipped the butter, added salt to the corn, and took a big bite. "This is like corn chowder on the cob," he said. Then he told Julie about his conversations with Vinny Hunt and Freddie Buckles and why he didn't think the tattooed man threw the Molotov cocktail.

He also told her he'd seen Henry, told her about Moog being there the night of the synagogue firebombing, about the mustard-colored Explorer in Moog's garage, and about Vinny Hunt telling him that Moog had planted a bug in the lamp in Julie's living room.

Julie's face drooped like a Salvador Dali clock, surreal wheels of betrayal spinning in her blue eyes.

"Moog was my . . . *partner*," she said, as if she were experiencing a sec-ond unfaithful spouse, another kind of painful divorce.

"He's involved in all this somehow, Jule," Tobin said. "In some rotten, lousy, treacherous way. Working with Cox, using you to get at me through our kids. All I know is that I believe Henry when he says he got to the syn-agogue fire twelve minutes after it started. But somehow LL sends me a photograph of a mustard-colored Explorer at the scene at the time of impact, time of explosion, and leaving the scene."

"So you think Moog—"

"There's a mustard-colored Explorer in Moog's garage," Tobin said. "Too coincidental for me. I think he drove it to the Sinai Torah Temple and firebombed the temple. Kelly took pictures. Then Moog drove the Explorer away after it was photographed. Then returned to work the inci-dent like a big fucking hero. . . ."

"Oh ... my ... God ..."

"What unit is Moog working in?" Tobin asked.

"He told me it was better I didn't know because it was deep cover," Julie said. "He said he was on vacation, anyway. But I had to figure it had something to do with the current terrorism stuff or guarding dignitaries or the mayor or something hush-hush and sensitive and that it was better that I didn't even know. I didn't *need* to know. I'm retired four years already, Hank. He's my *ex*-partner."

"You lost touch?"

"We stayed friendly, holiday cards, saw each other at weddings and wakes for other cops. But we sort of lost touch. He had his family, I had the kids and ..."

"When did he get back in *touch* touch with you?" Tobin asked. "As in 'I wanna touch what's in your pants' touch?"

"While you were away in the Middle East," Julie said. "He always had a sort of thing for me, you know. ..."

"Yeah, I know."

"Even though I was older than him. A lot of younger policewomen thought he was a doll, in that short hair, bull neck, muscles kinda way. To me he was just my partner. But after he got divorced he came around, with flowers and all that—"

"He isn't divorced," Tobin said.

"*What?*"

"You didn't check?"

"I'm gonna launch an investigation? Guy tells you he's divorced, you figure he's divorced. He was my partner, I trusted him. I mean what the hell, I trusted you, too."

"Well, Moog's still married. Vinny Hunt says Moog still very much has a wife *and* a mistress, too, and he was cheating on both of them trying to get in your tight little short-shorts, and planting bugs, and setting up our son to be framed at the same time. Real sweetheart."

Julie threw her kabob in the garbage as Debbie Hu and her kids raced up the wooden steps, carrying blankets and towels.

"I'm glad I don't have a gun on me right now," she said. "I might kill myself in shame. Or go find this son of a bitch and blow his heart out. How fucking dumb and trusting and gullible could I be, Hank?"

Debbie Hu reached the top of the steps and told the kids to run ahead. The kids raced down the boardwalk toward the defunct parachute ride,

Brooklyn's Eiffel Tower, which looked like it was ready to bend and topple in the blistering sun. Only the sea breeze offered any respite.

Tobin and Julie caught up with Debbie Hu. "We're going to Bay Twenty-two," said Debbie. "Serenity Beach. The only one without drunks. I feel safer there with the kids."

"That's where we used to go," Tobin said. "Of course we drank then. . . ."

Julie elbowed him. The sun roasted the boardwalk. Barefoot Latinas in string bikinis skipped along the sands as if negotiating beds of glowing coals. A lifeguard with Noxzema on his nose chatted up a platinum-blond hard-bodied girl with a chestnut tan. Kids ran in and out of the water. A plane flew by trailing an advertisement for Goumba Johnny, WKTU-FM—103.5 FM.

"You guys don't have to bullshit anymore," Debbie said. "I might not have been born in this country, but I've been a New Yorker for twenty years, so don't try conning me. I found out from a guy I know in the Lucky Seven who you two are. You're the Tobin guy who wrote the column. I can still remember the whiskey on your breath when you interviewed me."

Tobin cringed, and said, "I've cleaned up my act."

"Yeah, so did my husband," Debbie said. "You look better with a shave and glasses." Debbie turned to Julie and said, "And you're his wife. Where do you get your hair done? I like it."

"Rossi Salon. Ask for Tony or Mitchell Rossi," Julie said. "And that's *ex*-wife."

"You don't act it."

"Yes, she does," Tobin said.

"Is this like a lovers' quarrel? 'Cause if it is, it's way too hot. Are we gonna talk or what? If not, just leave me alone."

"No, we're gonna talk, Debbie," Tobin said.

"Okay, but look, I just got a call from my husband. He said you and another cop just hassled him. Threatened to violate him, trump up terrorist charges. This bullshit isn't right."

"You're right," Tobin said. "I think I picked on the wrong suspect."

"I'll say," Debbie said. "Just because he has a record and has tattoos people treat him like some kind of monster. He's not."

"He said the same thing," Tobin said. "What's this, a set routine with you two?"

"Hey, booze breath," Debbie said, "my husband might've done some stupid things in his lifetime. Maybe he's not perfect, like you, but he's a good husband. A very good father. He works hard. He saved my family's business. . . ."

"Yeah, smuggling cigarettes."

"Hey, he did a year in jail for that. Pled guilty. Like a man. Away from the kids and me. Isn't that enough? For what, felonious Marlboros? Look what the Wall Street assholes steal. Look how much the pricks at Tyco robbed. How about Enron, WorldCom, Merrill Lynch, Arthur Anderson, and all the other places that robbed from people like my father when they cashed out early and left people like him holding the bag? You get moral on me, I'll give you car fare, and you can go tell it to Wall Street."

"I've got nothing to add to that," Tobin said. "They're my sentiments, too."

Julie looked at Tobin and back to Debbie and said, "You're good."

"Come on, it's hot, I have PMS, ask your questions. You said you wanted to talk about the old fire. Talk. I have nothing to hide."

"Oh, no?" Tobin said.

"No, that's right. N o. What am I talking? Greek?"

"Your devoted husband got you pregnant at the same time as he got Erin Kelly knocked up, didn't he?"

Tobin saw a wave of old jealousy wash over Debbie Hu, as if it had risen right out of the deep Atlantic and crested on her face. "He mighta got her pregnant first. But my Freddie left that Erin bitch for me."

"Still president of the Erin Kelly Fan Club, huh?" said Julie.

Debbie Hu shrugged as they passed the Steeplechase Pier and the old Half-Moon Hotel where Tobin knew that a stoolie named Abe "Kid Twist" Reles, who was going to testify against Albert Anastasia of Murder Incorporated, went out the window on November 12, 1941, while he was being guarded by cops. The cops said he jumped. But Reles landed so far out on the parapet that investigators were convinced he was thrown to his death. Kid Twist's twisted corpse left an indelible historical example of what happens to rats in Brooklyn.

"I haven't seen her in ten years," Debbie said.

"She ever contact her brother, Billy?"

"How the hell should I know? My husband gave Billy a job washing dishes and cleaning floors. All I ever hear Billy say is he's sorry three hundred times a day if he did start the fire, followed by his prayers—"

"But you *do* know that he *didn't* light the fire, don't you, Debbie?"

"All I can tell you is my husband didn't do it. I want you off his back. I want that other Intelligence Division captain off his back. I don't want my kids to live without their father. They need him. I love him and I need him. My family needs him. So I need you people to leave my Freddie alone. No possible way he threw the gasoline bomb."

Tobin asked, "How do you know for sure?"

"I was baby-sitting," she said. "My parents were in the store. I got the kids to sleep. And Freddie was, well, Freddie was in bed with me. You know . . . what, I gotta spell it out? I'm in no mood, here."

Julie turned to Tobin, who looked unconvinced.

"I think maybe you're using Freddie to give yourself an alibi," Tobin said.

"*Me?* You think I firebombed my own friggin' house?"

"Yeah, maybe, because you were so mad jealous that Erin was also pregnant with Freddy's baby that you firebombed your own house to make it look like Erin did it. Then either you or Freddie planted the clothes and the gasoline in Erin's house, to make it look like she did it. Except the cops pinned it on Billy, the skinhead, an obvious choice."

Debbie Hu watched her kids race down the beach and open up their blanket, weight down the edges with their sneakers, strip to their bathing suits, and sprint for the shore.

"You need to take a Paxil pill, man," Debbie said. "Something wrong with your brain chemistry. You're paranoid. You hear voices, too?"

"As a matter of fact I do," said Tobin. "I hear a voice on the phone all week saying he's getting even with me for what I did to his kid ten years ago with a column about the fire in your house. He's making my son pay for whoever set that fire."

Debbie looked at Julie and said, "That true? You think your son's being framed for all that stuff?"

"Yeah, that's true," Julie said.

"Now you know how I feel when you people come around threatening to violate my kid's father," Debbie said.

Tobin and Julie looked at each other, sharing an abashed moment as waves crashed. He heard what he thought were mumbled prayers in the blinding sun. Tobin swallowed a dry, sandy knot. He realized that he was so self-absorbed in his own family he never thought about how he might be hurting yet another family. *I'm like Lenny Kelly to the Hus,* Tobin thought

Debbie Hu fell silent as Tobin and Julie followed her across the roasting sands. Different groups of Alcoholics Anonymous, Narcotics Anonymous, Gamblers Anonymous, and Overeaters Anonymous sat on flattened parachutes or on big bedspreads or on low sand chairs, "sharing" stories about their addictions and the various stages of their recoveries. Some said the all-purpose Serenity Prayer aloud. *"Lord grant me the courage to accept the things I cannot change, the strength to change those that I can, and the wisdom to know the difference."* Tobin knew it by heart, from rehab. It had helped save him from himself. Although he had stopped going to meetings after doing ninety meetings in ninety days after twenty-eight days of rehab, Tobin felt an affinity for these people who believed in redemption and making amends with people they loved whom they had hurt while lost in the vortexes of their own diseases.

No one played loud radios.

No beer hawkers.

No chicks in thong bikinis came looking for adventure here on Serenity Beach, the new Brooklyn oasis where the damaged and those on the mend flocked to schmooze and commiserate and search for peace one day at a time. Even the lifeguard was in his fifties and looked like a childhood Friend of Bill's.

Tobin and Julie trailed a mute Debbie Hu, passing people sitting alone in lotus positions, meditating, or facing the sun and chanting "om." Others did *tai chi.* Some held hands and participated in collective meditation. *Whatever gets you through the day,* Tobin thought, *clean and sober and alive.*

He wished he'd bought a sun hat on the boardwalk.

Debbie Hu walked closer to the shore, keeping an eye on her kids. Tobin and Julie followed her, sweat dripping off them under the high, intense sun as they trudged through the timeless sands where they had fallen in love in another century, in a different city and more innocent world over two decades before.

"I don't know if you guys are wired," Debbie Hu said. "You wanna talk more, meet me out there."

She ran into the surf, splashing with her kids, who squealed and giggled with their loving mom. She gave the oldest one finger-pointing instructions to watch the younger ones and then swam straight out into the sea toward a bobbing orange buoy. Tobin took off his shoes and socks and shirt, stuffed his wallet and keys and cell phones into his shoes, and put his faith in providence and the goodness of men and women engaged in self-salvation on Serenity Beach.

"You go," Julie said.

"You're the cop."

"I'm afraid of jelly fish."

He clutched Julie's arm and dragged her screaming into the surf.

"You son of a bitchin' bastard," she screamed. And he dunked her into the water. The Hu children roared with laughter, the youngest one missing front baby teeth.

When Julie bubbled to the surface, she said, "I'll get you for that, Hank."

"Promise."

"Up yours."

They swam out to where Debbie Hu clutched the orange buoy in the deeper sea. Tobin and Julie and Debbie held on to the buoy in what might have been the only place to have a private conversation left in New York. Tobin figured if they used the same meeting-spot twice, Cox or Moog would have a bug planted in the buoy.

"Listen," Debbie Hu said. "I told the cop that night what I saw."

"What did you tell him?" Julie asked, the steady wind blowing past them.

"I told him that I was with Freddie in bed," she said. "But I asked the cop not to tell my parents. It was one thing being pregnant. It was another thing still getting it on with him in their house before we were married. While I was watching the kids. The cop told me he would keep it quiet if I did."

"You remember his name?"

"No, but he was white, big, kinda cute," Debbie said. "He asked for the description of who I saw running from the house after throwing the fire-bomb. I told him it was a figure in a hooded sweat suit. But that it looked six sizes too big, the sleeves dangling, the pants legs both rolled up. And that the figure ran like a girl. Straight to the Kelly house."

"Oh, Jesus," Tobin said.

"My husband hates a rat more than he hates cops," Debbie said. "So if he ever asks if I told you this, I'll deny it. But there's never been an ounce of doubt in my mind that it was Erin Kelly who threw the Molotov through my window. Because she was jealous of Freddie being with me. Now, please, leave my Freddie alone. Leave me alone. Leave my family alone."

With that said, Debbie Hu kicked toward shore to join her kids.

Julie and Tobin stared at each other, treading water, clutching the buoy. As she turned, Julie grabbed on to Tobin's arm. He put another arm around her waist, her butt pressed against his groin. She felt perfect in his grip.

"What now?" she asked. "We need to go back to Erin Kelly? Confront her? Beg her to appeal to her father? Wherever the hell he is. What?"

"Give me a minute to think," Tobin said, unwilling to let go of Julie.

She spun. They stared into each other's eyes, the sun making tiny prisms of the beaded seawater on her long lashes. He kissed her. She let him.

"Not a bad move," she said, kissing him back.

Then in one fast flourish Tobin tore off Julie's halter top, leaving her bobbing and bare-breasted in the Coney Island sea, as he had twenty-three years before. Small rolling waves rose and fell, revealing the dark nipples. He waved the halter-top over his head like an adolescent male trophy, looking to the shore, hoping to get a testosterone-fueled chant of "Tits! Tits! Tits!"

But it was a different Brooklyn, a different Bay Twenty-two, a much different time. Tobin saw people holding twelve-step meetings where once they guzzled six-packs. One guy stood on a jetty like a whooping crane doing graceful *tai chi*. One big guy with tattoos led a prayer circle, as other men and women read from the Bible. An older, emaciated man with jet black hair and a black beard too dark for his age stood staring at his navel, doing rhythmic symmetrical twists, like a man keeping an imaginary hula hoop in motion.

"Give me back my top, you asshole," Julie said, laughing, looping her arms around Tobin's neck, and pressing her breasts against him. Instead of taunting her, Tobin surrendered Julie's top as his mood grew grave. He shielded his eyes with one hand.

Julie shaded her eyes with her top, following Tobin's line of sight.

"What?" she asked.

Treading water, Tobin felt a tingle slither his spine as if zapped by an electric eel. He shielded his eyes with both hands now, kicking to keep afloat, staring into the shimmering shore.

"Didn't Charlie Chan say Lenny Kelly always had sand between his toes?" Tobin said.

"The guy with the black wig and beard?" Julie asked, fumbling to tie on her top.

"He's doing *chi gong*," Tobin said, his words drowning in the sea wind. "And he keeps looking up at the guy with the tattoos in the prayer circle."

"Billy Kelly doesn't even know that his father is right there on the beach with him," Tobin said, and started swimming hard for shore, followed fast by Julie, husband and wife, mother and father, going after the man who held the fate of their son in his hands.

Going after Lenny Kelly.

FORTY

Breathless, Tobin trudged out of the surf, followed fast by Julie, who was in much better shape than him. They raced across the sand right toward the man with the black beard and wig. They zigzagged around beach blankets and spread parachutes, disrupting tranquil and emotional meetings.

"Hey, wrong bay for that guy," an older man yelled.

"Watch out for my kids," screamed a fat woman.

As he ran toward Lenny Kelly, Tobin kicked up sand and clumps of wet surf. Lenny Kelly *chi gonged* in sight of his only son, who stood some thirty yards away, leading a Bible class in prayer.

"Are you two crazy?" asked another woman.

"Sorry," Julie said, one of her breasts popping out of her half-tied halter top.

"Hurry, Jule!"

"Fuck!" Julie screamed, racing across the beach, trying to shove her breast back in the harness.

"Kids here," a young father yelled.

"Sorry!" Julie shouted.

"No nudity here!" screamed a fat woman.

"Shit! Shit! Shit!" Julie said, snaring one breast as the other popped out.

"Watch your language," shouted a man building a sandcastle with his kids.

The man stood in anger. Tobin tried to veer out of the father's way as he barreled toward him. Couldn't. Tobin banged into the man. Knocking him down. Crushing the sandcastle. Ruins. The man's kids cried.

"Son of a bitch!" said the man, tackling Tobin. "You asshole son of a bitch!"

"You . . . don't . . . under . . . stand," Tobin said.

"You bet your idiotic ass I don't, pal," the father said, as his kids sobbed.

The serenity of Serenity Beach shattered. The entire bay—twelve-step meetings, prayer groups, meditation rings, family picnics, sun-worshiping—came to a loud, aggressive, and vulgar halt.

Everyone watched Tobin and the angry young man wrestle in the wet surf.

Including Billy Kelly.

And Lenny Kelly.

Julie tried pulling her badge-wallet from her wet and skintight shorts.

"Cover your damned boobs with kids around," said the fat woman.

"I'm a cop," Julie said, yanking the badge out of her pocket. Tobin rolled into the surf with the young father. A crowd formed around them.

"What, an undercover hooker?" the fat woman asked.

Tobin shouted, "Jule . . . Lenny . . . Kelly . . ."

Julie looked up. Lenny Kelly gaped at her. And then at Tobin. And turned. And started to run.

Julie shoved her badge in the husky man's face.

"Yo, guy, sorry, but I'm a cop, and this is police business," she said. "Let . . . go of him . . . or I'm gonna lock your ass up."

The man let loose his grip on Tobin.

"Watch the language," the fat woman said. "What kinda cop are you? Curse like a trooper and do a striptease on a public beach in front of kids."

Tobin staggered out of the surf, panting, gulping air, pointing at the fleeing Lenny Kelly.

Tobin found the buried energy to give chase. The old man moved nimbly but slow, as if in pain, clutching the upper right side of his abdomen.

"Stop him," Tobin shouted.

"Police," Julie said, brandishing her mock badge, her right breast popping out again, lowering her arm fast.

Lenny Kelly ran to the end of the bay, toward the rock jetty. Tobin figured the sick and dying man would veer right, try to make it to Surf Avenue, and head into the projects and back streets of Coney Island.

But Lenny Kelly climbed up onto the rocks and made his way out toward the sea. *God almighty,* Tobin thought. *I blew it. I'm forcing him to kill himself a day early.*

"Please, Kelly, stop! Talk to me!"

He raced toward him through the blistering sand. And then Billy Kelly stood in his path. Big. All dancing, shiny muscles and garish religious tattoos, like a page of a comic book come to life in the shimmering heat waves.

"Holy shit," Tobin said.

"Nothing's holy to you, bro," Billy Kelly said. "You bother me at church. You bother the guy I work for. Now you're bothering me at my fucking Bible class, bro. Now you're botherin' some poor old guy who comes here minding his own business every day, doing his own peaceful, spiritual thing. . . ."

"That . . . peaceful . . . old man . . . is *your* old man, Billy."

Billy glanced at Lenny Kelly stepping across the jagged jetty, wearing sandals and shorts.

"My old man is dead and gone, man," Billy said. "You better learn some respect, hear me? I'm getting fed up with you. You can drive a guy to his breaking point."

"Don't be an asshole. That's your *father*. I swear to you."

Billy shielded his eyes as Julie approached, tying her blouse, gold shield flapping over her wet shorts pocket.

"It's true, Billy."

"Who're you?"

"I'm his wife. Was. Mother of his son. The one your father framed."

"My father had white hair," Billy said, walking toward the rocks where the old man picked toward the ocean end. "Bald before he died."

"It's him, in a wig and beard," Tobin said, brushing past him. "He comes here to be near you. He knows you wanted no part of him."

"Stop it!" Billy said, covering his ears. "It isn't him. Only Jesus can rise from the dead! Come near me again, and I will kill you. You are the devil, Hank Tobin! You stay away from me!"

He thumbed through his Bible, searching for salvation, as Tobin and Julie raced for the jetty. Lenny Kelly picked his way along the rocks.

"He's gonna throw himself off and let the waves crash him into the rocks," Tobin said. "Or get sucked into a riptide. If he goes off the end of the jetty, it's over."

"I wish I had the goddamned gun," Julie shouted, following Tobin barefooted on the slimy, slippery, algae-covered rocks, as swelling waves crashed around them.

"Kelly, stop, please," Tobin shouted. "Come back! Talk to your son! While there's still time! Help our son! Please!"

Kelly glanced over his shoulder, losing his footing. Wheeling for balance, his right hand knocked off his wig, baring his bald dome. He flapped his arms for balance, trying to recover the fallen wig, but saw Tobin and Julie advancing on him across the jetty.

"Stop, you crazy son of a bitch," Julie screamed and then slipped on a slick rock, sliding into a treacherous crevice. Tobin stopped, braced himself against a jagged rock, and grabbed Julie's hand.

By the time Tobin pulled Julie out of the void and back on top of the jetty, Lenny Kelly was at the very tip, doing a slow rhythmic *chi gong* dance on the final gray rock. At one with the sun and the sky and the sea and the wind. Oblivious to Tobin and Julie, summoning the remaining *chi* he had left through the last of his unclogged meridians.

Tobin shouted, "Lenny! For chrissakes, man. Stop! Please, just let us talk to you."

Lenny Kelly looked back once, clutching his liver.

"Billy didn't light that fire. I know that now. I got it wrong. You got it wrong. We all got it wrong. It was . . ."

But the words were lost in the crashing of the waves, the screams of the gulls, and on the steady zephyr blowing in from the blue-ruled horizon.

Then Lenny Kelly pointed to the sun, folded his hands as if in prayer, and dived from the last rock into the roiled sea.

"Oh, my God." Tobin could hear the hammering of his heart.

He gripped Julie's hand in the savage silence, gaping at the end of the jetty that was the edge of the world. Lenny Kelly had dived off, into the abyss.

Neither Tobin nor Julie had any words.

They stood there for almost thirty seconds, each moment crashing with the waves like tireless bombardments of eternity.

Then Julie said, "Let's at least look for him. If we prove he faked his death, maybe they'll believe everything else."

Dazed, bewildered, Tobin led Julie toward the end of the jetty, picking up the black wig along the way.

Then Tobin heard the growl of a motor coming to life.

Revving. Louder.

Julie's hand squeezed his hand as the motor grew louder. And louder. And louder and louder and louder, a still heart rallying back from the flatlined dead, until the growl grew into a roar. And then it came thundering in a deafening watery swoosh from the blind side of the jetty. Tobin pointed at the red WaveRunner spinning out in a sweeping arc into the deep blue Atlantic, leaving a white foamy chevron in its wake.

Sitting in the small sea craft was a black-bearded man with a shining bald head.

Tobin and Julie stood watching their only glimmer of hope race through the blinding waters, a disappearing speck of life heading for the Rockaway peninsula.

Tobin and Julie watched and listened until they could not hear or see Lenny Kelly anymore.

Tobin turned back to look for Billy Kelly on Serenity Beach. But he was nowhere to be seen. Tobin knew that Billy was too consumed with guilt to believe his father was alive. His sister, Erin, was too consumed with herself and self-preservation to want to know or to help.

Henry Jr. was facing life. Lenny Kelly was going to end his own life the next day.

Time was running out. Fast. Tobin knew that the time had come for him to do what Hank Tobin did best.

He had to go and write a column.

FORTY-ONE

Tobin drove to Julie's house and collected his Lexus. Reporters asked him if it was true that his daughter Laurie's arrest was imminent. Tobin said he had no comment for the moment and drove straight toward the *Examiner*.

On the way his cell phone rang.

LL said: *"Almost, Hank."*

"I only wanted to talk. To you. And your son. Together. To look at you and say I am sorry."

"You had all these years to do that. Too late."

"Your vindictiveness outweighs your righteousness," Tobin said. "You're as blinded by revenge as I was by ambition. What do we have for it? Two innocent kids who pay for our sins? Is this fair?"

Tobin was enthused by LL's brief silence. Then LL said, *"But you haven't paid the same price as I have. You never will. Your wife is too strong a woman to end her own life. Your son will still have her when he gets out. Unless you fall ill, your son will also have you. It's more than my son ever got."*

"You're a Mets fan, aren't you, Lenny?"

"Wrong name, but, yes, they're my team," he said, laughing. *"I'm going to miss the Mets. They've been like my family. They come to life every spring. But then when they disappear after the fall, it's another kind of death. Every season that passed reminded me of another season without my son."*

"We're both Mets fans. We're both from Brooklyn. We both grew up working class. We both had two kids, a boy and a girl. We even lived not far

316

from each other. We probably stepped in the same footprints on the same hot days in Coney Island over the years. We probably both drank in the same saloons at the same time. We have so much in common."

"Especially now, Hank."

"Yeah. Especially now. The point I'm making is that if your aim was to make me feel your pain, I feel it. I'll appear with you anywhere, in public, to admit I was wrong."

"You don't seriously expect me to believe that, do you, Hank? Too many other things had to be initiated. Sorry. I'll remain in control of the situation here. It's only another day. For me. Then my pain will end. And you will inherit all my pain. God help you. I'll say a little prayer for you before I depart. It's going to be an awful, awful life, Hank Tobin. Life without one of your children is a daily living death."

"Please, Lenny . . ."

But all Tobin heard was silence.

Tobin saw Phyllis Warsdale leaving the *Examiner* building as he entered. She didn't recognize him at first, but when he talked to her for thirty seconds, she realized he was Hank Tobin. He told her he didn't have time to explain his appearance. She said she was in a hurry but told him she had an interview scheduled with Judge Koutros the next morning.

"He finally agreed to talk to me," she said. "There's something desperate about him. I almost feel sorry for him. I've been looking at the two cases in which Koutros is accused of taking bribes. The original defendants are unreachable. Nowhere to be found. It took me three days to find out who the arresting officer was on the first one. Weird."

"Why?"

"Well, it was the same cop who arrested your son," she said. "Detective Mona Falco."

Tobin's skin itched like he'd walked into a giant, sticky cobweb. "She was the arresting officer in the old arson case," he said. "Who was the arresting officer on the second bribery case?"

"I dunno," she said. "NYPD is stonewalling. I'm waiting for the FOIL."

"An official Freedom of Information Law request to get the name of an arresting officer?" Tobin said. "That's strange. Unless it's connected to some secret investigation."

"I think I'll have it by tomorrow morning," she said. "But I thought I'd tell you about Detective Falco, same one who cuffed your Henry. Weird coincidence, no?"

"Yeah," Tobin said, thinking that it wasn't a coincidence at all.

"How's Henry doing anyway?"

"Could be better."

"I keep hearing rumors out of the federal prosecutor's office that your daughter, Laurie, might be getting locked up tonight, too. Any truth to that?"

"It's a witch-hunt. But, no, I didn't hear about the arrest coming tonight. Thanks, Phyllis."

"Remember, Hank, anything I can do."

"Where you meeting the judge?"

She gave him his beach-house address in Neponsit, not far from where Flight 587 crashed two months after September 11.

Tobin thanked Warsdale and hurried upstairs to the *Examiner*.

"I held your space," Tracy Burns said. "Something told me you'd be filling it."

"Thanks, Trace, you're a queen," Tobin said.

Then he sat down at his desk, called Clancy, left messages that Laurie might be getting arrested and the cell phone number for the phone he borrowed from Burns.

Then he wrote his column slug, with his initials and the next day's date. And then he wrote his lead. Mulled it. Made sure it was what he wanted to say to set the tone. And then, over the next ninety minutes, without referring to any notes, he banged out the most honest column he'd ever written.

TOB29JULY

BY HANK TOBIN

Ten years ago I helped destroy a Brooklyn family named Kelly with a reckless newspaper column in this space.

Now that column has boomeranged through time and come back to destroy my family.

A decade ago, a mixed-up nineteen-year-old kid named Billy Kelly went to jail for ten long, hard, innocent years. During his incarceration, his mother committed suicide, his sister disowned the family, and the father was reported missing in the World Trade Center on Septdmber 11.

I hereby take the blame for a lot of what happened to Billy Kelly and that family.

A decade ago I was still a drinking man, with a twisted romantic belief that when you mixed alcohol and ink it made you a better writer. It doesn't. I believed that the saloon was an extension of the column, a rich gold mine into which a columnist must plunge to dig for ore. It's not. For most writers, saloons turn them into braying, self-important fools, caricatures of themselves.

That would be okay if the only person you wound up hurting was yourself.

But it rarely is.

In my case, drinking while columning made me a dangerous drunk behind a very powerful wheel.

A newspaper column can be a mighty piece of heavy machinery. Used responsibly, a column is a plow to till rich soil, and it can be used as a combine to reap bountiful harvests. A column can be a backhoe to unearth buried wrongs, a jackhammer to shatter crooked politicians, a street sweeper to clean up a community mess, a steamroller to help pave a new street, a cherrypicker to put up a desperately needed traffic light.

A column can be a deafening public address system to make the voiceless heard, and a spotlight to give the little guy his deserved fifteen minutes of fame.

A tough column can help get an innocent guy out of jail, and a tougher column can help slam a privileged crook into one. It can save a working woman's job, make people think and laugh and cry.

A newspaper column can be a very powerful vehicle.

When a newspaper gives you the keys to a column, you take on a great responsibility. With it comes a strict set of rules of the road.

And some columnists abuse it. A column can turn a timid man into a bully. In the wrong hands this amazing machine can be transformed into a destructive weapon. It can be used to settle personal grudges, feuds, and jealousies. Say something nasty about someone enough times in a newspaper column and, whether or not what you say is accurate, you can hurt that person. You can hold that person up to public shame, humiliation, and ridicule. You can ruin his or her career, reduce someone to a pariah.

Sometimes, as in the case of my column about Billy Kelly and his father, Lenny Kelly, it only takes one column to do irreversible damage.

So a column can be an erector crane, and it can be a wrecking ball. It can run people over and knock people down. That's okay when the target is some smug, swaggering politician or an entrenched and arrogant institution that has a fighting chance to counterpunch.

But when a drunk gets behind the wheel of a column and aims it at a defenseless common man, it can flatten him.

Ten years ago a Brooklyn greengrocer named Hu had received repeated racially charged hate letters threatening him for daring to move his Asian family onto the lily-white block of W. Second Place. Then one terrible night someone threw a Molotov through the window of the Hu home.

On that night I was in a Brooklyn saloon when the city desk tracked me down and said there was a possible racially fueled arson in the Gravesend section of Brooklyn. Full of beer and myself and my own importance, I swaggered and staggered and got behind the wheel of my car and drove drunk to the scene of the alleged crime. When I got out and hung my press card around my neck, I also drove drunk behind the mighty wheel of this newspaper column, which, no columnist should ever forget, gets its power from the newspaper. Which in turn gets its power from you, the readers.

And with all that power of a newspaper and its million readers in my hands, I started the engine of my column, and I proceeded to run people down.

I committed journalistic manslaughter.

I reported the story, all right, but I violated a lot of the basic tenets of my profession. Oh, I got the address right, and the names of the victims are accurate. (The copydesk probably checked those facts for me against the hard news story and the AP wire reports and the police statements.)

But when I went looking for column color, for that special Hank Tobin insight, I popped into another nearby saloon so I could get a little more stewed as I took notes for my column.

In a ginmill called the Lucky Seven, I overheard a hardworking janitor named Lenny Kelly, who went by the unfortunate nickname of Lenny the Loser—he was about as good at gambling as I was at writing a column back then—brag about his son, Billy, torching the home of a Vietnamese grocer on W. Second Place.

Problem was he told me all this stuff off-the-record. My first journalistic sin that night was being drunk. Then I quoted a drunk. Who implicated his son (who, it was later learned, was also intoxicated and sound asleep at the time of the crime) in the hate crime in an off-the-record interview.

And then I quoted this father implicating his son for that crime in the morning paper.

I did a miserable job of hiding the father's identity, calling him Lenny the Loser, which is his well-known neighborhood nickname.

I printed a breadcrumb trail that led police right to his son's bedroom, where Billy Kelly was arrested for the arson.

Problem was, the cops arrested the wrong person.

And I can prove it. This time sober.

Billy Kelly, a poor kid with short-on-their-luck parents, could not afford a decent lawyer. Looking at twenty-five years in jail, with the circumstantial and physical evidence stacked against him, not even sure if he did the crime or not, Billy Kelly was convinced by his lawyers to cop a ten-year plea.

He did every day of that sentence, with six months off for good behavior, holding his father and me accountable for a good deal of his life of horror in a hellhole.

He was right.

Billy Kelly found Jesus in jail and came out to try to be a better man. He is a better man than I ever was or will be.

Now, as many of you may know, my own son, Henry, is neck deep in boiling water right now. He is facing life for hate crimes not unlike the one Billy Kelly went to jail for allegedly committing.

My son is as innocent as was Billy Kelly. His case is directly tied to Billy Kelly's.

I do not have the time or the space here and now to go into all the details of how I know that Billy Kelly was innocent. Or why I know my son is also innocent.

But if the *Examiner* will indulge me, if they do not fire me first, starting with this one I will present that story in a series of columns.

I won't lie and say that some of my motives are not selfish here. They are. One of the reasons I am writing this column is to help my son. I won't deny that. There are people out there, and they know who they are, who can help me, and I need them to come forward to help me right away. Today.

But this column is also an attempt to set the crooked record straight. The main purpose of this column is to apologize to the Kelly family, the living and the dead, that I have so badly wounded and helped destroy.

My apology can never undo what irreversible harm I have done to you, but I want it to serve in the eyes of your friends and neighbors and the people of this city as an official public declaration that I WAS WRONG and that I AM ASHAMED and I AM SORRY.

Of course, this also necessitates an apology to the editors, my fellow workers at the New York *Examiner,* and especially to my readers. I failed all of you miserably with my recklessness. I beg your forgiveness.

I also ask forgiveness from my own family, which is suffering the consequences of my irresponsible words and deeds.

To be continued . . . I hope.

In her office, with the door closed and the blinds drawn, Tracy Burns said, "I wanna go page one."

"Thanks," Tobin said.

"Of course it isn't up to me," she said. "Our fearless leader, and the publisher, and the lawyers will mull and vet and piss on and edit this until the Sports Final deadline."

"Tell them that if they don't use it today, I'll yank it and gladly resign," Tobin said. "And bring it somewhere else and rewrite it a little bit as a freelance piece. Maybe for my son's paper."

"My guess is our paper will know it's gonna cause a sensation, sell a zillion papers, become a national gab-show topic. There'll be book and TV movie offers for this Kelly kid. People will want to tune in for the next installments. They'll know if they don't print it, you'll get someone who will, and why wouldn't they? It's hot. It's sexy. It's ballsy. In an age of public apologies, it's a big shot eating crow and humble pie. It's a helluva read. And it's fucking news."

"Will you call me and let me know?"

"Sure," she said, her eyes glassy as if she'd been crying.

"Trace . . . you okay?"

"I just found out that my friend Claire from that fashion rag down the street is fucking my boyfriend. I swore to myself that I'd never fall in love with any guy, never mind one thirteen years younger than me. I promised myself that when I found out he was fucking around it wouldn't matter. Guess what? It does. Especially since Claire is fifteen years younger than I am. Two years younger than Himself. And it makes me feel like an old hag."

"You will find a better man, Trace," Tobin said. "You're a stop-the-presses, page-one lady. . . ."

"Please, don't reduce me to corny, fucking, newspaper metaphors."

"Okay, you're a great broad. If I wasn't already in love with someone else, I'd make a fool of myself chasing you around, even though you'd tell me to scram."

"Yeah?"

"Absolutely! But the next guy who does, for chrissakes, let him catch you, Trace. Go for it. You don't have to have kids for two people to call themselves a family. People need a family these days. Who else you gonna trust? Sometimes the strongest weapon around a man is a stiff ring finger."

Burns smiled, took a deep breath. Her eyes were puffy, probably from earlier tears. Tobin knew he could have fallen hard for her if he'd ever tried, and if she'd ever let him. But that was never their arrangement. And she just wasn't Julie Capone. No one else was Julie Capone.

Burns held up her naked left hand, nodded, and waved him toward the door. "No problem. Just keep my cell phone on in case I need to talk to you about the column," she said with a wink. "If they don't print this on page one, I'm resigning, and I'll marry the first bartender who calls me 'Baby.' "

"I'm sorry I can't be there for you tonight, Trace."

"Go home to Julie, Hank. You two need each other."

FORTY-TWO

After Tobin rang the bell a second time, Julie answered the door.

He asked, "Is Laurie home?"

"Up in her room."

"Good, because Clancy is gonna meet me here and—"

"Hank, I have company," she said. "Let me explain. . . ."

Tobin stepped into the living room. Zach Moog sat in Tobin's old recliner chair, the chair where Tobin had bounced his children on his knee, where he'd made love to Julie on countless better days. He held a sheaf of papers in his hand.

Julie said, "He's here about Laurie."

"You got an arrest warrant, scumbag?" Tobin asked.

Moog said, "No, I'm not here to—"

"Then get the fuck out," Tobin said.

Moog stood. Chest out, fists balled, he glared into Tobin's eyes.

"Hank, it isn't your house to tell him to get the fuck out of," Julie said. "He's here because—"

"Don't worry, I'm leaving," Moog said, banging Tobin's shoulder as he passed him.

Tobin shoved him. Moog shoved back. Julie jumped between them and said, "Assholes!"

Moog handed Julie the sheaf of papers and marched to the front door. He pulled it open, and Clancy stood on the doorstep amid a gaggle of reporters who were asking questions about the rumored imminent arrest of Laurie Tobin.

Moog left. Clancy entered.

Julie ignored him, shoving Tobin. "Who the hell do you think you are? You don't live here anymore, remember?"

"We better talk," Clancy said. "Where's Laurie?"

Tobin grabbed the living room stand-up lamp, yanked out the electrical cord, and carried it out the back door, banged it down on the stoop, went back inside, and slammed the door.

Tobin stormed back into the living room, still ignoring Clancy, pointing a finger at Julie.

"I told you that prick was treacherous," Tobin said. "He has some pair of balls showing up here! And you're worse for letting him in. You lied to me about him, didn't you? In the elevator, you lied to me."

"Can I talk to Laurie?" Clancy said.

Julie looked at Clancy, smacked the sheaf of papers that Moog had given her into the lawyer's hands. "Upstairs," Julie said. "Knock. Make sure she's dressed."

Clancy climbed the stairs, reading the papers. "Holy shit," he said.

Julie said to Tobin, "I did not lie! Moog came here to help."

"Help? Are you dumb on top of deaf? He's working for *them*. He planted a bug in your house. He set up our kid with a duplicate car. He's in cahoots with Lenny Kelly. . . ."

"I'm not so sure about—"

The doorbell rang. Tobin looked. "What, he forget his drawers in your bed?"

Julie slapped Tobin across the face and stormed to the door.

She yanked it open and said, "Stop ringing my fucking doorbell, you pack of vultures!"

Cox, Danvers, and Mona Falco stood at the door with Abel Winerib, an assistant United States prosecutor. The press popped flashes, beamed sun guns, shot tape, and shouted questions behind them. Mona Falco handed Julie a paper.

"Sorry, Julie, but we're here for your daughter, Laurie," Mona said.

"You're enjoying this, aren't you, Mona?"

"The Federal government has taken superceding jurisdiction because we feel it's tied to your son's case," Cox said. "This might come under the RICO statute if we can prove your children conspired together against people of a particular ethnicity."

Tobin shouted up the stairs for Clancy to come down, and he turned to Mona Falco. "One leaves," Tobin said. "Then the whole gang shows up. You will not destroy my family, Mona."

"Please don't take this personally, Hank," Mona said.

Julie looked from Cox to Danvers to Winerib. "How can we not take this personally when Mona Lisa Falco is my husband's spurned ex-lover?" Julie asked.

Winerib and Cox looked at Mona Falco. "In his dreams," Mona said.

Tobin said, "You're going to deny you ever went to bed with me?"

"I won't even dignify that with an answer," Mona said. "Now come on, get Laurie for us."

"Then how do I know you have a mole on a part of your, um, well, your vulva that can only be seen when you're fully naked?" Tobin said.

Cox looked at her, sweat springing from his brow.

Assistant United States Attorney Abel Winerib said, "If you have a conflict-of-interest charge to file, have your attorney file one. Meanwhile, let's just do this without any nastiness, okay?"

"I'm sure you wanna perp walk her out the front door, in front of all the cameras," Tobin said.

Winerib shrugged and smirked. "I didn't bring a helicopter, Tobin, to take her through the roof. Sorry."

Clancy walked down the steps with Laurie, from her upstairs bedroom.

"I think you might want to read this before you do anything, Abel," Clancy said, waving the sheaf of papers Julie had gotten from Moog. "Before you make an ass of yourself with this arrest. And I will be filing more than simple conflict-of-interest charges against Detective Falco. Starting with coercing witnesses."

"Oh, come on," Mona said.

Clancy handed Winerib the papers. Winerib shuffled through them.

Julie stared straight at Mona Falco and said, "That's a sworn statement from one of the Moroccan girls that my daughter is supposed to have assaulted during a racial tirade. She says that a police officer named Mona Falco coerced them into pressing charges and coached them into what to say to prosecutors after the fight."

"Bull . . . nonsense," Mona said. But Tobin knew she was nervous, her voice rising, eyes shifting from an already-shaken Cox, to a frazzled Winerib, to the ever-silent Danvers. "I took their statements, sure. But I never told either one of them what to say. The victim told me that she was on the Kingsborough College beach with her Moroccan friend discussing Henry Tobin Junior's case when Laurie called her a 'sand nigger,' and assaulted her with her pocketbook, which is a weapon."

"That's not how it happened," Laurie said. "No way."

Clancy grabbed her arm and told her to be quiet.

"But the other Moroccan girl says Laurie was taunted and called a 'white American motherfucker,' first," Julie said. "She says Laurie responded by *asking* how she would like it *if* she called her 'a dirty Arab sand nigger.' To which, according to your only witness, the Moroccan girl threw a handful of sand in Laurie's face, saying, 'Here's some sand from this sand nigger, you white trash American cunt.' "

"That's exactly what happened!" Laurie shouted. Clancy yanked her arm, putting a finger to his lips.

"So, Laurie swung her bag to defend herself, says the witness," Clancy said. "And the two of them wound up on the ground going at it. Punching, hair pulling, and scratching."

Laurie nodded her head up and down. Tobin watched Mona Falco's beautiful face tighten in dread.

Winerib shuffled through the papers, looking flustered, glancing up at Falco, who wouldn't look at him, glaring at Cox as the air hissed out of the prosecutor's balloon. "Why exactly am I looking at a birth certificate for your grandfather, Ms. Capone?"

"Because it proves that my grandfather's father was from a little island called Pantaleria, a spec of volcanic ash south of Sicily in the middle of the Mediterranean Sea. About twenty miles from Tunis. Where he met my great-grandmother. Who was one-hundred-percent Tunisian, or North African, which makes my daughter part Arab, or African American, take your pick, same as people of Moroccan descent. So even if what your complainant said was true, which my daughter and our witness says it's not, she couldn't commit a hate crime against a member of her own ethnicity, now could she, Ms. Falco?"

Mona Falco said, "This is absurd. . . ."

"I mean it would be no different than you calling Mr. Cox there by the N-word," Julie said. "Or would it be? Because while I was doing my genealogy research at the vital records office at the Italian Consulate, I took a fresh look at yours, Mona Lisa Falco *Lupo*."

Tobin watched Mona's face drop like the counterweight on a gallows.

"I also finally got your brother's military records, which are no longer classified because he's been dead since 1983. He died that year all right. But not in a Special Ops mission following the Beirut marine barracks, like you claim. He died in a car accident near where he was stationed in West Virginia."

"How dare you poke into my life," Mona said. "Into my family . . ."

Winerib glared at Cox and then at Mona Falco.

"You always claimed your mother was all white and father was black," Julie said. "Funny, but I couldn't find one drop of African blood in your family history, Mona Lisa Falco Lupo. You always claimed your father's name was John Wolf. But your father's name on your birth and baptismal certificates from Trapani, Sicily, is Gianni Lupo, which is Italian for John Wolf. Also odd that your brother never claimed on his military records that he was African American. He listed his father's name as Gianni Lupo. In fact, Gianni Lupo is still alive and well and living in an Italian jail, doing life for several 1970s assassinations for a right-wing terrorist organization called Propaganda Due that planned a coup d'état to have Sicily secede from Italy."

Mona Falco looked at Cox and Winerib and said, "None of this is accurate. . . ."

"Your old man is a Sicilian. So was his father and his father before him. Your father is just a dark, nappy-haired siggie. Like mine. Your mother is also one-hundred-percent Sicilian. The fact is, Mona, you're about as much an African Queen as Katharine Hepburn. You slithered up the ranks of the PD and now the JTTF on an affirmative-action scam."

"That's just untrue and silly," Mona said.

"Your whole career is based on a little *white* lie about being part black, isn't it, Mona?" Julie said. "You're a fraud. I bet you even got the JTTF gig because you're a *twofer*, a woman and a minority, which qualified you for all the Federal and NYPD racial and gender quotas. It also helps that you play poor Cox here like a skin flute. Sorry, is that politically incorrect of me? Let's just say you cocktease Cox into looking past all your secrets and lies. You're the daughter of a convicted terrorist, and you are one-hundred-percent Caucasian."

Mona mock-laughed and said, "My record speaks for itself. I have nothing to hide or to be ashamed of."

"To my lifelong shame, my ex-husband can attest to the fact that you're a *female*," Julie said. "But you are not an African American woman, are you, Mona Liar Falco Lupo?"

Tobin was tempted to throw what he'd learned from Phyllis Warsdale into the mix, but he decided to reserve it, like an ace in the hole. The way Lenny Kelly played his hand of ruthless poker.

"Yes, I am and proud of it," Mona said. "And neither me nor this contrived diversion are at issue here."

"No," Clancy said. "But the more serious implication here, Abel, is that Detective Falco threatened and coerced the victim and a witness. It's here on tape, Abel. Read the transcript and weep. According to our witness, neither girl even reported the crime. Falco found out about it, tracked them down, threatened to drag their families in for terrorist links, to scrutinize their legal status, to harass them."

Tobin stared at Mona and said, "Why?"

Cox stopped chewing his gum, looking at Mona with a cock of the head.

Mona Falco said, "Who took that preposterous statement?"

Winerib showed her the name on the bottom of the page. Mona Falco's face grew grave. But she swallowed hard, pulled out her handcuffs, and approached Laurie.

"Who signed it?" Tobin asked.

Falco rattled her handcuffs and said, "Laurie Tobin, you are under arr—"

Winerib held up a hand and said, "Hold on. In light of this new statement, I think we better reconsider this arrest warrant, Detective Falco."

Clancy pulled the statement from Winerib, who left in a hurry. Cox rolled his gum around his mouth, tying it in knots. Danvers looked at Tobin and Julie, nodded in his silent little way, and followed Cox out the door. Mona Falco glared at Tobin and Julie.

She turned and strutted out, her shoulders back, the round ass in the tight pants bunching. Tobin knew Julie saw him watching Mona Falco's exit.

"So long, honky," Julie said.

FORTY-THREE

A half-hour later Clancy was gone and a relieved Laurie asked if she could use the family's night visit to see her brother. Tobin and Julie agreed. Laurie left the back way, said she was going to visit her boyfriend afterward.

Then Tobin and Julie were alone.

In the house.

Julie poured herself a glass of Merlot. And rattled another sheaf of papers.

"Your editor, Tracy Burns, called and faxed your edited column."

"They're gonna run it?" he asked.

"Yeah."

"Good."

"I read it, Hank."

"What'd you think?"

She sipped her wine and said, "You grew your balls back."

"I just told the truth."

"That's what the old Hank Tobin used to do in every column. This one brought tears to my eyes because I knew you didn't write it for you. You wrote it for this kid Billy Kelly and his father. And you wrote it for Henry."

"I also wrote it for me. . . ."

She walked closer to him.

"Tracy Burns did a good job editing it."

"She's the best."

"She couldn't have said nicer things about you on the phone either. She sounded like a matchmaker trying to set me up on a date with my ex-husband."

"She's a corker."

"What exactly is your relationship with Tracy Burns, Hank?"

Julie was standing in front of him now, holding the faxed column in one hand and the wine in the other. Tobin stared into her intense blue eyes and thought hard about the answer.

"She edits me," he said. "She demands clarity, brevity, directness. Her motto is 'Details, details, details.' "

Julie sipped more wine and said, "Like vividly remembering the mole on Mona Falco's crotch?"

"I'm a writer, I notice everything," he said.

"Oh, what utter crap. You couldn't even remember writing the god-damned Billy Kelly column that wrecked his family. And ours. But a mole on Mona's mound? Unforgettable. Okay, surprise quiz: What're my secret, private characteristics?"

He rattled off a small Christmas-tree-like scar on her right butt cheek from where she sat on an escalator as a kid and got it caught at the top step. He touched it. She let him. He told her about a beauty mark on her left breast. He touched it. She let him. And a mole located somewhere even more private.

"Bullshit," she said.

"How would you know? You'd need a fish-eye mirror to see it."

"Believe me, I'd know."

"Maybe Moog told you about it."

"Moog did the interview with the Arab girl that just got our daughter out of an arrest, asshole."

"And what did Moog get for helping Laurie?"

Julie threw another slap at Tobin. He grabbed her wrist, yanking her to him. Wine spilled onto the floor. He bound his arms around her arms so she couldn't slap him again. He held her close, talking into her face. "I don't know just what Moog's act is, but I think he just threw us a very nasty knuckleball. My bet is Moog and Mona probably cooked up Laurie's bull-shit arrest together."

"What? Why?"

"To divert our attention away from Henry and what they're really up to. Mona gets Laurie in a jam. She even makes a weak federal case out of a bull-shit hissy fight between two teenage girls. But coupled with Henry's prob-lem, Laurie's looked bigger than it was. Got the press all riled."

"Yeah, that sure happened."

"Then Moog comes along and just so happens to save the day, looking like Julie's shiny knight on the white steed who rescues the distraught mother's child. Somehow he extracts a statement from a witness that gets our kid off the hook. A simple bullshit gesture that makes us put our defenses down."

Julie frowned. "You think so?"

"Wanna bet when I get my hands on the arrest file from the old arson that the cop who took and buried Debbie Hu's statement—describing a woman in a man's oversized clothes running from the scene—was Zach Moog?"

Julie started doing some fast math in her head. "Moog was still in uniform then. I know he was assigned to a Brooklyn precinct."

"Did he talk to you in the living room, near the bug in the lamp?"

Julie thought a moment and said, "No, matter fact he motioned for me to go in the kitchen."

"Like he knew?"

"Yeah . . . maybe . . . yeah, maybe like he knew."

"And you didn't think that was strange?"

"I had my mind on other things."

"I'm sure you did."

She wrestled to free herself from his grip. He clutched her tighter. "I fucking hate you," she said. "I cherish the day I divorced you."

"Debbie Hu said she couldn't remember the cop's name but that he was 'kinda cute,' " Tobin said, holding the bucking Julie.

"Which Moog is," Julie said, rubbing it in his face, an inch from hers.

"See, you were ready to die lying about humping Zach Moog."

"Not me, pal. But I saw the way you watched Mona Falco walk out of here," Julie said. "Like you wanted to put her between two pieces of bread."

"Shut the hell up."

"No, make me. . . ."

Tobin kissed her mouth to shut her up. He hadn't tasted wine in four years, since he stopped drinking, but on Julie Capone's tongue it made him want to fall face-first off the wagon. She struggled in his arms, glaring at him.

"Let go, Hank."

"No."

She looked him in the eyes. "Okay, if you're gonna hold me like this, make yourself useful."

He pulled her on top of him into his recliner chair, her wineglass crashing to the floor. They kissed and groped and got each other naked in a fit, in a heated race, in an outburst. He touched and kneaded and roamed and pinched and spanked and smacked and massaged her body. He kissed her from her ears and eyes and mouth and neck to the soles of her pretty small soft feet. He kissed each toe and her ankles and calves and thighs. And then Tobin kissed her wetter and longer in all the places he remembered she liked to be kissed most.

"Here's the mole I was talking about," he said. She yelped and growled and grabbed two handfuls of his hair until she levitated in sexual implosion.

Then she visited all his intimate places that she remembered he liked best and then she mounted him, easing him into her a mind-bursting millimeter at a time.

Buried deep inside of Julie Capone, he felt like a man who had chased and hunted and dug for his squandered past and had rediscovered it. And so he wrestled her to earth and clutched Julie Capone and wouldn't let go. They made love on the old recliner chair, the chair where he rocked his kids and slept-off old, unforgivable drunks.

They made love on the ottoman, and on the wine-stained rug, and over the kitchen table, and on a dining room chair. They made love on the carpeted stairs, leading up to their old bedroom. Then Tobin lifted her by the bare behind, still deep inside of her, her strong thin arms looped around his neck, and he kicked open the bedroom door with a splendid and very loud bang.

And then as his page-one column rolled on the New York *Examiner* presses in the night, Tobin and Julie rolled in the bed where they had created a family and where their love and marriage had gotten lost in the dirty linen, infected with the human jealousy virus.

"Right now, I need you to be a savage," she said.

And he was. And so was she.

And then they rested: two exhausted middle-aged lovers, reunited lovers, still-trying-to-be-young lovers.

And they conspired as reteamed parents of a son in very big trouble.

"I need to get my hands on the original case file from the Hu house arson," Tobin said. "I know Mona Falco was there. I need to verify Moog was the other cop."

Tobin explained that Mona Falco was also one of the cops involved in one of the two cases that led to Judge Koutros's bribery indictment. Julie said she had asked Moog to get her the Hu fire case. "He said it wasn't available," Julie said.

"You surprised?" he asked, telling her that one of the case files in the Koutros case was also unavailable to Phyllis Warsdale. "My bet is Moog's name is on both files. He helped set up Billy Kelly with Mona and now they're both somehow connected to the Koutros case."

"You think Lenny Kelly is blackmailing them, too?" Julie asked.

"I have to talk to the judge again in the morning."

"I'm gonna see Moog, surprise him. To pick his brains with what I know now."

"I'm gonna make you go bowlegged," he said.

"Put up, or shut up," she said.

They spooned together. "This time, do it like it was the first time, Hank," she said, turning onto her back, steering him into her, staring up into his eyes.

"Like the day when we came home from Bay Twenty-two?"

"Yes, like the first time you said you wanted me to be your wife and the mother of your children."

And Tobin did. This time slow and caressing, staring deep into her blue eyes, kissing her mouth, her legs scissored around him. And Julie's lovemaking told him that she still loved him back. As a man, as a husband, and as the father of her kids. They made that kind of limitless love until they were sore and spent and delirious with orgasm and romance and family, until they fell into sweaty sleep in each another's arms.

Tobin had no problem calling Julie by her right name.

FORTY-FOUR

Saturday, July 29

Tobin believed he was dreaming.

I must be, he thought. In the flannel-gray dawn, rain pecking the windows, he thought he heard a familiar doorbell. The doorbell of his old Marine Park, Brooklyn, house. And he thought he could smell Julie's perfume. When he half-opened one eye and saw Julie Capone sleeping in his arms, there was little doubt he was dreaming.

When Laurie's voice came through the cracked-open bedroom door, he was convinced he was deep in some devious REM fantasy.

Laurie said, "Mom, there's some big goon at the door looking for Dad. I told him he doesn't live here, but he won't leave and won't stop ringing the friggin' bell. . . ."

Laurie opened the bedroom door wider and yelped. "Oh . . . my . . . God . . . so sorry, Mom, didn't know you had company."

Tobin rolled out of Julie's arms and turned to his teenage daughter.

"Who's at the door?" Tobin asked.

"Daaaaad? Holy shit! Oh, man, this is like just *way* too *weird."*

"Time's it?" Julie asked, yawning, leaning up on an elbow, and seeing Tobin. "Ayyyyy!"

"Mom, you okay?"

"No! Yes!" Julie said, pulling the covers up over her bare breasts. "We just . . . he just . . . ya know, we sorta just . . ."

"We got it on," Tobin said.

"Oh, *God,"* Laurie said. "Even my shrink will be embarrassed."

Tobin said, "Who's at the door? A reporter? A cop?"

"No, a total wacko-weirdo. Don't get me wrong, there's nothing better than seeing my mother and father in bed together. But it's very weird. Weird-like-the-guy-at-the-front-door *weird.* He asked me to say the *rosary* with him in the rain."

Tobin asked Laurie to step out, and he jumped into his pants, and raced down the stairs to the front door.

Billy Kelly stood on the stoop in the morning drizzle wearing a yellow Brooklyn Cyclones rain slicker. He held a copy of the New York *Examiner* in his hands.

"Hey," Tobin said.

Billy Kelly held up Tobin's column on the front page and said, "I told you I was looking for a sign."

"Yeah. You said that, Billy."

Billy Kelly tapped the column with his index finger, the finger bearing the letter "E" from "J-E-S-U-S," and said, "That's a sign. That's a billboard thrown up by the Lord. It's a skywriter in the sky over Coney. Any man who risks his job and reputation and his future with a self-effacing public apology like this, is a man who believes in redemption, bro."

"Wanna come in out of the rain?"

"That isn't rain, bro. That's the Lord's tears of joy. No, I think you better get dressed and come out. If you're telling the truth about my father being alive, and if he's ready to kill himself before he can save your son, I think you better come out. With me. We gotta go find him. While there's still time for him to save your son, which will in turn save my father's soul. If he dies before he can clear your son, he will take an express elevator to Hell. So I have a chance to make my peace with my father *and* to help him save his soul before it's too late. There might even be time for me to tell him that I forgive him. Which just might set me free. This is a sanctifying crossroad in my life, Hank Tobin."

Tobin studied Billy Kelly's eyes to be sure there wasn't some psychotic messianic David Koresh/Jim Jones undercurrent in his spiel. There wasn't. He was just an earnest, God-fearing guy who believed that his crucifix was a master passkey to all the locked cell doors of this life and eternity.

Tobin said, "I'll be right with you."

"By the way, apology accepted," Billy said. "I mean, what the f—hell, right, bro? You put on the sackcloth and stood on the church steps of the city asking for forgiveness. Jesus forgave his killers. He gave executive pardons to the other two cons he got crucified with. I figure if Jesus could for-give Judas, Pontius Pilot, and a pair of second-story artists, I can accept your public apology. I talked to my pastor this morning about this. He told me if I didn't accept your apology, I'd be guilty of the sins of pride and vengeance and that I would still be serving time in my heart and my soul. He promised that if I accepted your apology and made peace with my father, I would be truly set free. So I accept your apology, Hank Tobin."

Billy Kelly held out his big, scary hand, the knuckles tattooed with the name of his savior. Tobin put his hand in Billy's hand. They shook. Billy almost crushed the bones of Tobin's hand. "That's what I wanted to do to your neck," Billy said, as if the Devil were whispering in his left ear. Billy eased his grip and slapped his other hand on top of their clasped hands. "Thank you for saving me from doing that. For saving me from myself."

"No, thank you."

"But tell me something," Billy said. "If I don't even know for sure, what makes you so sure I didn't torch the Hus' house?"

"Promise not to get angry at me again? For being the messenger?"

"Promise."

"Promise you'll try to forgive who did it?"

Billy Kelly thought about this for a long conflicted moment. He grasped his crucifix, closed his eyes, as if repeating a mantra, and said, "With Jesus's help, I'll try."

"I think it was your sister, Billy. I think Erin did it."

Tobin expected the big man to explode. Instead he clutched his cruci-fix, closed his eyes, blessed himself, and mumbled a silent prayer.

Lightning splintered the Brooklyn sky, followed by a wallop of thunder.

"We gotta find her," Billy Kelly said.

FORTY-FIVE

Tobin showered, dressed, and kissed Julie good-bye. It was 7:15 A.M., and she said she was going to find Moog, sit outside his Bay Ridge house, maybe tail him, and then confront him, to pick his brain and pull his covers.

Tobin made sure she took her .25 pistol.

Tobin jammed his pockets with two cell phones—his own and the one he'd borrowed from Tracy Burns. He was going with Billy Kelly to confront Erin Kelly, to see if together Lenny Kelly's kids could find their father and talk some reason into him before he decided to end his life.

Walking to his car, Tobin told the reporters who peppered him with questions about his explosive morning column that he would only be answering questions in his own future columns. Tobin and Billy Kelly then piled into his Lexus, and he sped down Flatbush Avenue to catch the Belt Parkway west toward Manhattan.

As he passed Kings Plaza shopping mall, his own cell phone rang.

It was Vinny Hunt. "Man, I can't thank you enough," Vinny said.

"Careful what you say on this line."

"Well, I don't kiss and tell, anyway," Vinny said. "I just wanted to say that I had the time of my life last night. That girl loved every minute of it. The ball game, drinks in Peggy O'Neil's, the Nathan's hot dog, fireworks from the boardwalks. Dani Larsen is everything I ever dreamed of."

"Great," Tobin said. "Listen, you ever get that other thing I asked you about? You know that thing on that old thing we discussed?"

Tobin didn't want to mention the Billy Kelly case file on the cell-phone line he was sure was tapped.

"What thing was that again?" Vinny asked. "My desk is piled with—"

"Remember the one concerning the guy we spoke to yesterday?"

"Yesterday . . . Oh, shit! Yeah. Sorry, man. I have so much on my plate and I've had Dani Larsen on the brain day and night. Promise, I'll get it today for sure. How soon you need it?"

"ASAP. I just need one detail from it."

"Give me an hour. Where you gonna be?"

Tobin's other cell phone rang, the one he'd borrowed from Tracy Burns. He asked Hunt to hold on and answered.

Phyllis Warsdale said, "I got this number for you from Burns. Hank, listen to me, you gotta get out here to Judge Koutros's house. Now! He'll only talk to you."

"I can't now. I—"

"I think he's suicidal, Hank. He keeps talking about how his life won't be worth living after noon. He has a gun on his desk, on top of a Bible. He keeps quoting Plato and Aristotle, about life and death. I don't think this guy's slept in days. He says he *must* talk to you about your son. What's this all about, Hank?"

"Can't you call the cops to stop him from hurting himself?"

"He doesn't have the gun to his head or anything. It's just a *vibe.* I can't call 911 on a *vibe.* He keeps insisting he's gotta talk to you. Only you. About your son. He threw me out. I'm sitting in my car, parked out front."

"I'll be right there. I'm maybe fifteen minutes away."

Tobin hung up with Warsdale and got back on with Vinny Hunt. "I have a bit of an emergency," Tobin said.

"Anything I can help with?"

Tobin said, "That judge I told you about."

"Judge?" Vinny said. "What judge? Never mind, tell me later. Anyway, thanks again for the Dani Larsen thing. I owe you. Big time. I'll get on that other thing right away."

"Thanks," Tobin said and hung up, passing the on ramp for the Belt Parkway west.

"You missed the turn," Bill Kelly said.

Tobin said, "Change in plans."

"Yeah?"

"We gotta go see a judge."

"Not my favorite people. Which one?"

"Koutros," Tobin said.

Billy Kelly clutched his crucifix in his big, balled fist. and cast his eyes toward the leaden skies. "Is this another test, Lord?"

Lightning scribbled in the heavens. Tobin glanced from the yellow-veined sky to Billy Kelly, his agnosticism shaken as he swished for the Marine Parkway Bridge to the Rockaways.

While crossing the slippery bridge, Tobin's cell phone rang. The one he didn't trust. It was Dani Larsen. He told her he'd call her right back from another line. He did, from Burns's phone.

Dani Larsen said, "Thanks for setting up the date from hell."

"What?"

"For four solid hours, nine innings of Cyclones baseball, three drinks at Peggy O'Neil's, a hot dog at Nathan's, a fireworks show on the boardwalk, and a stroll through the arcades of Coney Island, Mister Vinny Bashful Shyguy Hunt never once stopped talking."

"Really?"

"I was gonna buy him a snorkel because he never once came up for air except to yank answers out of me."

"Wow," Tobin said, as the wipers peeled away the building rain. "What the hell did he talk about?"

"You."

"Me?"

"He asked me a million questions about *you*. What your legal strategies were for your son. How you managed to get your daughter off the hate-crime assault. I told him I didn't even know what the hell he was talking about. I'd heard rumors she was gonna get arrested. I didn't know she got out of the jam. Did she?"

"Yeah . . . what time was this that he asked you about it?"

"Oh, maybe eight o'clock, about the fourth inning, and he was just getting started about you. . . ."

Tobin knew that the confrontation with the JTTF cops and U.S. Attorney Winerib didn't happen until about seven-thirty. Only Cox, Danvers, Winerib, or Mona Falco could've told Vinny about it so fast. *Or, of course, Zach Moog,* he thought.

"Well, he runs the Intelligence Division," Tobin said, trying to rationalize it for himself. "Intelligence cops ask a million questions. They feed on information."

"He asked me all about some cop named Zach Moog. I told him I never even heard of him. He didn't seem to believe me because then he asked if you ever mentioned that Moog and your ex-wife were an item."

Tobin's skin pebbled. He realized that Vinny Hunt was also investigating Hank Tobin the whole time he made him think he was an ally.

Clancy was right, he thought. *Trust no one.*

He had Cox and Mona Falco and the JTTF investigating him. And Moog. And now Vinny Hunt, whom he'd trusted, was sniffing behind his back. *The fucking Intelligence Division and the Counterterrorism Bureau and the JTTF are in competition to see who can nail me first,* Tobin thought. *To see who gets to stand at the press conference when they indict the whole Tobin family on some concocted conspiracy charge, some RICO or terrorism charges. They could charge anyone with anything these days. I confided in Vinny. Trusted him because he was a neighborhood guy. Godson of an old friend.*

Tobin's mind raced in paranoid circles, like a steer galloping through the pens to its slaughter. Billy Kelly sat next to him reciting decades of the rosary on his holy beads, clutching his crucifix. Tobin envied him. Envied the simple faith he had in anyone or anything, real or imagined. Tobin trusted no one now. Maybe Dani Larsen was fucking with his head, too. Maybe Vinny Hunt was using her, with promises of giving her big stories, to throw Tobin off balance. Maybe Dani was throwing him a curveball. Tobin didn't believe one word from anyone now.

Trust no one, he thought. *Except Julie.*

They have my kid in a steel box and now they're trying to box me. They tried to nail my other kid. Then a wild card named Moog bails her out to win brownie points with Julie. To misdirect my attention. Now Vinny Hunt is angling in at me from left field. All of them in a race to be the one to get Hank Tobin for obstruction of justice or some new-fangled antiterrorism conspiracy charge.

"You there, Hank?" Dani Larsen asked.

"Yeah."

"This Vinny guy walks me to my door. He's big and good-looking, sure. But he bored me so bad with questions about you that I didn't send out one signal asking him to come upstairs to my apartment. But he has the balls to say to me, 'Sorry, but I don't sleep with women on first dates.' I'm like, 'Who does this asshole think he is?' I told him how gracious that was of him. Hank, do me a favor, save him and me any future embarrassment and let him know that there isn't gonna be a second date, will ya? Tell him to lose my number and watch a different news channel."

"He ask you about anything else concerning me?"

"Yeah, he asked a bunch of times if you ever brought up a judge named Koutros. Isn't that the bribe judge in Queens?"

Tobin shivered in his seat, an involuntary rattle of the shoulders.

"Yeah," Tobin said. "What did you tell him?"

"I told him no, because you never did. Why? You know something about that? Is there a story I should know about here, Hank?"

There she goes, he thought, *picking my brains. Maybe for him. For Vinny Hunt. Get a grip. You're getting paranoid. But why shouldn't you be? This chick is ambitious. Like Mona. She's just starting general assignment on a local cable station. She wants networks to notice her. She goes along with a cop in the Intelligence Division to set up a guy who called her by his ex-wife's name in the sack. Who would have the last laugh if she broke the story about busting him and his wife?*

"No. Listen, Dani. You're breaking up. I . . . got . . . a . . . go. . . ."

"I can hear you fine."

Tobin disconnected and sped Beach Channel Drive, whispering the foggy road out along the rain-dimpled Rockaway Inlet, where sailboats, cabin cruisers, speedboats, and other pleasure craft rocked at marinas and mooring fields in the storm-tossed waters. Frantic gulls pedaled the morning wind. Foghorns grumped.

"Who you praying for?" Tobin asked Billy Kelly, whose fingers inched around the rosary.

"The judge."

"That's what I call turning the other cheek."

"I'm praying I don't fucking kill him."

Tobin prowled the beachfront block and found the address on Beach 151 Street in Neponsit that Warsdale had given him, a rain-stained, two-story brick bayfront home with a wooden dock big enough for two or three boats. A BMW SUV clogged the driveway. A Honda Accord idled at the curb, wipers flapping, bearing NYP press plates. Tobin pulled behind it as rain tumbled off Jamaica Bay.

"Wait here," Tobin said.

"Hurry up, I wanna find my sister. Maybe she knows where to find my father."

Tobin approached Phyllis Warsdale, who sat in the driver's seat of the Honda.

She powered down the driver's window and said, "Everybody's talking about your column today."

"The judge part of the story is still all yours."

"What the hell is going on, Hank?"

"I'm not really sure, Phyllis."

"He wants to see you and you alone. The door is open. In his study."

Tobin entered the house.

He moved through the forty-by-forty-foot living room decorated in a nautical motif, crowded with two facing oversized couches with deep olive-colored suede cushions and broad mahogany arms and coffee table and end tables fashioned from the hatches of old ships and dipped in heavy polyurethane. Original seascape oil paintings in ornate gold-leaf frames hung on the walls. Dark wide-plank floors mirrored the rain-beaded casement windows. The captain's clock on the mantel ticked to 7:34 A.M.

"Judge?"

Tobin heard no reply as he walked to the modern eat-in kitchen, peeking through the sliding glass doors onto the back deck that served as a barbecue area with picnic table and lounge chairs. Rain percolated in the hot tub fitted into one corner of the deck and one small cabin cruiser bobbed at its mooring at the end of the dock.

No Judge Koutros.

The low, persistent groan of a small motor, probably a twenty-foot cabin cruiser, rumbled out of the gaping gray mouth of Beach Channel. Tobin couldn't see the boat that was as loud and invisible as a small plane lost in low clouds. The horn of a commercial fishing boat steering out of Sheepshead Bay pierced the shrouded morning. He couldn't see that craft either, but Tobin guessed it was cleaving through the snotty tide toward the open sea, going for mackerel or blues.

"Judge?"

"In here, Hank," came a flat, defeated voice from an anteroom off the kitchen. Tobin hurried across the ceramic Mexican tile floor, down a small flight of oak steps, and through a half-opened oak door into a sunken, burnished-oak study.

Judge Nikolas Koutros swiveled in his forest green leather chair behind his teakwood desk, a cigar smoldering from his dry lips like a slow fuse to oblivion. Law books jammed floor-to-ceiling bookcases. One bookcase bulged with handsome leatherbound collector's editions—Greek philosophy, Greek myths, Greek culture, Greek literature, and Greek classic dramas, written in English and Greek. Plato, Aristotle, Euripides, Sophocles, Alexander the Great.

"What, no George Stephanopoulos?" Tobin asked, scanning the shelves and trying to lighten the somber smoky air.

An overhead fan blew the cigar smoke in useless concentric circles, like the desperation in Koutros's tired, bloodshot eyes. A Greek Orthodox Bible sat on the desk, emblazoned with gold letters that were obscured by a pearl-handled .38 Smith & Wesson revolver.

As time ticked away, Koutros had retreated to this windowless sanctuary, the last desperate watch pocket of the world to which the old-machine pol could run, his back to the sea, surrounded by volumes of immortal philosophy and the all-powerful American Law that had been his life. The fear of that same law was now the reason for the handgun on the Bible.

"Wanted to see me, Judge?"

"Funny title on Judgment Day," Koutros said.

"That thing loaded?"

"Always. I sent a lot of bad guys away in my time."

"They deserved it."

"As we both know, not all of them."

"Lenny Kelly still here?" Tobin asked.

The judge smiled, squeaking back in his swivel chair. "How did you know Kelly was hiding here?"

"It only occurred to me on the drive out here," Tobin said. "If he was blackmailing you, why not make you shelter and hide him?"

"I could have killed him, of course, but he has the e-mails programmed on an automatic send-later timer," Koutros said, shrugging. "He was more dangerous dead. Alive at least I got to plead with him every day. Lenny Kelly rather enjoyed it too. The judge pleading to the janitor for leniency. Me beseeching him to please keep my dirty record sealed. Begging at his dying feet for alternative sentencing. He has a wonderful sense of the ironic. He spent six of the last ten years going to college, reading everything, earning a master's degree in philosophy. The two of us would sit up all night sometimes, discussing Plato's ethics, Aristotle's rules of drama. I'd gulp cognac and he'd sip green tea, and we talked about our children, and how we'd failed them. He made me feel his pain, Hank. Like a transfusion of despair, a grief transplant. Speaking of which, I even offered to give him a portion of my liver. He laughed and said we were incompatible. And he's too far gone, anyway. But you know something? He was very touched by the offer. I thought I might have opened a clogged meridian to his heart. But, no such luck."

"He talked meridians and *chi* and Chinese Zen philosophy, too?"

"Oh, endlessly. Interesting stuff. I don't dismiss it, anyway. But clearly the man is not well in body or mind. He loved talking philosophy but said all in life boiled down to a single line in Albert Camus's *Myth of Sisyphus*. 'There is but one truly philosophical question and that is suicide.' He has been greatly disturbed by his hand in the incarceration of his son, which led to his beloved wife's suicide, and his daughter's lifelong shame."

"Which is why he intends to ruin us all before he kills himself, today."

"Yes."

"Why are you going to do the same?"

"He promised that if he got news of my demise by ten A.M., he would accept that I had assumed full responsibility for my actions against his son, and he would deprogram the e-mails to my daughters before he ended his own life," Koutros said. "And he would release the evidence that cleared me and therefore my family's good name instead. Suicide is shameful. But at least then my daughters would not have to live with the worst of the two shames of their father. If I don't kill myself, I will go to jail and lose all contact with my children and grandchildren, and wish I had. I would be dead, professionally and emotionally. There wouldn't be any reason to live. It would be worse than death. So I have accepted Lenny Kelly's alternative sentence. At least this way I get to do it here, on my own terms, by my own hand, surrounded by the sea and the law and the great words of great men."

"Why did you ask for me?"

"Because you deserve to know a few things before I go. I couldn't do this with a clear conscience if I didn't tell you who else is involved."

"Involved with who?"

"Lenny Kelly is blackmailing the others, too, of course."

Small hairs stood on Tobin's neck and arms like little electrified filaments. He heard another commercial fishing trawler blare its horn in the bay, probably warning off the motor of a smaller craft that crossed its course. Koutros yawned, mopping sleep from his tired face with his big sweaty hand.

"What others?"

"You don't know this?"

"Who?"

"The cops who rigged his son Billy's arrest?"

"You mean Mona Falco?"

"Yes, of course," Koutros said. "And her boyfriend."

"You mean the other cop who was there that night in uniform?"

"Yes. I don't know—it's on the arrest form, on the case file."

"We've had a hard time getting it. . . ."

"Same two cops who later made the blatantly flawed arrests I had to throw out of court," Koutros said. "Then they had money deposited in my accounts by the defendants whose cases I would have to dismiss."

"Who, Judge? Who?"

"I should have seen it coming," he said, blowing cigar smoke to the ceiling. "But who remembers the names of the arresting cops in a ten-year-old plea bargain?"

"I know that feeling. I forgot the goddamned column."

Koutros chuckled. "Lenny Kelly didn't forget."

"No, he did not. Neither did his son."

"The assistant district attorney on that case is dead, but Lenny didn't forget the two cops either," Koutros said. "They knew I was what you call a 'covering judge' and would catch cases while other judges were on summer vacations. I take my vacation in the winter. So Kelly and the two cops timed the arrests just right so the cases would have to pass by my bench. Mona Falco and her boyfriend set me up the same way they set up Billy Kelly that night. She wanted a much publicized hate crime to advance her career. The handsome young cop wanted *her*. She knew it, too. Still does. So she led him around by the short hairs. And still does."

"You mean, these two fucked up the arrests on purpose? So you'd have to throw out the cases on technicalities?"

"Yes," Koutros said. "But it was all Lenny Kelly's idea. His plan. He spent ten years, working nights, accessing computers, prying into people's lives, planning all of this. A janitor who spent his life cleaning up other people's messes was now cleaning up the biggest mess of his life. Getting revenge on the people he holds responsible for his son's imprisonment, his wife's suicide, his estrangement from his daughter."

"Where's Kelly now?"

"He left on the WaveRunner this morning. We had coffee together. He wished me luck, said he hoped I chose the honorable path. The same path as him. Said he had a very big day. He shook my hand, he embraced me, he said good-bye, and left on the WaveRunner, toward Brooklyn."

"Where does he intend to kill himself?"

"I have absolutely no idea. Noon, that's all I know. . . . You hear that?"

The judge stood, his eyes popping, like a man on a hallucinogenic drug.

Tobin said, "What?"

"You hear an engine idling?"

Tobin heard the small putter of something mechanical, but it was drowned in the wind and the rain and the foghorns and the gulls.

"Phyllis Warsdale is parked outside, her car's idling—"

"No, it's . . ."

"Judge, Mona Falco's boyfriend, Zach Moog."

Koutros's eyes bugged wider, spooked. "You don't hear that?"

He made a move toward the kitchen. Tobin reached for the loaded .38. Koutros dived for it. Koutros got to it first, pulled back the hammer. *Nuts,* Tobin thought. *He looks nuts.*

"Don't you fucking dare stand between me and my family's honor, Hank. I'm not a violent man, but I cannot let you stop me from stopping him. It's the only way."

"You're not thinking clearly."

"Yes, I am," Koutros said, his eyes wide and dilated, like a man who hadn't slept for days and so his brain forced its need for fantasy and dreams into his consciousness. "I've pondered Camus's single philosophical question, Hank. I've been forced to push Sisyphus's stone to the top of the slope a thousand times only for it to roll back down again and again and again and again before I get it to the top. There is only one answer to Camus's question. I don't want to, but I will kill you, Hank, before I let you stop me from killing myself. And don't tell me you don't hear that! You brought someone, didn't you, from the sea. . . ."

Tobin saw paranoia distorting Koutros's face the way alcohol disfigures an old rummy's, a beleaguered hound's mask of worry and stress and dread and defeat that had pushed him to the lip of his world, to the end of his life.

"Tell me more about Moog," Tobin said, trying to keep him talking. And alive.

"Moog?" Koutros said, climbing backward up the four steps to the kitchen, the gun trembling in his hand like a small, trapped animal. "What the hell is a *Moog?*"

"Mona and Moog," Tobin said.

Koutros looked over his shoulder through the glass doors onto his deck as rain blew in off Jamaica Bay in a surging gray onslaught. Tobin walked toward him.

"I don't know what the hell . . . you brought him!"

"Judge, you need sleep. Help. You're not thinking right."

"Stay away from me," the judge said, pointing his gun.

"You're not gonna kill me, for Christ sakes. You're not a killer. You're not even a thief. You're guilty of wanting human affection."

Koutros looked over his shoulder, out onto the deck, and tried to slam the study door. Tobin stuck his foot in the door. Stopped Koutros from closing it. Pushed it open. Koutros staggered back.

Then Tobin saw the figure in the rain.

Dressed in a hooded yellow poncho.

Tobin's heart leaped.

He thought it was Billy Kelly. Then Tobin saw the figure raise his arm. Gun in his fist. Aimed at Koutros. Tobin dived at the judge.

The shooter's bullet exploded through the sliding glass deck door in a gale of shards and splinters. The bullet tore into the judge's belly, the gun spilling from his hand. He dropped straight down, into a bed of glass. The second shot went high, hitting a copper-bottomed pan hanging on the wall.

The figure stalked toward Tobin, aiming the gun in the downpour. Tobin grasped the judge's gun, juggled it in his hands. He'd lived with a cop but had missed the military and never once fired a gun. He aimed with two hands as the figure approached the shattered bay doors. The figure dropped into a firing crouch.

Tobin squeezed the trigger. Felt the numbing metallic recoil. The bullet exploded the second sliding door into a glass storm. The figure turned and slipped and got up and ran for the end of the dock.

Tobin lay on top of the moaning Koutros, the gun gripped in his fist, as a motorboat roared off into the rollicking bay. Tobin scrambled outside, watching it spin away. But all he saw was the man in the hooded poncho sweeping from Neponsit, steering the boat in the rainy direction of Brooklyn.

Billy Kelly raced through the house, crunched into the shattered kitchen, followed by Phyllis Warsdale, who screamed at a 911 operator, demanding cops and an ambulance.

"Holy fuck!" Billy shouted. "Holy fuck!"

Tobin knelt beside Koutros, timing the judge's pulse. Still strong, but weakening. The abdominal wound pumped blood onto the Mexican tiles and broken glass, but Koutros was conscious, if delirious.

Tobin shouted, "Billy . . . clean towels . . . bathroom."

Billy hesitated, glared at the wounded man who'd sentenced him to ten years in prison, bucking and pumping blood onto the floor.

"I thought maybe *you* were hurt, Tobin. Not this piece of . . . not *him*."

"In the name of Christ, get me some fucking towels, will ya?"

"Well . . . you put it *that* way," Billy said, rushing to the bathroom.

Koutros bucked and said, "Don't write bad stuff about me in my obit, Tobin. Please. Stuff that would disgrace my family after I'm dead."

"You aren't gonna die, Judge."

"Please, let me die."

"Did you see the shooter's face?" Tobin asked Koutros.

"Sure," Koutros said. "He did me a favor. Tell him thanks."

"Tell who? I couldn't see his face from my angle. . . ."

"Mona Falco's boyfriend . . ."

"Moog? Cox?"

"What . . . the . . . fuck . . . is . . . a . . . Moog?"

"Cox, then?"

"Cox?"

"C-o-x as in Special Agent in Charge of the JTTF Cox. He's nuts about Mona Falco."

"I know that asshole, but he's not Mona Falco's boyfriend."

"Who is Mona Falco's boyfriend if it isn't Moog or Cox?"

Koutros said, "Big, good-looking, white guy."

"Yeah, that's Zach Moog. . . ."

"No, *Hunt*," Judge Koutros said. "Mona Falco's boyfriend, her partner in all of this, is Captain Vinny Hunt."

FORTY-SIX

Mona and Vinny, Tobin thought. *Working together. Against me. Against Julie. Against Henry. Against Laurie. Against my family.*

Nothing and everything made sense all at once.

Tobin said, *"Vinny Hunt?* You sure?"

The judge tried to speak, but the words clogged in his phlegmy, bloody throat.

Tobin told Koutros not to talk anymore. He pressed the towels on Koutros's belly wound. Billy Kelly blessed himself. "Lord have mercy on this son of a bitch," Billy said. "And give me the sanctified strength of forgiveness today."

Phyllis Warsdale gazed at Billy sideways, a look usually reserved for subway "wack-jobs" and scrolled her Palm Pilot with a stylus. *"Hunt,"* she said. "Hey, that's the name of the arresting officer on the other case the judge is accused of accepting a bribe on, in exchange for throwing it out of court. The arresting officer on one case was Mona Falco, the cop who arrested your son. The second one I couldn't get my hands on until this morning because it was held up for special circumstances by the NYPD Intelligence Division. It was finally e-mailed to me this morning from headquarters. Here it is, right here, arresting officer, Captain Vincent Hunt, NYPD Intelligence Division."

"No wonder it was held up," Tobin said. *"Hunt* held it up."

Tobin couldn't afford to be delayed by police questioning, paperwork, and eyewitness reports. It was 7:56. He had until noon to find Lenny Kelly. Tobin told Warsdale he had to run. She said she'd nurse Koutros until the cops and ambulance arrived.

350

*　　*　　*

Tobin stood under the umbrella as Julie splashed toward him on Fifth Avenue across the street from the Washington Square Orthodox Jewish Center. Billy stood alone in front of the temple in the falling rain, the drops dancing on the vinyl hood of his Cyclones rain slicker.

Tobin's watch said it was 9:28. The service would be finished by 9:30.

Tobin hadn't heard from LL all morning, and it was starting to get him nervous. *Maybe he knew I was on his tail and decided to kill himself earlier,* Tobin thought. Maybe he'd never call. Never give Tobin a last chance to help clear his son.

Julie was excited. She waved a file folder in her hand. Breathless. Wet. Gorgeous. "I tailed Moog," she said, adding that she followed him across the Brooklyn Bridge, straight to Internal Affairs, which was housed in lower Manhattan.

"Internal Affairs?" Tobin said.

"I confronted him," she said. "He said he couldn't tell me what he was working on. I cursed him. Then he handed me this, said it had sat in a dusty precinct file for ten years, told me to get lost, and walked through the door."

She handed the file folder to Tobin. The file tab bore the words: WILLIAM KELLY.

Now as they waited for Erin Kelly Levine to emerge from the temple on Shabbas, Julie traced a finger to the bottom of the Billy Kelly arrest form where Mona Falco's beautiful script was legible.

"We knew she made the collar," Tobin said.

Julie flipped a page of the file to a Xerox copy of a patrolman's logbook. It contained the details of a statement taken from then sixteen-year-old Debbie Hu by the first uniformed officer to arrive on the scene of the ten-year-old arson of her family's home.

"If Billy Kelly hadn't copped a plea, if he'd had a decent lawyer, this preliminary precinct file woulda been subpoenaed at trial," Julie said. "But because the police brass, DA, and his public defender basically coerced Billy into accepting a 'dime' or do a 'quarter,' the DA never even included this in their case indictment. But it sat there in an old precinct file folder, as many Xeroxed police logbook entries do, for years, forgotten."

"Like a little smoking derringer," Tobin said, scanning the logbook entry.

22:33 hrs. Fair weather. No clouds. Three-quarters moon. Victim and e/wit Debbie Hu describes seeing perp from BR window flee scene. "Hooded blue sweat suit, oversized. 6 sizes too big. Legs&sleeves rolled up. Perp 5 ft. 5, 120–130 lbs. E/wit. says perp 'ran like girl. long hair flapping from sides of hood.' Ran N. on W. 2nd Pl. approx. 21:12 hrs. E/wit appears sober, fright, cred. In bed W/BF at TOC. BF name Fred Buckles. Poss. skell. JH tattoos. Intox but no smell of alc."

It was signed by P.O. Vincent Hunt.

As Tobin read, Julie interpreted the logbook entry for him. "The night was clear and a distraught, credible, juvenile Debbie Hu told then-uniformed Police Officer Vinny Hunt that she had been in the sack with her adult, probably stoned, boyfriend Fred Buckles, at 9:12 P.M., the time of the crime," Julie said. "When Debbie ran to the window, she saw a figure in a dark hooded sweat suit six sizes too big, running like a girl north on W. Second Place, hair flapping from the sides of the hood. The suspect was described as five-foot-five, 120 to 130 pounds."

"Jesus Christ," Tobin said.

Julie nodded across the street to where Billy Kelly stood six-foot-four and 240 pounds and alone outside the synagogue, rosary beads dangling from his left hand, waiting to confront the sister he hadn't seen in ten years. Years he spent in jail for a crime she'd committed.

"He really fit the eyewitness description, huh?" Julie said. "And he was a skinhead then, so how did his hair 'flap over the sides' of the hood?"

"The poor son of a bitch never had a chance," Tobin said. "I don't know that I'll ever be able to forgive myself for my part in what happened to him, Julie."

"You had plenty of company," she said. "He did his *sister's* time. His *father* fingered him to you. Falco and Hunt falsified and buried evidence to frame him for a high-profile hate-crime collar. The DA just looked for a win with a tough election on the horizon. Judge Koutros never even reviewed the evidence, just accepted the plea and sent him away to clear the calendar, and make it look like the judicial system worked, swift and tough."

"Yeah, but it started with me, Jule," Tobin said.

"Bullshit, it started with Erin Kelly's Molotov," Julie said. "What you did sucks, but what Falco and Hunt did was way worse. Reckless as you were, as many rules as you broke, you *believed* Billy was guilty because even his father said so. But Mona read your column *after* she read Hunt's initial report and Debbie Hu's statement. Then, when she read your big loud column, causing a public outrage, she deliberately decided she could go big-game hunting by nailing a skinhead. With a swastika tattoo. Who was also an *adult*. Erin Kelly was a juvenile, a distraught pregnant teen in the middle of a lover's triangle. With no one hurt, a first offense, knocked up, and a crime of passion, Erin would have gotten Youthful Offender status, a sealed record, and maybe six months in juvie hall. It wouldn't have advanced Mona Falco one notch up the ladder. But falsifying it as an adult hate crime, coming off the high publicity heat of your column, it was a great collar. Especially for a self-created minority woman. It won Mona Falco major points in the evermore politically correct NYPD that was desperate for minorities and women in ranking positions. When your name is in lights, in a high-profile case, and you're a minority and a woman, you get promotions, baby."

"So she cockteased Vinny Hunt into burying his report," Tobin said. "Mona convinced Debbie Hu that it was better for everyone concerned that they arrest Billy Kelly instead of Erin. She probably told Debbie Hu that if she stuck with her original story, they'd have to arrest Fred Buckles for statutory rape. Then the father of the baby she was carrying would be in jail until the kid blew out his fifth-birthday candles."

"And Mona probably threatened to tell Debbie's parents that their precious daughter was banging Freddie Buckles in their house while she was supposed to be baby-sitting her siblings," Julie said. "And that's why Erin Kelly, also knocked up by the same skank, threw the Molotov through Debbie's window. Hey, when I was sixteen, if I was knocked up, and I knew the prick who did it to me was down the block banging another knocked-up chick in her bedroom, I'd have lost my fucking mind. Erin Kelly knew Buckles was in there humping Debbie while she was home vomiting, her childhood gone, her Harvard scholarship going south."

"Plus, Mona scared sixteen-year-old Debbie into believing that the insurance company would never pay the premium unless she kept quiet about seeing a suspect 'who ran like a girl' run away," Tobin said.

"Right, and so she said the original statement she gave P.O. Hunt would be downplayed, buried, but that if she was ever asked about it, she should say she was confused. They stuck with the dark hooded sweat suit, which they found in Billy Kelly's house, reeking of gasoline."

Tobin looked at Billy Kelly standing in the rain, saying his prayers, trying to salvage what scraps were left of his demolished family. "This poor son of a bitch was robbed of a decade of his life," Tobin said.

"But I'll tell ya," Julie said, "it must've driven Hunt crazy when he lied to help Mona frame Billy Kelly, and then watched her take all the public credit for the collar."

"He probably got a promotion out of that collar, too. He went on to become a captain, for chrissakes."

"Yeah, maybe, but he saw her get the headlines, promotions, praised in your column, and then she dumped him for *you*. Because she knew she could go further on your coattails, Hank."

"Don't make me any sicker than I already am, Julie."

"It's the truth. She fucked Hunt to make him falsify an arrest. She chased you for columns, big stories, to get her name in the paper, to get promotions. How do you think this makes me feel? My husband, the bimbo?"

"How do you think it makes me feel, Julie?"

"So, was she good in bed, Hank?"

"Stop."

"Was she better than me?"

"No one ever was or will be. Besides, I couldn't get it up for her."

Julie stared at him in the downpour. It was the right answer, but the old pain was still not vanquished.

"I can't believe I slept with you again. I must be getting early Alzheimer's."

"I half-wish that was true."

Julie took a deep breath, shoved the arrest file into the back pocket of her snug dungarees, and said, "When Lenny Kelly reunited Hunt and Falco, Hunt was probably glad. Probably took a perverse pleasure in going after you. He's clearly still nuts about her after all these years. Mona is his one that got away. He wants her back. And he's got a hair up his ass for you for taking her away the first time around."

"And for Cox," Tobin said. "He blames Cox for his surrogate father's death, my old friend Jimbo. Mona knew that and that Hunt was still nuts about her. And she knew Cox was nuts about her, too. So she led them both around by the dick."

"Sounds familiar."

"Stop there, Julie."

The worshipers streamed out of the temple, popping umbrellas, and walking in family units through the streets. Billy Kelly clutched his crucifix for courage when he spotted Erin Kelly Levine in the crowd, with her husband, Barney, each holding one hand of their little blond-haired daughter.

"Lenny Kelly hasn't called yet," Tobin said.

"Erin might be our last chance."

Billy Kelly waved to Tobin and Julie, nervous and filled with hope. They crossed the street to join him at the curb on the corner.

"God, my little niece is adorable," Billy said, rain popping on the hood of his rainslicker. "Whadda I do? Whadda I say?"

"Whatever comes from the gut," Julie said. "Even if it's silly, at least it'll be the truth. Don't tell her she looks older or fatter. Tell her she looks pretty."

Billy looked at Julie and then at Tobin. "You trust this broad?"

"I don't trust anybody else," Tobin said.

"I need somebody to trust," he said. "Here goes, bro."

Billy waited until the family walked a full block from the temple before approaching them on the street. Tobin and Julie followed.

"Shamrock, we need to talk," Billy said. Tobin knew Billy had called Erin by a childhood nickname that had probably tickled chills up Erin's spine.

Erin froze. Hunched her shoulders.

Barney Levine spun. Jumped. Waved as if for bodyguards. *A rich man's paranoid reaction to a stranger,* Tobin thought. The startled blond-haired girl clutched Erin's legs. Her prolife-champion husband placed himself in front of his wife and daughter. Tobin admired him for putting their safety before his own. *That didn't come from money,* Tobin thought.

Screaming bodyguards, guns drawn, splashed toward the Levines. From behind Tobin. From a parked Town Car. From across the street.

"Hold it," one bodyguard screamed.

"Stop right there," said another.

"Hands where we can see 'em," a third bodyguard said.

Tobin made them for retired cops. Julie spread her arms away from her sides, shouting, "Retired from The Job!"

Billy held his hands aloft, rosary entwined in his left hand. Tobin stood motionless beneath his umbrella. Erin looked from Tobin, to Julie, to the bodyguards, to her husband.

And then to her brother, Billy.

A confrontation she had long dreaded had arrived.

"You know this character?" Barney Levine asked Erin.

"You don't look old or fat, Shamrock," Billy said.

Julie grabbed her forehead. Billy said, "In fact, you look real pretty, Shamrock."

"Thanks, Spud," she said, using her own pet name for him.

"We need to talk about Daddy," Billy said.

Barney Levine said, *"Daddy? Spud? Shamrock?* Who is this kook?"

"Barney, darling, meet my brother, Billy."

"Brother? I thought you had no living family?"

"It's a long story," Erin said, waving for the bodyguards to put away their weapons. "But I do now."

"We don't have time to explain it all," Billy said, holding out his Jesus-tattooed right hand to Barney Levine. "Nice to meet you, bro."

The rich man looked at the tattooed knuckles, and at Erin, and shook Billy's hand. "Shalom. I'm sorry . . . about the bodyguards. But I attract nuts because of my politics, my religious beliefs, and my money. It's a complicated world. You understand."

"I'm with you, bro," Billy said. "You have no idea some of the dudes I bunked with. And thanks for taking care of my sister. But I need to borrow her. We got lots to catch up on. And very little time."

Barney looked at Erin, palms up, asking her to reply. She said, "I'll explain later, darling."

The Kellys sat in the back of the Lexus. Tobin drove with Julie next to him.

Billy looked at Erin and asked, "You know Daddy's alive, don't you?"

Erin drew her lips into her mouth, stared out at the rain, and nodded. "He called me," she said.

Billy asked, "When?"

"Once a month since he faked his death."

"Did you talk to him?"

"Just once, to tell him to stop calling."

"What did he want?" Billy asked.

"He wanted to see me and his granddaughter," she said.

Tobin looked up into the rearview mirror and said. "Where are we going? Do you know where to find your father, Erin?"

She nodded, looked at her watch. "Start driving downtown," she said.

"Where to?"

"Take Broadway, and I'll tell you as we go. I don't trust you not to call and tell the police to go there first. They'll kill him."

"Listen to me, Erin," Tobin said. "I don't have time for rich-bitch games. We have a son in the middle here."

"Don't talk to my sister like that," Billy said. "Understand?"

"Don't you talk to my husband like that," Julie said.

"I could say that to you about the way you're talking to my brother, lady," Erin said.

"All of a sudden you care about him?" Julie said. "Don't make me laugh, little sister."

Tobin took Eighth Street east to Broadway and made a right.

Billy clutched Erin's trembling hand to steady her. She said, "Your husband's column helped frame him."

"There wouldn't have been a fucking column if you didn't throw a goddamned gasoline bomb into Debbie Hu's house. Which you let your brother, who you're so quick to defend now, take the fall for."

"That's it, stop the car," Billy said, reaching for the door handle. "You talk to my kid sister like that, fuck you and fuck your kid."

"All right, everybody shut up!" Tobin said, hitting the button that locked all the doors. "We all have beefs with each other. But look at the cards on the table. Right now. I got a kid in the can. You have a father ready to kill himself. Let's focus on saving your father so he can save my kid. Agreed?"

Silence fell as the wipers flapped and the tires swished downtown, crossing Houston Street, through artsy Soho and trendy Tribeca.

"She's right, Billy," Erin said. "You fell on my grenade."

Billy said, "You don't have to do this in front of them."

"No, it's time."

"I want you to know, whatever it is, I'm gonna forgive you, Erin. You're my kid sister. I want you back."

"You might not say that by the time I'm finished," Erin said.

"The statute's run out, and the Lord'll decide that."

"I dressed in your clothes so they'd think it was a man who did it," Erin said. "I never intended to implicate you. I would have gotten away with it, too. After I threw the Molotov, I ran to the next block, ran through the yard, up the fire escape, and into the house. Dad was out getting shitfaced, as usual, betting the rent. You were zonked out on beer and Mom's goofballs. Mom was fast asleep on her sleeping pills, too. She was already upset with me. Mom was the only one, besides Freddie Buckles, who knew I was pregnant."

"You were *pregnant?*"

"Freddie Buckles had me and Debbie both knocked up," Erin said.

"I'll kill him," Billy said. "I'm washing dishes for a mother jumper who knocked up my kid sister! I'll kill him!"

"Not a good idea," Tobin said. "The law and the Lord wouldn't approve."

"I was the honor student who'd gotten accelerated," she said. "I had the scholarship from Harvard."

"You were Mom and Dad's pride and joy," Billy said. "And mine! You were the only success story coming out of our house. I was so damned proud of you. I was a shithead, skinhead, pill head. Dad was a gambling fool and a boozer-loser. . . ."

"And when Tobin's column appeared in the morning, quoting Dad in the bar, saying you did it, and the cops were outside ringing the bell," Erin said, "no way was Mom going to let *me* get arrested, go to jail, blow the scholarship. She also wasn't going to let me have Freddie Buckles's baby. Mom made all the decisions."

"Somebody had to, Erin. You were our lucky charm, our four-leaf clover, the family Shamrock."

"I told her I threw the Molotov. I told her about the gasoline-soaked clothes. And with the cops pounding on the door, she made a decision. She stuffed the clothes under *your* bed. They also found your typewriter *I* used to write the notes. They found the gasoline can where I put it in your closet. They found you sleeping. With a swastika on your arm. The really pretty female cop, the kinky-haired one, kept staring at me, like she knew I did it. She said Mom had a choice, Billy."

"You or me," Billy said, nodding.

Erin nodded, big round tears dropping over both lids at once, onto her high cheekbones. Billy wiped them with his thumb tattooed with the letter "J." He took Erin's collapsing face in his big, scary hands and held it together, kissed her nose and her forehead.

"Mom made the right choice, Shamrock," Billy said.

Tobin glanced in the rearview mirror, watching Erin shake her head, watching her gulp hard, swallowing ten years in which she had gotten a Harvard education, a high-paying prestigious job, married a billionaire, had a baby, and lived like royalty while her brother did her awful time.

"No, she didn't. It was wrong and unfair, and she knew it."

"You don't know that," Billy said.

"Yes, I do."

"Come on, it's a long time ago. We have plenty of time left. I'm gonna be the best uncle that little girl ever saw. I guess it's okay she's a Jew, but she better not be a Yankee fan. . . ."

Erin smiled and gazed out at the rain. "Make a left on Chambers Street," Erin said. Tobin did until he approached the Municipal Building, requiring a left or right turn.

"Take the bridge," Erin said.

Tobin took the right off Chambers Street onto the rain-ghosted Brooklyn Bridge, which looked the way it must have a century before.

"Why do you think Mom killed herself, Billy?" Erin said. "She was a mother faced with a King Solomon decision. One of her two children was going to go to jail. Either her drugged-out, skinhead son, Billy, or her precious little scholarship-winning Erin. She chose you for jail and me for a life of privilege. The day they sentenced you she swallowed a jar of her Seconals as soon as she got home from court. She didn't tell Dad. He went straight out to the bar. By the time Dad got home from the Lucky Seven and found her, it was too late. The date was July 29. The coroner determined the time of death was noon. It was listed as an accidental suicide. A letter she wrote to me came in the mail two days later, explaining why, begging me to leave Brooklyn and the family behind, to start a new life with a new name for myself. Dad never knew the real truth why she did it."

"Just as well," Billy said.

"No, it's not, Billy. No, it's not. Dad thinks Mom was driven to her grave by an unjust system, because of Hank Tobin's column, and a rotten judge and crooked cops. That was only part of it. Mom and me were part of it, too. We all sacrificed you. But Mom wasn't finished saving me. Three days after they arrested you, she took me to Planned Parenthood and got me an abortion, which was against everything she believed in, everything Daddy believed in, everything that I believed in, to save me from another of my big mistakes. We never told Daddy. We never told you. And after you went to jail, I dealt with my own rotten guilt with . . . what? Denial, delusion, rationalization. Like Mom, I convinced myself that you were destined for jail or the cemetery anyway. That maybe jail would even save you. . . ."

"Maybe it did, Erin. Maybe if it wasn't for jail, I never woulda found the Lord."

"Later it was easier to just pretend that you and Dad were dead. I put my family behind me, like Mom suggested, because I couldn't face any of you. So I started a new one. With a new name. A new religion. A new baby. Because I destroyed this family, Billy. Not you. Not Dad. Not Mom. *Me.* So it's not okay that Dad doesn't know all that. Not anymore. Not when he's playing with other people's lives, blaming them for things that I did, that I caused. I had no idea. . . ."

Billy looked at her, as earnest as a Jesuit, and said, "I just hope that before you turned Jew you went to Catholic confession?"

Erin half-smiled and said, "Some sins are unforgivable, Billy."

Billy lifted Erin's chin, looked in her tear-stained eyes, and winked. Tobin watched in the rearview, then stole a glance at Julie.

"I forgive you, Shamrock," he said. "And if I do, so will Jesus. Or, ya know, whoever it is you Jews haggle with up there."

Billy held open his arms, and Erin fell into them as Tobin exited the bridge.

"Where we going?" Tobin asked.

"The day we buried Mom," Erin said, "Dad said that he would join her on the ten-year anniversary of her death. When Billy was a free man. After all those responsible paid for what they had done to her."

"He said that all the way back then?" Tobin asked.

"He was half-drunk, as usual," Erin said. "I didn't take him serious. But after the priest was gone and we were alone, he made it like a vow over Mom's grave. He said, 'Ilene, I failed you in life, but I vow to you now that I will join you in exactly ten years from the moment of your death, when both of our children are once again free, and all the wrongs against our son are made right. On this I will not fail you.' "

"He cared that much about me?" Billy asked.

"I remember it clearly because he read it aloud from a paper. He'd thought about it, long and hard, and I remember thinking how pathetic he was. Drunk. Still a loser. He'd probably forget he ever made the promise by the end of one good bender."

Tobin's cell phone rang. The one he didn't trust. He answered.

"D-day, Hank," said LL.

"Hello, Lenny."

"Call me what you want. It's our last call."

"The judge is dead." Tobin was lying, but he hoped he could determine if LL had any reason left in him.

"Hmmm. Sad, but noble. I'm sure he'll rest in peace."

"Can you offer me the same deal?"

"Sorry. There's a ten-year deficit that must be filled to make things right. I might arrange for it to come to light then, posthumously. The way you did for Billy . . . for mine. That was an amazing column. It makes the transition easier. I wish there was more I could do for you."

Tobin fitted the cell phone into the speaker-phone rack and let everyone in the car listen. He watched the reactions of Billy and Erin in the rearview mirror. Julie turned in her seat to face them.

"You can do something for me, Lenny," Tobin said. "You can clear my son."

"That I cannot do," LL said. *"I need your son to counterbalance what you did to mine. To put the* yin *and* yang *in harmony."*

"You're bastardizing Zen philosophy the way maniac suicide bombers corrupt Islam and the Koran," Tobin said. "You want an eye for an eye, take both of my eyes. Not my son's."

"It doesn't work that way," LL said. *"You put a pox on my son. I put one on yours."*

"How can you go to your grave knowing my son is being railroaded?" Tobin asked.

LL's mechanical voice crackled in the car. Erin and Billy leaned forward and listened.

"I explained to you, it's the yin *and* yang *of life, Hank. One injustice will balance the other."*

"You really believe two wrongs make a right?"

"The second wrong has already taught you right from wrong," LL said. *"Evidenced by your morning column. A noble gesture but ten years late. Not sufficient to give back a young man ten years of his life which you helped take away."*

Billy said, "Dad? It's me, Billy. Wassup? We need to do some serious talking. But listen up, I'm the one who did the ten years. I'll decide who pays for it."

Silence and heavy breathing crackled over the speaker. *"This is a very cheap trick, Tobin,"* LL said.

"Dad, it's me, Spud."

"Silly time for tomfoolery, Tobin," LL said.

"Dad, it's me, your lucky Shamrock," said Erin. "Dad, I need you to listen to me. To Billy. Please. For our sakes. For your sake. For the sake of Mom's memory, please listen to us."

"Tobin, did you really think I'd be fooled by this nonsense?" LL asked.

"You used to hide your Four Roses bottles in the milk box on the stoop so Mom wouldn't find them," Billy said.

"You used to take me with you to OTB as a good luck charm," Erin said.

LL said, *"You'll be sorry for trying to play games with my final hours, Tobin."*

"Dad, I want you to know that I forgive you," Billy said. "I want you to forgive yourself. I want you to forgive Hank Tobin."

"Nice try, Tobin," LL said. *"Put together a couple of your Hollywood actor friends, read a few old diaries, try to fool me. I admire you fighting for your kid all the way to the end. But in exactly one hour and eighteen minutes I'm out of here."*

"Please don't hang up," Tobin said.

"Dad . . ."

"If my daughter is really there," LL said, *"she'll know where to find me."*

"Lenny, please . . ."

LL hung up.

Tobin looked at the clock on the dash. It was a quarter to eleven.

"Take the Gowanus Expressway," Erin said, and Tobin floored the Lexus, hydroplaning onto the highway.

"No more games," Tobin said. "Where the hell are we going?"

In the rearview he saw Billy nod to Erin. And she told Tobin where her father had said he would end his life.

Tobin lifted his cell phone, the contaminated one, and dialed Julie's number. Laurie answered. Tobin told Laurie exactly where he was going. He gave the time. He said that if Vinny Hunt called to tell him where he'd be.

FORTY-SEVEN

The man in the dark black wig stood over the grave of Ilene Kelly, head bowed in the noon rain. A hundred yards away a small burial was in progress in Greenwood Cemetery, mourners in dark clothing standing around an open grave under umbrellas, listening to the prayers of an old, fat priest.

A cemetery security Bronco with two uniformed square-badge cops squished past on the muddy road, wipers flapping, the windows beaded with fresh rain. A gravedigger roped off another open grave some thirty yards away, awaiting a second cortege that approached on the serpentine road, wiping his muddy hands on his soiled green uniform.

Rain pelted the roofs of the elaborate, two-story mausoleums surrounding the lawn where Ilene Kelly was buried in a humble family plot, and where a matching headstone marked the fake September 11, 2001, passing of Leonard Kelly.

Tobin's watch told him it was exactly 11:38 A.M. when he heard a car park on the cemetery drive, listening to car doors opening and closing. He heard figures squeak across the sodden lawn and heard Mona Falco say, "Okay, Lenny, we've done everything you asked. The judge is dead. The Tobin kid is going, going, gone. We couldn't make the charges on the daughter stick, but two out of three ain't bad. Give me the disc. Then we'll leave you to your good-bye, hello, whatever you want to call it."

Tobin felt the rain peck the fake scalp of the black wig that he'd retrieved after Lenny Kelly dropped it the day before while fleeing along the rock jetty of Serenity Beach. Tobin kept his back to them, bowed over Ilene Kelly's death stone.

"Come on, Kelly, Tobin and his crazy fucking wife are on the way," he

363

heard Vinny Hunt say. "They have odds and ends. But without you or the judge or that disc, they can't prove anything. Give us the disc. And you can get on with your . . . *business.* And we'll get on with ours."

Tobin turned and faced Mona Falco and Vinny Hunt.

"Your business is standing right behind you," Tobin said.

Vinny and Mona both reached for pistols, but Julie cocked her .25 and placed it at the base of Mona Falco's skull.

"This could be the last *head* you ever give, white girl," Julie said.

Behind Julie an opened mausoleum door creaked in the storm wind.

"You're holding a gun on two cops," Mona said, as Julie took Mona's .38 and jammed it in her back waistband. "Even for *you,* this is dumb."

"Shut the fuck up," Julie said, kicking Mona so hard in her tailbone with her construction boot that she collapsed into the mud. Julie pinned her muddy boot on Mona's face and ground it into the mud.

"When you seduced my husband, it was degrading to me," Julie said, bending over her. "Fucking with my kid is suicide."

"You better put that gun down, you crazy bitch," Vinny said. "I'm a fucking *captain* in the Intelligence Division and . . ."

Julie turned, took a deep breath, glanced at the stormy sky, and kicked Vinny in the balls.

"Cap'n Crunch," Julie said. Vinny doubled over in pain. She shoved him down on top of Mona, slamming his face into the back of Mona's skull. Vinny's nose burst blood. He moaned, dazed. Astonished.

"You already hurt my child. I'll kill you if you give me one more shitty reason," Julie said.

"Enough, Julie," Tobin said. "Just handcuff them."

Julie removed Hunt's 9mm Glock and handed it to Tobin. She grabbed Mona's handcuffs, yanking her arms behind her, crunching a cuff so tight on Mona's left wrist that it caused the beautiful detective to yelp. Tobin found Vinny's cuffs and was about to handcuff him when they heard the man's voice above them.

"This is not in my plan," he said, his voice a wheezy whisper.

Julie turned, training her .25. Lenny Kelly, dressed in the gravedigger's soiled green uniform, stood above them. He pointed his own small .32-caliber pistol.

"You shouldn't have come here, Hank," Lenny Kelly said, his face gaunt and jaundiced, the color of butterscotch. His teeth looked loose and horsey from radiation. His hair, including his eyebrows and eyelashes, had been obliterated by chemotherapy. He looked much worse than he had only two days earlier when he was dressed as a parkie in the Marine Park playground.

Tobin said, "I had no choice, Lenny."

"You hurt my kid, you sick twisted fuck," Julie said, pointing her .25. "I'll fucking kill you."

Lenny Kelly laughed, pointing his .32 at her. "I have six minutes before I die, and I'm supposed to be afraid of that? So I rejoin Ilene a few minutes early, she won't mind. Go ahead, shoot. And I'll shoot you both. And your son won't have a mother or father to come home to. Just like Billy. Now throw the guns over here."

Tobin tossed the Glock toward Lenny Kelly. It splashed in the mud. Julie hesitated, glaring at Lenny Kelly who aimed his .32 at Tobin.

"I'll kill him," Lenny Kelly said, bending to pick up the Glock, still aiming his .32 on Tobin. "I'll kill the man you never stopped loving, Julie, the way I never stopped loving my Ilene."

Julie's eyes danced, looking from Lenny Kelly to Tobin. She swallowed and lobbed her .25 toward Kelly.

Vinny Hunt pushed himself to one knee, his face a muddy, bloody easel, and moved toward Julie's .25. He glared at Julie and said, "Okay, cunt-cop, now I'm gonna pull down your pants and do things that'll make you beg me to kill you."

Mona Falco rose to a seated position, spit mud from her mouth, glared at Vinny Hunt, and said, "Shut up, you big vile moron." She turned to Lenny Kelly and said, "Thank God you showed up."

Mona scrambled for Julie's .25, looked around, saying, "Where's my—"

Lenny Kelly cut her off: "Leave it alone. Sit back down. You too, Vinny. Both of you, take a moment to make peace with your higher power. Before I join Ilene, you two are going to die. That was always the plan."

"No way," Mona said, tears leaking onto her muddy face. "You promised you'd give us the disc with all the information."

"We made a deal," Vinny said.

"Oh, that? You mean my word? My promise? My oath? Like the one you two made when you pinned on the badge? Sorry, I'm breaking that trust. Just like you two did every day for the ten years my son paced a human zoo."

Lenny Kelly jammed one gun in his belt and held up a computer disc packed in a clear plastic case. "I could understand if you only did it to my son, a mistake, youthful ambition," he said. "But both of you falsified one arrest after another, framing poor kids for crimes they never committed, coercing witnesses, manufacturing evidence, perjuring yourselves at dozens of trials, all so you could climb the ranks. It took me nine years to find out everything I needed to learn about you bastards. By that time my son was almost finished with his sentence. He didn't want my help, wouldn't talk to me, refused to talk to lawyers. He did his time while you two wrecked people's lives for your own ambitions, your own promotion. Well, here you are. The ultimate promotion day."

"Lenny, don't die as a cheap killer," Tobin said. "Some lousy, embittered, vengeful subhuman. Find the peace within. Punish them by setting yourself free."

"You talk the good talk," Lenny said. "But I have to walk the walk to eternity. I need to mete out justice myself. I can't rely on a corrupt system. I used these two to set up your son and the judge because they had practice. And now they're finished with their chores and errands, and they have to pay for what they did to Billy, to Erin, to Ilene. To my family. Sorry, Tobin, you and your wife don't get off so easy. You'll watch your son rot in a cage for a long, long time. That's a much worse punishment."

Tobin looked past Lenny Kelly.

Erin and Billy had drifted from the other funeral when they saw their father appear at their mother's grave. They now stood two feet behind him.

"Dad, put the dopey pieces down," Billy said.

"Don't do this, Daddy," Erin said.

Lenny Kelly turned to his two children standing in the rain. His rheumy old eyes narrowed, like dimming yellow penlights.

"I have shamed and ruined you both," he said.

"It wasn't your fault, Daddy," Erin said. "It was mine."

"Yo, gimme those stupid guns, Dad," Billy said.

As Lenny Kelly reached out the guns to his big son, Vinny Hunt sprung from the ground like a nimble tackle. He slammed into Billy Kelly, grabbing the 9mm. Billy and Vinny wrestled in the mud for control of the 9mm.

Mona lashed a handful of mud into Julie's face and scrambled for the loose .32.

Tobin dove for the same gun.

Mona got it. And rolled through the mud. Then pointed it directly at Julie, who pulled the .38 she'd taken from Mona from her back waistband. Julie fired her gun. The shot ricocheted off Leonard Kelly's headstone. The mourners at the distant burial scattered, some screaming.

Mona came up firing at Julie. Julie dived behind a stone angel. Tobin rushed at Mona. She swung her pistol toward Tobin and said, "You hurt me once, Hank. That won't happen again."

Vinny rammed the barrel of the 9mm to the base of Lenny Kelly's skull. "You demented old rat, you fucked everything up!"

Then he was distracted by the roar of a motor.

Mona's eyes popped when she heard the cemetery security Bronco race up the hillock toward the gravesite.

The Bronco skidded in a lawn-gashing swerve. Danvers and Moog jumped out of either door. Aiming semiautomatic weapons.

"Freeze!" Danvers shouted.

"Don't move a hair," shouted Moog.

"No way," Vinny said, aiming at Danvers, ready to fire. Billy Kelly detonated his tattooed right fist onto his jaw. Vinny Hunt's shot flashed high. Danvers returned fire, ripping a diagonal line across Vinny's torso. He died sitting up. Then he fell sideways with the weight of his lifeless head, making a small, final splash.

Mona Falco pointed her pistol at Moog. "I won't go to jail," she said.

Too late. Julie squeezed a single round into Mona Falco's head.

The three Kellys sat on the grave of Ilene Kelly, locked in a family embrace as the rain fell on top of them.

Moog moved toward Lenny Kelly with the handcuffs.

"Give them a minute together, Zach," Julie said.

"They haven't had one in ten years," said Tobin.

Moog nodded.

Danvers spoke into a police radio, calling for crime-scene investigators and a morgue wagon as Tobin approached.

"Where's Cox?"

"He was recalled to Washington this morning," said Special Agent Danvers. "I expect he'll be asked to retire."

"You knew everything all along?" Tobin said.

"The bureau suspected that Special Agent in Charge Cox was being compromised and manipulated by his affections for Detective Mona Lisa Falco," Danvers said. "I was sent in by the Office of Personal Responsibility to monitor him from inside the JTTF."

"OPR? FBI Internal Affairs?"

"Yes, to watch and listen and monitor," Danvers said. "Detective Moog was assigned by NYPD Internal Affairs to monitor Mona Falco. When Cox brought her onto the task force, we worked together. We knew there was a private agenda going on. Her background didn't match what she'd been telling NYPD over the years. I was impressed that your wife found out that she was not even of African American extraction. We also knew that most of everything you and your wife were saying might be true. But we needed to investigate it from inside. Sorry."

"While my kid sat in a cage?"

"What's it been? Six days to save him from a life sentence? We needed proof, Mister Tobin. Not hunches. Not emotions. Don't forget, the stories your son printed about innocent Arab Americans who were framed by Lenny Kelly, Mona Falco, and Vinny Hunt, also led to some egregious arrests. Some of those people have to be set loose now, too."

"God, I didn't even think of that."

"They and their loved ones sure have," Danvers said. "A lot of innocent people have been hurt here. We knew for sure that Captain Hunt was deeply involved in your son's predicament when we placed him under sur-veillance and saw him transport and place a stolen mustard-colored Explorer in Detective Moog's garage. Just to keep you confused. To keep you from suspecting him long enough to get what they obviously needed from Lenny Kelly. Little did Hunt know that Moog and I were watching him at the time. And then later he directed you to follow Moog, where you would see it. Clever. But arrogant. He thought because he was running the Intelligence Division, that no one was doing intelligence on him."

"And you've been following us all day?"

"Just from Manhattan. We were actually following Hunt and Falco but lost Hunt when he boarded a boat. And couldn't get a helicopter recon in the storm."

"He used the boat to shoot Judge Koutros."

"I know. I hear he's gonna be okay. But we stayed on Mona Falco. She led us here. We overheard the same bugged phone call they heard, about where you all would wind up."

"What about my son?"

"Your son will be going home today as soon as we debrief Leonard Kelly."

"You better do that fast," Tobin said. "Lenny Kelly is dying."

Tobin turned. Julie stood in front of him. She had listened to their conversation.

Tobin looked at her, standing wet and numb in the mounting rain. He draped his arm over Julie's shoulder and looked to the lifeless bodies of Mona Falco and Vinny Hunt.

Billy Kelly said a rosary with his father and sister over the grave of Ilene Kelly.

Then Julie said, "Hank, let's go home."

EPILOGUE

Saturday, August 19

Tobin stood on the stone steps as Billy Kelly helped carry Lenny Kelly's coffin out of Immaculate Heart of Mary church to the waiting hearse.

Tobin stared at Erin Kelly, dressed in black, who stood with her husband and her daughter on the other side of the church steps. They followed the coffin to the sidewalk.

Tobin had come alone to the funeral of this tormented man whose life had been changed by a Hank Tobin column. And who in turn had forever altered the life of Hank Tobin and his family. Lenny Kelly's revenge had almost cost him a son. But instead it had given him back his wife, and the life he had thrown away for fame and nonsense.

He had not asked his wife, Julie, or his children to join him at the funeral for this man who had caused them so much pain. Tobin had simply risen early on this sunny Saturday morning in his old Marine Park home, donned a black suit, and left a note that said he would come home after the funeral.

Now, as he watched the coffin carried from the church, he felt someone clutch his right arm. He turned and gazed at Julie's strong and beautiful face.

"Shut up before you say 'boo,' " she said. "I'm not here for the sick old 'wack-job.' I'm here for his kid."

Tobin turned and on his left Henry stood with Laurie.

"Me, too," Henry said. "I can identify with Billy Kelly."

"I'm just here because Mom said we should do this as a family," Laurie said. "Personally, I don't give a hair rat—"

"Dummy up, girlfriend," Julie said. "Or no new car."

Laurie drew an imaginary zipper across her lips. Tobin smiled and draped an arm around Laurie's shoulder and kissed her on the top of the head.

The hearse doors closed, and Tobin punched Henry Jr. lightly on the shoulder and nodded for him to follow. Then father and son descended the church steps together and approached Billy Kelly.

The two young men looked at each other and nodded. Tobin introduced them.

"Sorry about your loss," Henry said.

"Sorry what my father did to you," Billy said.

"Sorry what mine did," Henry said with a nervous laugh. Tobin looked at his shoes. He needed a shine and didn't care.

"I'm sorry for what I did to both of you," Tobin said.

Billy shrugged, his polyester suit gleaming in the August morning sun.

"I'm just glad I had a few weeks to let my father know that I forgave him before he kicked the bucket," Billy said. "Maybe he got to save his soul."

"That's good," Henry said.

Billy whispered in Henry's ear, "I'm fucked up enough already without walking around blamin' all my troubles on the sins of my father, know what I'm sayin'?"

"I hear ya," Henry said.

"I got my sister back, a beautiful little niece, and Jesus in my life now," Billy said. "My rich Jew brother-in-law's giving me a job. I got a life to live. You gotta be thankful for what you got now. Bitchin' about the shitty past keeps you there."

"Yeah," Henry said. "Good attitude."

"Thanks for coming," Billy said, shaking Henry's hand with his Jesus-tattooed right hand. "See ya around. Peace, bro."

"Yeah," said Henry. "Same."

And then Billy Kelly climbed into the limo behind the hearse, joining his sister, his niece, and his brother-in-law.

Tobin watched the hearse and the limo pull away toward Greenwood Cemetery, where Lenny Kelly would be joining his wife, Ilene, in the Brooklyn earth. Then Tobin felt his son drape his arm over his shoulder. It felt like the hand of absolution.

"Thanks for coming," Tobin said.

"Thanks for picking me up, Pop," Henry said.

Father and son looked at each other and nodded.

Julie and Laurie joined them on the sidewalk.

"How about breakfast at the Greek diner?" Henry said.

"I'm thinking of a proper brunch somewhere nice," Laurie said.

"Come on, let's pick up bagels," Julie said. "I'll make breakfast at home."

"I can't think of anything better," said Hank Tobin, who went home with his wife and kids.

ACKNOWLEDGMENTS

I would like to thank my brother Joe and my daughters, Katie and Nell, for their notes on the early draft. And gratitude to my editor, Mitchell Ivers, who gave me his encouragement and suggestions when this was still an idea—and for his great notes when it became a book. And as always, thanks to my agent, Esther Newberg, who made it happen.